# Ack

MW01129234

Anyone can write, even if just scribbling on paper, a wall or Aunt Dolly's antique coffee table. But to make it more clear and entertaining, the story has to unfold easily. So, I would like to acknowledge all the people who helped me unfold this story.

My daughters, Alaina and Gillian, provided the character profiles, dialogue, and countless hours of plot discussions (while driving to and from school, dance and swim practices).

My husband, David Ruby supplied instant medical information. When it wasn't so instant, he provided the appropriate medical reference books.

My sister, Sue, and her friends provided a great deal of the bizarre humor and entertainment (like that classic game of Uno we played so long ago).

My mother-in-law, Delores Ruby, spent countless hours proofreading my early manuscripts, although she claims that she was running out of reading material at home and pushed me to finish. Her red pen and literary savvy were invaluable.

Dominique, Taylor, Bryce, Katie, Kevin, Savannah, Tatum, Aunt Toni, Mrs. McNair and Mr. Billar let me integrate their personalities into great fictional characters.

Lisa and Alan Minker relayed stories and provided priceless photos of the many trails within the Grand Canyon. I loved their story about Kathy, the wild turkey, who now probably has many generations of little Kathies rooting around somewhere in Indian Gardens.

Ken Euge, my consulting geologist (who also doubled as the geology teacher in this story), checked over my descriptions of Grand Canyon geology. The textbook he loaned me as well as occasional explanations of terms kept my understanding of the subject clear.

Mr. Erasmo Luna, both my daughters' Spanish teacher, was very patient with my pestering him on several occasions in order to keep the Spanish dialogue correct in this story.

Frank Ybarra not only *stomped his artistic skill* in designing my book cover illustration, but he also let me write him in my story. His amazing artwork is immortal, but now his fictional character is too!

Katie Dimpfel reviewed my original manuscript for credit in Mr. Billar's Social Studies class. Her feedback was invaluable.

Ruth and Joe, my parents, brought me into this life and deeply ingrained a *finish-what-you-start* work ethic.

Finally, every author/scribbler has at least one teacher that made a difference. Being a professional college student for at least two decades, I've had multitudes. But if I had to mention only one, it would be my freshman composition professor, Dr. Vetrick from Lakeland Community College (Mentor, OH). He was the first one who successfully convinced me that writing research papers could be fun. Back then (late 1970's) my paper, *The Molecular Basis for Memory,* involved collecting information from some obscure and antiquated library sections. One library on the campus of Case Western Reserve University (Cleveland, OH) had several floors that were accessible only by ladders, and the floors were actually slats, allowing views from floors above and below.

Although I am forever thankful for search engines and the Internet, I nevertheless miss the physical hunt for reference material from those old libraries. They helped fuel my own mental search engine, which to this day has not extinguished. The hunt for knowledge is just as rewarding as getting it.

# THE AZURITE ENCOUNTER

### JANE FRANCES RUBY

iUniverse, Inc.
Bloomington

# The Azurite Encounter

Conventional Books and eReaders can be ordered from most online retailers: Amazon.com, BarnesandNoble.com, etc.

iUniverse books may be ordered through booksellers or by contacting:

iUniverse
1663 Liberty Drive
Bloomington, IN 47403
www.iuniverse.com
1-800-Authors (1-800-288-4677)

ISBN: 978-1-4502-3854-0 (sc)
ISBN: 978-1-4502-3853-3 (hc)
ISBN: 978-1-4502-3852-6 (e)

Library of Congress Control Number: 2010908677

Printed in the United States of America

iUniverse rev. date: 8/31/2010
Second revision date: 3/18/2013

Please visit my website: www.TheAzuriteEncounter.com

# Azurite

- A blue ore of mined copper; copper carbonate hydroxide, $2CuCO_3 \cdot Cu(OH)_2$

- A semiprecious gem from copper ore found in Arizona and other Southwestern states

- The most popular blue pigment in European painting through out the Middle Ages and Renaissance

- Considered by Native Americans as a sacred stone and used to connect to spirit guides

- Recommended by Edgar Cayce for psychic development, and advised direct skin contact for best results

- Thought to help heal sinus problems, throat disorders, spinal alignment problems, circulatory disorders, and spasms

- Believed to be beneficial for amplifying healing ability and energy, gaining insight, mental clarity and control

- Provides assistance when expressing deepest thoughts or feelings

# Chapter I

Despite having great speed and agility, the ill-fated prey could not avoid his predators. He tried everything. He hid among the structures, blending in with the scenery, but the predators had keen eyesight and found him. He retreated back to what was once safe haven on familiar grounds, but they quickly caught his scent and followed him. He even bluffed an attack, but they weren't intimidated.

He was running out of tactics and time. His approaching enemy countered every strategic move that he made. Ultimately he was surrounded, and escape was impossible. He coughed. He choked and gasped for air as his enemy pounced on him.

"Checkmate!" Candice cried and looked across the table for her opponent to concede. Desiree glanced at the board, looking for any possible escape from her king's apparent capture, but she had to concede.

"Well, Candice Carter, you are indeed a ruthless hunter, but I admire your integrity," said Desiree as she stood up and slowly bowed to her best friend. Candice popped up from her seat and snatched up Desiree's king. Clenching it in her fist, Candice raised it high above her strawberry-blond hair as if to show power and superiority over Desiree and the rest of the world.

"Oh, yes! That's why I'm the most worthy opponent in this club," Candice proudly decreed. Her wavy, layered hair ruffled with every turn of her head. She then addressed the other players. "By the way, the same goes for the next fool who challenges me!"

Moans spontaneously rose from some of the other tables, but all heads remained bent over chessboards that topped several classroom tables. The reaction could have been in response to Candice's threat, or perhaps because other kings were in jeopardy. Desiree reached up to retrieve her king piece from Candice's grasp.

"It sounds like the rest of the club doubt your malice," Desiree said while using her long, strong fingers to pry open Candice's hand. Candice wanted to savor her victory, so she tried to hold on a little longer.

"Ow! Desiree, not only are you breaking my fingers, but you're also spoiling my victory dance, " Candice complained. She was much shorter than Desiree and had less leverage to keep her captured prize. But she finally gave in and released Desiree's king. She then put her hands on her hips and danced a brief jig while circling in place.

"Oh, yeah, look at me, I'm the best, in the West, no doubt, hear me out," she chanted, but this time her disturbance generated a few derogatory comments along with the moans.

Desiree politely flashed a smile as she gathered the rest of her chess pieces. She placed them carefully into a black, velvet sack. They were the typical size and weight of chess pieces with no fancy motif. But the dark pieces were actually a deep blue, and the lighter pieces were cream-colored with gold flakes. They were a special gift from her beloved grandfather for her sixth birthday. She wasn't interested in chess at the time, but she still found the pieces intriguing as well as the story behind them.

Her grandfather found them in a remote slot canyon he discovered in the Grand Canyon National Park. She remembered his tale of that canyon; how he saw the most strikingly blue-colored mineral in the wall. He fancied off-trail hiking and never mentioned where this particular canyon was or how he happened upon it. Maybe he took a wrong turn. Maybe a sudden flash flood washed him there—she heard news reports of those kinds of mishaps during the Monsoon Season. He never chipped the pieces from the canyon wall. Instead, he found them lying on the ground. He said they seemed to be placed in an odd array with the creamy-gold nuggets opposite the blue ones—almost like chess pieces on a board. That's where he got the idea.

She loved his story telling. He always had a fantastic tale of adventure to accompany each souvenir. Whether the story was true or made up didn't matter. When she first got the chess pieces she sat for hours on the backyard tire swing just holding them and reminiscing his adventure. He promised to take her to that hidden canyon when she got older, and she couldn't wait for that day.

But just before she entered ninth grade he died from a blood infection. She didn't understand all the complicated, medical issues. All she knew was that he got an infection from a simple stupid prick on his finger while pruning rose bushes in his backyard. It wasn't fair that he died that way; he was so much bigger, stronger and braver than those heinous, thorny plants. Her long-awaited opportunity to hike with her grandfather vanished like a krill in the jaws of a whale. Even now as a high school senior, she still mourns his death and her unrealized dream.

A tear trickled down her cheek as she finished bagging the chess pieces. She sniffled while tightening the chess bag cord.

Candice noticed and stopped dancing. She gently wrapped one arm around her opponent's shoulder. "Sorry, Desiree, guess I overdid it. I never thought you'd take defeat so badly."

Desiree's image of her wiry, leather-skinned grandpa with bright turquoise eyes whisked away like smoke from a gust of wind. An annoyingly boastful classmate replaced it.

Desiree wiped away her tear before glaring back. "Candice, I'm not going to get over it because, as they say, what doesn't kill me will make me want to beat the tar out of you next time."

Candice stopped to think about Desiree's twisted saying and asked, "Desiree, shouldn't it be *what doesn't kill you makes you stronger?*"

"Yeah, that, too," Desiree replied as she packed her school bag.

Confused, Candice first scratched her head and then hugged her best friend. By this time, the shushing from the other players was accompanied by death threats, causing the two girls to pack up and head for the exit.

As boastful as Candice was, Desiree still cherished her friendship. Candice helped Desiree get through a few, troubled teenage years. They've only known each other since ninth grade. They attended different middle schools, so their paths had never crossed until they stumbled upon each other—literally—at their adjoining, high school lockers.

On that day, Candice had just opened hers to get a notebook, and all her softball equipment tumbled onto the hallway floor. It piled in front of Desiree just as she was running to class. With a resounding gasp she stumbled over the bats and softballs, sending them into other lockers with loud, metallic *bangs*.

Desiree tried her hardest to maintain balance while negotiating all the rolling and bouncing hazards under her feet. All the noise she generated set off the security alarm. She fell to the floor while trying to grab any arm from the sea of students standing nearby. Miraculously Desiree landed softly onto her back. She hid her face, hoping that no upper classmen noticed the commotion.

Fat chance! Everybody in the hall pointed and laughed at Desiree, who was now buried in equipment, wearing a catcher's mitt on her head. Candice, herself, couldn't help laughing. When she finally caught her breath, she extended her hand to help Desiree.

"That would be my fault." Candice confessed.

"Which senior set you up for this?" Desiree asked as she reached for Candice's hand.

"They could never be this creative. My name's Candice, by the way. Any broken bones?"

"Mine's Desiree, and, no, I don't think so," Desiree replied as she sat up and removed the mitt from her head, "but this hat I'm wearing is way last season."

Candice took the catcher's mitt from Desiree. "What's worse—green rawhide just doesn't work with your pale skin or your blue eyes."

They both laughed louder than the crowd and the security alarm combined.

That was four years ago. Since then they've been the best of school buddies, even though times were rocky for Desiree. She was still bereaving her grandfather when her parents separated. She felt helpless watching her family fall apart. She lost concentration at school and dance practices.

Candice realized this during their casual discussions at the lockers between classes. She would just listen to Desiree's problems fly from her lips like the flight of hungry bats from a cave at dusk. Any typical teenager would have ignored Desiree or suggested counseling. But Candice was not typical. She had a special gift of listening. Instead of impressing Desiree with all her athletic achievements, Candice would render her undivided attention to Desiree.

Most of the time Desiree's troubles were resolved or at least minimized by class change, and Candice would end the chat with a smile or a few words of encouragement. That was all Desiree needed to feel better.

Outside school, however, they led different lives. Candice was a gifted athlete. She earned varsity letters in every sport that she played. Her favorite, however, was fencing. She felt as a *lefty* she had the advantage over the right-handed fencers.

Desiree, however, preferred the fine and performing arts. She learned to play piano when she was six-years old. Her mom enrolled her in ballet and tap classes soon after she learned to walk. She always landed major dancing or musical parts in school performances.

Desiree and Candice had only one other thing in common besides adjacent lockers—the chess club. It was an opportunity for them to chat while sitting across a chessboard. Desiree was by far the most experienced player in the club. But on this particular day she let Candice win, although not too handily. Desiree loved to see Candice's freckled face light up with glee. And, of course, there was the victory dance that followed, which today was not appreciated by the rest of the club.

"Haven't you two left yet," an annoyed chess club member mumbled from the array of heads.

While at the door Candice brazenly advised, "We'd better hurry before these losers throw us out." More growling resulted, and the girls quickly slipped out the door.

The February sun hung low in the sky casting a reddish glow through the small windows of the doors leading to the parking lot.

Candice pulled out her sunglasses. "Never thought I'd need these just before sunset," she said. "It must be murder driving west on the expressway at this time."

Desiree agreed, and likewise put on her own sunglasses. "Yeah, for once I'm glad I don't have to drive through all this glare," she said.

Their figures cast shadows that trailed and refracted across the floor behind them like a large, two-headed serpent. The girls whispered and giggled as they came to the exit doors.

A few yards before they reached the exit doors, a raspy voice came from behind them. "You need to control your emotional outbursts in the chess room, or else there will be carnage where you stand."

Both girls stopped but did not turn around to see who it was; they already knew.

"Hey, Wesley," replied Candice, who didn't so much as flinch from his threat. "My outburst didn't mess up your concentration, did it?"

Wesley jumped in front of them. "Well, as a matter of fact, Candice, I lost my match way before your outburst—but enough about me. Are you two doing the field trip next month?"

"Field trip?" Desiree turned to Candice. "What field trip?"

"Desiree, I put the permission slip in your folder right at the end of geology class today," Candice replied. "Remember? No, I guess not because you were too busy gazing at the rocks in the display case."

"They're not rocks; they're crystals," corrected Desiree.

"They're not crystals," interrupted Wesley, who was just dying to get into this argument. "They're special lenses that diffract Desiree's focus in class."

"Wes, you're such a dweeb," Desiree replied as she gently punched Wes in the arm. "But seriously, where's it this time? I hope it's not to a museum or dairy farm."

Candice and Wes paused and faced each other, and Candice spoke first. "What's wrong with museums—I love museums!" she cried. "My favorite was the Hall of Flame Museum. They have the best fireman's pole for sliding."

Wes ignored Candice, pulling on Desiree's arm and twirling her back towards him. "And what do you have against those all-important, dairy farms that produce bone-strengthening nourishment to millions of calcium-deprived Americans? Good nutrition is very important don't you—?"

"Wesley, STOP!" Desiree cried, cutting him off before he gained momentum in his hideous monologue.

Wesley pulled out his lower lip and scowled. Then he looked down at the floor, and turned towards the exit doors in complete dejection. Desiree and Candice followed him out and laughed as they skipped down the outdoor steps to the parking lot. Both girls were just about to call for rides, but Wes was way ahead of them.

"Will you both be nice to me if I drive you home?" Wes offered, "I just had my truck cleaned, and it's got new car, air-freshener."

"Really—that's a first," Desiree remarked with sarcastic enthusiasm.

"OK, we'll be nice, if you'll be quiet," Candice answered.

"Deal!" Wesley cried. Candice and Desiree laughed and flanked him. Wrapping arms around each other's waist, they skipped like giddy first-graders down the paved walk towards Wesley's truck. Being seniors meant they could act this way without ridicule from any lower classmen. It was a senior privilege.

Wesley Ward was another good friend of Desiree's, who accompanied her to sports games or school plays. He was more cerebral and sensitive than most guys at school. She really enjoyed his odd sense of humor. He seemed comfortable with his teenage awkwardness, and he used it to make fun of himself and guys in general just to amuse her.

He weaseled out of early boyhood troubles with his quick wit because the neighborhood bullies had no ammunition for teasing. If they made fun of his tall, skinny build...

*—Hey Scarecrow, where's Tin Man?*

Wesley would come back with an even funnier reply:

*—I would know if I only had a brain!*

If they picked on his bottle-thick glasses...

*—Do those double as binoculars?*

His comeback was even funnier:

*—Binoculars? More like replacement lenses for the Hubble Telescope!*

The bullies would laugh even harder.

He had no social problems at elementary and middle school because he was home-schooled like all his siblings. His dad owned a consulting business and was always traveling. His mom ran the household as well the schooling for all six children. They were amazingly smart and socially adjusted because she impressed the importance of teamwork, patience and tolerance. When Wes was old enough for high school, his mom turned him loose in the world of public education. He fit in perfectly—just like his older siblings.

Wesley's frame filled out with lean muscles after many years of competitive swimming. Contact lenses replaced his eyeglasses, and the world finally saw his pale-green eyes. They especially attracted Desiree because the color resembled the large crystal in geology class. As a self-proclaimed late-bloomer Wesley had to fight off all the high school girls ("because they're only after one thing" he would say to Desiree) and used his quick humor to keep Desiree's other chess club friends amused. Wes has won the Class Clown Award since ninth grade and will most probably win it again this year.

"So, Wes, about the field trip," continued Desiree, "any idea where it's at?"

"Neither museum nor dairy farm," answered Wesley. "It's a geological study at the Grand Canyon."

They all sat in the front seat of a large, pickup truck that Wesley inherited from his dad. It used to carry all his dad's construction equipment, which many times came straight from a dusty or muddy site. Wesley had the truck for over a year, but he never found time for custom detailing. As a result some of the construction artifacts still remained in the carpet and on the seats. Wes opened his window, and dust from the graveled parking lot blew into the truck's cab.

"Ugh, now I have to vacuum in here again," he grumbled.

Desiree coughed a little as she tried to fan some of the road dust away from her face. "The Grand Canyon—you're kidding, right?"

"*Moi*? Have I ever?"

"*Vous*, and, yes, most of the time."

Wes answered her using a booming voice and sounding like a game show host. "Well, not this time, *mon cherie*. The field trip is for Mr. Roeser's geology students. It's his annual project for seniors only. You camp for three days and nights with several of your best friends in the beautifully majestic but mysterious Wonder of the World—"

"—Wes, you need to reboot," Candice said, interrupting him.

"Sorry," replied Wes. "Guess I got a little carried away—like I always do."

But Desiree was intrigued. "No, tell us more," she insisted, "Did Mr. Roeser mention exactly where?" She was hoping maybe the field trip would be along one of the trails that her grandfather travelled.

"In the Grand Canyon, of course," he replied.

"It's a big canyon, Wes. Any idea *where* in the canyon?" asked Candice.

Wes now took the role of an unfortunate infidel undergoing a Spanish Inquisition. He pulled his right arm behind his back as if it was being twisted, and he pleaded with them as if in pain.

"Please, don't hurt me. I'll tell you all I know. My older sister went on it last year—Ow! You're hurting me—and my older brother the year before that. But they both camped in different spots—North Rim, South Rim, Phantom Canyon, Lava Canyon, I don't know. Maybe Roeser changes it every year. We won't know until the hike stops. Please, I'm telling you everything!"

During all this Desiree and Candice turned to each other, exchanging their usual fish stare—like they've done several times before—when Wes went off in his monologues.

"Oi," said Candice in reaction to Wes' melodrama. She looked back at Wes. "But that kind of field trip requires strength, fitness and youth. Roeser is as old as the Grand Canyon."

"And he looks twice as eroded," added Wes.

"How can he hike a steep trail, and, at the same time, handle a bunch of seniors on spring break?" Candice asked.

"Anyone, young or ancient, can hike the trails," Wes said, "but it's not age that's the problem. It's the lack of planning that can kill you. At least that's what my brother and sister said. They told me about hikers going in without enough water. Then during the hike out they run out of water. They end up dehydrated and start to puke—oh, the horror—and need medical help."

"I'll bet Roeser uses a mule to carry his provisions; that's how a lot of folks do it," said Desiree. "My grandpa sometimes took a mule for his stuff."

"Your grandpa hiked the canyon?" Wes asked.

"A lot, ever since he was young." Her eyes lit up as she got a chance to reminisce his life. "He used to tell me stories of exploring the smaller slot canyons. Once he discovered a hidden canyon that had blue- and white-striped canyon walls."

Candice was intrigued. "That sounds awesome. Did he ever take you to this hidden canyon?"

Desiree's gaze went out the window. "No, my mom thought it was too dangerous," she said, and then sighed. "She'd never let me go anywhere with Grandpa unless both my parents came. It seemed like they were protecting me from his adventures—like they would be disastrous. But they never were. Each time he came back I'd get a great story about river running, rock climbing or just hiking trails. It sounded like fun, and he came back with all his limbs. OK, maybe he got few scratches—but everybody gets those. So why wasn't it safe enough for me?"

There was a long silence because her best friends had no answer. They arrived at Desiree's house, and Wes turned into the driveway.

"Did your grandpa ever keep a journal of his Grand Canyon hikes?" Wes asked. Desiree got out to get her backpack out of the back of the truck before coming back to Wes' window.

"Journal?" Desiree asked. "Hmm. Well, I never saw one. But that's not to say he didn't keep one." She stuck her head into Wes' window and quickly kissed his cheek. "I'm going to find out. You're a genius, Wes!" She then ran towards the house.

From her window Candice called out to Desiree. "And what am I—chopped liver?" Desiree turned back around and saw Candice sticking her head out the window with her eyes closed and puckering her fat, pink lips.

Desiree laughed. "Oh, sorry, Candice," she said and blew her a kiss, "you're the best chopped liver ever!"

# Chapter II

A middle-aged, slightly arthritic woman wandered alone. She explored this area countless times before, but for some reason she couldn't recognize her surroundings. The patterns on the walls did not look right nor did the textures on the ground. She plodded along with her bulky load of provisions. The ground was level, and there were no hazards nearby.

She stopped to check her watch. She took a quick drink of water before continuing her search, hoping for any glimpse of familiarity. She turned and proceeded through a different passage now that raised her comfort level. With a burst of energy she quickened her pace. A glimmer of hope shined upon her. But then she collided with an unrelenting wall that reached up into oblivion. She sidestepped and circled it but could not find a path around it.

It was another dead end! Hope crumbled from her spirit like bark from a decaying tree, and she started to panic. Her anxiety level rose, her breathing increased, and her palms started to sweat. She doubled back and proceeded again towards another path scanning high and low with desperation in her darting eyes. A broad, shapeless figure was crouched down in the recessed corner of the wall. She felt his presence, but resolved her defeat and prepared herself for the inevitable confrontation.

"Hey, handsome, can you point me to the jarred popcorn?"

"Third aisle, left side, about halfway," the store clerk cheerfully replied as he pointed behind her. "Can I show you?"

"No, thanks, sweetie," Janelle replied, turning her shopping cart. "You've helped me enough, and I appreciate it." The milk carton slid, and a few apples rolled across the bottom of her cart as she sped towards Aisle Three.

Just then her cell phone rang. It was a cutesy hip-hop tune with a female group:

*Baaay-beh, yer just no good for me. Mama sez you
ain't reality...*

The woman stopped her cart, fished inside her purse, and pulled out her phone before the whole grocery store heard the next verse of the song.

"Hello, this is Janelle...Oh! Hi, Desiree. How was school today? Did you have a good chess match?"

Desiree had a detailed reply as her mom continued towards Aisle Three.

"So you let Candice win. Wasn't that nice of you, Desiree? But you're clearly the better player than she. You shouldn't let her think that she can win at everything. She's going to develop a false sense of success. Then when she goes out into the real world she's going to think she can beat everybody at everything." She waited for another long reply. "Field trip? Where? The Grand Canyon? Oh, no—I mean—oh, great!"

She rocked the shopping cart back and forth slowly, and looked around as if she forgot to do something. "Travel journal?

15

Well, I wouldn't know, Desiree, maybe you should ask your dad." She stopped rocking the cart. "…Because he lives at your Grandpa's house, and a lot of his stuff is still there. Why can't you use your own car?" A loud reply blurted from the speaker. "Oh, yeah. That's right—it's still in the collision repair shop," Janelle replied cynically. "You know, life in our household would run so much easier if you could learn to drive more defensively…I know that it wasn't your fault, sweetie, but geez, maybe next time you see the Light Rail crossing signal you can stop and let the car behind you take his chances over the tracks…All right… Fine, just make sure you're super careful." Janelle snapped her phone closed, and shoved it in her purse.

She quickly hobbled towards the popcorn, snatched up a jar and dropped it in her cart. The jar landed with a loud pop but miraculously didn't break. The clerk heard the commotion and peered around the corner. He worried about the next item she was shopping for and prayed for a softer landing.

After ending the heated discussion with her mom, Desiree hung up the phone and unloaded her backpack. After some rummaging she pulled out a spiral notebook with *Geology* scribbled on the top, outside cover. She opened it to the inside pocket and pulled out several loose papers. She carefully fingered through them until she found the *geology field trip* permission slip. She carefully pulled it out and flattened it on the kitchen counter, smoothing out its wrinkles before reading the trip's details.

*Location…location…where exactly is this field trip?* Desiree asked herself as she perused each paragraph and turned to the back of the page. *Come on, why isn't it the first thing printed on this stupid slip? Maybe I missed it.* She flipped the page back over slamming it on the counter. She read it from the top again.

"Dizzy, is that you?" her brother called from his bedroom.

Desiree carefully slid the permission slip back into her folder and answered her brother. "Royce, you had better be dressed for swim practice because Mom will be home soon, and then we have to fly. I have to be at the library."

"Know what the tie said to the hat?" he asked, suddenly appearing in the kitchen doorway. "*You go on a head, and I'll just hang around*, get it?" He was dressed in his warm-up suit with a swim bag strapped over his shoulder.

Even though Royce was her kid brother he was already taller than she. He was a freshman at the same high school and swam for the varsity swim team. Royce never had the awkward underclassman beginnings like his sister.

"I'm getting a ride tonight, so you can go on ahead—get it, *a head*?" Royce lightly jabbed her arm.

"Only if you quit the quirky jokes," replied Desiree, as she blocked his jab and tickled his well-chiseled abdomen.

He flinched and guarded himself with both arms. "Hey, cut that out, Dizzy—tickling isn't fair."

"Being ticklish is your Achilles' Heel, Baby-bro," teased Desiree. "Don't ever get caught in a dark alley with thugs who tickle."

Suddenly a car horn sounded from outside. "That's must be my ride—and in the nick of time—so got to go," Royce said slipping past his sister while still protecting himself. "I'll call you if I need a ride home." He darted out of the house and ran to the car.

Then the phone rang. It was Desiree's mom, and she was running a few minutes late.

"That's OK, Mom, I don't have to drive Royce to swim practice. He got a ride, so I'll have some extra time before I go to the library. Is there anything I can eat for dinner?" She waited for a reply and walked to the freezer. "No problem, I'll just heat it.

Thanks, Mom. See you in a bit. And, Mom, sorry I upset you on the phone earlier. You know how I get when talking about Grandpa." Desiree hung up phone and powered up the TV.

Her mom left a travel channel on, but Desiree didn't change it because she just wanted to listen while eating dinner. She went back into the kitchen, opened the freezer door, and grabbed the dark, green plastic container. She popped open the plastic lid.

Lasagna! Desiree loved her mom's homemade lasagna. She missed it for dinner yesterday because she had dance practices all night. But it always tasted better as a leftover. Desiree placed the lasagna in the microwave and set the cooking timer. The microwave confirmed her settings with the usual *beeps* and ran its program.

Desiree went back into the family room and turned up the TV's volume. The program showed a mule team carrying tourists down a trail of the Grand Canyon. She heard the tour guide mention *Bright Angel Trail* and walked back into the kitchen. She pulled out her dinner from the microwave, and set it down on the counter. She poured a glass of milk and grabbed a fork before sitting in one of the four barstools at the long counter that separated the kitchen from the family room.

The tour guide on TV was describing how the mule team walks the narrow, unpaved trail while carrying tourists down to the Colorado River. She watched intently with her dark-blue eyes fixed on the screen. She slowly absorbed into the program. She pictured herself stepping over the loose rocks and tree roots. At times she gazed at the monstrous yet monumental canyon walls.

She didn't notice that her mom arrived home and walked through the back door to the kitchen. Desiree didn't even look down at the large chunk of lasagna she had on her fork. She needed to cut it before putting it in her mouth. But her eyes were glued to the treacherously steep and descending trail. Just as she raised the noodle to her lips, a sudden gust of wind blew up from the abyss and knocked her off the path over to the ledge. Fearing the worst she grabbed for a tree root, which jutted out from the nearby rocks. The thin, vine-like root suddenly snapped, and she slid down the loose rocks. She jabbed her fork into a crack to avoid falling into the abyss. Then she felt the saucy, noodle drop to her chin, slide down her neck, bounce from her chest and finally tumble into her lap.

"See? This is why you still have to sit in the kitchen when you eat," her mom nagged from the back doorway.

"Oh, hi, Mom, sorry about the mess," Desiree replied, "I slipped off the trail and was falling down the cliff." She removed the piece of lasagna from her lap, replaced it in the bowl and grabbed a napkin from the dispenser. She wiped her lips and the saucy trail down the front of her clothes. "Guess I was careless."

"Were you in one of your fantasy worlds again?" her mother asked as she entered the kitchen with her groceries.

Desiree still daydreamed a lot about grandpa's adventures in the canyons. He'd been gone now for about four years, but whenever she had a moment to herself she daydreamed about his hiking trips. She imagined hiking with him and finding the chess pieces.

"Well, as soon as you're rescued from the crevasse would you please give me your top and jeans so I can launder them?" Both her kids were still messy when they ate. She prays for a day without spills or accidents.

"Sure, Mom, as soon as I'm done," her daughter replied. "So, how was your day?"

"OK, I guess," her mom answered as she emptied the grocery bags on the same counter. "I got all my errands done, but

I'm afraid the car needs gas." She handed her daughter some money. "Would you mind getting some before you go anywhere?"

"No problem; I'm just going to the library tonight. I'm meeting with Taylor and Dominique. We're going to work on our English Lit paper for a couple of hours. After that I'll come straight home unless Royce needs a ride after his swim practice."

Her mom put the jar of popcorn away and then sat next to Desiree. "I can't wait for your car to get out of the shop," she replied in frustration. "Letting *you* drive my car can sometimes drive *me* nuts."

"I'm sure I'll get my car back soon," Desiree replied before gulping down the rest of her milk. She then grabbed her dinnerware and placed them in the sink. "Maybe I'll get it back before our field trip next month."

"Oh, that's right—the field trip. Where are you kids going again?" Janelle asked.

"Somewhere in the Grand Canyon National Park," answered Desiree. She walked back to the counter and pulled out the permission slip from her folder. "But I checked the info, and it didn't say exactly where. It just had the park office phone number."

Janelle read the slip. "Hmm…I don't see the location either, but maybe you'll find out later. Do you have to drive all two hundred and some odd miles to the National Park?"

"No, Mom, the school always uses a bus," said Desiree. "I was just hoping to get my car back, so I can shop for stuff beforehand—you know, sleeping bag, sunscreen, hiking boots. This could involve some serious drive time to the mall and the surrounding stores."

"I'll bet it could," her mom replied. She read over the date of the trip. "Next month, huh?"

"Yeah, over spring break, so I've got a whole month to prepare. Mr. Roeser listed all the stuff we need."

"I just read that part. But now I'm reading the part about rock picks, ropes, and beacons. What kind of trip is this?" her now worrisome mother asked.

Desiree was still watching the mule team travel the switchback trail on TV. "Mom, I doubt Roeser would put us in danger. I'm guessing he just wants to be prepared in case of an emergency." She got up and walked towards her bedroom. She stopped at the hallway mirror and looked at the lasagna stains on her shirt and jeans. *Yikes! I'm a mess*, she thought. Then she yelled back to her mom. "I'm sure he wants us to have a safe and educational trip."

*Educational, huh?* Desiree's mom asked herself. Her attention went to the TV, which showed hikers emerging from the canyon trail. Each one wore a backpack and several pieces of gear strapped upon it like a totem pole. All wore wide-brimmed hats and heavy hiking boots. "I'm not so sure you should go on this field trip, Desiree," her mom called out to Desiree. "This kind of hiking looks pretty intense. And I don't see a whole lot of guardrails along the main trail. Accidents can happen when ya least expect them."

Desiree was already in her room removing her soiled clothes. She quickly slipped on a dark blue T-shirt and matching sweatpants. "Mom, accidents can happen just walking down our driveway," she yelled back.

Her mom walked toward the doorway to the hall. "That may be true," she agreed. "But if you trip on the driveway you only fall a few feet—not thousands of feet."

"Mr. Roeser has this field trip every year," Desiree said, trying to ease her mom's mind. "Wesley's brother and sister went on it, and Wes said they had a blast." She returned to her mom with the lasagna-stained clothes. "I'll be super-careful. I might get sore muscles or a few scratches, but it's the Grand Canyon, Mom. This is the adventure of a lifetime. I'll be with all my friends. Can I go, pretty please?"

Her mom took the clothes from Desiree. "Does your Dad know about this trip yet?"

"Not yet," answered Desiree, "but I'll call him tonight, I promise."

"Well, I never did let your grandfather take you on his crazy excursions, but now I suppose you're old enough to go with your class."

Desiree's face lit up like a casino marquis in Las Vegas. "Mom, really?" She then hugged her. "You are absolutely epic! Thank you!"

Her mom never felt such an exuberant hug before. She caught her breath and stepped back. "But you have to promise me you'll be more careful eating, and you have to promise to avoid the train crossing."

"I promise to be clean, neat, and dent-free!" Desiree shouted gleefully, taking the keys from the counter. She grabbed her school bag and headed out the back door. Then she turned back to her mom. "Oh, yeah and thanks for saving the lasagna for me; it really hit the spot!"

Janelle watched Desiree leave before looking at the soiled clothes in her hands. "Yes, it hit a few spots," she mumbled as she walked to the laundry room and placed the clothes in the washer. She heard Desiree start the car and drive off. It was already twilight, so Janelle turned on the outside lights then walked back towards the family room.

The Grand Canyon program was showing an interview with one of the park rangers. "...Of course there are dangerously steep areas. But we can't put up guard rails on every trail in this park..."

Janelle walked up to the TV screen, and started talking to the uniformed gentleman. "And why the hell not?" she asked.

"...Because there are just too many trails. We don't have the resources or the money to safeguard every trail down to the Colorado River. Even if we did, it would no doubt spoil the canyon's natural beauty."

"I'm OK with a little spoilage," Janelle answered.

"...We have a few checkpoints and ranger stations along the major trails. We also have signs throughout the park and on the maps helping visitors along. But they need to follow the basic safety rules like carrying adequate water, staying on the trails, hiking with a buddy, and using common sense..."

"And if they don't, you escort 'em out, right?" she asked.

"...We have all the campers register and detail the trails they intend to use..."

"Yes, but you didn't answer my question."

"...This helps us locate them in the case of an emergency..."

"Emergency, huh? Like what? Skinned knees? Broken bones? Death?"

"...Trying to completely safeguard the entire park makes as much sense as building a stairway up to the summit of Mt. Everest..."

"No stairway? I'll bet there's a lot of accidents there, too, not to mention lawsuits."

"We're not a theme park; we're a nature park."

Janelle giggled through her nose. "That means no Fast Pass, right?" she asked jokingly.

"Most of the safety measures have been in place along the South Rim's heavily visited areas, and—"

"—I hope that's where Desiree's campsite will be," she said.

"—In order to safely enjoy the breathtaking views you must follow the rules," the ranger said as video camera cut away to a trail which seemed to snake endlessly down to obscurity.

Janelle sighed and switched to another channel, which showed a snowstorm in the upper Midwest.

She sat down at the counter, pulled out her planner and turned to the first day of spring break. She scribbled in *Desiree's Field Trip* as the first entry. She looked for other entries hoping to find conflicting events, which would cause her to cancel Desiree's trip like perhaps senior prom, a wedding or distant relative's birthday party. But the pages were empty. She sighed and reached for the permission slip that was still on the counter. She signed it and left it for Desiree to find in the morning.

Janelle and her children live on a farm in the central corridor of the city. She represents the fourth generation of proud, organic farmers. Her great-grandparents purchased this five-acre farm to grow crops easily adaptable to the desert climate. They built giant compost bins to generate natural fertilizers. They used water from the local canal system to irrigate their crops like the many generations of farmers did before them.

Her family also established a cooperative network of farms, suppliers, and distributors, making local farming more economical. When growing organic became popular again business boomed, but growth was limited by subdivisions and strip malls that eventually surrounded the property. A small number of farmhands either live nearby or take the city bus to work. Her parents, though retired from full-time duties, still consult on production and accounting.

She even started an organic farming camp for the local school kids to teach the next generation of organic farmers in exchange for free labor.

She hopes that some day her own children will take over the business, but she knows that they will have their own paths to follow. Right now they have to finish high school and not eat so sloppily. She loves her kids and doesn't want them to grow too quickly, but at the same time she wishes they each had cars. And—more importantly right now—the Light Rail Train won't be running this evening.

Less than a mile away, Desiree pulled into the gas station. She ran to the cashier, paid for gas and returned to the car. While filling her gas tank, a Jeep Wrangler pulled alongside and two girls called out to her.

"Hey, Desiree!" It was Dominique and Taylor, her English literature classmates. Dominique jumped out to pay the cashier. "We'll see you at the library after we get some dinner," she said.

"We just got out of volleyball practice and we're starving," Taylor remarked from the passenger side, grabbing her stomach. "I think I'll have a double order of fries with my cheeseburger."

"It will never beat out my mom's leftover lasagna," Desiree replied, "You guys should come over and try it sometime."

"Sounds like a date, but only if your brother is there," said Taylor. "He's so dreamy and cute!"

Dominique heard her partner while fueling her jeep. "Taylor, you got the hots for a frosh?"

Taylor spun around in her seat to answer Dominique. "So what if he's a frosh. I don't care. I saw him in first period P.E. class, and wow! I hear he's on the swim team; bet he looks great in a swim suit!"

"Calm down, Taylor," said Desiree, as she finished pumping gas and returned the nozzle to the pump. She then walked to Taylor's side of the jeep. "He's my baby brother, and I'm very protective."

"Do you have an older brother?" Taylor asked.

"No, just Royce—and that's enough for me."

Taylor snapped her fingers. "Damn! I never get a break," she cried. "Oh well, you can't blame me for trying."

"Maybe you can find someone closer to your age," said Dominique, "like those cuties that practice in the court next to us. You'll never find an ugly, volleyball guy."

"Yeah, like that middle-hitter with the dreamy brown eyes," replied Taylor. She turned back towards the front of the jeep and took a deep sigh. "He's so tan and island-looking."

"I think he's Samoan, and there's no such thing as an ugly Samoan guy," said Dominique. "Maybe that's why he plays volleyball."

"So, which came first, the chicken or the egg?" Desiree asked.

"Huh—what do you mean?" asked Dominique.

"Does he play volleyball because he's cute, or is he cute because he plays volleyball?"

"Does it matter? So, what about the chicken-egg thing?"

"Ugh, never mind," said Desiree in frustration as she turned back to her car. *Maybe this is the reason why I don't hang out with these girls too often. But at least they're good for getting schoolwork done,* she thought. "So, how long will you be?"

"Oh, we shouldn't be more than fifteen minutes behind you," said Dominique as she got back in the driver's seat. "We need to get our papers started tonight, so we'll make it quick."

"OK, See you there," replied Desiree as she got back in and started her car. She drove for a few blocks before pulling out onto a quiet street towards the library. The streetlights cast an orange glow down to the Bougainvillea shrubs and Palo Verde trees. The air felt especially crisp this evening, so she didn't see too many people walking dogs or strollers.

She pulled into the parking lot of the library. It began as a driveway lined by desert shrubs and squat, multi-trunked trees. After a few yards it broke off into a set of parking aisles. Each aisle was joined by a common walkway, which also was tree-lined to offer shade for day visitors. However, at night, small can lights in the ground pointed upward, illuminating the trunks and lower branches. It gave them an eerie glow, making the walkway appear like the throat of a spiny, prehistoric creature.

Desiree parked in the aisle farthest from the building, so that she could enjoy the long walk. She pretended getting lost in the creature's throat as she darted and dodged every branch, looking for escape.

But it came quickly as the walkway soon opened to a wide crosswalk just a few yards from the building. As she crossed, she could see the single story, cinder block building accented by large wooden panels. Each panel had an earthy color of purple, gold, red, or brown. The windows between the panels stretched from floor to ceiling but had thin openings to minimize the radiant heat from the unrelenting, desert sun. Thin, vertical strips of silvery metal shaped like small chevrons stacked upon one another protected the glass. The décor reminded her of some futuristic civilization living in harsh, stone-age times.

Desiree proceeded to the front entrance, which was fortified by panels made of steel rebar that encaged river rock. She stopped to inspect one cage. It had rocks of different sizes and color. She reached in with her hand to brush her fingers over the rock surfaces. They all felt smooth and round although each had a unique color and shape. *No two are the same; just like snowflakes,* she thought.

Before she headed to the entrance doors, she stopped and turned back to view the journey she just completed. *If this wasn't a library it could be an ideal hideout—just like one of Grandpa's secret slot canyons,* she thought. She grabbed two rocks and imagined climbing a rock wall, but, before she could reach the top, two kids darted out of the sliding door. She let go of the rocks and slipped through the door before it closed again. *Whew! Good thing I got out before the entrance sealed. I could have been trapped forever,* she thought.

In the library Desiree immediately searched for the reference section and sat at the nearest round table. She grabbed her notebook and looked for the assignment. Her teacher wanted the class to review a book from an English or American author, but she couldn't start until she got the outline from her classmates.

Her choice for the review assignment was a work from her favorite author, William Shakespeare. The only problem was she couldn't decide which of his works to review. She had so many favorites. Her dad read most of them to her as bedtime stories when she was younger. He loved getting into each character. He used so much drama when he read the lines, and she would laugh hilariously at the voices he used to depict each character. It was especially funny when he would try to portray a child or fairy with a high-pitched voice. She took delight hearing it from a man so big and masculine. He didn't mind; he loved hearing his daughter laugh.

She missed her dad not being at home. He felt that the blood infection responsible for grandpa's death was preventable.

Her dad's guilt was so strong, that it consumed him, and he withdrew from the family. He stayed at his dad's house for several hours each day. Sometimes he didn't come home until after midnight.

This frustrated Desiree's mom, and she urged him to undergo counseling. They both went, but after a few weeks her mom was the only one going. Finally she gave him a choice: to either move past his guilt or move out. He chose the latter, living and working out of his dad's house. It has been over three years that they've lived apart.

In her heart Desiree hopes their separation is only temporary. She loves both of them and can't bear to see them apart. Both try to spend more time with her, and that helped a little. But while in school Desiree needed to be with her friends, especially Candice. She once told Desiree at the ice cream shop that ninety percent of all families were dysfunctional. Desiree wasn't sure where Candice got her data, but just hearing all Candice's crazy facts was great therapy.

That and Shakespeare. Desiree read as much as she could between dance classes and school. Sometimes after reading a few passages she would close her eyes and picture her dad's attempt at play-acting. She interjected Shakespearean quotes in her everyday conversations. When she cursed she used Shakespearean curses, which at times creeped-out her friends. Luckily they understood what she was going through and that quoting Shakespeare helped her through some troubled times.

Dominique and Taylor, when not busy with volleyball, were her main study buddies. They wanted grades as high as their volleyball skill level. They realized both would increase their chances for college scholarships. Desiree also wanted to attend college but didn't have any specific one in mind. She just knew that she was interested in geology. Maybe her grandpa's stories influenced her, and maybe a couple of her trips with her parents to the Grand Canyon did also. But her study buddies motivated Desiree enough this year to focus on academics.

Right now, though, she needed that outline. She got up from the table and looked towards the entrance. No study buddies yet. She then meandered around the library aisles, stopping the *Local Topics Section*. There she saw colorfully covered books on the Mogollon Rim, Petrified Forest, Native American Country, and the Grand Canyon.

She picked up a book that contained several depictions of the Grand Canyon by local artists. The front cover had a cubist impression of the North Rim. She ran her fingers across the surface, hoping to feel the textures of the rocks as the colors and shadings suggested. But the depiction deceived her since she felt only a flat, smooth surface. She paged through several illustrations of many local artists, hoping to find a canyon with blue- and white-striped walls.

She found fascinating representations of vegetation, weather and landscapes, but she didn't see anything similar to her grandfather's canyon. In frustration she forcefully closed the book, causing wisps of hair to puff away from her face. *Oh well,* she thought, *maybe these artists never saw Grandpa's hidden canyon.*

She then found a book describing all the documented deaths in the Grand Canyon. She paged to the flash floods chapter. She read how slot canyons drain rainfall from the high plateaus down to the Colorado River. She raced through some stories where the rainstorms were ten or more miles away from the unfortunate hikers who got caught in the ensuing floods. *Yikes, it was a good thing that Grandpa never got caught in those,* although she remembered one of his adventures about escaping rapidly rising water. *He always returned to tell the tale, so maybe he stayed on the higher trails,* she thought. Suddenly she was startled by a backpack dropping loudly on her reading table.

"Desiree, you can't write a review of the Grand Canyon," said Taylor.

Dominique sat down next to Desiree. "Taylor, you never know; maybe some obscure British poet visited the park and wrote a poem about it."

Desiree smiled at them both. "Hey—that didn't take long. You guys were quick!" She then led them to the round table that she had set up for the study session.

"Actually we took longer," said Taylor as she placed her backpack on one of the chairs. "We were still hungry after our cheeseburger combos, so we went back for dessert."

"And you didn't even notice our extended absence," Dominique complained as she stepped in front of Taylor. "That cuts us deep, Desiree, really deep."

Desiree didn't know what to say. Dominique looked dead serious so must have been insulted somehow. She has been known to fly off the handle.

"Did I seriously insult you?" Desiree asked. Dominique never changed her expression while continuing her glare.

Finally Taylor popped up from behind her. "No," Taylor answered and then laughed.

"Gotcha," said Dominique, cracking a sly smile. But after a few seconds she scowled. "OK, enough screwing around. We need to started on this paper," she said as they all pulled out pens and paper. "We got lots to do and this place closes in two hours."

"No, it closes in one hour," interrupted the librarian, who overheard them while pushing a cart full of returned books past their table. "Due to cuts in the state's budget we had to shorten our

31

hours. We turn off the lights and lock the door one hour early Monday through Saturday. We're also closed on Sundays now."

"Ouch," exclaimed Dominique. "Now *that* really cuts us deep," she said while pulling out the assignment outline. Then she asked the librarian, "Copy machine still costs the same, right?"

"Yep, so copy 'em while you can still afford it," the librarian replied as she pushed her cart over to the *State Government* section.

"Guess I'd better hurry," said Dominique, as she clenched her coins, took the outline and turned toward the copy machine. She then bent over and tucked in her cache, looking like a thief right after a burglary and hurried towards the copy machine. Taylor rolled her eyes, hoping that no one else in the library saw Dominique's theatrics.

Desiree laughed. She wasn't sure if Dominique was really serious or not, but it didn't matter. "I'll bet her drama on the volleyball court is a real scream," Desiree commented to Taylor.

"That's where she got it," Taylor replied. "She's the captain of our team, and that means she's the official spokesperson on the court while we're playing. No one else can call the time-outs or question the referee's call but her. But when she contests a call she has to sound all polite and sportsmanlike. If she doesn't she can get kicked off the court—or even worse—the other team gets a point."

Desiree laughed again. "The opponents' point is worse than losing your own captain? Sounds like you don't value her much."

Taylor smiled and answered. "We do; she's the best captain we've ever had, but don't tell her that."

"I won't—I promise," giggled Desiree. "But with her low boiling point how does Dominique question a call without getting upset?"

"She's learned how to pretend really well. She puts on her happy hat, and she politely questions the call and punctuates it with a *please*. After the ref explains the call, she comes back with a *thank you, and have a great day* reply. She could be as mad as hell about the call, but she never raises her voice or cusses. She does it well, but sometimes it can sound pretty sassy. The rest of us are laughing behind her back, but we can't get penalized for laughing. It's such a funny ruse. What it really does is calm us down, so we can play a better game."

"I need to come to one of your matches sometime and see this in action," Desiree replied.

Dominique soon returned with three copies of the outline. "So, did everyone miss me?" she asked.

"Only because we couldn't gossip about you anymore," replied Taylor.

Dominique took a heavy and rough-sounding gasp. "No! You promised to keep it all a secret!"

Taylor was right about Dominique's theatrics, and played along. "Yeah, but Desiree bribed me with a lot of money," she said while winking at Desiree.

Dominique quickly switched to her normal tone of voice. "OK, that's cool, Taylor, but we're splitting the money, right?"

Taylor smiled. "Like always," she said.

Dominique then passed out the outlines. They read the first question—*State the title and author of your book*—and began writing.

A few minutes passed before Desiree asked Dominique, "Which book did you choose?"

"Agatha Christie's *The Mystery of the Blue Train*," she answered. "Because I love mysteries, and it's the best one." Then she turned to Taylor. "What about you, partner?"

"I'm doing my paper on Charles Dickens' *Great Expectations*," said Taylor as she held up her paperback version of the classic book. The cover was bent and wrinkled with several dog-eared pages.

"That must be your personal copy," surmised Dominique. "It has seen better days."

Taylor giggled. "As you can tell I read it a lot," said Taylor. "And you can just imagine what my copy of Dickens' *The Christmas Story* looks like."

"Pretty worn out from all the Christmas season readings?" Desiree asked.

"You know it," Taylor answered. "It's even got traces of milk and cookies that we used to put out for Santa."

Dominique laughed before looking over at Desiree, who was already on the second question: *In no less than one page please summarize the story.* "So what are you doing yours on, Desiree?" Dominique asked. "No, let me guess; Shakespeare, pray tell?"

"*O! She doth teach the torches to burn bright,*" Desiree answered, quoting Shakespeare. "How did you guess?"

Dominique and Taylor laughed. But all the laughing caused the librarian to glare at them. They mouthed *sorry* back at her and continued chatting in a softer volume.

"That you'd pick Shakespeare for your review? Oh, just a lucky guess," Dominique whispered back, winking at Taylor.

But Desiree felt a need to explain herself. "Look, I know you guys think I'm crazy about Shakespeare, but he really was the best writer ever. He had the most incredible imagination, and he used the most amazing language."

"Well, I read some of it once," admitted Taylor. "But I couldn't understand anything he said. His sentences were kind of backwards—like how *Yoda* talked in *Star Wars*."

"Not all the time," said Desiree. "In fact some of his quotes are used in everyday language. Dominique just quoted Shakespeare when she said that Taylor's book has seen better days. The phrase, *seen better days,* was used in *Othello,* and *As You Like It*."

"Damn—I quoted Shakespeare and never even read his stuff!" Dominique exclaimed.

Although still whispering, Desiree's voice escalated while defending Shakespeare's writing style. "You also have to understand that he wrote in verse—like everything was a poem. Once you get used to his style then you can understand how beautiful his language was."

"OK, maybe I should give him another try sometime," said Taylor trying to appease Desiree.

"Sure, how about when we have nothing else to do—like on the field trip to the Grand Canyon, perhaps?" Desiree proposed.

"You're going on the field trip?" Dominique asked.

Desiree stopped writing and leaned in closer to her study buddies. "Yeah, my mom is letting me go—all by myself. I can't wait." Her voice rose even louder. "So what do you say? Promise you'll let me read you one, short Shakespearean play. Then you can decide."

Taylor and Dominique both knew about Desiree's rough times. They wanted her to be happy, so they considered her offer.

"OK, but promise—just one play," Dominique said.

"I promise," Desiree answered, rapping the table with her palm. "And if I can't convince you that Shakespeare was the greatest romantic author of all time, I'll buy dinner after your next volleyball match."

35

Both Taylor and Dominique agreed, "Oh, yeah," giving each other a high-five.

The librarian's tolerance for the noisy students wore out, and she immediately intervened. "Look, I'm all for Shakespeare, but you girls need to keep quiet, or you'll have to leave," she said, pushing her empty cart past their table.

"Oops, sorry," apologized Desiree lowering her volume. "Shakespeare and I are practically best friends."

"Understood. I'll let it go—but this is the last time," warned the librarian as she headed towards the *Returned Books* table.

Taylor started writing her summary. "This is going to be a fun paper to write, I loved Charles Dickens ever since my dad read his books to me at bedtime when I was little," she whispered.

Desiree looked up from her paper. "My dad read me Shakespeare, but you probably could have guessed that."

"Well, I can't say the same for Agatha Christie," said Dominique. "I guess my taste for *Aggie* developed when I grew older." Her pen raced across her notebook answering the next question:

*In no less than a half-page critique the book. Did you like it or not? Why or why not?*

"So, Dominique, what were your bedtime stories?" Desiree asked as she continued writing.

Dominique put down her pen and gazed at the ceiling searching her memories. "In the beginning they were fairytales that always had a happy ending. But over time I got jaded and asked my parents to read real life stories—you know, stories of courage, intrigue, and cleverness. I realized that folks in real life don't automatically live happily ever after. They usually have to work for it."

"Cinderella worked really hard to get what she wanted," Taylor argued. "Remember she cooked and cleaned for her stepfamily."

Dominique continued writing as she argued Taylor's point. "Yeah, Cinderella worked hard all right—building an unhealthy codependence with her stepfamily, who had no clue about domestic chores," said Dominique. The librarian overheard and chuckled, but Dominique continued. "If I were Cinderella I would have left those abusive slackers and let them fall flat on their faces."

"But maybe in those days young women didn't leave home," Desiree argued. "With all the invasions and crusades going on maybe it was too dangerous."

Taylor put down her pen to voice support of Desiree's explanation. "And besides it was Cinderella's dad who owned the house. Her stepfamily was infringing. She wasn't going to leave her own house."

"Besides she was out-numbered," added Desiree. "So Cinderella probably had to wait for a chance to break free—like when the royal ball was announced. And remember how hard she worked to make her gown."

Blood rushed to Dominique's face, as she continued to hotly argue her point. "Recall also that she used her stepsisters' stuff to make the gown, and we all know what happened when they found out. Geez-o-man, no one that stupid deserves to attend a royal ball. She would not have made it without her fairy godmother." At this point her reddened face was turning blue. "Come on, who has a fairy godmother in real life?" Then she caught her breath enough to pose one last question. "What was her name, anyway?"

37

"We called her Catalina," answered Taylor. "At least my mom did."

"Catalina?" Dominique asked. "What kind of a name is that for a fairy godmother? Isn't that the name of an island somewhere?"

The librarian pretended to be busy, but she couldn't help overhearing the ridiculous analysis of *Cinderella*. She pushed her cart slowly around the book aisles to stay within earshot.

"Catalina is as good a name as any," replied Taylor. "We couldn't just keep calling her *fairy godmother* all the time. The poor woman needed a name. The whole story had taken place in Europe somewhere, so why not Italy and why not an Italian godmother named Catalina?"

"You could have called her Antoinette—that's a good European name," answered Dominique. "My mom's family is Italian, and her sister is my godmother, Aunt Antoinette. When I was younger I couldn't pronounce it very well. So I shortened her name to just Aunt Toni."

"Antony? Like *Marc Antony*?" Taylor asked.

"No, two words—*Aunt* and *Toni*."

"Definitely easier than Aunt Antoinette," Desiree remarked.

Dominique then put down her pencil and continued describing her beloved godmother. "She didn't seem to mind when my sibs and I called her Aunt Toni. She and her husband had no kids, so she treated us like gold. She was always very nice to us—always taking care of us when my parents were away. The only weird thing about her was she dressed nicely all the time. She looked like she was dressed for church even if we were going to a picnic. I remember that she always wore a pill hat and gloves and carried a matching purse! She must have had coordinating outfits for every day of the week. I guess it was fashionable at the time.

Kind of reminded me of what Jackie O used to wear when she was the first lady," she said.

"Her name was Jackie Kennedy when she was first lady," said Desiree, correcting Dominique.

"Then she'd be Jackie *K*, and that's not as cool-sounding as Jackie *O*," Dominique argued.

The librarian burst out laughing. She tried stifling it by covering her mouth, but it went through her nose and was still loud enough to be heard. She turned and walked farther back in the aisle, hoping not to disturb anyone. But the sound pierced every book in the reference section, causing all three girls to stop talking. They stood up and looked in that direction, but the laughter finally stopped, so they resumed their conversation.

"Does you're Aunt still wear those outfits?" Taylor asked Dominique.

"I don't know for sure. I haven't seen her lately. After my uncle died she retired to her vacation cabin up in Tusayan—that's really close to the Grand Canyon Village. My mom goes to visit her every now and then, but I've been too busy with volleyball these past few years to go. I'd love to see her again just to see what she wears."

"Or how she accessorizes," added Taylor.

"Anyway, getting back to fairy tales," Dominique continued. "Some really have value in teaching morals, but then there are others that depict characters having really dumb luck to live happily ever after. I loathe those stories."

Desiree already finished the first three questions and took a break to rejoin the conversation. "But you have to admit, Dominique, that even in real life there are times when people catch a lucky break by being in the right place at the right time," she argued.

"Yes, that's true," admitted Dominique, "but they didn't plan it that way, and no one should. There are times when you just have to create your own lucky break, you know? I'm not going to wait around for it. I'll make it myself."

"And you will," Taylor said. "Because you always work hard at everything—especially holding your rage from the referee after a bad call." She then giggled.

"Thanks, Taylor, I think," Dominique commented. "Now I need to get back to my paper." She again picked up her pencil. "We have only twenty minutes before this place shuts down."

The librarian returned to her desk and sighed aloud, relieved that the fairy tale review finally ended happily ever after.

Desiree and Taylor finished answering the last question and packed up to leave, much to the chagrin of Dominique. "Wait, you guys are finished already?" she asked.

"Oh you know what they say: *Time flies when you're writing about something you really enjoy*," Desiree replied.

"That's not how the saying goes," Dominique argued.

"You know what I mean," Desiree answered. "Anyway, I'm not completely finished; this is only my first draft."

"Yeah, me too," said Taylor. "By the time I start typing this I'll find tons of errors."

"But you'll wait while I catch up, right?" Dominique pleaded. "I really enjoy reviewing books with you guys. It makes my homework just fly."

"Sure," said Desiree. "I've got no pressing engagements; I'm just going home after this." Suddenly her cell phone sounded. She opened her phone and saw the photo of a chubby baby sitting in a bubble bath and holding a rubber ducky. "Oh, foul-smelling flesh monger! It's my brother calling—I'll be right back." She walked towards the exit.

Taylor's face lit up. "Royce can ring my chimes any day of the week," she said. "Sure wish he was a senior."

Desiree soon returned to the table. "Sorry, I have to leave this party; Royce needs a ride home."

"Send him my love and phone number," said Taylor.

"Taylor, you need a cold shower," Desiree joked as she began to leave. "Hey, Dominique, thanks again for the outline."

"Bye, Desiree," the volleyball girls yelled back. They didn't get reprimanded from the librarian this time since they were the only ones left in the library.

"Lights out in five minutes!" the librarian announced from her desk. She didn't care anymore about being quiet either.

"Five minutes—more than I need," said Dominique as she started answering the final question: *Describe the topic of the book. Did you agree with the author?* Taylor finished packing her supplies and waited for Dominique to finish. The librarian went to power down the computers.

Taylor grumbled about Desiree's parting comment. "I don't need a cold shower," she said feeling offended, "You can't blame me for having a crush on a freshman like Royce. He's got what senior guys only dream of having: good looks, a great body, and brains—I'm sure. He would be the perfect hero in my fairy tale." She then turned to Dominique who was just finishing her last sentence. "So, Dominique how is it that all Samoan volleyball guys are cute?"

Dominique commented while still writing, "Taylor, you really *do* need a cold shower."

Desiree was already on her way to the local pool, where Royce's club team was practicing. He had qualified for state championships and was doing double sessions in order to get faster times. He wanted to better the times from his high school season, which ended a few months ago.

The swimming pool was so close to the library that Desiree could see the pool's outdoor lights from the parking lot. But she had to drive through a convoluted roadway before crossing the wretched train tracks. While doing so, her phone went off. The ringtone was a classic George Thorogood song:

*The head nurse looked up and said, "Leave this one alone."*
*She could tell right away he was bad to the bone...*

"Hi, Dad," she said. "So good to hear your voice."

"Hey, how's my little girl?" Walter asked.

"Great, I'm just leaving the library now to pick up Royce from swim practice. How was your day?"

"A good one, sweetie. I got three more bookings for next month. People sure want to see Arizona with the great weather we're having."

Walter Sumner ran an outdoor adventure/cookout business. He was a native Arizonan who loved to go off-road and explore the desert. After he graduated from Northern Arizona University with a recreational management degree, he started his business. He took out a loan to buy a custom-made touring van along with gold panning equipment. He then hit the ground running and has been busy ever since. His tours drew tourists from around the world. He paid off all his business and student loans in two years. His business grew to owning three off-road coaches and a barbeque catering service.

"That's great your business is doing so well, Dad," Desiree replied. "Hey, I have some awesome news."

"Hit me," he said.

"Next month we have a field trip to the Grand Canyon."

"Great! For which class?"

"Geology. We're going to examine rock layers and formations and stuff. They do this trip every year."

"Don't tell me; it's Bradley Roeser's field trip, right?"

"How'd ya know?"

"Why, that crazy fool goes there all the time lookin' for somethin' that ain't there. And now he usin' you kids as an excuse for his wild goose chases."

"He's using us—for what?"

"Oh, uh, it's a long story; has somethin' to do with Dad—I mean—your grandpa."

"Really, like what?"

"C'mon over, and we'll talk about it."

"I've got a better idea," she proposed. "Can you take me shopping for camp gear?"

"Camp gear? You don't need any gear—I got plenty of stuff for you—tents, sleeping bags, flashlights, all kinds of outdoor gear—"

"—Dad, that's great, but I'm a girl."

Walter paused for a few seconds. "Uh, you lookin' for a girlie tent with Barbie Doll curtains?"

"No, that's not what I mean. I want my own stuff. I want my own sleeping bag. It's kind of like underwear."

"Like underwear—whatcha mean?"

"Well you don't wear anybody else's underwear. I think sleeping bags should be personal—just like underwear."

"I don't understand the underwear thing, but if it makes you happy, we'll get your own personal sleeping bag."

"Great! So when can we go shopping together?"

"Well, my Saturday's free. Does that sound good?"

"Sounds like a date, Dad. But let me check with Mom first, and I'll get back with you."

"Can't wait, baby girl, I love you."

"I love you, too, Dad. Bye."

Desiree closed her phone and pulled into the pool's parking lot. Royce was waiting at the curb. He didn't hear the car—he was listening to his music player. She then honked the horn and startled him.

"Hey, I'm rocking here!" Royce yelled. He grabbed his swim bag and walked to the car. "You don't have to blow out my brains with the horn."

"You have brains?" she asked.

"Very funny," he answered, as he opened the passenger door and jumped inside. He threw his swim bag onto the back seat and buckled his seat belt. "I'm starving, Dizzy. Can we swing by the drive-thru?

"Sure, but you'd better call Mom and tell her where we're going," Desiree said as she handed Royce her phone.

He did so just as Desiree headed for the nearest fast food restaurant. "Hey, Mom," he said, "I'm done with practice, but I'm gonna grab some grub on the way home…Yeah, practice went good. Coach is working us really hard. That's why I'm hungry enough to eat an elephant right now."

"Let me talk to Mom," Desiree said, interrupting him. Royce motioned for her to wait while he was still on the phone.

"Yeah, I got my homework done—before practice. Hey, Desiree wants to talk to you." Royce gave the phone to his sister.

"Hey, Mom, can Dad take me shopping for camping stuff this Saturday? Well, he wanted to loan me his smelly, dusty sleeping bag, but I told him I wanted my own…Yes, I'll help you in the early morning, and he can pick me up right after…Great.

Thanks, Mom. See you soon." She closed the phone and put it in her bag.

"What was that all that about?" asked Royce.

"Dad and I are going to shop for camping stuff," answered Desiree.

"Doesn't he already have a lot of camping stuff?" asked Royce.

"Sure, but I want to get my own—untouched and unscathed."

"Until you touch and scathe it."

"But it's my touching and scathing, Baby-bro. His stuff has to be at least twenty years old. It probably still has mud and rattlesnakes from his first outing, yuck! I want a nice, clean-smelling sleeping bag and a backpack with no scorpions hiding in the pockets." Desiree finally pulled into the restaurant's drive-through.

"Dizzy, get me a double combo with a chocolate milkshake," said Royce, handing her some money. "And my treat if you want something."

"That's OK, I'm good; I finished Mom's lasagna leftovers tonight." She then ordered Royce's food then pulled around to the delivery window. "Oh, that reminds me—my friend, Taylor, has the hots for you."

"Which one is she?" Royce asked.

"She's the short girl with the light brown hair, and she plays varsity volleyball," answered Desiree.

He suddenly perked up with interest. "Is she a senior?"

"Yes, why do you ask?"

"Because senior girls usually have nothing to do with freshmen unless they're trying to direct us to some imaginary classroom in the middle of the football field," he answered. Then

45

he slumped back in his seat. "Wow—a senior! Maybe she'll ask me to prom—wouldn't that be cool!"

Desiree pulled up to the cashier window. "Cool your engines, Baby-bro," she warned, "I told her you already have a violently jealous girlfriend."

He jumped up in his seat, almost hitting the roof of the car. "Why did you do say that, Dizzy?"

"Because I don't want anybody breaking my baby-bro's heart, that's why." She grabbed the food bag and handed it to Royce. "Especially one that's so young and naïve."

"My heart is not that young and naïve," he argued, "It'll be sixteen by summer." He then pulled out his sandwich from the bag.

"Why can't you just date girls your own age?" Desiree asked as she pulled out onto the main street.

"Because *they're* hearts are young and naïve. I want age and experience," he answered, unwrapping his sandwich and taking a big bite.

"Oh, no you don't; not while I'm alive."

While chewing his burger he replied, "Then I'll make it look like an accident."

"Oh, come on, Baby-bro, you don't want to kill your only sister," Desiree replied while reaching over to tickle behind his ear. She always tried tickling at his most vulnerable moments—like this time, when both his hands were holding the sandwich.

"Hey, that's not fair. I can't defend myself," he protested, trying to elbow her tickling fingers away from him.

"Exactly," she replied smugly.

"Well, if you were really sharp you'd keep both hands on the wheel while I'm eating, so we don't crash mom's car. Oh, look, it's the train crossing," he said while pointing at the gates. But there was no train in sight.

"Now that's a cheap shot," Desiree declared, looking both ways before pulling out from the Light Rail depot. "I should make you get out and walk."

"OK, Let me out here, so I can check out all the senior chick hangouts at the mall."

"Never mind, young stud," she replied and accelerated past the giant discount store, causing Royce to drop a french fry in his lap. As he leaned forward to get it, she snatched up a few of them from his food bag.

"Hey!" Royce cried, grabbing the bag and putting it on his lap, "You're depriving me of energy for tomorrow's workout. Wait till I tell your boyfriend how cruel you are to me."

He was, of course, referring to Wesley, who was on the very same club swim team. They were the best of teammates because they both swam on the same relay team that won the high school state title.

"Wes is not my boyfriend—at least not in the normal sense," retorted Desiree. She knew what kind of argument Royce was heading for and put on her Mona Lisa hat.

"OK, then he's your *abnormal* boyfriend," he said, teasing her.

Desiree was not surprised by his mode of attack, and, like a chess game, she was ready to counter his offense. "You mean abnormal like your brain?" She stopped at the traffic light and turned to her brother. "No, our relationship is purely platonic."

Royce finished the rest of his fries then picked up his milkshake and gestured to Desiree with his straw. "What kind of guy wants that kind of relationship? There's no passion or sex."

Desiree felt a need to stop his rather awkward questions about sex. "You're right, Baby-bro, not too many guys want a platonic relationship. Most guys are like dogs and want to *facilitate*

47

as many females as possible. They then have to battle for dominance, and perhaps getting an ear chewed off or an eye scratched. You may satisfy your primal sexual drives, but you end up hurting people including yourself. Where's the romance in that?"

"It's great, short-term romance," he replied.

"It sure is," she agreed. The light changed and she accelerated through the intersection. "And that's why the dogs have to keep the cycle going. Soon it just becomes a cycle they're romancing and not the female anymore. Most girls aren't like female dogs. Their feelings get hurt when caught up in this kind of cycle. They lose their self-esteem and go into a downward spiral of short-term, sexual relationships with no sense of true romance. Some guys and girls realize this cycle and avoid it—like Wes and I. We really want a relationship based on having fun and enjoying each other without all the heat and hormones."

"Wow, sis, you speak with a lot of experience!"

His sister laughed. "Not really, but people talk. You hear stuff. Word gets around."

"I haven't heard all that."

"Not yet; you're just a freshman, but in time you will."

"So, will you ever have sex with Wes?"

Caught off guard by this question, she slammed on the brakes. Luckily there was no traffic behind her. "Royce, that's not an appropriate question. That's it; I'm telling Mom on you."

"Here we go again," he complained, "You can never win these arguments by yourself; you always have to pull out the *Mom Card.*"

"OK, I'll rephrase that," she replied, continuing to drive. "If you don't quit this line of questioning, then I won't introduce you to Taylor," she said. Royce gasped before swallowing his bite of sandwich, and started coughing. Desiree laughed at his response.

"Really, you really will?" Royce asked, and she nodded. "OK, no more sex-with-Wes questions, I promise. So when will you introduce me to Taylor?"

"Oh, in about three years," Desiree said then laughed as she pulled the car into their driveway. "I didn't promise I'd introduce you right away." She got out, grabbed her backpack, and ran towards the back door.

"Arguing with older sisters suck—they never fight fair," Royce complained while grabbing his swim bag from the back seat before following her into the house. She heard him and turned back to him.

"*Fair is foul, and foul is fair*," she replied, quoting Shakespeare.

"Who needs you anyway; I can introduce myself, *myself*," he resolved.

They both entered the kitchen still arguing, while their mom was sitting at the counter with her planner, organizing her next day's activities.

Desiree put her bag down and gave her mom a hug. "Hi, Mom, missed you," she said. Then Desiree walked into the hallway leading to her room. Her mom approached Royce for a hug.

Royce was still a little perturbed by his sister, but hugs from his mom always made him feel better. "Did you miss me?" he asked, giving her a hard squeeze.

His mom exhaled forcibly. "Unh! I miss you every minute you're gone," she said. "So what's with all the bickering?"

Royce stepped away, grabbed his swim bag and headed for the laundry room. "Oh, no biggie, you know how we always fight about stupid stuff," he replied. He pulled his towel and swimsuit

49

out of the bag. Then he filled the rinse tub with water in and threw in his suit.

"Yes, but it usually ends up in a nasty scuffle," his mom said.

After Royce threw his towel in the dryer he came back to the kitchen. "But we're maturing, and we can handle our little spats."

"Especially since he's gotten used to losing," Desiree said, interrupting the conversation as she returned to the kitchen. "Hey, Mom, did you finish washing my jeans yet? I want to wear them tomorrow for school."

"They're folded on the ironing board," her mom answered. "Wait a minute; don't you have other jeans in your room? Why do you need this particular pair?"

Desiree went to retrieve them from the laundry room. "They're my favorite right now," she answered, brushing the denim across the side of her face. "And they get softer every time you wash them."

"I can get your other jeans softer, too. But you'd have to wear them first and get 'em dirty, so I can wash 'em," her mom said.

"But I can't wear stiff jeans," Desiree argued. "Can't you just wash them a few times first, so that they get softer?"

"Not if they're not dirty. I'm not wasting precious, desert water on clean jeans." Janelle made it clear over the years that she was very conservative with her laundering.

"Well, how can I get soft jeans if you won't wash them, if they're not dirty, if I'm not wearing them to get them dirty?"

Royce couldn't stand the argument anymore. "Ugh, I need to leave; my head is starting to hurt," he said, walking to his bedroom.

50

"Wait, Royce," his mom called out. "Don't leave; you never told me what the fight was about."

"It's not as important as Dizzy's stiff jeans, so goodnight."

"Yes it is," his mom answered. "Come on, super swimmer, you can tell me."

Royce stopped, turned around, and returned to the doorway. "Mom, Dizzy won't introduce me to one of her girlfriends," he said.

"What do you need your sister for—you can do the introducing yourself," said Janelle.

"Sure, but I don't know who she is, and Desiree won't point her out to me. She's making me do all the work," Royce complained.

"That should make the hunt more challenging," said Janelle.

"Yeah, Royce," his sister added. "You freshmen dogs live for this sort of thing."

"Wait, a minute," said Royce. "I thought you said you didn't want me to date older women."

"What you do is your own business, Baby-bro, I'm just not helping you," she replied while heading for her room. "Good night, Mom, and thanks for the jeans."

"Let's see how long we can keep them clean this time," Janelle yelled back.

"Oh, Mom," Desiree whined before closing her bedroom door. But her mom wasn't listening. Instead she walked over at her son.

"Let's see how you did today," she said as she inspected his warm-up suit. "Oh, tsk, tsk, you've got grease and dairy spots on your sweats. Please change out, so I can launder them."

"What's the rush, Mom—I won't need them tomorrow."

"I still want to pretreat them tonight before I launder them," she said, "You want them clean and neat in case the TV stations show up at your next swim competition. Ya just never know."

Royce figured she was right and went into his bedroom to quickly change. He then returned, wearing his favorite loungewear—boxer shorts. "Thanks, Mom, you're the greatest," he said while handing over his sweats. "And don't worry about tomorrow morning; I'm getting a ride from Wes to practice and school."

"I love you too much not to worry," said her mom as she stole another hug from him. Royce was so much taller than his mom now. Her head nestled right inside his shoulder and chest. "But worrying is my job, and I love doing it."

"If I don't see you at breakfast then I'll catch you after school," said Royce as he let go and turned towards his bedroom.

"I just may catch you," replied his mom. "I have a breakfast meeting with the other co-ops before the weekend market, so I'll be up early."

She grabbed Royce's warm up suit and went to the laundry room. She unrolled the warm ups and inspected the fabric, which was green and black with white letters spelling *Vikings* in a half circle on the back of the jacket. In the front on the upper left side was *Royce* embroidered in white along with a splash of pink, dried-out milkshake. She smiled, feeling proud of her son's swim accomplishments but not his sloppy eating habits. She then grabbed the pre-wash solution and sprayed the jacket before placing it in the hamper.

Feeling tired from a busy day, Janelle decided to retire to bed. She grabbed her planner, turned off the kitchen light and entered the hallway. The lamp table separated two bedroom doors and flanked a half-length mirror. She carefully put her items quietly on the heavy, oak table.

She looked towards her son's room, which was at the end of the hall. The crack below the door was dark, so his light was out. She then looked at her daughter's room. No lights either. They had both gone straight to sleep. No more fights, and no more messes!

She looked at herself in the mirror, pulled her hair away from her face, and leaned closer to inspect her eyes. No surprise that they were bloodshot, but she also noticed a serious need for calming, soothing replenishment around her eye sockets and cheekbones. She resolved that a visit to the local spa for a mudpack facial should be on her agenda for the next day—if she could just find the time.

# Chapter III

While Desiree slept, a putrid life form stirred in the dark waters. The sleazy, slimy mass of gelatinous protoplasm moved gently in the waves and eddies of its aqueous environment. Life was quiet and serene now, but action was inevitable. The protoplasm started to writhe and roll. Then it jerked. The water rose and fell with greater amplitude each time the jerking strengthened. Air mixed with the water causing it to bubble and spit.

Desiree rolled onto her back, letting out a quick dry cough. The waters stopped for a moment as if disturbed by her sounds. After a minute, the bubbling and spitting resumed. Desiree opened her eyes and sat up from her bed. She threw off her sheet, slipped into her flip-flops, and walked to her door.

She peered out towards the kitchen. She could not recognize the sound, so she slowly entered the hallway to investigate. She walked quietly. That part of the house was still dark, but the noise seemed to be coming from the kitchen. Desiree cautiously proceeded there. A sharper, louder sound caught Desiree by surprise. She covered her mouth and gasped. The sound stopped again. She grabbed a skillet from the stovetop and tiptoed past the laundry room towards the back door. She opened the door slightly and peered outside. Maybe it was an urban coyote that was raiding the trashcan outside. She carefully scanned the entire area while listening for sounds of scampering feet.

Suddenly something cold and wet landed on her shoulder. She looked down to see a dripping, green and black glob. She jumped, hitting her head on the top of the doorframe.

"Ahh!" she screamed, dropping the skillet on the floor. It landed with a loud *gong* and spun on its edge several times before coming to rest.

Royce appeared a few feet behind her. "Hey, Dizzy, how do you like our new team swimsuit?"

Desiree checked her head for blood. "Royce!" She pulled Royce's dripping suit off her shoulder and whipped it back at him. He ducked, and it soared over his head towards the back wall, briefly sticking onto the wall's rough texture then falling to the floor in a rumpled ball. "Not only did you give me a heart attack, but you practically fractured my skull!"

"OK," he agreed, and went to retrieve his swimsuit. "Does that mean you *don't* like our new team suit?"

"I am so going to get you for this!" She picked up the skillet and threatened him with it. "You could have killed me!"

Royce backed away slowly. "What—with my innocent, little swim suit?" He quickly picked up the suit, rolling it in his towel and stuffing it in his bag. "Maybe I should register it as a lethal weapon."

Suddenly their mom appeared, turning on the kitchen light. "What's this talk about a lethal weapon?" She was already dressed, wearing an ankle-length Navajo-woven skirt with matching short-wasted jacket. "From my bedroom it sounded like a killer skillet with built-in, blood-curdling screams."

"Mom," said Desiree while pointing an accusing finger at Royce, "he's trying to kill me! He snuck up on me and slapped his wet swim suit on me." She pointed to the wet spot running from shoulder. "See where it hit me?"

"Yes, I do," her mom answered as she took the skillet from Desiree. "But, I don't see any blood or bruising. Hey, Royce, is this your doing?"

Royce was clearing his cereal bowl and juice cup from the kitchen counter, trying to hide his smirk. "All I did was show her my new suit and asked if she liked it." He grabbed the dishcloth that was hanging over the sink and walked back to the counter where he ate. "I just got it last week, and I can't wait to wear it at my next swim meet." He wiped up the splashes of milk and drops of juice he made while eating his breakfast earlier.

To his mom this display of clean up—something that he seldom did—was a sign of guilt. "If that's all you did then why all the noise?" Janelle asked.

"It was dark, and she couldn't see it, so I laid it across her shoulder," he said.

Now his explanation was bordering on absurdity. Desiree knew it and went back to her room with a smile of satisfaction. Her mom continued questioning Royce.

"And I suppose you also wanted her to see it with an extra element of surprise," she said while looking in the direction of the hallway waiting for Desiree's bedroom door to close. Looking back at Royce she said in a lower voice, "Not bad, kid, but next time you want to kid with your sister, please do it more quietly." She then changed the subject while giving him a hug. "You all packed for the day?"

Royce wrapped both his long and strong arms around her. "Yep, all set. Got my breakfast finished and cleaned. My suit is packed in my towel. Got my books, too."

She abruptly broke from his hold. "Wait—your new suit is in your towel?" she asked.

"Yeah, I just rinsed it out this morning, and I'm drying it in my towel."

"Sweetie, you can't be wearing your new suit to practice. Please hang it over the sink and get one of your practice suits."

"But, Mom, I like my new suit," he protested.

"It's a competition suit that's supposed to be worn in competition," his mom replied. "If you wear it at practice everyday it will be worn and tattered before your next swim meet."

Royce groaned while returning his new suit to the laundry room. He then came back to the kitchen, holding two of his older suits that were worn thin. "But look at these, Mom, they're falling apart."

"Yes, they are, and that's why you wear them to practice. That's how you recycle your old competition suits."

"But Mom, they practically fall off when I swim."

Janelle smiled. "Honey, that's 'cause you swim so fast. Tell you what—when your dad takes Desiree shopping this Saturday, I'll take you to the swim store for some new, practice suits. How's that?"

Royce stuffed the old suits into his bag and looked back at his mom. "That would be totally epic," he replied, pleased by her decision.

"Meanwhile promise me that this new suit stays home until your next competition," she said, negotiating with him.

"OK, I promise," he said.

A horn sounded from the driveway. Royce picked up his backpack and swim bag and headed for the door. "That's my ride, see ya later, Mom!"

Just as he left, Desiree returned to the kitchen, dressed for school. Of course she was wearing her favorite jeans that her mom washed the night before. She also wore her favorite white-laced tank top with a brown, fur-lined hoodie. February mornings in the low deserts of Central Arizona were still pretty chilly, and Desiree loved this particularly warm hoodie.

Her mom saw the familiar jeans and sighed, hoping that someday the other jeans would get worn. She went to the sink to fill the coffeemaker with water. "So, Desiree, have you fully recovered from your brother's little prank?"

"Recovered for now, but not forgotten, Mom. But right now I'm more interested in typing my book review," Desiree answered. She put her laptop on the counter and pulled out a stool. "It's not due until next week, but I want to get it out of the way."

Her mom hadn't heard words like that from Desiree in a long time. "Getting homework done ahead of time—that's wonderful!"

Her daughter grabbed a notebook out of her backpack and paged through to the notes she had written last night. "Well, it helps when the homework is something I'm interested in—a review of *Macbeth*. There's nothing like Shakespeare to get me in a good mood."

"You're not angry at your brother anymore?"

"Nope," Desiree answered. "But you know what they say, *what goes around* comes back with vengeance."

"No, *what goes around comes around*," her mom said, correcting her daughter.

"So, you approve of my quest for vengeance," Desiree said as she propped up her notebook next to her laptop and started typing. Soon her fingers flew over the keys as she transcribed her answers.

Her mom couldn't believe what she saw. "Shakespeare must be magical," she remarked before getting a commuter coffee mug from the cupboard. "He gets you happy and your homework done—all at the same time."

"Amazing, huh?" Desiree replied, getting more absorbed in her typing.

"What about the rest of your homework—did you get it done?"

"Yep; finished it during chess club practice."

"Guess that puts you ahead of the game."

Desiree wasn't sure what her mom was talking about. "No, I lost my match to Candice, remember?"

The coffee maker started hissing as the hot water percolated through the coffee grounds. Janelle stood in front of it waiting with her cup. "Not the chess game, honey—the homework game," she said.

Her daughter's mind was getting more deeply immersed in Shakespeare. "Sure, Mom, whichever."

"Oh, never mind," replied Janelle, "I can see that you're busy, so I'll pour my coffee and head off to the meeting. You can leave the coffee maker on for your grandma when she arrives."

Desire mentally popped out of her book review. "What? You have a meeting?"

"It's a breakfast meeting with the co-ops at the Squaw Peak Resort. We each report on the previous quarter's results." She filled her cup with freshly brewed coffee and capped it.

"Sounds like fun, Mom. Hope the food's good—I heard they serve good breakfast," Desiree replied.

"I hope so, too," her mom answered as she went back to the mirror in the hallway and checked her hair. "It better be as good as my report. Our profits were way better this quarter than last year at this time." She grabbed her purse and planner. "Oh, by the way, the market opens one hour earlier this Saturday, so you need to get up earlier on Saturday morning. Hope you didn't have any late Friday night plans."

Desiree finished typing her review, closing both her notebook and laptop. "I'll be at Candice's fencing match, then the ice cream parlor. So, I should be home around dinner. Please say the creature from the slimy lagoon isn't joining us."

Her mom laughed. "If you're referring to your brother, he will be joining us after his swim practice," she said while putting the planner in her purse before slinging it over her shoulder.

Just then her cell phone rang. "Oh, *tsk*, just when I'm trying to get out the door!" She put her purse down to pull out her phone then walked everything over to the kitchen counter next to Desiree. She answered her phone as she returned her purse back on her shoulder. Before grabbing her coffee she gave Desiree a half hug with her other arm.

After her mom left, Desiree went to the refrigerator and pulled out a pitcher of orange juice. Their farm had a bumper crop of Sweet Arizona oranges this season, so her mom had extra for the family. Desiree grabbed a glass from the cupboard and poured out the sparkling, fresh morning elixir. The sun had already risen above the citrus trees that grew on the eastern half of her family's farm. The first rays flooded the kitchen and swirled inside her juice glass. But before she could take a sip the phone rang.

"Heritage Farm, this is Desiree," she greeted cheerfully. "Hey, Wesley! Wait—aren't you supposed to be at swim practice? You are. So what's up? Uh, sure, that sounds yummy. How about a couple of glazed, doughnut holes...OK, see you at first period. Thanks." She hung up and smiled again. Despite her shaky start this morning she's got freshly squeezed orange juice, Shakespeare, and doughnuts waiting for her at school!

She skipped over to the family room and turned on the TV. Her mom had left the channel on ME-TV Network, and the *I Love Lucy* program was on. In that particular episode Lucy and Ethel were arguing about what to eat first at their picnic. Suddenly a flash of lightning made the whole discussion pointless. They both threw tablecloths over their heads and ran back to their cars. A gust of wind inflated Lucy's tablecloth like a huge windsock, and she started to sail up into the air.

Ethel jumped up to grab Lucy's ankles only to go airborne also. They both sailed for a minute screaming for their husbands before getting snagged by the lower branch of an oak tree. Their husbands shouted from the ground as both women lay on their stomachs across the branch.

Desiree laughed almost on cue with the canned audience. *Who could ever get in such a crazy predicament?* She went back to the kitchen to drink more juice. The wall clock showed plenty of time before school, so she sat back down at the counter. It was almost eight o'clock, and the women had to get rescued soon.

Then an old-fashioned fire truck pulled up to the tree with firemen extending a ladder to the branch. *Oh good; this will be a slam-dunk; they'll get down before the commercial. Uh-oh, both are too petrified to climb down. What a bunch of wimps!* The fireman finally talked Ethel down, and then asked Lucy to try. She reached for the ladder and got it with both hands. Another wind

61

gust blew her off balance! Her foot slipped through the ladder wrung. Like a monkey she wrapped both her arms around the ladder while trying to get a foothold. The fireman below tried to guide her leg back through, but she lost her grip and dropped upside down, hanging by her knees!

Desiree laughed again, but this time spraying the juice from her lips and onto the counter. Unfortunately some of it also got on her tank top and favorite jeans. *Oh cursed—not again! Eh, that's OK; I'll change after Lucy gets rescued.*

Meanwhile, Lucy was bear-hugging the fireman while hanging upside down from the ladder. Desiree grabbed a napkin to sop up the juice from her jeans. Then the phone rang again. She leaned over to answer it while still cleaning up.

"Heritage Farm, this is Desiree...Hi, Dad! Yeah, I checked with Mom; we're starting earlier on Saturday, so I should be done by around one o'clock...Can you pick me up there? Great. This'll be fun... Thanks, Dad. I love you... Bye."

Desiree hung up the phone and glanced back at the TV. Lucy was being led down the ladder in bare feet while wearing a tablecloth over her head. With canned applause the network cut to a commercial.

Desiree looked around at the mess she made. Juice was on the floor, the counter, her clothes, and the phone. She finished cleaning up then hurried to her bedroom, stopping at the mirror. The jeans weren't too messy; the juice drops will dry quickly in the desert air. She only needed to change her white tank top, which had several orange spots. She grabbed a towel from the bathroom and tried blotting out the spots.

"*Out, damned spot! Out, I say*," she said, quoting Shakespeare. The liquid came out, but the orange color remained. She slipped out of her hoodie while going into her bedroom.

62

She imagined herself in a situation comedy. A dust devil unexpectedly blew through her room. She held onto her hoodie by the sleeves, letting it inflate like a windsock. It swooped her off her feet. She tumbled and twirled with each gust. After a few seconds the wind died down, and she landed on her bed. The hoodie deflated over her face and she laughed. She pulled it off her face and glanced over at the alarm clock.

"Oh, fracking fudge ball—the bus will be here soon!" She pulled off her tank top and tossed it in the corner. Then she went to get a clean one out of her dresser. She didn't have time to coordinate the colors, but luckily everything goes with jeans. She pulled out a dark red tank top with a narrow lace lining the straps and neckline. *Close enough*, she thought and slipped it on just as she heard a knock on the window.

"Morning, sunshine!" called out a voice that followed the knocking.

Desiree, greeted voice while opening the blinds. "Hi, Grandma! You're right on time."

Her mom's parents always came to the farm early in the morning, and this routine always included a knock on Desiree's window. She's been awakened this way ever since she was a child, when her grandparents still lived on the farm. Desiree's bedroom window looked out the front of the house facing west. It, like all the other bedrooms, were on the front wall of the house, so everyone in the bedrooms would hear the knocking.

Desiree opened the window. "I'm still getting dressed, so let yourself in."

"Nobody else home?" Grandma asked.

"No. Mom had an early meeting, and Royce went to swim practice."

"OK if we put the coffee on?"

"Mom already made some for you."

As her grandmother walked around to the backdoor, Desiree closed the window and continued dressing. She pushed one arm through the sleeve of her hoodie and looked in her mirror. Her long hair was in several tufted wads that looked like a swallow's nest woven by a confused spider. She grabbed her hairbrush and started working out the tufts.

She must have been thrashing from all that noise Royce made while rinsing out his swimsuit. She caught a big snarl on her right side, the side on which she sleeps. She tugged a bit at mid-length. She thought about how little brothers can be such a pain. *That's why he was put on this earth—to irritate me by tangling my hair.* The snarls began to loosen. *Maybe I was put on this earth, just so he had someone to irritate.* She finally worked her brush up to her scalp. Her brush found the tender spot where she hit the doorframe.

"Ouch!"

Her grandma heard her. "Are you OK in there?"

"I'm good, Grandma!" Desiree shouted back. She tilted her head and parted her hair to look for injury, but she saw nothing and only felt a small bump. She continued brushing. *If Royce weren't annoying me all the time, he would be out on the streets causing trouble and ending up in juvenile detention. Then Mom would really be mad.* Desiree stopped brushing. Miraculously all her long brown hair fell in place with a sheen that showed perfectly tamed hair. Pleased by it, she smiled and grabbing it from underneath and flinging it behind her shoulders. *It's a good thing I'm his older sister. I'll keep him out of trouble.*

Soon Desiree heard the school bus revving its engine as it rolled up her street. She ran to the kitchen just as her grandmother was pulling out some coffee mugs from the cupboard.

"Just heard my bus, Grandma, so gotta go," said Desiree while giving her a quick hug.

"Have a great day, cupcake," her grandma replied.

Desiree grabbed her school bag and ran out the front door. She waved to her grandpa who was still out by the car, which was parked by the tool shed. He waved back as the bus stopped with one, metallic-sounding shriek.

She got on and noticed that most of the seats were occupied by underclassmen. *I'm the only senior on this bus—yuck! I really need to get my car back,* she thought.

Later, at school, Candice was at her locker, stuffing it with her fencing clothes. Desiree cautiously approached, watching Candice cram each piece of padded clothing into a narrow space.

"Candice, it's not going to fit—you have so much junk in there already," said Desiree.

Candice didn't even turn to her friend. "Oof," she grunted, "It fit yesterday, and, oof, it's gonna fit today." She pushed with both hands then turned around and pushed with her shoulder and hip.

"Maybe, if you remove the equipment you're not using— like your basketball and softball stuff." Desiree helped push Candice to get in the fencing outfit. But the compressed equipment looked like it was ready to bounce back.

"Back off; I'm gonna close the door," Candice warned, her shoulder still pressed against the clothes. "I close on three. One...two...three!" Desiree backed off as Candice spun around to slam the locker door shut. It closed and clicked, sounding like it locked. "There. I told you it would all fit. Am I good or what?"

*"What's done is done,"* answered Desiree, quoting Shakespeare. "Until you have to get back in your locker again, of course."

"Won't be doing that until after lunch. By then I'll empty out my fencing gear, so it'll close more easily." Candice checked her backpack. "For now I got all my books for class."

"If you say so," Desiree said tentatively. She quickly pulled out textbooks from her locker and slammed the door. "Then I'll see ya at lunch—bye."

Just as she turned to leave, Candice cussed out loud. "Oh, shingle sheets, I left my binder in there." Desiree backed away, but her best friend stopped her. "Desiree wait, can you help me?"

"I don't think I want to be around for this, Candice," said Desiree, "Your locker is a ticking time bomb."

Candice pulled on her sleeve. "Come on, Dizzy, we've done it before, and we'll do it again. You help me this time and I'll buy ice cream on Friday."

Desiree couldn't pass up the offer, so she walked back to the locker. "OK, I'll do it for a sundae," said Desiree.

"Thanks, pal," said Candice, as she began redialing her combination lock.

Wesley showed up unexpectedly behind Desiree. "Got your doughnut holes!" he announced.

Desiree turned around just as he held out the bag. But before she could take out her glazed doughnut holes, Candice's locker door popped open, pushing Candice back into Desiree, who fell into Wesley. He dropped the doughnut bag in an attempt to catch both girls, but he fell backwards onto the floor. The bag had tipped over, spilling out the doughnut holes, which rolled a few feet down the hall.

Candice tumbled onto the thick padded fencing suit and sat up unscathed. As Desiree rolled off Wesley, however, she fell facedown into a jellied doughnut that was perfectly nestled in the fencing helmet. She pushed herself up while wiping the jelly off her nose.

Wes complained to Desiree, "Hey, that doughnut was supposed to be mine."

Candice saw the gook on Desiree's face and laughed. "Yeah, but red jelly goes better with her red tank top and brings out her blue eyes much better, don't you think?"

Wesley laughed, grabbing a towel from his swim bag and handing it to Desiree, who was licking her fingers. "Here, it's still a little wet from practice, so it should wipe up the jelly better."

"Thanks, my pastry-packed prince," she said looking up to Wesley while wiping the tip of her nose. Then she looked down at her tank top. "Did any of this get on my clothes; I promised my mom I'd stay clean for a week." She pulled it away from her ribs for his inspection.

He took this opportunity to gaze at her smooth long neck, which gracefully ran down to the laced neckline of her tank top. His eyes fell on her chest and absorbed all the red color that played off her curves. He finally stopped at her long, elegant fingers that were pulling out the lower half of her tank top. He looked back up to her shoulders and pulled her hair back. It fell effortlessly through his fingers.

"Yeah, you look great," replied Wes, marveling at the amazing sight before him. "I mean—uh—no jelly there."

Candice laughed at Wes' awkward reply before picking up her equipment from the floor.

Royce happened to come by just in time to see Desiree and Wes still on the floor. "What's all this?" he inquired. "A platonic display of romance, perhaps?"

"More like an explosive display," Candice said to him while jamming her equipment back into the locker.

Desiree realized the embarrassing predicament she was in. "Royce, it's not what you think," she said.

"Of course it is," interrupted Wes—not knowing what she was talking about. He then looked up at Royce. "Uh, what does it look like?"

"Nothing like what Desiree said about your relationship with her—"

"—Royce, cut it out; you're embarrassing me," she said, interrupting him. She quickly jumped up and straightened her hair and clothes, knowing that it wouldn't erase what her brother just saw.

"Yeah," Royce replied, nodding his head and smiling snidely. "I *am* embarrassing you. This is awesome."

More students came over to see the commotion—including Taylor. "Hey, Desiree," she said, "What happened to you?"

"Oh, uh—nothing really." Desiree replied, blankly. She didn't want her brother to know that this was the senior who had a crush on him.

"Hey, sis, is that Taylor?" Royce asked, trying to maneuver in front of his sister. Desiree quickly pulled Taylor aside while pushing Royce away, not wanting the two to meet.

"Yes, but this is not the Taylor you want to meet," she said, hip-checking him into the locker.

But Taylor heard Desiree. "Yes, I am!" she exclaimed, trying to maneuver around her to get closer to Royce. "I'm Taylor Mayer, Desiree's best study buddy." She then flirtatiously tossed her jaw-length hair back from her face.

Royce gleamed at Taylor while wrestling with his sister. "Hi—I'm Royce Sumner, Desiree's best and only brother," he replied, picking Desiree up under her arms, and dropping her behind him. He muttered to her, "I'm also the official spreader of sibling scandal around school."

She was now in a bigger jam than the stuff she just cleaned from her nose. Desiree hissed at her brother. "Don't you get any ideas," she warned.

Taylor returned Royce's smile with a bigger one. "I know who you are," she said, "I've seen you in P.E. class. Aren't you on the varsity swim team?"

"Yes, I am," he said, standing tall and sucking in his gut, trying to impress her with his physique. "And you're a senior, right?"

"Yep, and very eligible for the upcoming senior prom," she replied, trying to impress him with her social privileges.

During this time Candice was repacking her locker. It closed for a few seconds before popping open again—this time with her helmet falling on her head. Desiree noticed and giggled to herself. *Candice doesn't know futility if it hit her in the head,* she thought. Then she saw her brother and Taylor exchanging phone numbers. *Maybe I don't know futility either.*

Wes gently nudged Desiree's arm. "Hey, why so glum, Desiree? Taylor and your brother would have met eventually. But don't worry; Royce is a big boy and can take care of himself."

Desiree glanced back at her brother then sighed. "You're probably right, Wes," she said, leaning into him. "But he's my only brother, and I feel he should have a few, awkward relationships with girls his own age before moving up to the senior level."

Wes, who had never before discussed romance with Desiree, pulled her in close and, with his sparkling pale-green eyes, tried to dispel her worries.

"Look, you know Taylor fairly well, right?" Wes asked.

"Yes, we're study buddies," she answered.

"So, as a fellow study buddy, she has to be nice to Royce. And since she lives to gossip, she couldn't help telling you about their budding relationship."

Desiree paused to think. *Wes is right again, and I sure love this bubble we're both sharing!* "So, maybe I should back off—I mean—with Royce, huh?" Desiree asked.

It was Wes' turn to pause. *Yeah, with Royce, but never with me!* "Dizzy, if you want I can keep an eye on him and be his confidant at the same time," Wes offered.

She sighed, feeling more relieved. "Thanks, Wes. Your offer sounds great. But you don't have to act like his older brother."

"Why not—I almost look the part," he said and jumped back, looking down at himself. "We're both tall, and incredibly buff."

Desiree laughed. "Yeah, and you're about as humble as he is, too," she said. Then she stepped back, so that she could scan his body from head to feet.

He enjoyed her eyes cast upon him and raised both his arms, flexing his biceps. Other girls in the hall noticed and whistled at him.

"Uh-oh," he said, retracting his arms while glancing at the girls. "Now I have to protect both him and me."

Desiree laughed at Wes. "That could be a tough job."

They both watched Royce and Taylor end their encounter. Royce left first, wondering into the mass of students.

Taylor watched him disappear before heading back to Desiree. "Wow! I can't believe I finally met him," she said, excitedly.

Desiree could see her study buddy's starry eyes—getting even starrier. "Taylor, please be gentle with him—he's my little brother," she said sounding extremely concerned.

Taylor reassured her. "Yeah, I know. Don't worry; I'll take good care of him," she said then sighed. "Ooh, I just can't wait to see him again."

"And when is that?" Desiree quickly asked. "Did you two make a date?"

"Why, yes, we did! We have the same lunch period, so we're meeting in the cafeteria," said Taylor. The stars finally left her eyes, and she stepped back. "Well, I have to get to geology class, so bye!" She turned and skipped down the hall.

*Boy, they don't waste time*, she thought. She conked herself in the head. "Yikes, what have I done?"

Wes laughed and hooked his elbow lightly around her neck. "You let life progress as it should," he replied. Then he put on his theatric face and started to sob. "Oh, I'm so proud of you!" he cried and gave her a contrived hug.

She rolled her eyes. "*Ugh, The course of true love never did run smooth*," she said, quoting Shakespeare.

Morning classes went on as usual at Sunnyslope High, but lunchtime was a little different. Royce met Taylor for lunch leaving Dominique by herself. She decided to eat with Desiree, Candice and Wes. Initially Dominique enjoyed the change of company because volleyball wasn't the topic. Instead it was the upcoming field trip.

"So, does anybody know the exact location of this field trip?" Desiree asked.

"Wes said that it changes every year," replied Candice as she pulled her grilled cheese sandwich apart and scraped out the cheese with her teeth.

Dominique grimaced at her strange eating habit then began eating her own lunch. "Anywhere in the Grand Canyon is cool with me," she said. "It should be really fun—no matter where."

Wes pointed to Desiree's cottage cheese that was garnished with several thin peach slices. "Hey, you gonna finish that?"

Desiree glanced at it and sighed. She apparently had other thoughts on her mind. "No, you can have it," she answered, sliding it over to him. "Guess I wasn't that hungry."

Wes immediately grabbed her spoon and scooped up a large amount of cottage cheese. "You know, both my brother and sister did this trip, and both camped in different places," he said. "There are plenty of canyons for everybody." Then he shoveled the cottage cheese in his mouth.

"Roeser probably wants all his classes to have different areas, so that no two are alike," said Dominique.

"And if he gives us a test on it we can't cheat off anyone else," agreed Wes. He then scooped up a peach slice and slurped it into his mouth.

Dominique became more disgusted by this group's eating habits. She glared at Wes before rolling her eyes. Wes smiled at her while holding the peach slice in front of his teeth. She then turned to Desiree, who was quite tolerant of Wes' antics.

"Yeah, Wes, you could be right," said Desiree. "But the other night my dad complained about Roeser using the students to help him find something. Maybe Roeser camps in different locations because he hasn't found what he's been looking for."

"Hmm," said Dominique. "If that's true then maybe there's a pattern to his searches. If we could plot the area of his previous trips, then maybe we can figure out where our trip will be."

Candice put down the grilled bread that was completely gutted of cheese. She then licked her fingers before using her napkin. "Great theory, but how do we get that info?" she asked. "We'd have to hunt down a bunch of alumni," she said.

Wes finally swallowed the peach slice and cleared his voice. "We've already got two former students: my brother and sister," he answered. He looked at Candice's bread and reached for it, but she slapped the top of his wrist.

Wes' crude table manners were really annoying Dominique at this point. "Geez, Wes, you're like a scavenger! Do you always eat everyone's food?"

Candice laughed at Dominique. "What do you mean, *like*? He *is* a scavenger!" She then burped loudly and unexpectedly. "Oh, excuse my piggishness," she said while lightly covering her mouth.

Dominique realized why she never sat with this group before. *These guys have to be the biggest slobs in the cafeteria! But at least the conversation is more interesting*, she thought, so she tried ignoring their vulgar table manners. "We'll still need a few more locations in order to find a pattern," she said.

"I've got it!" Candice cried. "We'll get the info straight from the horse's mouth—Roeser himself!" She slammed her napkin on the table, got up and twirled around. "I am such a genius!"

Everyone at the table watched her victory dance, but didn't understand why she was doing it.

"Explain, please," Wes inquired using a high-pitched synthetic voice.

Candice quickly sat back down and leaned across the table, so that all could hear. "OK—here's what we do. We have Roeser's class this afternoon, right?"

Everyone nodded.

"During class we ask him where our field trip will be, and if he dodges our question, then we start asking about his past trips. We record them so we can establish a pattern. It's a more indirect way, and may take longer, but at least he won't get too suspicious."

"That could work," Desiree commented. "And maybe if we're lucky we can figure out the location of our *own* trip."

"Genius," said Dominique. "Pure genius." Then she thought to herself, *these guys may be slobs, but at least they're clever slobs!*

Mr. Roeser taught morning and afternoon geology classes. The latter one was the worst because students were weary by the day's end, having no mental or physical energy left for learning. Some students would just watch the clock while others would work on homework. Their lackluster attitudes usually frustrated him.

But not on this particular day. The students filed quickly through the doorway and took their seats. Their teacher, who was sitting at his desk, noticed their higher energy level.

Candice hurriedly sat in a desk up front, and Wes sat in one in the middle of the classroom but off to the left. Dominique chose a similar spot off to the right, and Desiree sat in her usual desk in the back corner by the large crystal display.

Mr. Roeser scanned the class then addressed the students. "Before I start with today's lesson I have a quick announcement." He got up from his chair and walked to the door. Some of the students were still chatting softly. He checked the hallway for latecomers, and then closed the door. "If you're planning to attend my field trip to the Grand Canyon, I must have your permission slip by next Tuesday…"

He had a dismally small number of responses to this trip and was hoping to entice more students to sign up before the deadline.

"…Park Service needs a final number, so I cannot accept any late slips. Of course you can always bring them in before Tuesday—like Mr. Ward did." He nodded at Wes who then raised his hand. "You have a question?"

"Yes," Wes replied. "Where in the park are we camping—you know—in case my parents need to reach me?"

The class fell silent. Candice looked back at Wes, who smiled, sure of what he was doing.

Mr. Roeser answered him without hesitation. "As stated on the permission slip the contact number is the park's main office. If your parents need to contact you, they'll have to call that number. Cell phone reception is limited, but I always carry a walkie-talkie that's tuned into to the park rangers' frequency. In the case of an emergency they will be notified."

"Great, but where are we camping?" Wes asked, obviously not satisfied with his teacher's answer.

Mr. Roeser turned on his projector. He then reached over to his laptop, which was connected to the projector and keyed in some commands. A map of the Grand Canyon soon appeared on the large screen.

"We'll travel by bus to the South Rim Village. We'll hike down the Bright Angel Trail to the River Trail." He stood in front of the map and traced the trail with his hand. "From the River Trail we'll cross the bridge over the Colorado River and proceed to the Phantom Ranch. We'll camp there for the first night."

Candice raised her hand. "Just the first night?"

"Yes, Miss Carter. We'll use it as a base camp. You'll want to recover after hiking more than nine miles the first day. We'll explore some areas close to the ranch, but I don't want to overdo it on the first day. The next morning we will break camp and hike a little farther out. At that point we'll camp where we study."

Mr. Roeser turned off the projector and went back to his desk to get the day's lesson. "Now while we're at it, let's talk about the geology of the Grand Canyon." He handed out lecture notes that contained several illustrations of sandstone and shale layers.

Dominique wasn't satisfied with her teacher's response. *The little dodger is not going to give us a direct answer, so we'll have to go through the backdoor.* She then raised her hand. "Are all these rock layers found in every canyon?"

"Pretty much, Dominique, yes," he answered.

"Then what we see at one place we'll see at the next, right?" she asked.

Roeser paused before answering. "Well, it depends on each canyon's depth. They all have similar components of shale and sandstone. But the deeper you go the more layers you'll see. And, depending on the erosion, some will differ slightly in color and pattern."

Desiree looked over to Dominique and gave her the thumbs-up. It seemed that everything was going according to plan.

"How long have you been doing this study with your classes?" Wes asked. "I mean—you must have explored a lot of canyons."

Mr. Roeser finished handing out the lecture notes. He went back to his desk to pile up the extras then walked over to the projection board where he presented the first illustration.

"Son, there are more canyons than both you and I have years to study them. The area has three hundred miles of the Colorado River and countless tributaries doing the chiseling—not to mention the wind, rain and other natural forces."

"So you explore different canyons each year?" Candice asked.

"I try to," he answered. "Each has its own, unique character, and no two are alike. They're kind of like—"

"—River rock?" Desiree asked. The rest of the class whispered or mumbled about her strange answer. She looked at her friends and shrugged her shoulders.

"Well, I was going to say *snowflakes*," her teacher replied, chuckling, "but river rock is actually another good comparison. Some have different composition—that's why they have different colors. But even the same colored rocks can be affected by erosion differently and over time can develop different shapes and textures."

"Really? How?" Bryan asked from the back row. He usually spends this class period memorizing lines for the upcoming school play, but this time he was more interested in his teacher's lecture.

"Let me explain…" Mr. Roeser directed the class' attention back to the projection. He explained how rocks erode in the waterways.

While this was happening Desiree laughed to herself. It only took four students to ask questions, and all of a sudden the whole class got interested. Of course it helps when the Grand Canyon sits in their home state.

Mr. Roeser digressed from his lecture but didn't care. He discussed past field trips and any humorous mishaps that occurred.

"So, anything funny from my brother's trip two years ago?" Wes asked.

"Let's see…two years ago…. hmm. Your brother's name is William. He has sandy brown hair—about as tall as you. Loves to play practical jokes on the class. Wet his pants after we rafted through some whitewater."

The class laughed.

Wes was amazed how much Roeser remembered about his brother. But at the same time he wanted to save his brother's reputation. "Yeah, but I heard everybody got soaked because the raft turtled in the rapids," he said.

"We do rapids?" asked Aaron, normally a non-participant in this class until now. "My uncle did, and he says those puppies are butt-wicked."

"Butt-wicked?" Mr. Roeser asked. "I don't think I've ever heard the rapids described that way, Mr. Howard." The teacher laughed, looked down and shook his head. He then walked down Aaron's aisle. "And I've heard 'em called pretty nasty names."

He noticed everyone's attention on the map. Even Desiree's eyes were glued on it, instead of the crystals on a nearby table. He was happy about their attention and continued.

"Aaron, I guess the butt-wicked factor depends on how much the river drops in elevation from one point to another and how much water is flowing. The midstream obstacles—like boulders or snags—also play into it. Some of rapids can be hair-raising, but most are tame enough to carry you safely through some of the most breath-taking views of the canyons."

He walked back up to the screen and pointed to the area from Horn Creek to Monument Creek. "That's where William Ward's class did some rafting. It was crazy-fun until everybody got wet. Had to hang clothes out to dry for a half day before we continued. But to answer your question, Aaron, we may have a chance for you to run the mighty Colorado if the conditions don't get too *butt-wicked…*"

The four students immediately jotted down the area Roeser mentioned. Wes was ready to ask about his sister's field trip just last year, but Roeser was ahead of him.

"…Then last year we were in a bit of a drought, and Phantom Creek was running slow through this area," he said pointing to an area of waterfalls. "Too many rocks and not enough water to raft. Heck, the falls were barely dripping, and the wading pools were just puddles. Good thing we were there in May 'cause I heard there was a big ol' gully washer in August that flooded the whole canyon. Really good thing we weren't around when that happened!"

Again the four students noted the area. Desiree, getting thirsty from all her note taking, took a sip from her water bottle.

At around the same time Dominique raised her hand. "Mr. R., is there a pattern to the areas of your studies?"

Desiree gasped while sipping her water and started coughing. Candice also gasped at Dominique then gasped at Desiree, whose coughing had worsened.

"Miss Sumner, are you OK?" Mr. Roeser asked, rushing back to her desk. With the entire class' attention on Desiree, Wes got up and threw a large wad of paper at Dominique. She ducked, but she was hit squarely on top of her head. She popped back up and gave him a confused look. He put his finger to his lips as if to shush her. Realizing her mistake, she cupped her hand over her mouth.

Desiree soon recovered from her coughing spell, and Mr. Roeser returned to the front of the class.

"I'm sorry, Dominique, I forgot your question," he said.

Dominique picked up Wes' paper wad and squashed it between her one hand and the desktop, hoping her teacher hadn't seen it. "Well, Mr. Roeser, I was asking about your past field trips. No matter where you went, the students encountered some sort of hazard. I'm seeing a pattern of disaster here—or aren't there any safe canyons to study?" She looked back and gave a thumbs-up to Desiree, who was already breathing normally.

"Miss Cruseaux," replied her teacher, "it's a hazard just to cross the street in front of our school."

"Yes," agreed Aaron, who couldn't help jumping into the discussion. "But what are the odds of getting hit by a flash flood in front of Sunnyslope High School?"

"OK, you got me," Mr. Roeser admitted. "The odds are greater in the Grand Canyon National Park for rock slides, flash floods, and turtling from butt-wicked rapids than they are standing out on Dunlap Avenue." The entire class laughed as he continued, "But a great deal of the beauty and science is explored by thousands of visitors every year who come prepared and leave with great memories. I've had field trips in these areas—"

He pointed to Lava Canyon, Nankoweap Creek and Carbon Canyon.

"—Without incident. Those were also areas where Mother Nature could have gotten a little feisty, but we were prepared and had a great trip. That's the key—being prepared."

Just then the bell rang. Usually the class jumps up to leave, but this time no one moved. Mr. Roeser saw nothing but spellbound eyes still fixed on him. *I can't believe I still have everyone's attention,* he thought. "OK, you can all leave now."

But they weren't ready to go. "Tell us more about the feisty canyons," pleaded Jeremy, another non-participant who sat in the front row.

Mr. Roeser smiled. "OK, two more minutes," he replied, pleased by the class' interest. "The geology of the Grand Canyon is incredibly fascinating and can excite anybody of any age. You just have to go and experience it," he said. "Five years ago we explored…"

Everyone listened attentively while only four students feverishly took notes. When he finished, a few more students asked for field trip permission slips. Mr. Roeser then dismissed the class and cheerfully handed out more permission slips.

Dominique, Desiree, Wes, and Candice slipped into the hallway and huddled together. They looked at each other smiling just like cats that found a big bowl of cream.

"Let's go to the shrine," Wes suggested, and he led them down the hall.

Wes was referring to the sports shrine, which originally started out as a narrow hallway with several trophy cases bolted to the wall. However, over the years, the amount and size of the trophies increased with the success of the sport teams. The trophies outgrew and overloaded the existing cases. A few fundraisers raised enough revenue to build a large foyer with aisles of tall-standing cases arranged in a rectangular labyrinth.

Some cases included digital photo frames presenting slide shows of recent sport seasons. The men's varsity swim team was displayed this way chronicling their road to the state championship. Other cases contained retired uniforms of stellar athletes who went on to become professional players. At the center of the labyrinth was a seating area consisting of two black leather couches and matching sofas facing each other. A darkly stained coffee table sat in the middle of this grouping, and small end tables with reading lamps anchored the grouping at the corners. This was a perfect refuge for alumni to reminisce during sport events as well as for small class gatherings during school hours.

Wes and Desiree sat together on one couch. Candice plopped into one of the sofa chairs, and Dominique circled to the opposite sofa chair.

Wes looked around, making sure their teacher wasn't nearby. "It looks like he's not going to directly tell us where we're camping, so we'll just have to figure this out by ourselves," said Wes. Everyone nodded.

"If we're going to find a pattern to his trips, then we need a comprehensive hiking map of the Grand Canyon," said Candice.

"Hey, I saw one in a book at the library last night," said Desiree. "It's one of those fold-out types that the National Geographic always inserts in their magazines.

"The library sounds like a good place to start," Wes decided. "Maybe we could all meet there later tonight. I've got swim practice in another hour, but I'm willing to duck out early if everybody else can make it."

"I've got volleyball practice within the hour, but I'm done by six o'clock," Dominique answered.

"I have a dance class, but I'll be done by six, too." Desiree said. "What about you, Candice?"

"My fencing practice starts early and ends early," she said. "I'll just grab a quick meal at home before going. I can get some homework done until everybody else shows up."

Taylor suddenly appeared from behind one of the trophy cases. "Hey, where's everybody going?" she asked, stopping at the swim team's trophy case to view the swimming slide show.

"Taylor, how was lunch today?" Dominique asked while turning to wink at Desiree, who was dying to know the same thing.

"Great," Taylor answered then exhaled with fervor. "I've had quite a day." Her gaze remained on the swim photos for another few seconds before turning to Dominique. "I'll tell you all about it in the car."

"No, tell us now," insisted Desiree as she straightened up in her chair. Wes' knee nudged Desiree's. She looked at him and he glared back at her.

"Down, girl," he commanded firmly, sounding like a dog trainer.

"Or not," said Desiree, looking frustrated at Wes.

"Good girl," he said while patting her on the head. He was right; she needed to calm down.

"Don't I get a treat for good behavior?" Desiree asked. He smiled down at her then turned to address Taylor.

"You have geology in the morning, right?"

"Yep, first period."

"Awesome. By any chance has Mr. Roeser mentioned any past field trips to the Grand Canyon?"

"Not yet."

"Then we could use your help. Can you join us at the library tonight?"

"I go where my captain goes," said Taylor, eyeing Dominique who nodded.

Wes stood up and offered to pull Desiree up from the sofa. "I suppose you want me to heel, too," she said sarcastically. She then took his hand and pulled herself up. He patted her head again.

Candice laughed at their antics. "Well, I'd love to stay for the rest of this obedience lesson, but I have to go defeat my next fencing opponent. See ya!"

Just as she took a few steps, her fencing helmet fell out of her unzipped gym bag, and it rolled a few feet in front of her. She was still looking at the group and didn't see that she accidentally kicked it. "Oh, shish kabobs!" she remarked, watching it soar into the air. It clipped a table lamp farthest from the seating area then ricocheted off a trophy case. A digital photo of a past tennis champion was knocked from its stand.

The helmet continued to wobble and turn like a penguin with a short leg. Candice grabbed the helmet before blasting through the gym doors, so she missed the cascading effects. The table lamp tilted precariously. Desiree saw it and bounded towards the lamp, hip-checking Wes onto the couch. His one leg caught her foot and she tripped. She stumbled and fell as she reached for the lamp, trying to catch it before it hit the floor.

But the lamp never fell. It merely rocked a little before returning to rest. Dominique and Taylor both walked over to Desiree, who was on the floor between the coffee table and couch. They peered over the couch and laughed. At the same time Wes rolled to his stomach and likewise looked down at Desiree, who managed an awkward smile up at all of them.

"I'm OK, I'm OK," she said through some of her long hair that had fallen over her face. Wes sat up in the couch, got his footing, and pulled Desiree to her feet.

"Now that trick really does deserve a doggy biscuit," he remarked. She tried to throw her tangled hair back over her head. A few strands hung over her face looking like sagging jungle vines. She tried to blow it out of her face without success. Wes reached down to help detangle her jungle. They all laughed at the situation then parted ways; they had lots to do in so little time, especially with the shorter library hours.

# Chapter IV

*This place is cozy, dark, and safe! It's so nice being with others who enjoy the same. It's much better than the forceful chaos before this. But for now it's a wonderful solace with a gentle sway. If only a lullaby could accompany the swaying. It's nice to snuggle up against others having so many facts. Wish it all could be imparted in a tranquil and quiet place—housed on high shelves like our distant brothers and sisters. But, it matters not; our world has never been more pleasant than this.*

*Oh no! The sudden drop, and sharp gnashing sound of metal teeth disturb us. Again our ceiling rips apart so violently. And here comes the intense light blaring in like a loud trumpet. Hey, take it easy! Stop shoving and slamming us together. Oh, when will this wretched cycle ever end? We have so much knowledge to impart, yet we get so little respect.*

Candice fingered through each textbook in her backpack smacking one against the other. *Where the heck is that math book? I know I put it in here,* she thought. She was ready to flip the next textbook but stopped at her chemistry book. *Well, I know I have homework in this.* She pulled it out and slammed it on the table. The sharp noise echoed off several walls, startling a few of the students at the computer station.

The librarian looked up from her desk and glared at Candice. "Shh!"

Candice then realized the disturbance she caused. She wasn't in the boisterous study hall at school—a place where nothing was quiet.

She looked back at the librarian. "Oops, sorry," she whispered and offered a remorseful-looking grin. The librarian returned a *just-don't-do-it-again* look.

Candice pulled out her three-ring binder and gently placed it on the table. She then pulled out a few more supplies before finally finding her math book. *I knew it was in here*, she thought, sighing with relief, *now if I can just remember which problem set I was supposed to do.*

Before starting her homework she counted the chairs that circled the table. *I guess this should be enough for everybody.* She placed each of her books on the table in front of each chair took look like someone was occupying that space.

Just then a high school student walked through the entrance. Candice didn't notice since she was still busy arranging the table. He circled around the computer section but found no empty seat. Then he noticed Candice and walked over to her table. She stepped back to view the whole table arrangement.

"There! That should do it," she said aloud.

"Hi, I'm Aaron Howard from geology class."

Initially startled by his sudden appearance, Candice jumped backwards. Then, as if greeting a fencing opponent, she robotically offered a handshake. "Hello, Aaron, what's going on?" she asked.

He shook her hand, although he was a bit surprised at her instant congeniality.

"Oh, just dropping by to surf the net," Aaron answered. "I don't have a computer at home, so I use one here. But right now there aren't any available." He looked at her table, noting its arrangement. "Looks like you're having a study group."

"Yeah, with some school friends," she said. She didn't know Aaron and wasn't sure she should tell him about the study group. After all, he could be a spy for the enemy. She continued rearranging notebooks and pens for each place. "We get together every now and then to make sure everybody's doing OK and nobody's flunking." She even started to dust off the seats with the sleeve of her shirt. "I guess we're a little nerdy about that."

"It's for geology, right?" asked Aaron.

Candice looked surprised. "Why would you guess that? We don't have any tests coming up, do we?" He started to follow her around the table—his light brown hair with unkempt bangs flopped in and out of his face with each step. But he stayed at a comfortable distance from her.

"No tests that I know of," he answered, "but we do have a field trip coming up. I noticed your friends were asking specific questions about Roeser's past field trips."

She stopped arranging and cleaning. "Not really," she said disagreeing, "the permission slip never gave an exact location of our study." She tried not to reveal any new information. "Some of our parents wanted to know." She went back to the seat where her backpack was placed. She went into it looking for anything else for the study group. She started to anxiously look towards the front entrance. *I'm gonna have to block and parry with this guy for a while until reinforcements come*, she thought as she checked the time on her cell phone.

But Aaron persisted. "Oh, really? Then why all the theatrics when Dominique asked about a pattern to his camp site selections?" He widened his hazel colored eyes enough to catch the incandescent light shining above him. "Why would that question make Desiree choke and Wes bean Dominique with a paper wad?"

Like a 3-D movie, his eyes seemed to project out and probe into Candice's eyes. "Sounds to me like you're up to something," Aaron said while slowly approaching her. She held her ground but moved behind her chair for protection from further mind probing.

"Aaron, uh, I don't know what you're talking about," Candice nervously replied. "A bunch of us are meeting to discuss homework, projects, and that sort of stuff." She then pointed to the computer section. "Hey, there's a computer station open now— weren't you waiting to get on one?"

Aaron never looked at the computers and instead kept focus on her eyes. "Yes, after you reveal your intentions of the study group," he replied. He widened his eyes even more. Her eyes widened, too, as if she was becoming hypnotized.

Then she blinked and cocked her head. "Aaron, you're creeping me out," she said.

Wes then appeared behind Aaron. "Who's a creep? You guys aren't talking about me, I hope," he said.

Candice gave out a huge sigh of relief. "Wes, glad you're here. This guy is trying to crash our study group," she said, fidgeting the waves in her red hair.

"Aaron? No, Candice, he's not crashing—he's *joining* our study group," Wes replied, giving Aaron a high five.

Candice came out from behind her chair. "He is?" she asked in disbelief.

Wes explained, "Aaron's a friend of mine, who just signed up for the field trip today," he said, placing his arm on Aaron's shoulder. "So, I invited him here. We drove up together. We could really use his *I.T.* skills. The more brains the better, I always say."

Candice eyed Aaron suspiciously. "Yeah, but you know what they say: too many chickens spoil the pot—or something like that."

Aaron laughed quietly at her obviously misconstrued proverb.

"Isn't she cute?" Wes asked, whispering to Aaron. "She's the biggest brain in this group, which is why we so desperately need you." Wes then addressed them both. "So, let's get started, shall we? I'll go find some books about the Grand Canyon."

Candice returned to her chair at the table. "Go for it, Wes. I can use the time to get some homework finished," she said. She then collected some of her schoolbooks and piled them in front of her chair.

Aaron started to clear the table area opposite her. "Here, let me help."

"No, Aaron, you don't have to," she said.

"It's the least I can do for creeping you out," he said, smiling.

"You really weren't," she replied, "I knew the whole time what you were trying to do."

"Oh, you did, huh? Is that why you were dodging my questions?" Aaron asked.

"Dodging? I never, *ever* dodge anything. I live for full-frontal confrontation," she boldly claimed, throwing her hair behind her shoulders.

"Great, then I can join this group without anymore grief from you, right?" he asked.

She smiled at him. "Sit right down, buddy-boy! I'll even share my pencil leads," she said.

Accepting her invitation, Aaron smiled down at her. He wasn't as tall as Wes but still taller than Candice. He placed his backpack on the floor and sat next to her. He then pulled out his textbook, paper and pencil.

Candice had her materials ready but noticed that Aaron had the very same textbook. "You in Algebra-Trig, too?"

"Yes, first period," he answered. "It has to be the toughest time of day. I'm hardly awake for this class and no way ready to grasp mathematical concepts."

"I have it fifth period—right before lunch. My brain works, but my stomach complains the whole time. Hey, do you know which problems we're supposed to do?"

"My notebook says *page two hundred eighty-five, problems one through twenty-one, odds,* but your class may be ahead of mine."

"Let me check." She flipped through to page two hundred and eighty-five. "That's where we're at, too, so that's gotta be my assignment, too."

Aaron was not really listening; his attention was already on his homework. He wanted to get his homework done quickly, so that he could help Wes with the group's mission.

Candice noticed Aaron's pace and decided to race him. They both rewrote the first problem on the first line of their loose-leaf notebook paper. Obviously they both thought it was an easy problem, so they each raced to the second line to solve the problem. They both finished and circled the answer simultaneously. They both looked up at each other then proceeded quickly to the next problem.

Again it was an easy problem for Candice, but Aaron was stumped and had to flip back to the explanation in the chapter. Candice smiled, knowing she finished first and circled her answer. Aaron finally got to the method of solving Problem Three in the chapter and started to scribble down his solution, but in the process of hurrying, he had to erase the entire second line.

Candice heard the erasing and laughed. He glanced over to see her smirking. Aaron flushed in embarrassment, hoping that Candice hadn't noticed. He rewrote his second line and emphatically circled the answer loud enough for Candice to hear.

Candice, meanwhile, was stumped on Problem Five and had to flip back to the chapter's explanation, but Aaron raced to catch her. He circled his answer before she did. Not to be beaten by Aaron she finished Problem Five, but she broke the lead on her pencil. She pumped it to replace the lead, but ran out of lead. With an exasperating groan she reached over to her pencil case and pulled out a new one. She quickly replaced it and proceeded to the next problem.

By that time Aaron was on Problem Nine and well ahead of Candice. He put his pencil down, leaned back in his chair and stretched. Annoyed by his display, Candice glared at him before racing to Problem Seven. He noticed that she didn't stop to check his progress, so he quickly copied Problem Eleven. Candice circled her answer to Problem Seven and raced through Problem Nine, circling its answer.

Beads of sweat were now rolling down Aaron's forehead as he circled his answer to Problem Eleven and copied Problem Thirteen with break-neck speed. Again Candice caught up to him.

By this time Wes found three books and proudly walked to the table to show them the fruits of his search. "You gotta see this stuff; I got some great books we can look at—"

But in the heat of battle both math competitors rudely yelled back at him, "Not now, Wes!"

The librarian looked over and shushed everyone at the table, but no one noticed her. She then got up and walked over to the table. She repeated her shushing, and finally all three looked up.

"What?" Wes asked.

"You didn't hear me?" asked the librarian.

"Hear you what?" Candice asked, putting down her pencil.

"My shushing," the librarian answered.

"Why did you shush?" Aaron asked, finishing his last problem. He apparently was oblivious to the commotion that he and Candice caused.

"You were loud—all of you, and we're not to be loud in the library," she answered.

"I wasn't loud," Wes contested. "I was just getting books." He sounded like a little schoolboy trying to declare his innocence.

"The table was loud, and I was shushing the table," she said. "If this table cannot stay quiet, then you'll all have to leave."

"But I wasn't loud," insisted Wes. "Can I stay?"

"Are you with the table?" she asked.

"What if I sat at a different table?"

The librarian heard this type of ridiculous plea-bargaining a million times before, but it was usually with younger kids who would say anything to get out of trouble.

"Then you could stay so long as you're quiet," she decided. The group giggled quietly to themselves. The librarian returned to her desk, annoyed by the snappy, know-it-all seniors.

"We can't afford to get kicked out before the rest show up," Wes warned in a whispering voice to his friends.

"Well, then, Mr. Varsity Swimmer, go sit at another table," Aaron whispered back. Candice heard Aaron and giggled. *Not only is this guy competitive, but he's also stupid funny,* she thought.

By the end of the Algebra-Trig problem set, Aaron and Candice finished in a dead tie. Candice was a little miffed that she didn't beat him but challenged Aaron to a rematch. Aaron gladly accepted, and the two exchanged phone numbers to form their own, homework group.

Soon the rest of the group finally arrived. They viewed the books that Wes retrieved from the reference section. Aaron found an open seat in the computer section and researched *Grand Canyon Hiking Trails*, printing out a few results. They placed stickers on all the areas that Mr. Roeser mentioned in last period geology class.

"He didn't lecture on any Grand Canyon trips yet in first period," said Taylor, "but it sounds like he's getting closer. This morning's topic was *Sunset Crater*, and that's just outside Flagstaff."

Dominique opened her laptop that contained notes she took that day. "So far the only area in common with all the trips is the Phantom Ranch," she said, scrolling down her screen. "It's probably where every class camped on the first night then hiked other trails."

"Yes, but the study areas are located both up and downstream of the ranch," said Desiree as she paged through a Grand Canyon hiking book. "There are a whole slew of canyons in between."

"We gotta get Roeser to talk about more trips, so that we can get more stickers on this map," concluded Aaron.

"It sure was easy today," said Wes. "He couldn't wait to talk about some highlights and mishaps. But if we keep sapping him for information, he may end up getting suspicious. We've got to find another source of information."

"Wait a minute," said Desiree rising from her chair as if she just had a revelation. She looked up at the library check out desk. It was made of hardwood with a wide rail. Buckshot and knife carving stressed its surface. It reminded her of the information desk she saw at one of the canyon lodges where she stayed with her family when she was younger.

"Just give me a minute to figure this out." She then walked towards the desk. Her classmates watched her. The faux fur trim on her hoodie fluffed with the blowing air from the overhead fan. Her long hair, still braided from dance class, swung like a pendulum across her back with every step.

She approached the desk and ran her hand along the surface of the wooden rail. The librarian was busily checking out books but then noticed Desiree's strange behavior and began watching her.

"Hopi House, maybe," said Desiree, running her fingers along the imperfections. "El Tovar—no wait…" All the while she had quick flashbacks of her last childhood trip with her family including her grandpa at the lodge in the South Rim Village. "…Maswik, that's got to be it!"

Desiree's sudden outburst startled the librarian, who jumped in her seat. Desiree noticed and whispered a quick apology before walking back to the study table.

"No one can camp overnight without a permit from the Back Country Office at the Maswik Lodge," she told them. "My grandpa always had to get one, and he had to list the areas he intended to go plus how long he intended to stay. It didn't matter who you were—local folk or international visitors, Boy Scouts or

94

high school seniors." She stopped at Wes' chair and looked at every member of the table. "If we can get a hold of that permit registry, then we could find all the places where the geology field trips camped."

"Great, but is it public record?" Dominique asked.

Aaron shot up from his chair and darted back over to a computer station. Another elementary student was just about to take the seat, but Aaron got it first. The elementary student frowned, but Aaron pointed him over to another empty seat. The child smiled and skipped over to it. Aaron then began tapping on the keyboard.

Meanwhile the discussion at the study table continued. "It has to be public record," said Desiree. "Safety forces need it to find campers or hikers who may be in trouble or missing. I'm guessing families and friends would also need it, so it's got to be public record—"

"—And publicly accessible," Aaron announced from his computer as he hit the *enter* key. He spun around to face the group. "You guys have to see this." The students got up and filed over to the computer station where Aaron was sitting. They formed a semi-circle behind him and peered over his shoulders. On the screen they saw several lines of data containing names of camp permit applicants. "Am I good or what?"

"How did you get this?" asked Wes.

"Well, I sort of hacked into the website and got the *PDF* files in the registry."

"Wow, there's people from all over the world listed here," said Candice, leaning in more closely to the screen. She grabbed the computer mouse and started scrolling down the list "… Japan, Nepal, Netherlands, Norway, Argentina…"

Aaron felt Candice leaning into him more as she eventually blocked his view. He then leaned back and let Candice's wavy hair whisk his face. He inhaled deeply, smelling the fresh green tea and cucumber scent of her hair conditioner. Then he exhaled and closed his eyes, enjoying her intrusion.

"There must be hundreds of people who register, and look—some are hiking from rim to rim," Candice said. She pointed at a group from New Zealand who intended to hike down to the Colorado River via the South Kaibab Trail, camp overnight in the Bright Angel Campgrounds, and then hike back out via the North Kaibab Trail. "That's got to be more than twenty miles of walking. Sure hope they packed extra shoes."

"People hike rim-to-rim all the time," said Desiree. "My grandpa once mentioned that thousands of people camp, but thousands more just hike down and out in a day. He called them fools for not taking time to view the beauty. But the registry will only contain those who camp overnight."

Candice turned from Aaron's screen back to the group. "Maybe we can narrow our search using Roeser's name or Sunnyslope High School," she suggested.

Aaron gently pulled her aside. "Excuse me, please," he said politely. She moved with her eyes still fixed on the screen while he continued his analysis. "This registry is not a spread sheet, so I can't do any sorting or searching. We'll have to print it out and do it manually. This could take several hours or even days."

"Well, there's seven of us, so we could split up the search," said Taylor. "We're a team, you know. And if Royce helps we can make it a team of eight."

Before Desiree could comment on Taylor's suggestion, the librarian rang a hand bell for several seconds to announce closing time. Like a group of trained kindergarteners they immediately broke out of their huddle, walked in orderly fashion to their table and packed to leave.

Aaron closed the registry, deleted the address and ended his internet session. "We still need to narrow the search," he told them. "Each photocopy is prefaced by date, so I can go by that then print out the page for that date. Then I'll divvy up the pages for everyone to check." He rejoined the group at the table. "The only problem is I need to use some one's computer."

"So you really were telling the truth about not having one, huh?" asked Candice.

"Really and truly," Aaron answered as he packed his bag and slung it on his shoulder. "I'm saving up to buy one of those smartphones."

"So, there *is* honor among hackers," she said smiling at him, "I like that! If you want, you can use the computer at my house," she offered. He, of course, accepted.

"We can narrow the search even more by choosing registry dates from March to mid-May," Wes said to Aaron, "but how many years you reckon we should go back?"

"As far as necessary," said Dominique, "until we have enough points on the map to figure out a pattern."

"We could still try to get more info from Roeser," said Taylor. "I have lab tomorrow; I'll see how much info I can suck out of him."

The group quietly packed up and left the library, not wanting to further stress the librarian. But as soon as they filed through the exit doors they literally exploded with excitement. They screamed and laughed like first-graders at recess. Solving this mystery made geology their new, best class of the term!

# Chapter V

The entrance to the chamber opened. In tumbled the joyful little critters. Happily they thrashed and bounced off each other as they looked for a spot. Some needed gentle persuasion to either stack up or conform into a particularly shaped slot if they couldn't do it by themselves. Eventually everybody settled. They've waited forever to grow and mature. Then they were processed and inspected. The ones who made the grade shined and rolled with glee. The race to this chamber was the last stage of their long journey. They instinctively ached for it like salmon fighting upstream to return to their birth pond to spawn. They had such perfect shapes and smooth textures. Anticipation ran high. Soon the critters felt an urge to dance. The floor beneath them started to move, and the waves of energy flowed through them. Their excitement rose with each second. A few hopped while others tumbled. No one could stand still. Man, this place was really cooking!

Janelle shook the pot over the burner until the popping slowed down. With the lid still on she carefully carried it over to a large, stainless steel bowl before lifting the lid and pouring out the puffy and steamy indulgence. Some kernels were still popping and jumped out of the bowl. She quickly retrieved them, tossing them into her mouth before getting lemonade from the refrigerator. The TV was tuned into *The Weather Channel*, which was airing stories of natural disasters. It showed a person trapped inside a car on a flooded street in Las Vegas.

*That could be Highway 51 under Highland Road during the monsoon season*, she thought. She then got her planner and sat at the counter. On TV the rescue helicopter spotted the stalled car, which was starting to drift with the currents of the rising floodwaters. She pulled the index tab of her planner over to the page where the *Farmers' Market* event was listed. She started checking off completed tasks and reviewed the uncompleted ones. Then the phone rang.

"Heritage Farm, this is Janelle, good evening," she said. "Hey, Royce. You need a ride? Oh, you got one... No, you come right home. I've got tons of snacks here...See ya soon." She hung up the phone and looked over at the TV again. The car's driver was now climbing out onto the roof just as the water was rushing over the hood.

*People just don't realize how deep floodwaters can get. And they're warned all the time. Sure hope my kids know better than that*, she thought as she poured out some lemonade. The exhausted driver was lying across the car's roof as the helicopter hovered overhead. A rescue swimmer with an extra harness was lowered.

Janelle grabbed a kernel and tossed it into her mouth. The kernel bounced off her front teeth and landed on the counter. On TV the victim reached for the harness, but a gust of wind blew it just out of reach. Janelle picked up the kernel and tried tossing it again, but she missed again. The victim's second attempt at the harness was also unsuccessful. The water was now rising up to the car's roof! Time was running out!

Getting frustrated, Janelle picked up the pesky kernel for the third time and placed it into her mouth. She crushed it between her teeth and yelled at the TV.

"Come on, try something else!" Just then the rescue chopper dropped lower, and a rescue swimmer jumped into the water. He paddled to the car. "Yes, the direct approach is always more effective," Janelle remarked as she grabbed a few more kernels and placed them in her mouth. The rescue swimmer pulled the harness over the victim. Soon they both ascended slowly, and after a few seconds the chopper flew them to dry land. "Hooray!" Janelle grabbed her lemonade glass and toasted the successful rescue.

Desiree arrived home and ran up to the house. She couldn't wait to find out about Royce's lunch date with Taylor. At the same time she was exhausted from everything else that day. She opened the back door and immediately caught the aroma of fresh popcorn.

"Oh, that smells so good!" Desiree exclaimed as she dropped both her school and dance bag on the floor just inside the doorway.

"I'll share this with you, but it'll cost a hug," said her mom. Her daughter promptly ran into her outstretched arms. "Dizzy-girl, it seemed like a really long day without you."

Desiree thought so too, and she wanted to tell her mom everything about the day. But for now she enjoyed the embrace. "I missed you, too, Mom," she said.

For them the simplest pleasures during the calmest moments can soothe all ills. Desiree forgot about her frustrations of the school bus ride. She forgot about all the tortuous stretches and monotonous routines from her dance class. She even forgot about Royce's lunch date with Taylor.

"So, Mom, how was your day?" Desiree asked.

Her mom stepped over to get the popcorn bowl then slid it to her daughter. "Great—I presented my report at a rather tasty breakfast meeting. Most of the farming folks are doing OK, except gas prices are going up. So the distribution folks will be charging more, but hey, what can I do?"

"Deliver your produce by horseback, maybe?" Desiree suggested as she popped some kernels into her mouth.

Her mom laughed. "That's a good one! But I'm not all that worried; our profit margin is big enough to eat the rising fuel cost. Just want to make sure they're not gouging us. Your grandpa is a good birddog. He'll watch the books and keep 'em honest."

The two sat at the counter and munched on more popcorn. Janelle asked about her daughter's day—about school, dance class and the library.

Desiree summed up her day, leaving out most of the details—except for one. "We also found out where we'll be camping during our field trip."

"Where?"

"Phantom Ranch the first night, and then we'll hike out the next morning."

"Hike out to where?"

"The dismissal bell rang before our teacher could tell us, but we'll try to find out in the next few classes."

"Maybe your teacher doesn't really know," her mom guessed. "Maybe he plays it by ear. Conditions down there can change at the drop of a hat, so maybe he's not dead set on a location.

Desiree went to the cupboard for a small glass. She then poured out some lemonade—not spilling a single drop. Her mom smiled as she noticed Desiree's neatness.

"He mentioned a few past trips but never to the same canyon twice," said Desiree. "Dad thinks Mr. Roeser is searching for something that has nothing to do with geology." She took a small sip of lemonade and, enjoying its fresh taste, took a larger sip. "Hey, Mom, this stuff is great! Did you make this with our lemons?"

"Yep," answered her mom cheerfully. "The secret is in the coffee grounds. We just spread it right under the tree. It nourishes the soil and holds in the moisture. No fancy, high-tech stuff. You just can't beat the basic elements of Mother Nature."

"Mom, coffee grounds are from the local coffee shop, not Mother Nature" she disputed before taking another sip.

"Maybe so, sweetie, but Mother Nature produced the coffee beans in the first place. Besides, we got lots more than just coffee grounds; we also got mulch from last year's Christmas trees, last season's leaf litter, leftovers from your dance class picnic—"

"—I get it, Mom, thanks," Desiree said, politely ending the argument.

Her mom smiled and munched on more popcorn, and then glanced at her planner. "By the way, I told you that the Farmers' Market starts at sunrise and ends at noon, right?"

"Right," answered Desiree. "That usually means we have to be there at least one hour earlier, right?"

"Afraid so, sweetie. My parents have all the tables and chairs, but I'll still need some help getting the produce packed in the truck."

"No problem," said Desiree. She finished her lemonade, got up and went to the sink. She placed her cup in it, and went back to her mom. "I'm going to bed, Mom. I had a busy day, and I'm tired. Thanks for the popcorn and lemonade."

"Sure thing, pumpkin, goodnight," her mom replied then kissed her daughter's cheek. After Desiree left Janelle sat back down at the counter and closed her journal.

Just then the crunching sound of tires rolling over the gravel driveway announced the arrival of a car. She could hear voices and a car door closing. She went to the cupboard to get another glass just as Royce came through the backdoor.

"Everybody's home, right?" he asked.

"Yep," replied his mom. He turned off the outside porch light then went into the laundry room. "And how was your day, handsome?" Janelle asked while following him.

"Pretty cool," he replied. "I had lunch with a senior." This shocked his mom—not news about lunch—but more details about his day.

She could hardly catch her breath. "So you found Taylor, huh?" she asked.

"Yeah, it was a weird circumstance, but I found her at Desiree's locker this morning." He circled back to the kitchen, and she followed closely behind while sniffing the air.

"Royce, did you shower after practice?"

"Yeah, Mom, I always do."

She sniffed around him more. "Then why do you smell like bleach? Is that pool water going funny again? Maybe you'd better try using soap next time to get out that pool smell. No girl, especially a senior, is gonna be charmed by a walking bleach bottle."

"Yeah, but I'm the only bleach bottle with six-pack abs," he said, while showing them off in front of his mom. She couldn't help lightly jabbing them. But he flinched and jumped back.

"Oops, sorry; couldn't help myself," his mom confessed.

"That's OK, Ma, at least you don't do it as much as Dizzy does." He then sniffed the air. "Hey, I smell popcorn. Is there any left?" He sat at the counter and looked in the bowl which had only a few kernels left.

"Don't worry, Mr. Six-pack, I can make more," his mom replied.

"Great, so while I'm waiting…" Royce went to the freezer and pulled out a carton of key lime sherbet. He then went to the fridge and got some leftover melon, strawberries and orange juice. He assembled the blender and added all the ingredients. After he turned on the blender he reached into the cupboard for a jar of wheat germ.

His mom had already poured more popcorn seeds into the pot on the stove. She then watched Royce add a palm-sized portion of wheat germ into the blender.

"Now why would you wanna wreck such a yummy smoothie with *that* gunk?" she asked while sliding the pot back and forth across the burner.

"This gunk is good for me," he answered. "Besides I thought you wanted me to eat healthy foods."

"I do," she admitted. "Just remind me next time not to watch you make your healthy snacks."

He grabbed a carton of egg substitute and poured some of it in the blender. "OK, I will," he said while watching his mom wince.

Back in her bedroom Desiree slipped into her flannel pajamas, crawled into bed and pulled Shakespeare's *Macbeth* down from the bookshelf. Her leg muscles were especially sore, so she propped up her knees with a few pillows. Then she lay back and read a few scenes from the play.

She heard the whirring sound of the blender in the kitchen, but it didn't seem to disrupt her peacefulness. She closed her eyes, and, instead of picturing a murderous scene in *Macbeth*, she pictured her dad reading it while sitting in the wooden chair, that creaked only when he turned each page.

She readjusted the pillows under her legs, but some of the overworked muscles twitched in protest. After a few more adjustments she was finally in the perfect position of repose. She set her book on the nearby nightstand and turned off the light. Then she stretched both arms over her head. Lacing her fingers together she slid her hands under her head. Then after a long yawn she relaxed all her muscles and drifted to sleep, breathing slowly and deeply.

Back in the kitchen, Royce was happily sipping his smoothie at the counter and munching on a fresh and hot bowl of popcorn. He described his lunch date with Taylor. He would have loved a date with Taylor on Friday night, but his mom reminded him about being home early. Disappointed, he retired to his bedroom.

The next morning was busy for Janelle. She had to collect all the produce from the farm for sale at the next day's market. Her parents arrived early—as usual—with shipping cartons. Winter produce like citrus, carrots and broccoli were easy to collect and store for transport in cool temperatures, so they did it a day early.

Royce was the first one out of the house. He left his customary trail of clothes and breakfast tidbits all over the kitchen and laundry room. His mom quickly made coffee and cleaned the kitchen before her parents arrived.

Desiree got up and dressed at her usual time. She greeted her grandparents at the window and let them in the kitchen for coffee. She got a phone call from Taylor wanting to talk to Royce, but Desiree politely informed her of his early swim practice schedule. Taylor reminded Desiree about having lab that morning, and that she was getting second thoughts about tricking Mr. Roeser into revealing past campsites. Desiree said she'd meet Taylor outside the lab door.

Excited about going to Taylor's lab, Desiree hurried to get her schoolbooks. She made it to the bus stop on time and without a spill or mess!

"Those kids of yours are growing up fast," Janelle's dad remarked while warming his hands around his coffee mug. "I can remember taking them for tractor rides when they were only knee high." He was looking out the kitchen window at a nearby tree that still had the tire swing hanging from the lowest branch. "Now they're out the door before we can get a chance to measure their height."

Janelle smiled and poured herself some coffee. "Now they both can drive and repair the tractor," said Janelle, "and both are much taller than you."

Janelle's mom was reading the local news section of the newspaper that was lying across the café-sized table in front of the window. The sun was barely creeping in, but she had enough light to see the print. "Janelle, there's an ad in here about the market tomorrow, and look, they even listed the participants!" She flipped down her glasses so that she could read the finer print. "Heritage Farms," she said. "How about that!"

"We'd better be; I paid good money for that ad. Hope it's big enough to see without a magnifying glass," said Janelle with biting sarcasm while walking to the table. She leaned over the newspaper and viewed the ad. "Well I'll be—I can almost see it without my reading glasses!"

Her mom looked up from the paper. "Of course you can, dear, but do we really need to advertise? Our produce is the best in the area. It's always been that way, and everybody knows it."

Her daughter sat down in the chair across from her mom. "You are—as always—correct, Mom," Janelle said. "We're a great farming family with the best team members."

Her mom smiled back, before taking a sip of coffee from her cup. Then she sighed. "Do you think the kids will want to run the farm after we retire to the old folks home?"

Janelle looked up from the ad. "Can't say for sure, Ma. Desiree wants to study geology and maybe minor in performing arts—that doesn't sound a whole lot like farming." Then she looked out the window. Through the trees she could see a city bus letting out two passengers at the street corner.

"What about Royce?" her mom asked. Janelle was still gazing out the window when she answered.

"Well, Ma, he maybe more the farming-type. He's interested in biology and botany, but he's too young right now to make a career choice," she said. "He's having fun being a high school freshman and an outstanding swimmer." She then looked back at her mom. "It would be nice if they both could run the farm, but right now they have a hard time working together. They're constantly at each other's throats. They only act civilized when I'm around."

Her dad fed a slice of bread into the toaster. He stood and watched it while philosophizing. "Well it might just be a stage in life for them—being teenagers and all, and we can only wait for their acts to end then exit," he said chuckling. "All your brothers and sisters got along at that age."

Janelle turned to her dad. "We didn't fight all that much, Pa. We were either too busy working in the fields or too tired when we got done."

Her dad smiled. "Exactly," he said. "That was the idea. Your mom and I kept you kids busy or exhausted as much as we could."

"Well," said Janelle, "now it's our turn to get busy this morning. We gotta load our produce onto the truck. Jake and Javier are coming up the driveway now," she said pointing out the window at the two farm hands reporting for work.

Her dad raised the toaster lever. "In that case I'll have my bread lightly-toasted this morning." He quickly buttered the bread, folded it in half and took a large bite. He then stuffed the rest of it his back pocket, grabbed his coffee mug, and walked out the back door. Janelle and her mom both followed him.

At school Desiree met Taylor, who was carrying a lab notebook and rock pick, at the geology lab door. She wore safety goggles atop her forehead and a shroud of doubt on her face.

"I'm not sure I can get Roeser to switch the topic from *hydrous aluminum silicates* to past Grand Canyon field trips," she said.

Desiree gave her an encouraging pat on the shoulder. "Taylor, sure you can; you have the gift of gab," she said. The sun was already shining through the door of the classroom opposite the geology lab, and it showed her short, round face with a pert nose powdered perfectly with peach blush. "You also have the gift of schmooze—you can start a lively conversation with complete strangers. Don't think of him as a teacher. Think of him as the pivotal point of this school's rumor mill."

"Now *that* I can do," Taylor said as her cheeks started to glow even brighter than her pink rouge. "I'll start with some idle chit chat, and—just leave it to me. This'll be fun!" She opened the door and ran into the lab.

"Don't forget to take notes," Desiree added. Taylor popped back out into the hall to thank her friend.

"By the way, aren't you dying to hear about my lunch with Royce?" Taylor asked.

"Oh, yeah—lunch with my brother," Desiree replied blankly, "Well, Taylor, to be honest, I was going to wait until it reached the end of the rumor mill. By then the story would have gotten pretty juicy."

Taylor giggled. "Oh, Desiree, you're so funny," she said, "but you can hear it from me first; your brother is not only a hunk, but he's fun to talk to—kind of like you."

"What—I'm a *hunk*?" Desiree asked. "What do you mean by that?"

"No, no, no; not the hunk part—the fun-to-talk part. See, there you go again," she said tapping Desiree's arm while giggling again. She then turned and entered the lab.

Mr. Roeser was already in the lab talking quietly on his cell phone. "Hey, Tom, this is Brad. Did you get my message? OK, meet us at the Phantom Ranch that Friday morning…No, only two mules this time. I've got a small group this year…You're right, it'll make the search a little more restricted, but we'll search as much area as we can. Make sure you and Bessie bring extra batteries and memory chips for the cameras—just in case we find a few of them. Hell, the whole tribe would be nice."

He saw Taylor and closed his phone. "Good morning, Miss Mayer, you're here bright and early."

She walked over to her lab table and unloaded her equipment. "Yes, I am," Taylor proudly replied. "I wanted to be awake and ready this time."

Her teacher was pleased. "That's good to hear. But I'm curious as to why this particular time."

Taylor opened her notebook and pulled out her pen. Then she took a deep breath and nervously brushed her wispy, jaw-length hair behind her ears. "Well, you see, I wanted to catch you before class so that I could ask you a few questions about the field trip…"

Meanwhile Desiree walked down the hall towards her locker. Wes was waiting in the recessed part of the next classroom door and jumped out to surprise her. He had just arrived from swim practice. His hair was still damp and tucked under the hood of his sweatshirt. Each time he moved, however, she smelled a fresh, herbal scent.

"Hey, I had a chance to talk with your brother this morning," he said. "Do you want to hear how his lunch date with Taylor went?"

Desiree wasn't listening; she seemed more interested in his aroma. Leaning into his arm she inhaled deeply through her nostrils. "Mm, you smell like a rain-washed desert," she remarked. As they walked slowly down the empty hallway, she stayed cozy with the varsity swimmer, and he welcomed it.

"Does that mean you *don't* want to hear about Royce?" Wes asked.

She stopped and looked up into his eyes. They were outlined by red wear marks from his swim goggles. She laughed to herself, and her dark blue eyes twinkled as she answered him.

"Sure, I'd love to hear a guy's angle on how this lunch date went," she answered, "but it can wait. I am enjoying my morning with you right now." She closed her eyes and took another whiff. "Your cologne smells wonderful but strangely familiar."

"As the matter of fact, it's some shower gel I borrowed from Royce after swim practice. The pool water has been getting pretty smelly lately—like a bleach bottle." He leaned into Desiree and opened his jacket exposing a blue and white tie-dyed T-shirt. Another puff of eucalyptus-mint bathed her nostrils. "Do you like it?" he asked.

She inhaled again while watching his chest rise and fall with each slow breath he took. Her senses were exhilarated from the blue shades of his shirt, the aroma from his skin, and the expansion of his amazing chest! She enjoyed everything about him right now. She wished she could be imprisoned in his jacket forever.

"Dizzy?"

"What?"

"Do you like how I smell?"

She paused before answering his question. "Yes, I do. What's it called?"

"I think the label said, *Monsoon Shower.*"

"You mean *Desert Monsoon?*"

"Yeah, that's it—*Desert Monsoon.*"

Desiree suddenly spun away from Wes. She transformed from a mesmerized quarry to a vengeful witch. "That white-livered lout; he stole my shower gel! Ooh, I'll so get him for this," she said, seething.

"Hey, give your brother some slack," Wes said, gently pulling her back into his jacket again. He held her there with his wonderfully captivating arms tightly wrapped around her, trying to extract her rage. "Come on, Desiree, he probably wanted to smell nice for Taylor." He then fanned the aroma from his chest and neck. "It worked on you, right? You like how I smell, right?"

Desiree stopped seething. She closed her eyes and inhaled Wes' aroma again. Once again, he was right. She really liked how it was working on her.

"Yes, I like how you smell, Wes. I just wish Royce would use his own shower gel. I think his stuff is called *Pheromone Phever* or something like that," she said.

Wes laughed. "You mean *Forever Evergreen*, and he's not going to use that. It actually smells like a pine tree. It attracts guys, especially hunters. I don't think your brother wants to attract them. Did you ever smell that stuff?"

"Can't say that I have. He's never used it," she answered. "Hey, how do you know about all this gel stuff anyway?"

"—From my older brother and sister," Wes answered, hooking an arm around her waist. "They fill me in on all the aphrodisiacs."

The two walked together through the quiet corridor, enjoying each other's company until they passed through the double doors to the main hall. There the noise level shot up a few hundred decibels as hundreds of students talked, laughed, and slammed locker doors. The couple headed for Desiree's locker and saw Candice trying to arrange the contents of her locker. She was pulling out her sports equipment to make room for her backpack and water bottle.

"Hey, guys," Candice greeted as she dropped her catcher's mitt on a pile just in front of her locker. "Just doing a little spring cleaning, so be forewarned."

"OK, we'll steer clear," said Wes as he sidestepped her locker area. Desiree then opened her own locker. She gently kicked aside Candice's fencing helmet that was on the floor, pushing it closer to Candice's pile.

On the inside of Desiree's locker door was a small mirror, which had a cosmetic pouch attached. She glanced in the mirror then opened the pouch and pulled out a tube of lip-gloss. Wes watched her as she slowly applied it to her lower lip then upward across her top lip.

"I love watching you pretty yourself for me," he said as Desiree blushed. "Let me guess," he said bending down so that his chin lay right on top of her shoulder. Both their faces filled the mirror. "Your lip gloss is called *Goal-essence*, right?"

She pressed her cheek onto his. "That's right—how did you know?"

Wes likewise turned to her while staying in the mirror's frame. "That's the same stuff my older sister uses. She says she likes the deep rich shimmers but no real color. Hey, I don't know what all that means. I just know she looks natural, and it seems to make her whole face glow when she smiles."

"So what about me?" Desiree asked. "Do I glow like your sister?"

"Uh, let me see," he said. He tried to push his face over Desiree's shoulder more. At the same time he squinted his eyes to look at her lips. She giggled as he looked because he now had to hold her by the shoulders to keep from falling. She was caught up in his aroma. *Boy I could stay in this mirror with Wes forever*, she thought.

Just then their coziness was interrupted by a hand that slowly drifted between them. Then it opened to catch a softball that came from out of nowhere. Wes and Desiree backed away and saw that it was Aaron's hand.

"Dude, back off," Wes barked. "I wasn't finished checking my girl's make up."

Aaron tossed the ball back and forth in his own hands. "*Her* make up? I thought you were checking *your* make-up," he joked.

Irritated by Aaron's remark, Wes grabbed the ball in mid-air and faked a throw at his buddy's face. "I think you could use some black and blue eye shadow," he said as Aaron ducked.

Candice, who came up next to Wes, quickly jumped up and snatched the ball from Wes' hand. "Not with my softball you don't," she said, tucking it back into her locker. "And by the way, both your make-up jobs look just fine."

Both guys looked into Desiree's mirror to check. Just watching them fight for mirror space made the girls laugh.

"I think Wes finally has some competition for this year's Class Clown Award," said Desiree.

Candice agreed. Then she pulled Aaron away from the mirror. "Now, handsome, can you please help me with this equipment?" Aaron happily obliged and shifted next to Candice.

Wes stayed with Desiree and whispered in her ear. "It looks like Candice has everything in control."

"Control of which—the equipment or Aaron?" Desiree asked as she took another long whiff from his shirt.

"Both," he answered, putting his arm around her. They stepped back and watched Candice and Aaron organize the top shelf of her locker.

"They do make a cute couple," Wes commented. He and Desiree exchanged smiles then just stared at each other for another minute. Both were probably thinking the same thing about each other, but neither had the courage to say so. The school bell then interrupted their interlude.

Before leaving Wes reminded Candice and Aaron to meet up at lunch period for Taylor's report from geology lab. Desiree told them that Taylor should be bursting with information.

Desiree breezed through all of her morning classes. She had a test in precalculus and finished before anyone else. She scored fairly well in archery class, outscoring even Candice. In English literature class Desiree handed in her book report ahead of the deadline. Her teacher was a little surprised until she saw that it was a review of *Macbeth*. Desiree was feeling so cheerful that she just had to call her mom.

"Is something wrong—are you OK?" Janelle anxiously asked.

"Mom, everything is fine. I just had to tell you how well I did at school so far," answered Desiree. She then spent the next few minutes describing her best morning ever.

"That's nice, Desiree. I'm glad you called to tell me, but you never do this. Are you really OK?"

"I don't know. I just feel happy that everything's going well. I haven't felt this way in a long time."

"Well, I ain't gonna try and figure it out. I'm just happy 'cause you are. But I have to cut you off, now; I'm getting the farm produce packed for tomorrow. I love you!" Janelle closed her phone and continued working out in the backyard by the shed.

"Was that Desiree?" asked Janelle's mom. "Hope she's OK."

Janelle loaded a small crate of oranges onto her truck then turned to her mom. "I'm not so sure," said Janelle. "She never calls me from school unless there's an emergency. She sounded amazingly cheerful."

Janelle's mom cracked a wide smile. "She must be in love."

Back at school Dominique and Taylor joined Desiree in the hall right after English Literature class.

"Wow, you sure got your book review done fast!" Taylor exclaimed.

"It's easy when you're inspired," explained Desiree. "Sure wish all my assignments were like this."

"My paper's finished, but I need to rewrite it," said Taylor.

"Me, too," said Dominique. "But we should have plenty of time to revise between matches at our volleyball tournament this weekend."

"And if we make it to finals we'll have extra time."

"Speaking of time—did you get a chance to talk to Royce this morning?" Desiree asked Taylor.

"Barely. I caught him in the hallway leading to the gym. He was on his way to the track. He said he'd meet us in the cafeteria at lunch."

"OK, see you all there," said Desiree. "My next class is on the other side of campus." She took off, pushing through the congested flow of students.

Dominique then turned to Taylor. "Meet me at the shrine after class and we'll walk to the lunchroom together, OK?"

"Aye-aye, captain!" Taylor replied eagerly before the two parted ways.

At lunchtime Candice was first to arrive at the cafeteria and ran to the nearest unoccupied table. She reserved it with her books and half-kneeled on a chair to look out for her friends. Desiree was the next one through the doors, and Candice waved her over to the table.

"Nice going on the archery field," Candice said, greeting Desiree.

"So you're not upset that I beat you?" Desiree asked.

"Of course not," Candice replied. "It's my mission to be competitive, but it's my goal to elevate everyone's potential. If they beat me then I've done my job."

116

Candice, indeed, was the most competitive person Desiree ever met. She almost seemed too competitive—like she wanted to beat the world in everything. But Desiree hadn't realized that Candice was just trying to help other people—not beat them. Desiree smiled while putting down her school bag.

"Candice, this is why you're my best friend. How about if I get your lunch while you hold the table?"

"Sure." Candice pulled out a few dollars from her sports' bag. "Get me the chicken strip basket and a side of fresh veggies."

Desiree refused her money. "No, I'll buy it this time. Save your money for the ice cream parlor tonight," she said as she walked towards the lunch line. Candice stuffed her money away and climbed up on the chair again. A few minutes later she saw Aaron and Wes. She waved to them, too, inviting them over.

But then Taylor came rushing in and ran to the table, gasping for air. "Royce won't be here right away; he's at the nurse's office," she said.

"What happened?" Wes asked, jumping up to pull out a chair for her.

"I'm not sure," she said as she sat down. "I saw him lying on a cot in the dispensary. I poked my head in to see if he was OK. He said that bees attacked him while running on the track field. Then the nurse sent me out while she was pulling out the stingers."

Wes laid his hands on Taylor's shoulders, trying to calm her. "You relax and catch your breath; I'll go tell Desiree what happened," he said then headed to the lunch line. He met Desiree at the register, and told her about Royce. Soon they both hurried back to the table.

"Don't let Wes get near my lunch; I'll be back soon," Desiree said, placing her food tray in front of Candice then leaving the cafeteria. Candice pulled the tray closer and took the basket of battered fried chicken strips.

Aaron looked surprised. "Candice, are *you* stealing Desiree's lunch?" he asked.

"No, Aaron," she said while pointing to Desiree's plate. "Hers is this over-cooked, and rather blasé pasta, while mine is this crispy and totally yummo chicken strip basket. Give me a break; I'm a scavenger, but at least I have taste." She then picked up a chicken strip and started gnawing away the breading.

Aaron hadn't yet gotten used to her bizarre eating style. He watched her while opening his lunch cooler and almost dropped it.

Dominique finally showed up and pulled out a chair next to Taylor. "I thought we were going to meet at the shrine," she complained while plopping down in the chair. "Thanks for stiffing me, partner!"

Taylor gasped. "Oh! I'm so sorry—I forgot. I was at the nurse's office," she said. "Royce got stung by bees."

Dominique's face changed from anger to concern. "Huh? No kidding—is he OK?"

Taylor pointed at the exit doors. "Desiree just left to find out," she said then turned back to her best friend. "I was so worried about Royce—I forgot all about meeting you."

Dominique reached around Taylor's neck. "I can see that you're upset, so I'll excuse you this time," she said with an understanding smile.

"Thanks—you know I'd never abandon my captain on purpose," said Taylor.

As the lunch period progressed, Candice finished gnawing all the breading off her chicken strips and piled them back on her plate. Then, using her fork, she stabbed one and dredged it across her ranch dressing. Aaron stopped eating his leftover pizza and watched Candice slowly coat the chicken on both sides before popping it in her mouth.

Dominique laughed at Aaron. "If you watch Candice eat the whole time, you'll starve to death," she said. He agreed and resumed eating his own lunch.

Desiree finally returned the cafeteria this time with Royce whose arms and neck had several welt marks that stood out from his sun-tanned skin.

Wes got up first to greet him. "Yowch! You look painful. Those bees sure did a number on you."

"Yeah, and the number was ten—stingers, that is," Royce replied. "After the nurse pulled them out, she sprayed some medicine on me, so I guess I'll live."

"How did it happen?" Candice asked as she finished her last bite of chicken.

"Did you disturb a beehive?" Dominique asked.

Royce answered while dropping his backpack under a vacant chair. "No, I was minding my own business, jogging around the track. There were no trees around, but I did notice a field of clover inside the oval, so maybe that's where they came from. After I went into the first turn I saw a few buzzing around my head. I kept running, but they kept following me along with few more of their friends." He then sat down at the table. "Next thing I knew they lit on my T-shirt. I ran as fast as I could to the locker room."

Dominique, who sat next to him commented, "Bees can be attracted by bright colors or pungent scents." Then she sniffed around his collar. "Were you wearing any cologne?"

"Actually it's shower gel," said Royce.

Desiree clarified his statement. "Yeah, *my* shower gel," she said.

"Well, sort of," her brother admitted.

"He let me use the same shower gel after swim practice, so why didn't the bees ever go after me?" Wes asked.

"You probably rinsed it all off," Desiree guessed.

"*I* rinsed off all *mine*," Royce said. Then he paused to think. "Well, it really smelled good, so I put a few extra dabs on my shirt," he confessed.

Wes laughed. "Well, there you go; the bees liked Desiree's shower gel too," he said.

"Yeah, they probably thought you were one butt-ugly but sweet-smelling blossom," Aaron added. Everybody at the table laughed—even Royce, although it hurt when he did.

"Oh, Royce, you poor thing," Taylor responded sympathetically as she leaned into him. She almost hugged his upper arm but then saw the shiny smear of ointment on his neck and recoiled. "But anyway," Taylor continued quickly, "can we change the subject and get to my notes from geology lab? I got some hot info about past field trips." She then scooted her seat in a little closer to the table.

Desiree was surprised by Taylor's attention rapidly switching from Royce to the field trip. Royce, feeling neglected at this point, got up to get a fruit smoothie. When he arrived at the counter a group of freshmen girls surrounded him. He chatted with them, showing off his sting marks. Desiree watched him and laughed to herself. *Some freshman dogs never change,* she thought. She then turned her attention back to Taylor.

"Go ahead, Taylor, we're listening," said Dominique.

Taylor went to her backpack and pulled out a notebook that was speckled with crystals and jewels. She opened it and waited for everyone's attention. Wes quickly pulled a map of the Grand Canyon out of his book bag. Aaron meanwhile had finished his first piece of pizza and opened his soda. Desiree was hungrily diving into her soggy, pasta lunch special.

Candice was jabbing the large, black olives from her relish plate onto the tips of her fingers. Then, one-by-one she ate them off her fingers. She then noticed Dominique and Aaron both staring at her. "What—don't *you* eat your olives this way?" Candice asked.

"No," they answered.

Taylor loudly reprimanded the group. "Hey, I'm reporting here!" Candice continued eating her olives as everyone else turned to Taylor, who read from her notebook. "OK, so we'll be hiking down the Bright Angel Trail and crossing the bridge to the Phantom Ranch."

"Taylor, we already knew that," said Dominique.

"Yeah, but I didn't. Anyway, his past camps were at Nankoweap, Pipe, Havasupai, Lava, and Bright Angel Creeks..." Wes applied stars to those areas on the map as fast as he could peel them from his sticker sheet. Taylor glanced over at the map to make sure Wes caught up then quickly resumed her report. "...Zoroaster, Phantom, Lonetree, and Cremation Canyons."

The group, astounded by the amount of camp areas, stopped eating. Dominique dropped her fork, and Desiree dropped her jaw. Candice dropped one of her olives that rolled across the map. Wes quickly snatched it up and popped it into his mouth. By this time his map was covered with so many stars that it looked like a mini-Milky Way Galaxy around the Phantom Ranch!

Taylor punctuated her report by snapping her notebook closed and slamming it on the table. Then she flittered her heavily made-up eyelashes at everyone.

"Taylor, you're amazing!" Dominique exclaimed. "How did you get all that from Roeser?"

Taylor smugly answered her. "You won't believe it when I tell you—I kind of tricked him. I'll explain later."

Then Wes proudly announced, "OK, I've got 'em all stickered." His voice changed into a TV game show host. "And *heeere* they are!" He turned the map around and pushed it towards the center of the table. Some of the group had to make room by removing lunch trays. Wes had small, gold, red, and silver stars on all the camp areas that Taylor reported.

"Hey, there are no green stars," Candice remarked. "Why no green stars, Wesley?"

"Because this was all my mom had before I stole them from her," he said.

"Awh," she replied, whining with disappointment.

All eyes were fixed on the map. Candice's eyes got bigger and she tilted her head to the side.

"You know, it kind of looks like an elephant with pointy ears," said Candice.

"No, not an elephant," argued Wes, "It looks more like a serpent that just ate a car. What do you think, Aaron?"

Aaron shook his head. "You two are seriously simplistic," he replied. "The stars aren't outlining anything."

Dominique was relieved. "Well, Aaron," she said, "at least there's one normal brain in this group."

Aaron smiled back at her. "Thanks, Dominique," he said. "Then you'll agree with me when I say it looks more like the Fourth of July than anything."

Dominique hit herself in the head. "Ugh, I'm drowning in a sea of absurdity," she said.

Aaron laughed then explained himself. "Chillax, I'm just messing with ya, Dominique. The locations aren't an outline of anything—we hoped it was that easy," he said.

Just then the school bell rang. Wes rolled up the map and put it in his school bag. "We need to study this more," he said.

Taylor packed her notebook away. "Dominique and I can't do Saturday. And remember the library is now closed on Sundays," she said scratching her heavily powdered nose.

"Hey, how about Sunday at my house?" Desiree offered. "I can check with my mom and call everyone for an exact time."

Everyone agreed. Candice licked the last of the ranch dressing from her plate and placed it on the return tray. Wes checked the plates for uneaten food. He found a few morsels, and then stacked the rest of the plates. Royce barely had time to finish his smoothie but kept slurping it as he grabbed his backpack. Taylor offered to carry it for him, and Royce graciously accepted. Then they both headed for the cafeteria door.

Desiree ran up to join them. "So, Taylor, how did you get all that info from Mr. R.?"

"You were right, Desiree. It was so easy," Taylor answered. "All I did was tell him I work for the school newspaper, and that I was gonna write an article featuring his field trip in the next issue."

"So that's why you wore all that make-up," said Desiree. "You look very professional, by the way."

"Thanks, I wanted to look like an anchorwoman on the six o'clock news—just like all the other girls on the newspaper staff," Taylor replied, giggling.

"And you wear it so well," Royce added. He wanted to hug her, but then winced in pain.

"Thanks, Royce," replied Taylor as she batted her eyelashes at him. Just then some of her dried mascara dropped into her eye, and she started to blink uncontrollably.

"Taylor, are you alright?" Royce asked.

"I think I wore too much make-up today. Give me a second," she said as she wiped her eye. It started to tear and the mascara was now smudging. "Anyway, Mr. Roeser was so happy about my writing the article, he unloaded information like a freight train. He talked so quickly—I could hardly keep up with my notes." Then she rubbed the lower lid of her smudged eye. "Ugh, excuse me—I gotta wash off this eye make-up." She handed Desiree her brother's backpack and left.

"OK, so I'll call you!" Royce shouted out to Taylor, but his voice only bounced off the lockers as her body integrated into the cluster of wayfaring students. He then turned to his sister. "Well, so much for this romantic encounter," he said glumly.

She looked up at him with her caring eyes. "Oh, Baby-bro, there's plenty of time for you and Taylor."

Royce was pleasantly surprised. "So you're OK with my seeing her?" he asked.

"Of course I am," she answered as she smiled. "She's my friend, and you're my brother. I care about both of you, but not so much as to interfere. It's your business not mine, and I trust that you both will stay out of the dog house."

Royce gazed through her as if she was the gateway to total bliss. "Wow, Dizzy, that's really nice of you!"

But she stepped back from him. "Savor this moment, Baby-bro. It wouldn't be fair to fight when you're full of bee venom. But be on guard; I still live under the same roof as you. To quote Shakespeare: *I am a little more than kin and less than kind.*"

He laughed. "And may I also quote: *To mourn a mischief that is past and gone is the next way to draw mischief on.* Hey, I remembered some of that stuff Dad read to you," he said smiling before wincing again from the pain. Proud of her brother, Desiree faked a tickling jab at him before accompanying him to his next class.

Candice's fencing match was held right after school. Her parents attended as did Desiree, her number one fan. Royce was too sore for swim practice so he also attended. Much to Candice's chagrin Aaron showed up. They sat together, chanting *Lefty*! This was the first time Candice had a substantial fan section. She saluted them as well as the referee and her opponent.

Her match was challenging because her opponent was also left-handed, so Candice lost her psychological edge. With less than a minute in the match the two were tied. Then, in a flurry of attacks, her opponent accidentally swiped the side of Candice's neck. She retreated, feeling her neck for blood. Her parents gasped, and the referee called a time out while issuing a warning to the opponent. Aaron jumped out of the bleachers and ran to Candice.

Her coach assessed the injury, but it was superficial—looking much like a long welt. But the stinging pain remained, motivating her to win even more. Aaron offered some encouragement and patted her back. He returned to his seat, and Candice again pulled on her mask. She gave a thumbs-up to her parents and they applauded. She walked back to her position on the court and glared at her opponent.

The referee sensed Candice's intensity as he invited both fencers back on the court. He paused for a moment, hoping that the extra time would calm Candice's storm. The referee then took a deep breath and restarted the match.

Her opponent attacked first, but Candice instantly blocked and countered with a *coupé* towards her opponent. Caught off-guard, her opponent couldn't fend off Candice's advancing foil. The electronic detector signaled a touch, and the referee stopped the match.

Candice won! In jubilation she pulled off her helmet and quickly shook hands with her dazed opponent. Like a pogo stick she bounced her way off the court towards her coach. She gave him a spirited hug then turned to acknowledge her fan section. Aaron responded so wildly that he fell backwards. He grabbed Desiree, and they both rolled into the next row of bleachers. Royce, forgetting his pain, tumbled on top of them just to make it unanimous.

Candice saw the resulting body pile, dropped her equipment and ran towards them while laughing hilariously. She tried to pull Aaron out, but he pulled her back in the pile. Her parents stepped politely aside to avoid any possible contact.

For Candice this was the best match ever. She found Desiree and hugged her tightly. Aaron sat up, grabbed Candice's head and put it in a wrestler's hold. He then rubbed her head with his knuckles. Candice was so happy celebrating with her best friends. It eventually ended when Candice's parents coaxed them down with a promise to buy them all hot fudge sundaes.

Back on the farm Janelle, her parents and farmhands got the farm produce packaged and ready for transport to the next day's market. Janelle cooked up a big pot of chili along with homemade cornbread and invited everyone to stay for dinner. Jake and Javier respectfully declined dinner in lieu of catching the next scheduled bus, so she packed both of them dinner in large containers for them to take home.

By the time Royce and Desiree arrived home, their mom just finished pulling out the tableware. "How was everyone's day?" she asked. She then handed Desiree the red and white-checkered tablecloth for the porch table.

"I got stung by a bunch of bees," said Royce.

Janelle ran over to check his sting marks. "Oh, no! That must have been that first message on my voicemail. I was so busy here all day I forgot to review my messages," she said. "Are you OK?"

Royce recounted the painful details while Desiree went out to the back porch table. It was long and sturdy. The blond, butcher-block surface had cuts, scrapes and even bite marks from several generations of use. Two high-back chairs were at the ends, and two, long benches ran along the sides that could each seat six or seven hungry adults.

She yelled to her mom through the open window while smoothing out the wrinkles out of the tablecloth. "Did Royce tell you that the bees were attracted to my shower gel? He wanted to smell nice for Taylor, but the bees got to him first."

"They must have thought you were a flower 'cause you're so sweet," Janelle said, reaching up to pinch his cheek. But then she held back when she saw the welts on his face.

Grandma and Grandpa came in from the backyard, stopping at the porch to greet Desiree before walking into the kitchen. Grandpa walked over to Royce and shook his hand. "Long time, no see. Heard someone say you ran into some bees," he said.

Royce extended both his arms on the counter in front of his grandpa. "Wanna see, Grandpa? The nurse pulled out ten stingers. But it felt more like a hundred."

"Looks like you're gonna survive this time," replied his grandpa, who then turned to Janelle. "My hands are a little grimy from the farm produce, so I'm gonna wash up before dinner."

She pointed him to the laundry room. "I left a big bar of soap and some extra towels for you."

"Hope there's no flower-smelling, bee-attracting shower gel in there," he joked as he sauntered towards the laundry room.

127

Desiree heard her grandpa's comment from the back porch. "It's called *Desert Monsoon*, and it was *my* shower gel!"

"It sounds like that stuff is pretty potent," her grandma remarked.

"Only if you apply it full-strength on your clothes," added Royce.

"And you go jogging past a field of clover full of bees," his sister added.

"Don't think I'll be doing that anytime soon," their grandma replied, "and yer grandpa neither."

"What?" Grandpa called from the doorway. He's a little hard of hearing, but everyone is used to repeating for him.

"I said, you don't need to worry about using the shower gel while jogging past a field of clover!" she yelled.

"Jogging? Now why would I want to go jogging just before dinner?" Everybody laughed—including Grandpa.

They enjoyed their meal while watching the late winter sky darken. A few early stars and planets already began their nightly vigil over the cool, Arizona sky. Desiree made a temporary truce with her brother, which pleased her mom immensely. The grandparents caught up with the grandchildren's lives, commenting how they've grown. Afterwards, they called it an early night, so they could rest up for the Farmer's Market early next morning.

# Chapter VI

*Zero. Zero. Zero...I'm still zero...Hey—I'm doing zero, here! Ooh, did I feel something—maybe a cool breeze? One tenth. One tenth. No, Zero. Zero again. Hey c'mon! Zero. Ooh, One half. One half...hey, three quarters, this is great! Three quarters. Three quarters...ONE! We got one! No, nine tenths, nine tenths. Eight tenths. Three quarters, no, eight tenths. Wow, One and a quarter! One and a tenth. Ohh, one and a tenth. One. One. Nine tenths. No, One. One. One. Oh-oh....Zero! One tenth, zero. Zero. Zero.*

"There you go—exactly one pound. That'll be one dollar," Desiree cheerfully announced, taking some bright, orange-colored tangelos off the weight scale and placing them in a paper bag. She then sniffed the top of the bag. "Mm, they sure smell sweet...Oh, you'll take another pound? You bet, wanna pick 'em out? No problem." She then yelled back to Royce for more tangelos.

He ran to the back of the truck to get more. "Need anything else while I'm back here?"

Janelle, who was out in front of their produce display, heard them. "What's left?"

"Not much, Mom, maybe a few dozen lemons, a crate of grapefruit, and another of broccoli," Royce yelled back.

"No, that's it. Let's call it a day. You can box them all together and we'll haul 'em over to the food bank truck." Janelle turned to her parents who were sitting in the back of their tarp. "You guys hear that?"

They nodded, although Grandpa needed it repeated. He rose from his chair and walked to the table. He complimented Desiree on her excellent salesmanship then went to the back of the truck and offered to help Royce. Grandma closed and locked the moneybox and carried it to her car, which was parked next to the truck.

Janelle unsnapped a corner of the tarp and pulled it down. "Desiree, sweetie, you can start taking everything back to the truck."

"Not much to take, Mom, we practically sold out," she replied, grabbing a half-filled box of assorted citrus and heading back to the truck. Janelle folded the tarp and placed it in its sleeve. She then gathered up her brochures and business cards and tucked them in her backpack.

Janelle's mom came over to help. She seemed pleased about the family's sale. "We started with twenty boxes of produce, and we've only got two left. I'd say we've done well."

"Well, Ma, we could do better at the local groceries, but I like the business we do here," Janelle said. She looked over at her dad and kids at the truck. "Family help is so cost-saving."

"We're also reaching out to the community. We're putting our faces in front of the Heritage Farm."

"And that's always good business," added Janelle as she put an arm around her mom. They watched a car pull up to their truck. Janelle then yelled back to her daughter.

"Desiree, your dad's here!"

Desiree grabbed her backpack out of the truck and ran back to kiss her mom. "Thanks, Mom, see you tonight." She hurried to the passenger side of her dad's car.

'Hey, Dad!" she called out to him.

"Hey, baby cakes I missed your face!" Walter yelled through the window as he rolled through the parking lot. It was mostly gravel, but some Bermuda grass grew within the ruts. The grass kept the rough pavement more tempered—especially in the summer when temperatures soar. But today the air was pleasantly cool. Desiree waved to her mom and grandparents before opening the car door.

"I missed you too, Dad," she said, jumping inside. She took off her hat and let her braided hair down. Then she leaned back and let out a big sigh.

Her dad looked over at his seemingly drained daughter. "Were you folks busy?"

Desiree pulled down the visor mirror and checked her lips. She then pulled out her lip-gloss and applied a thin coating. "We sure were, Dad. Royce and I did most of the stocking and selling. Grandma and Grandpa sat the whole time, handling the money. Mom, of course, did all the talking." She then folded up the visor and put her lip-gloss back in her pocket.

"That's why your produce sells so well," he said as he smiled at her, "and that's what keeps you busy."

"Great, I guess, but feel I've gone through a whole day already. I wish I could sleep late just one Saturday morning."

"There's plenty of Saturdays for that, li'l darlin', but right now that farm needs you—your mom needs you."

"She needs you too, Dad."

He paused for several seconds before asking, "Is that what she told ya, or is that what your own heart's saying?"

"Both," she answered without hesitation.

"How is your mom?"

"She's as busy as ever with the farm and classes. But I guess she does all that to keep herself out of trouble, and from thinking about you."

Walter took in a deep breath and vented his thoughts. "Well, I do think about her a lot. I sometimes wonder how we both drifted apart from each other, especially at a time when we needed each other the most. I guess it was mostly my fault."

Walter pulled out of the parking lot and onto the busy thoroughfare, which got busier as they approached the satellite stores of the shopping mall.

"I just wanted time to work things out after your grandpa died. Being an only child, I suddenly felt very alone in this world. I know it sounds crazy, but he was all that was left of the Sumner side of the family. I wasn't prepared for his leaving. I buried my sorrow in my work. It was easy—maybe too easy. I didn't realize that I was shutting out the rest of my family."

They pulled into the driveway of the outdoor outfitting store.

"Anyway, I realized that important things don't come easy. You have to work for them. I'm ready to work—to take that healing road, if your mom will go with me."

Happy tears fell from his daughter's eyes. "Dad, I always wanted to hear you say that," she said. "But it was frustrating not to hear it right away."

Walter pulled into a parking spot and turned off the engine. "Sometimes healing doesn't happen overnight, baby doll. For boulder-heads like me it can take forever. And for kids like you it's hard to wait." He smiled and pulled his daughter over to his shoulder. "Sorry I made you wait so long. Will my spending a huge amount of money on you make everything better?"

Desiree turned and gave him a long sobering look. "Dad, spending all the money in the world can *never* make everything better," she began, "but, spending it with *you* can," she said, smiling at him.

They left the car and walked arm-in-arm towards the door. The early afternoon sun shined brightly in the clear blue sky. A cactus wren sounded his territorial song in a nearby mesquite tree as Desiree took a few quick steps ahead of her dad to grab the door handle. He bowed graciously but then insisted on letting her go first. She curtsied then went inside.

The store was full of shoppers. Most of them were families with young children. It was a perfect, outdoor playground for the kids to explore the tent and watercraft displays.

"I remember when you used to do that," said her dad, pointing to a preschooler paddling inside a kayak.

"I still have the urge every now and then," she confessed.

They walked arm-in-arm around the store planning what to buy. Then they focused on sleeping bags. Desiree found one without the girly colors. Instead it was a deep, shimmery blue with creamy white lining. It reminded her of the colors of grandpa's chess pieces. Her dad was more impressed by the bag's durability and low-temperature rating.

When it came to hiking boots, however, her dad wasn't going to compromise function for color. "Color is not important. You need leather boots with steel shanks, and I don't care if they

133

look like army boots. Fashionable boots won't keep your feet adequately supported for long hikes," he advised. He headed towards the dark brown, high-top mountaineering boots that were in the men's section.

Desiree didn't follow and instead called out to him, "But, Dad, I can't wear those; they're not for color-coordinating girls like me," she protested.

A salesgirl overheard their discussion and jogged over to Walter. "Can I show you and your daughter a compromise?" She then led them to another section of hiking boots, which were mounted on the wall. "All of these have a waterproof leather upper, with breathable mesh and a Gore-Tex liner to help keep feet dry. As far as support they have a quarter-length, steel shank in the sole." She pointed to several of the more popular jewel-tone colors.

Desiree's eyes beamed with interest. "Oh look at these," she said grabbing one from the display. "They're sapphire-blue to match my sleeping bag!"

Her dad looked a bit skeptical. "Will they be good enough to hike down the corridor trails of the Grand Canyon? And do they have enough flexibility to climb cliffs?"

Desiree interrupted her dad's questioning. "Dad, I'm not planning on climbing cliffs—just hiking trails."

"Darlin', you just never know," he said. "It's better to be prepared for anything and everything."

The salesgirl took a deep breath and described all the boots' features, sounding much like a TV commercial. "These boots will be more supportive than day-hiking boots while being lighter than the heavy mountaineering boots. They will keep feet dry and comfortable for the long hikes when carrying loads heavier than the typical daypack." Desiree was already sold on the boots, but the salesgirl added a last comment, "*And* they have soles flexible enough for cliff-climbing."

"Can I try on a pair?" Desiree asked her dad. He took the sample boot from his daughter. She pleaded with her big dark-blue eyes while pulling out her pouty lower lip. "Pretty please?"

"Oh, all right," he said, caving in to her. He looked at the salesgirl and remarked, "She always does this to me."

The salesgirl smiled. "They do it here all the time. You wouldn't believe how many guys do the same thing."

The saleslady brought back a few different colors of the hiking boots, but Desiree instantly fell in love with the blue ones. She wore them for the duration of the shopping trip. They strolled throughout the store, trying out all the new camp gear. Walter told her stories of Grandpa Sumner's camping in the *good old days,* when he packed a just few bare essentials: hammock, army knife, rain poncho, matches, water and candy bars. It was a good time for both to reminisce about Grandpa Sumner.

But it was finally time to check out. They both left the store carrying several bags of gear back to the car.

"Never have I shopped so much for just one person," her dad jokingly commented as he opened the trunk of his car.

"Maybe I can get a mule to carry all this down the trail like Grandpa did," she said.

Her dad laughed. "Dizzy-doll, your Grandpa Sumner rarely used a mule. Most of the time he carried everything on his back."

She leaned against the window but stared straight ahead. Her eyes drifted into space as her mind traveled back in time. She pictured her Grandpa Sumner unloading gear from his old jeep. She remembered sitting on the tire swing, waiting patiently for him to finish. When he did, he usually pulled out a little souvenir for her. Then she'd jump off the swing and run to him. He could have gotten her a rock, arrowhead, or old horseshoe—it didn't matter. What really mattered were the stories that he told.

"Dad, did Grandpa ever keep a travel journal?"

"Yeah, but not for every trip."

"I'd love to read it sometime. Do you know where it's at?"

"Sure I do. I have it at locked up home."

"Locked up? Why?"

"Well, it's in his old foot locker that *he* kept locked. He didn't want anybody stealin' his notes—like they were deep, dark secrets or something. He did a lot of off-path hiking and found all sorts of old stuff—tin cups, canteens, and knives—that other hikers lost or left behind. Sometimes the stuff was really old. He documented all the places where he found his so-called treasures. They could've come from hikers or victims.

"Victims?"

"Yes, victims. People die from falls, heat stroke, drowning, suicide, and natural causes. Your grandpa once found a plane propeller—don't think that was from a natural cause, though."

"He really found a propeller?"

"From a plane that crashed in the canyon. Sometimes the investigators don't recover everything. The waterways can move wreckage long distances from the crash site. Your grandpa found part of a propeller in an obscured ravine, way off the beaten path. He tried to sneak it out of the park, trying to avoid the park rangers, but propellers are pretty hard to conceal in a backpack. He was caught red-handed and had to hand it over to the park authorities. Boy, was he ever mad!"

"So Grandpa collected wreckage and other people's junk, huh?"

"Ya know, darlin', there's a park rule that says whatever you bring in, you have to take out. There are no trash pick-up

136

services in the remote spots. But a lot of visitors don't know that rule and leave stuff behind. The stuff your grandpa recovered could have been decades old. So not only was he interested in stuff, but also how it got there. He was a sort of forensic, junk collector. He kept detailed notes of what he found and where he found it."

"What was his most valuable find?"

"Those chess pieces he gave you. He snuck 'em out of the park because he felt that they were an incidental find—sort of like pebbles getting in your boots. As the matter of fact, he hid them in his extra socks!"

Desiree laughed, and then turned to her dad. "Those are great stories, Dad," she said smiling.

"Glad I could share them with you," he said, smiling back.

They soon arrived at the farm. Desiree jumped out first and ran towards up the porch steps to the back door. No one was home. She ran back out to her dad, who was unloading her bags.

"Mom must be still out with Royce. Can you stay for awhile—maybe for dinner?"

"Love to, baby, but I think it's your mom's call," he said. "Let's not rush this."

Desiree thought about it for a moment. He was right about young people not having patience. "OK, so maybe next time?"

"Tell your mom what I said this afternoon. I'll keep my cell phone next to my heart," he answered. She hugged him long and hard, not wanting to let go.

"Can I stop by tomorrow for the journal?"

"Sure, but make it early. I have to pick up tourists at noon."

"I'll be there by nine. I love you, Dad," she said, finally letting go.

"I'll always love you, princess," he replied.

She grabbed all the bags and ran back up the steps. He pulled away and honked the horn. She then unlocked the door and went into the house.

Suddenly her stomach grumbled from hunger. She had such a great day but forgot to eat! She quickly ran the bags into her bedroom then returned to the kitchen to grab a few shortbread cookies from the cookie jar.

Then she heard a car pull into the driveway. She looked through the back window and saw her mom and brother walking up to the house. Through the window she called out to them, "You guys just coming home *now*?"

Royce proudly held up his shopping bag. "I got some new swim suits." He brought them into the house and headed back to his bedroom.

Desiree acknowledged him, but wasn't too impressed. "Great, just keep 'em dry and away from me," she said.

Janelle then walked up the porch steps. "And how was your day, dear—did you get all your camp gear?"

"Sure did," her daughter replied. "Dad is really smart about this stuff, so it was tough getting what I wanted instead of what he thought I needed. But we compromised a little. You must see my hiking boots." She walked out to the porch to show her. "I also got a rain poncho, fleece socks and a sleeping bag to coordinate with my boots."

"Wow, matching camp gear," Royce commented indifferently as he entered the kitchen. He also grabbed a few cookies from the jar before heading for the family room. He turned on the TV and surfed all the channels but nothing interested him, so he left on a movie channel and retreated to his bedroom.

Janelle inspected Desiree's new footwear while heading for the kitchen. "Those boots are very nice," she said before dropping her purse on the kitchen counter and checking her watch. "Oh, shucks—it's almost dinnertime, but I'm too exhausted to cook." She then kicked off her sandals towards the doormat.

"Hey, Mom, how about we order pizza?" Desiree suggested.

"Oh, I don't know," answered Janelle tentatively as she went to the refrigerator for lemonade. "The last time we ordered pizza, the delivery guy screwed up the order, and we had to wait forever for the second delivery."

"Yeah, the last time they forgot the anchovies on my pizza," Royce yelled from his bedroom.

"Don't worry, Mom," replied Desiree, "I'll make sure the delivery guy gets everything right this time." She got on her cell phone and went to her bedroom. It wasn't long before she returned to the kitchen.

"All set. The pizza should be delivered shortly," she announced.

Desiree and her mom went into the family room waiting for the pizza.

Janelle had her feet propped on a pillow. A modern, romance comedy was airing on the movie channel.

"Mom, Dad asked about you," said Desiree.

"What did you tell him?" her mom asked.

"Well, I kept stuff generic."

"What do you mean?"

"Mom, do you miss him?"

Janelle was still watching the screen as she answered her daughter. "I miss the dad you had before your grandpa died. But I guess people change. I miss what he was but not what he's turned into."

"Mom, he said he was a boulder-head."

"A boulder-head. He called himself a boulder-head," her mom said, repeating in disbelief.

"Yes, Mom, a boulder-head—a very big rock that resists budging. But when it does the earth shakes! He said he wants to heal the wounds he's made. He told me today he's ready when you are."

Her mom didn't reply right away. She just sat and watched the TV screen. The girl in the movie was rescued by her romantically wounded—but incredibly rich—consort. "That must only happen in Hollywood! She's a simple hooker, and he's a ruthless and successful businessman. How could they possibly live happily ever after?"

"This movie has a great theme, Mom, the characters learned to better complement each other's life," her daughter explained. "She learned how to dress, act and dine elegantly. He learned to enjoy simple pleasures and to help people in financial trouble. People will change for the better if you let them."

Her mom watched as the man jumped out of his limo and climbed up to the balcony and rescue the lady, who turned around and rescued him.

Janelle smiled from the movie's ending and then sighed. "Well, my life ain't a Hollywood movie, babe, but I guess nothing's impossible. I'm ready to listen to your dad if he's ready to talk," Janelle said.

Just then the doorbell rang.

"Mom, I'll bet it's the pizza," said Desiree. "I'll get Royce."

Her mom grabbed her purse and headed for the front door. She muttered about getting the correct order while opening the door. She then saw her husband standing on the steps holding two pizza boxes.

"Here's your dinner, nice and hot!" Walter announced.

Janelle couldn't believe her eyes. "Walter! When did you start working at the pizza place?"

Before her husband could answer, Desiree ran to the front door. "He doesn't, Mom, I asked him to get us pizza for dinner," said Desiree.

Royce brushed past his mom and ran down the steps to his dad. "Did you get my favorite?" he asked.

His dad opened the lid of the top box. "Large, double cheese, sausage, bacon, ham, pepperoni and—*yuck*—anchovies, right?" Royce grinned as he grabbed it and ran back into the house.

Janelle held the door open and motioned for her husband to enter. "Are you here to rescue me from my too-tired-to-make-dinner-after-a-busy Saturday?"

"No. I'm here to say I'm sorry," Walter replied. Janelle could hear the movie in the family room ending with music playing. A tear came to her eye maybe from the movie's happy ending—or maybe not.

They walked into the kitchen where Royce was already devouring his first piece. Janelle moved his box aside to make room for the other box.

Desiree, who was sitting at the table, sprang up for a slice. "Just cheese, right?" she asked her dad.

"Just the way you like it, sweetheart," he said. He turned to get a glass from the cupboard just as his wife was turning from the utensil drawer. They gently collided and immediately turned towards each other.

"Oops, sorry," they both said simultaneously.

"Um, maybe we should hold our apologies for awhile," whispered Janelle to her husband.

"Yeah, you're right," he whispered back. "The kids will think we're some boring, romance movie."

"I like boring, romance movies," interrupted Desiree, who was sitting at the counter and listening to their every word.

"Maybe later," her mom said, rolling her eyes. Her husband smiled then grabbed a slice of pizza.

"OK, later," answered Desiree, "but I get to keep my front-row seat for next time."

"Next time," said her dad just before he took a bite of his piece.

They enjoyed pizza and lemonade with no further apologies. It seemed like old times for the Sumner Family, although everyone was exhausted from the day's activities. The night ended early, and everyone walked out to Walter's car. After thanking him for dinner Janelle and Royce went back into the house, but Desiree stayed with her dad.

"Thanks for everything, Dad," she said offering him a hug.

"No big deal. I got a two-for-one special on the pizza," he replied pulling her into his arms.

"Yeah, but your being here was super special," replied Desiree. "See you tomorrow?"

"Nine o'clock," said her dad. Desiree waved as he pulled out and drove away. She smiled, skipping back to the house.

The next morning Desiree drove out to her dad's place. It was a modest mobile home that used to belong to her grandpa before he died. Her dad moved in after the separation. It was located in the northern fringes of town where horse ranches and grazing land dominated the area.

Desiree turned off the highway and onto a gravel road that was full of chuckholes from the seasonal rains. She proceeded slowly as her mom's sedan bumped and bounced along with the gravel and small stones kicking back up in her tire wells. Soon she saw her dad's place.

He was outside, cleaning one of his off-road passenger vans. When he heard her coming he grabbed a towel to wipe his face and hands. She pulled up and turned off the engine. She walked over to greet him, but he backed away, since his clothes were already soiled from early morning chores.

They walked through the front door, which was flanked by a wooden coyote and an old wagon wheel. Just inside a small Navajo rug welcomed her dusty sandals with rich earthy colors. He led her to the first room that was used as an office. He went to a short table and removed piles of paperwork exposing his dad's footlocker. It was painted army green with white numbers painted on the lid.

"This was your grandpa's army footlocker," Walter told his daughter. "He never talked much about his time in the service, but he sure liked the equipment he was allowed to keep." A huge padlock hung from the front buckle. He unlocked it and slowly raised the lid. The stale smell of mud and damp leather filled the air.

Desiree peered in and saw a pile of small tools, tarnished utensils, and bottle openers. "Wow, look at all this old stuff!" She inspected dozens of articles, which sent her back to another time. She found a rolled map containing hiking trails in the Grand Canyon. It was old but in very good condition. Along the margins were simple pencil sketches of rock formations and some local flora. Finally at the bottom of the footlocker she found what looked like a college composition tablet with ruled pages enclosed by the black-spotted cover.

"That was your grandpa's travel journal," he said. She carefully pulled it out and inspected it. On the title line was the word *Stuff* scribbled in pencil. She opened it and found carefully handwritten accounts that were dated and sometimes contained

143

several pencil sketches similar to the ones on the map. She closed the book and looked at the title again. She laughed and guessed that *Stuff* wouldn't reveal anything about the vital information inside.

"Can I take this home with me?" Desiree asked. Her dad put his arm around her.

"Your grandpa treasured that journal more than anything. You can have it if you promise to take good care of it," he said.

"I promise, Dad," she said returning the map and tucking the journal under her arm. "Hey, Dad, the other day you mentioned that our teacher is using us to help find something that isn't there. What were you talking about?"

"Aw, nothing really, darlin'," he answered.

"Come on, Dad, you sounded angry, so it really has to be something," she said.

"Yes, I was angry, but I'm not sure I ought to be telling you my suspicions."

"Facts or suspicions, I'd still like to know."

Her dad really didn't want to explain Mr. Roeser's ulterior motive for the field trip, especially if it weren't true.

"Nah, I don't want to put stupid ideas in your head. I'll tell you after you get back—I promise. Now off you go," he said, guiding her back to the front door. "I got an early desert adventure with some tourists from the resort."

She kissed him and went out the front door. "You're still the best, Dad." Then she turned and walked back to her mom's car.

"I know," he said as he watched her start the car and roll out of his driveway. She forgot about the chuckholes and raced down the street, throwing dirt and gravel behind her like a quarter-mile drag racer at a green light. Her dad watched the cloud of dust and scratched the back of his head; it was no wonder that her car was in the collision shop!

Later that afternoon, Heritage Farm was quiet and peaceful. Janelle decided not to unload the truck or clean up any of the supplies left over from the farmer's market. Instead she just walked the perimeter of the gardens, checking the irrigation system. She made mental notes of valves or hoses that needed maintenance. She really enjoyed working this time of year in the sunny, cool weather.

Her cell phone went off with the ring tone of Roy Orbison's classic, *Pretty Woman*, which had the same name as the movie she watched the day before. At first she was confused, having never heard that particular ring tone. But then she saw her husband's name listed as the caller and answered her phone with a few chuckles.

"You sound quite jovial today," said Walter. The sound from his end had intermittent buzzes or whooshes, which meant that he was traveling in his adventure van with the windows down.

"Oh, your daughter had changed a few of my cellphone ringtones," Janelle replied.

"Then I take it she made it back without wrecking the suspension in your car," he guessed.

"Why—are the chuckholes pretty bad out there?"

"The winter rains make some deep ones. You can get swallowed by one if you're not driving a high-clearance vehicle or a military tank."

"Great," Janelle replied. "Next time your daughter goes out there I'll get her a Humvee," Janelle replied. From the other end she could hear her husband laugh loudly then cough. "Walter, are you OK?"

"I'm fine, thanks. Rollin' along the unpaved roads by Lake Pleasant is murder on the mucous membranes. Been doin' some exploring around the cliffs," he answered.

"Well, you be careful," she said.

145

"You know it. Hey, I should be swinging back to the resort by six, so I'll be on your side of town. Think we could have a casual dinner together?"

Just then Janelle bent down to pull off an emitter from her irrigation line. The phone wedged between her jaw and shoulder slipped, and she momentarily lost contact with her husband.

"Wait just a second," she said straightening up to get a new emitter out of the pocket of her gardening apron. She grabbed a handful of various-sized emitter heads and fingered through the one she needed.

Walter felt that her long silence meant he needed to explain further. "I mean, if you think I'm pushing you too quickly, I'll understand if you decline. You just let me know when's a good time to talk with you again."

Janelle finally found the right-sized emitter and bent back down to install it on the hose. She then realized that she couldn't hear her husband anymore since the speaker slid past her ear. She repositioned the phone by her ear.

"Sorry, Walter…" She was trying to finish her sentence, but her husband responded to her first two words.

"Then some other time?"

"…My phone slipped from my ear. You were saying?"

"Did you want to go some other time?"

"No, that's not—"

He misunderstood her because he didn't hear her entire sentence. "I'm sorry you feel this way," he said sounding disappointed.

"Wait. Stop; let me finish," she said.

"We're finished? I thought you wanted to start over—"

"—Walter!"

"Yes?"

"Listen. Wait till I'm done talking. Dinner tonight would be wonderful!"

"Oh, so you *do* want to have dinner with me."

"Yes, absolutely!"

Like the selection button on a music player, his disappointment switched to jubilation. "All right!" But it caused him to cough few more times.

Janelle patiently waited for her husband to recover. "What time works for you?"

"Not sure exactly, but I'll call when I get closer to town," he answered.

"OK, babe, will be waiting to hear from ya—bye."

He closed his phone, feeling relieved that the cell phone had caused all the confusion. *Man, cell phone reception is tricky! Ya gotta be patient when using these gadgets,* he thought as he pulled on his headset and addressed the tourists riding in his van. "This is Wally-Ray again calling to your attention to Lake Pleasant over to the left, and if you look really far beyond it you'll see the dam that they built several years back in order to…"

# Chapter VII

*I can be fast or slow, loud or soft, back or front, bright or dim—so many choices. Mario and Luigi were real heroes. They helped Princess Peach battle that terrible, giant turtle with their sledgehammers. Sometimes all they did was stomp the creature to nothingness!*

*Wish I could lose that stupid dog that always ran from ghosts or zombies and saved the day only to get a snack! So glad he was damaged and had to leave. All I kept hearing was "Let me guess— because it's haunted. Shaggy how'd ya know? be— Shaggy, how'd ya know? be—Shaggy, how'd ya know?" So annoying!*

*How about those dancers? So much glamour and so much energy. Wow, that's really a dress? How does it stay on? No, Sabrina from the Cheetah Girls did not get voted off! What is this world coming to?*

*Master Hand approaches. What will he require
now? Wait, he's making his choice. What will it be?
Ooh, advanced boxing! Great selection!*

"Dizzy, where's the other controller?" Royce asked as he grabbed the remote and switched from cable TV to video games. "I feel like beating on *Geek the dwerb*."

His sister peered out from her room and shouted to her brother, "I never use it. Ask Mom—she was on the system last."

"*Mom*? When did *she* start playing video games?"

Janelle was in the kitchen and heard him. "Are you kidding? I use the stepping fitness program every day, but my favorite is slalom snowboarding. It's great for core muscle toning and balance."

She walked over to a drawer just below the game system and pulled out the extra controller. "Any remotes or cables or games that you can't find will always be in here," she said, handing him the controller.

"Thanks, Mom, you're a lifesaver," he said as he hooked both controllers together and loaded up his game.

"You can show your gratitude by putting everything back in this drawer when you're done." She then walked to her bedroom. "If anyone needs me for anything else, I'll be in the shower."

"Going somewhere tonight?" Desiree asked from her bedroom doorway.

"I've got a dinner date," her mom answered. "With a tall and handsome stranger."

"It's Dad, huh?" Royce asked from the family room.

"Can't fool you guys," his mom answered. "How'd ya guess?"

149

"The *tall* and *handsome* clues," said Desiree. "Oh, by the way, Mom, can I have a study session with a few friends tonight?"

"Study session? Sure. Just have the food off the ceiling and the empty beer bottles in the recyclable bin before I get back."

"Mom, it's not a party; we're going to be studying," Desiree insisted.

Her mom laughed. "Sweetie, that's what they all say." She then retreated to her bedroom and closed the door.

Royce was curious about his sister's plans. "Study session—is Taylor coming?" He was still seated on the couch with his eyes glued on the game screen. He went into a series of jabs and uppercuts on *Geek the dwerb*.

"Yes, Taylor is coming," answered Desiree. "So you may want to clean up and get dressed."

"Humpf!" Royce grunted as he punched *Geek* in the stomach and knocked him out. The sound of a body hitting the floor and a bell ringing bounced off the stone-lined walls of the family room. "I'm already buff and tough. What more do I need to impress my almost-girlfriend?"

"I don't think she's all that impressed with your boxing abilities—OK, maybe how you look in your boxers, but we need to keep this place G-rated for Mom and Dad, or else they won't let any of our friends over."

"Hmm," he thought while still waiting for the score from his last round. He then sniffed his sweaty T-shirt and grimaced. "Yeah, you're probably right, especially since I'm just a mutt from the dog pound." Desiree walked to the couch and plopped next to him, bouncing him up from the cushion. She always tried to distract him while he was playing.

"Right now, Baby-bro, you look *and* smell like a mutt from the pound." She punctuated her evaluation by tickling his waist. He grabbed her fingers but almost dropped the game controllers.

"Hey, cut that out! I swear, Dizzy, I am so gonna get my revenge on you."

She laughed, then got up and walked towards the hallway. "Sure, so long as you don't use your brand new swim suits on me."

"Thanks for the idea," he said, pausing the program and heading for the hallway shower.

Desiree went to her bedroom to get her grandpa's travel journal. She had it propped on the top shelf of her bookcase. She just loved his title, *Stuff,* and knew just what he was thinking when he scribbled it across the front title line. *He certainly was secretive,* she thought. She opened the journal to the first page in which he had a short but acute disclaimer:

> *This notebook is the property of Joseph Sumner and is not meant for anyone else unless duly permitted by said owner. All accounts here are not to be taken as God's awful truth since Man has messed with His truth for way too long.*

She turned the page and read:

> *October 3, 1969. Many paths but which to take? Weather is perfect for jeans and light jacket. Saw some scavenging birds at canyon's mouth. Maybe something dead down here. Will investigate.*

She was intrigued and read more:

*Found a woman's jacket, vest and boots but no tools or utensils. Will look farther downstream. Some evidence of flooding with heavy delta at confluence of two creeks. Stuff could be under it.*

She laughed to herself about how he used the term, *stuff*. Maybe he meant *treasures*—just like the treasures in his trunk. She kept on reading not realizing that the time of her study session was quickly approaching. Her cell phone went off. The ring tone was from a Venetian Princess popular tune:

*"He's got me rocking like Steven Hawking, Check out his hard drive, sets me to warp five...*

She placed the journal on her bed and answered her phone. "Greetings, my handsome and brave aquatic warrior."

"More like handsome and brave *delivery boy*," Wes replied then chuckled. "Hey, Dizzy, I'm at Chin's Restaurant taking orders for the study session."

Desiree then looked at the clock on the kitchen wall. The group was scheduled to arrive in twenty minutes. "Oh, ah, how about a small won ton soup?"

"Won ton soup it is. My car soars like a chariot driven by four noble steeds with hoofs of fire. See you in a bit."

Desiree laughed. "You're too funny, Wes!" She closed her phone and returned the journal to her bookcase. She then went out to the kitchen where her mom was already dressed and wiping up the countertops.

Desiree took the cleaning cloth from her mom's hand. "Here, let me do that. You're dressed for a date—not for house cleaning."

152

Looking terribly shocked, her mom clutched her chest. "Be still my beating heart!"

"Oh, *Mom*," Desiree whined. "Come on; I clean up sometimes—although probably not enough." Desiree started cleaning while her mom went to look out the front door.

"Your dad should be here anytime now. He just called me from the resort." Then she walked back to the hallway mirror and checked her clothes and hair. The sound of her suede, high-heeled boots lightly clicked over the tile floor as she walked. She wore a blue denim dress with silver studs decorating the yoke and neckline.

Her son just entered the hall from his room neatly dressed and groomed. Both stared at each other and whistled.

"Mom," he said, "you look sah-weet!"

"You look pretty hot, yourself," his mom replied. "You must have a date, too."

"No," he said, looking into the same mirror and straightening his shirt collar. "I'm just trying to dress up Dizzy's study group." He ran his fingers through both sides of his head past his ears then fluffed up his spiked, dark-brown hair. He then checked his nostrils for any stray nose hair.

"Taylor must be coming tonight," she said hugging his back then brushing loose hair from his broad shoulders. He smiled at her reflection through the mirror.

From her bedroom window Desiree saw her dad's van pull up the driveway. "Hey, Mom, Dad's here!"

Janelle quickly smeared the lipstick between her lips and walked to the front door. Royce and Desiree followed closely behind her.

Walter was already waiting at the base of the steps. "Sorry I didn't have time to change, but they did let me wash up a bit at the

153

resort," he said. When he saw Janelle along with his kids standing on either side, he smiled. "Now don't you all shine-up like a family portrait."

"Now that you're here, yes," said Desiree, smiling back.

Janelle started down the steps but turned back quickly with stern instructions for Royce. "Make sure your sister's friends don't wreck the place while we're gone," she said.

Her son grinned. "No problem."

As their parents drove away another vehicle rolled in. It was a familiar-looking jeep with the top down and two girls inside with hair flying in the breeze.

Royce's eyes bulged practically out of their sockets. "It's Taylor!" He turned to his sister and nervously straightened his shirt collar. "How do I look, Dizzy?"

"Like a jittery guy on his first date," she answered. She then faked a tickling jab to his ribs. "C'mon, Baby-bro, when did you ever worry about your looks?"

Flinching from her attack, Royce answered, "Never—until now." He smoothed his hair once more and ran back into the house.

Dominique and Taylor had the radio blasting as they slowed to pull into the driveway. Their heads were bouncing with a heavy metal beat that was booming from the speakers. Then they each gave Desiree a victory sign.

She walked over to greet them. "You guys are sure rockin' out! You must have done well at the tournament."

Dominique jumped out first. "We placed seventh," she proudly boasted.

"Which is better than eighth," added Taylor wearing a triumphant, toothy smile as she got out from the passenger side.

"So we're getting better each time we compete," Dominique concluded.

154

Another vehicle soon pulled up the driveway. It was Wes' pickup truck with Aaron and Candice as passengers. They all jumped out, each carrying cartons of Chinese food.

"Anybody hungry?" Wes asked. Desiree led the group into the house.

Taylor ran up to Royce. "Hey, you going to hang out for our study group?" she asked.

"Only if it's more interesting than my boxing match with *Geek the dwerb*," he replied flirtatiously.

"We shall see," she said, hoping to take up his challenge.

Royce led the guys into the family room to view his boxing opponent, who was lying on his back with his face battered, ribs bruised and stars circling over his head. The guys each found a place to sit around the big screen.

Meanwhile the girls went into the kitchen and opened the food cartons. Desiree offered plates and utensils. Most declined—they were experts at chopsticks. The girls then took the food out to the back porch table, which was decorated by several strings of festive mini-lights that spiraled around the support pillars. Hanging between them each was a paper lantern that gave a glow of red, green, and yellow.

"Desiree, your party porch is amazing!" Candice exclaimed as she ran out to it with her chow mein. She sat on the bench that was closest to the green lantern. "I wanna come here and study every weekend!"

"Dinner is served!" Desiree called out to the occupants of the family room. They streamed out and into the kitchen. Royce paused the video game and followed them. He immediately went into the fridge.

"Royce, there's plenty of Chinese food if you're interested," Wes offered.

"Nah, I still got lots of leftover anchovy pizza, because no one else in my family will touch it," he replied.

Taylor, who was in the doorway, overheard Royce and came into the kitchen. "Did someone mention anchovies? I just love anchovies!" she cried.

Royce's eyes sparkled. "Well then, little girl, come on over here," he said, taking her hand and leading her to the pizza box on the counter. "There's plenty for the both of us."

Soon after dinner was served, Wes, the unofficial group leader, started the brainstorming session. He rolled open his map on the table.

"I brought this, and Aaron has some pages from the permit registry," he announced. Aaron laid out several pages containing past field trips that were brightly highlighted.

"I got just a few more locations," Aaron reported. He read off the areas and Wes stickered them with more stars on the map.

"Wait," Royce said, interrupting the star-sticking process. "It looks like an airplane with Scooby-Doo hanging on the tail." He looked across the table, hoping for laughter. Instead everyone groaned, including Taylor.

"Royce, we've already played the what's-it-look-like game," she said.

Royce was surprised. "What? Someone else saw Scooby-Doo, too?" he asked.

"Oi," Candice remarked to Desiree.

"Royce, no one's amused. I think I hear *Geek the dwerb* calling you back for a boxing rematch," his sister said as she got up to turn on the overhead light. It lit up the map much brighter, making the stars glimmer even more.

"We already know it's not an outline of anything, but I'm sure that if we nosh and mull over it for a while we could come up with something," said Wes.

"Yeah, the brain works better when the stomach is fed with awesome, Chinese food and perfect lighting," added Candice as she tapped the green lantern.

No one spoke for the next several minutes. The porch area was quiet except for the occasional slurping of soft noodles or jousting of chopsticks as hungry students jabbed for food from the same carton.

Aaron crunched into a fried won ton and chewed for a second before sliding it into his cheek. "Well, we could analyze this systematically by stating the obvious—like, what do we know about all these stars?"

"We know that none of them are green," Candice complained as she glared at Wes. Everyone else groaned.

"Thanks, Candice, but that's not helpful," said Aaron.

"Well," said Dominique, getting the ball started. "They're all in the Grand Canyon National Park."

"And they're all in a canyon that's in the Grand Canyon National Park," added Taylor.

"And they're all by a creek that's in a canyon that's in the Grand Canyon Park," said Desiree.

Not wanting to ruffle any of the upperclassmen's feathers, Royce remained silent this whole time while eating his anchovy pizza. But the logical flow of the discussion seemed so simple. He just had to add his two cents' worth. He swallowed his last bite, stood up and spoke.

"*And* the stars are all by a creek, that's by a creek, that's in a canyon, that's in the Grand Canyon National Park!" He smiled and bowed, pleased with his helpful contribution.

But no one else thought so. The jousting and slurping stopped, and the porch area fell silent except for a few crickets chirping in the backyard. Royce didn't have to see more than a few scowling faces before quickly sinking into his seat.

Desiree rose from her chair and pointed towards the door. "Royce, you really need to go back to your video game now," she vehemently insisted.

Feeling bad for him, Taylor looked down. Through the groans and threats of Royce's expulsion, she glanced over at the ends of her hair that were slightly frizzed from the hot curling iron she used earlier.

She grabbed a small section of her hair and noticed a few split ends. Then all of a sudden her face lit up. With a loud gasp she sprang up from her seat.

"Wait, you guys," she said looking at Royce. "Split ends!"

He looked puzzled. "Huh—split ends? I don't have split ends; I visit the barber regularly."

"Not your hair, silly; the creeks!" She looked at Wes to explain herself. "The camp locations are where the creeks all split. As dorky as he sounded, Royce may have said something helpful!"

Wes didn't get what she meant either. "Taylor, just because you're practically his girlfriend, doesn't mean you have to stick up for his quirky comments," he said.

"They're not quirky—look," said Taylor, pointing to the stars on the map. "Each star is on or close to a confluence—you know, *confluence*."

"Uh, what's a confluence?" Wes asked.

"Confluence," Candice said, repeating the term while tapping her chopsticks on the top of a food carton. Then she started tapping them on her head. "Confluence—I know this is a term from geology class—"

"—It's a split in a creek or river," said Dominique, who understands the term because she is acing this class. "It's where two waterways come together." She looked down at the stars on the map and pointed at each one. "Look, confluence: here, here, and here. They're all at confluences!"

Wes followed Dominique's pointing finger then looked up at Royce. "Dude, you're a genius—a pure, freaking genius!"

Hearing what he said, Desiree looked over to Wes. "Huh?"

Royce looked at her, too, grinning. "See, Dizzy, I'm a pure, freaking genius."

"Pure freak, yes," she replied, "but I'm not convinced about the genius part."

Aaron stood up and summarized the brainstorming. "So, let's assume Royce is both a freak and a genius for right now, and there is some correlation between Roeser's past field trips and the split ends—I mean—confluences." He stopped behind Candice who was eating the tiny Chinese corn in horizontal rows. He paused to chuckle at her eating manner then posed a question to the group. "Knowing what we know now, can we predict the next area he would choose as a campsite?"

"We first need to know more about confluences," answered Desiree.

"There's a whole section of it in our textbook," said Candice as she licked her fingers and fished out the geology book from her book bag.

Wes folded his map and tucked it back into his backpack. "Desiree, did you ever find out if your grandpa had a journal?"

"Yes, he did," she answered. "I just got my hands on it this morning, but I've only had time to read a few entries. He collected tools or utensils that were left behind by other hikers, but that's as far as I got."

"Did he mention any splits or confluences?" Wes asked. Desiree took a slow slurp of soup. Then she quickly swallowed before answering. "You know what—he did," she said as she sprang up from the table, "I'll be right back." Then she ran to her bedroom.

She soon returned with the journal and opened it in front of Wes. "It was the very first entry I read, and he mentioned not finding anything at the confluence of two creeks." Wes pushed the open book around the table for everyone else to see.

"Hey, your grandpa did some pretty cool illustrating," Candice remarked, pointing to a pencil sketching in the margin. "Look at that canyon wall with all the detailed sediment layers."

"Yeah, he's got a bunch of drawings," said Desiree, "But this one happened to be at a confluence."

Candice turned to the next page and found another sketch. "Wow, check out this eagle ripping into a freshly-caught fish! Your grandpa really captured the ferocity of nature."

Desiree agreed but then pushed the journal towards Aaron. He read a few entries while Candice leaned over to catch a few last glimpses before he pushed it over to Dominique.

"This journal can be better than a map with his descriptions of the areas. It could come in handy for our trip," said Dominique.

"He had a map, too," Desiree said, "but it didn't look anymore detailed than the one Wes has."

"This journal is more than enough," said Aaron. "The text details his surroundings as well as the drawings."

"Detailed? More like obsessive," remarked Taylor. "It says here he found this compass buried three-point-five feet in the silt on the north side of the creek twenty-one paces from the canyon's mouth."

"Yeah, that's a little obsessive," admitted Dominique, "But I'll bet he wanted to be very exact in case he ever returned to look for more stuff."

Royce leaned over Taylor's shoulder and put his left hand on top of hers, which was still holding the journal. He smiled when she looked up at him. Then he slid off her hand and found an edge of the outside cover to grab. He motioned for the journal, and she smiled with approval. She reached from behind to grab his right hand and wrapped it around her. This pulled his chest into her back.

Caught by surprise Royce swallowed hard. He wasn't prepared for her flirtatious move. She smiled at him again then let go of the journal and slid her hands onto his. He returned a nervous smile and picked up the journal up over her head. She could feel his heavy breathing against her back and giggled. She knew he was just as excited about their brief, physical encounter as she was.

Only Desiree noticed them and giggled. *I see this kind of flirting at school all the time, but watching it happen to Royce is pretty funny,* she thought. Meanwhile her brother shook off his awkwardness, took the journal and briefly paged through it before giving it back to his sister.

"But if he wasn't so obsessive this journal wouldn't be so detailed," said Desiree as she closed it and returned it to her bedroom.

"Agreed," replied Wes. He watched her disappear through the doorway then turned to the group. "We've got a lot of good ideas."

"But there's a lot more work to do," said Aaron as he sat up taller in his seat. "We need as much info about confluences since it seems to be a focal point for Roeser's trips."

"Since some of Grandpa's junk was found in similar areas," said Royce, "maybe the confluences are the best places to look for anything lost in the creek or canyon. I don't know—maybe the currents catch stuff and deposit them close by."

Wes offered a high-five to Royce. "Too bad you're not a senior, Royce. We could use you on this trip," he said as they slapped hands.

"Just save some of the mystery for me when it's my turn to go," Royce joked.

Soon after the food cartons emptied, the meeting adjourned. The cool desert evening was quiet except for an occasional cricket or barking dog. Royce walked Taylor to the jeep. They took slow deliberate steps since the vehicle was parked fairly close to the back porch.

"This field trip sounds like fun—wish I could go with you guys," said Royce.

"It would be much more fun with you," Taylor answered as she placed her books onto the back seat. She then walked to the passenger's side and leaned her back up against the door. He stood in front of her. He impressed by her earlier and wanted to impress her more.

"So what is it you like about me, my body or my brains?" He moved closer to her. His taller stature towered over her. He leaned onto the roll bar to shorten himself slightly so that he could get closer to her face. She felt a little intimidated by his question and his closeness, but, being more experienced, she answered casually.

"Royce, it doesn't really matter."

Her response caught by surprise. He backed away, hoping she would have said *both your body and your brains*.

"No, I guess it doesn't matter," he answered, and then looked down, feeling disappointed.

Taylor tried to cheer him up and took both his hands. "Tonight I thought you deserved more credit than your sister gave you, especially in front of her friends." With that she pulled him down and gave him a slow, soft kiss on his lower cheek. Her lips felt soft and—oh, so very sincere! Then with her lips still touching his skin, she lightly tracked up to his ear and whispered, "It probably killed her to see your display of genius." The *s* sounds from her teeth in his ear made him shudder. All of this plus her smile sent him into orbit. This was quite a new sensation for him!

Feeling exhilarated at this point, he popped his long-awaited question to her. "Then can we go out sometime?"

"Sure," Taylor answered without hesitation, "but I'll have to check my schedule first. I'll text you." Just then they heard Dominique come down the porch steps. Royce then opened the door for Taylor. Dominique stopped a few feet away so not to intrude.

But Taylor knew her captain was near. "Hey, Dominique, we were just saying goodnight," she said then motioned to Royce to come closer. She embraced his face, kissed her two fingers and planted them on his lips. "This isn't our first official date yet, so no kissing on the lips. But feel free to call or text me anytime when you want to chat."

With a blissful smile Royce stood back and closed her door. *I think I actually have a senior girlfriend,* he thought. "Sounds awesome," he finally answered.

Dominique got in and started the engine. She pulled her jeep around the horseshoe driveway then onto the street, and Royce watched as the hard rock music resumed loudly from the car speakers. Soon both girls' hair again flew wildly in the breeze.

Wes, Candice and Aaron walked down the steps towards the pickup truck.

Wes then patted Royce on his shoulder. "Hey Royce, you need a ride to practice tomorrow morning?"

"Sure," Royce replied coolly as he rubbed his lips with his fingers. He could detect a slight aroma of freesia from the cologne that Taylor wore, and, at the moment, it was the best aroma ever!

"How about six-fifteen?" Wes asked.

"Yeah, sure," Royce replied, hypnotized by the taillights as they faded into the darkness. He stood motionless—like he was entranced—even after the jeep was gone.

Wes looked into Royce's face. "Hey, buddy, you OK?"

"Not sure," Royce answered still gazing. Candice waved her hand in front of Royce's face, but he didn't blink.

"I've seen this look before," said Candice. "Royce is bewitched—"

"—By a senior," interrupted Aaron. "How cool is that?" Desiree was still up on the porch turning off the party lights. She then came down and called out to Royce.

"Planning on waiting up for Mom and Dad?" she asked. Not getting a reply she came down the steps and nudged her brother in the arm. "Royce?"

"He can't do anything right now," Candice explained. "He's zoning." Everyone looked at his cosmically nebulized eyes and his warped smile. His fingers were still pressed upon his lips. Then he snapped out of his trance and turned to his sister.

"Dizzy, I need to get my own bottle of your shower gel," he said as he turned and ran into the house. Everyone but Desiree, who had no clue what happened, laughed at Royce.

Wes, still chuckling, turned to Desiree. "Tell Royce I'll pick him up for practice tomorrow morning at six-fifteen in case he didn't hear me—and I don't think he did."

Desiree was still not sure what had transpired. "Why didn't he hear you, Wes—what just happened?"

"Looks like Royce got stung by more than just bees this week," he replied, throwing his backpack into the payload area and circling back to Desiree.

"I guess so—sure hope he can handle it," she said.

"Time will tell," Wes replied while gently embracing her shoulders. Then using a heavy, foreign accent he played the role of a psychologist using broken English. "*Deez crush ding—is indeed stahdange ahnimal.*"

Desiree laughed at his bad impression. "And you know all about crushes, because—?"

He glanced up at the stars that were already twinkling in the evening sky. Then he cocked his head to the side and looked down at her, using his normal voice.

"I really can't say. The only crush I've ever had was on my ninth grade biology teacher because she was the first female teacher I've had besides my mom." They both laughed then walked to his side of the truck. "Thanks for letting us meet here." He bent down to kiss her cheek. She wanted to grab his face and kiss his lips but instead returned his affection with a tight hug.

"Anytime, Mr. Chinese food delivery man," she said.

"Yeah, Desiree, thanks from me, too," Candice yelled through the window. "I wanna study over here again real soon."

Desiree let go of Wes and stepped back from the truck. "Sure, Candice," she replied. "I'll see if I can find some more green party lights for you." Candice gave her a double thumbs-up.

Aaron finally climbed inside next to Candice and closed the door. Wes pulled out and drove slowly down the driveway. Desiree waved briefly then went back to clean the porch. Royce was already filling a large trash bag with the empty food cartons.

"Baby-bro," she said to him, "Are you seriously OK?"

He walked to the opposite side of the table loading empty food cartons into the bag. "Nope, I feel so strange." He sat on the bench and stared at the paper lantern that swayed with the cool gentle breeze. "I never really talked to a girl like I did with Taylor tonight. I'm usually so busy building myself up like a superhero. Tonight it seemed easier to just be mild-mannered."

Desiree sat next to him. "You mean you're not always a superhero?"

He wrapped one arm around her back. "No, not since I lost my flying cape during the last rescue mission," he joked. They both laughed, and Desiree put her head onto his shoulder. Obviously the pain from the bee stings was gone.

Not long after, their dad's safari van pulled into the driveway. The headlights were shining like two brilliant stars converging into a stellar collision. The siblings ran down the porch steps just as the van stopped. Both doors opened at the same time as their parents jumped out laughing. Walter moved quickly around his van to catch up with Janelle then took her hand. They both walked up to the porch step, giggling.

"Dinner must have been good," Royce called out to them.

"Not bad," his dad answered.

"Did you guys have a good time?" asked Desiree.

"Well, we argued the whole time," confessed her mom "but it was some of the best arguments we've ever had."

"Yeah, we got so loud the couples at tables around us kept edging away, thinking we'd be throwing chairs any minute," said her dad while bending over and hooting. Janelle was laughing so hard that the silver studs on her dress quaked, glistening in the headlights like a disco ball.

Confused by their parents' answers, Royce and Desiree just stood and watched their parents laugh and fall into each other's arms. It seemed strange that they were so happy together.

"Maybe we should leave them alone in case they get all mushy and stuff," Royce told Desiree. She agreed, and they walked together back into the house. Their parents exchanged a quick hug and kiss. Walter jumped back into his van, and Janelle walked up the porch steps.

Desiree waited until her mom stepped inside the door. "So really, Mom, how did it go?"

Janelle wiped a tear from her cheek. "We had such a good time, we decided to get together again," her mom replied as they both entered the kitchen.

"Together—like a family again?" Desiree asked as she grabbed the trash bag and walked back out to the porch.

"No, not like that, at least not yet. We both decided that we still need time and space to figure out if we could make this work."

Royce came up behind his mom as she continued. "We both agreed to see each other and discuss our relationship." She gazed at the lanterns and Royce gently nudged past her to help his sister with the cleaning. "Gosh, it almost feels like we're dating again. I'd forgotten how much fun that was. We were so immature and short-fused. Yet we both enjoyed each other's shortcomings. Guess that's why we were meant for each other."

Then her gaze changed to the cleaned-up porch area. "What kind of boring party was this—no beer keg? No passed-out bodies? No footprints on the ceiling?"

"Mom, I told you—this was a study session," insisted Desiree.

"Yeah, and Taylor wants to date me," Royce bragged to his mom.

Delighted by his news, she ran over to hug him. "That's my little Romeo," she said. "You must have won her affection by your charm and wit." He smiled, accepting his mom's compliment.

After they finished cleaning Desiree told her mom what was discussed during the study session. Royce, of course, had to boast about his valuable contribution much to the disdain of his sister.

# Chapter VIII

*They come, go and cycle but not before being counted. This is so terribly necessary. After all, someone may need to know how many there are. What's more, they may want them straight and orderly, and what better way than to number them. Lives can depend on them. Blocked and divided— that's the best way they'll know how many there are and who follows whom. They all get a name and a number. That's the way to do it–it's got to be the best system! So much depends on them. Life just wouldn't be as well planned or predictable without them. And when enough have been together, ordered, counted and cycled for quite some time, they all disappear in one, gigantic rip off the face of existence. This momentous event is approaching soon, so get ready!*

Taylor's index finger tapped over to the current day on the school's calendar. It was the last Wednesday in

February. Her eyes raced over the title and headings of the overly embellished presentation in the school's colors. She ran her finger down to the end of the page. She flipped the page and continued tapping. She flipped one more time and finally stopped at twelve taps to the senior prom. Then she heard a set of feet stomping down the hall. She looked over and saw Dominique rapidly approaching. She quickly flipped the pages back and tapped out the number of weeks before the geology field trip. Then she turned to her best friend whose ears were as red as burning charcoal.

"Dominique, look—only three weeks before the field trip," she said.

Dominique neither looked at the calendar nor at Taylor. She dropped her pack, unrolled a three-page report out of her hand, and let out a loud grunt of disgust. An underclass girl poked her head out of the washroom door and, after seeing Dominique, quickly retreated.

Then Dominique glared at Taylor while shaking with rage. "Look at this grade! Would you just look at it? I can't believe it!" She then stuck her English Lit paper right in front of Taylor's face.

Taylor crossed her eyes slightly to shift her focus on the large *A-* and *Great Work* printed at the top of the page. She was about to congratulate her captain, but Dominique exploded first.

"This sucks worse than a toilet plunger!" Dominique then rolled it up and jammed it into her pack.

Taylor couldn't understand her teammate's reaction. "But, Dominique, an *A-* is a pretty decent grade," she said.

Dominique paced back and forth, stomping each foot on the concrete floor. "No, it's not; I don't do *A-* work." Her voice escalated. "I'm gonna have a nice, little chat with Mrs. McNair."

"But, don't you see; she liked your paper, or else she would not have written so many positive comments."

"If she was so positive, then why not an *A* or *A+*?"

The girl from the washroom peeped out again before cautiously sliding into the hall. Her back was pinned against the wall, trying to avoid detection. But Dominique saw her and stomped an aggressive foot at her. Startled, the girl shrieked and ran. Taylor knew Dominique was rapidly approaching a meltdown.

"Captain, if it makes you feel better, Mrs. McNair gave me a *B+* along with a half page of nice comments. She's always been a tough grader, but at least she's a nice, tough grader."

Dominique took a deep breath for composure then smiled at Taylor. "Well, OK—I guess I shouldn't complain since I only spent one hour in the library and another one at our tournament playoffs," she decided. Then, with her emotions switching like the channels of cable television, she looked up at the school calendar. "So, anything interesting going on this week?"

Taylor sighed with relief. "Yes, if you're into getting a flu shot, going with the Spanish Club's dinner trip to Macayo's Restaurant or having your class picture retaken." They both laughed.

"Is our field trip listed?" Dominique inquired.

"Yes—it's right here," her teammate replied while tapping onto the date. "Only three weeks away. Got all your hiking stuff?"

"Most of it. I just need to get a rain poncho and a flashlight," answered Dominique.

"Don't forget trail food—we'll need lots of that," Taylor reminded her.

"Are you kidding me—I'm the wilderness food expert," Dominique bragged. They started walking to their lockers, while Dominique continued. "Our pantry at home is full of granola, trail mix, protein bars, beef jerky and dried fruit." She pulled out a granola bar from the front pocket of her backpack. "This stuff has the shelf life of a few decades, so even if we get lost for any extended period of time the food will still be good."

They stopped at the water fountain and Taylor got a drink. She was very thirsty, and after several swallows she filled her water bottle.

Dominique noticed. "Boy, Taylor, you sure drink a lot of water," she said.

Taylor capped her bottle and turned back to Dominique. "It must be this dry, desert air. Takes all the moisture out of me. Sometimes during volleyball practice I get so thirsty I just want to jump into the nearby irrigation canal and suck in all its water."

"Better stick with water from your bottle," Dominique advised. "Those Central Arizona Project canals run fast and furious. You don't want to deal with the strong currents or the cold temperatures. I know—I once fell in one. Even in the summer, the water can be freezing."

"OK, I'll stay out of the canals, if you'll help me with my meal selections for the Grand Canyon hike," Taylor said.

"Love to," Dominique replied. "They have an amazing selection at the hiking store and also at the nearby supermarket." We can go after practice some night if you want."

"Sounds like a date." They started walking slowly down the hall.

"Speaking of dates, has Royce called you?" Dominique asked.

"Well, I did get a few text messages from him Monday and yesterday."

"That's great!"

"I guess so. But each message is a piece of his life story. I think he wants me to know all about him before we even go out."

"What's wrong with that? It saves you a lot of time trying to find out if he's the right guy."

"Yeah, but that's the fun part about dating. Who wants to sit at dinner with nothing to say, because you know everything about your date?"

"Hell and Hades! You don't try to know *everything* about him before your date. Just the important stuff like—is he buying? Does he have a clean car? Does he like kids?"

"Why would I want to know about his liking kids? I'm not interested in marriage and family—just a fun night out."

"Taylor, it's not about getting married and having a bunch of kids. You want to know if he likes kids because then you'll know he has compassion, patience, sensitivity, playfulness, and fairness—important qualities. In my experience the guys who take care of younger siblings or coach sports' teams also respect their dates."

"That's so profound but weird," Taylor concluded.

173

"That's why I check out the volleyball guys. A lot of them come from big families with younger sibs. Some hang out to help coach the younger teams. I see how they treat the younger players. If they show great care for them, then I'll know they'll do the same for me."

"But you haven't dated any volleyball guys yet."

"No," Dominique admitted, laughing. "Because I have yet to see any of them driving a clean car—my second-most, important qualification." Both girls laughed.

Taylor's cell phone went off. She pulled out her phone and saw a message on her screen. "It's Royce again." She opened the message. "He's at school and wants to meet before class at the sports' shrine. That's on my way to geology, so see ya!"

"See you at lunch!" Dominique replied. "Wait, I forgot—catch!" She tossed the granola bar at Taylor. "Let me know how you like it."

Taylor caught it and smiled back at her captain. "Thanks," she said, stuffing it into the back pocket of her jeans. She then turned and blew through the double-hallway doors. A few other students standing on the other side dodged her. They got caught up in her breeze of flying hair and clothes. The notices pinned on a nearby bulletin board flapped from the draft she caused.

One of the girls walked over to Dominique and introduced herself. "Hi. I'm Gillian Lyght, editor of the Searchlight." She then offered a handshake. "You're Dominique Cruseaux, right?"

Dominique shook the editor's hand and replied, "Yes, I am. Sorry about my friend zipping past you. She should be more careful in these hallways."

"No problem," Gillian replied. "You both play volleyball for the school, so I expect you to be fast, but that's not why I'm here. I heard that Taylor wants to write an article about the Grand Canyon field trip. Did she mention anything about it to you?"

Dominique gasped. Someone heard about Taylor's ruse with Mr. Roeser and told the editor!

"Well, sort of," Dominique tentatively answered as she looked away.

"That's good because we want to support her project. No one on our staff is going, and we'd like a representative there."

Dominique tried to keep her composure. "Look, I can't speak for Taylor. You need to ask her yourself."

Gillian flashed a smile. "Great, can you let her know for me?"

"Uh, sure," she said pulling out her cell phone. "Let me have your number."

Gillian gave out her number and added, "Tell her to call me ASAP. This could be so awesome for our school and the world beyond!" Gillian then turned to walk back to her friends, waving slowly as if greeting thousands of fans. She rejoined her small circle of friends—not thousands of fans—huddled together a few yards down the hall. Dominique stared at Gillian for a moment then texted Taylor, prefacing her message with *URGENT!*

Meanwhile, Taylor was heading down the hall towards the sports' shrine. The hallway had a few upper windows that were opened by the janitors to better dry a freshly mopped floor. A gentle breeze rustled the palm trees growing just outside the windows. She felt the cooler breeze

175

brushing her face and caught the lemon-scented aroma of the floor cleaner.

The ambiance reminded her of last year's trip to Rocky Point, a Mexican tropical resort town, where the winds blew off the Gulf of California through the tropical palms, and over the sandy beaches. She stopped to smell, feel and hear the next breeze before spotting Royce at the swim team trophy case.

He was standing by the digital photo frame, staring at the photos, cycling through the most recent swim season. His hair was still damp from the morning practice, but his spirits seemed even more dampened.

"Hey, Royce, how's it going?" Taylor asked.

He looked up and saw her slow approach. "Hey, Taylor," he replied, running his fingers through his hair, trying to dry it in the hallway's breeze. "Sorry I look like a floor mop; I just got out of swim practice."

"No, Royce," she assured him. "You look fine but maybe a little tired."

He backed away from the trophy case and yawned. "I am tired," he said. "We're now practicing at another pool that's twice as far from home. So that cuts more into my snooze time."

"What's wrong with your regular pool?" she asked.

He stretched his arms and arched his back before answering. "It's closed for draining. I guess the water chemistry went bad. The aquatics director thought it was a good time to drain and update the plumbing, so we have to use a different pool for the next few months. It's only been two days, but already the longer drive time is killing me."

Taylor took his hands and pulled him closer to her. "Of course you can, Royce; you're a varsity swimmer. If you can swim eight bazillion yards a day then you can handle anything."

He gently gripped her hands and managed a weak smile. "Thanks, Taylor, but my studies and all this extra traveling is really messing up my social life."

"Hey, sometimes you do what you have to," said Taylor as she smiled, looking up at his pale-blue eyes.

But he didn't understand what she meant. He let go of her hands and stepped back, his tanned face going white from shock. "What—does that mean we're breaking up before our first date?"

She again pulled him back. "Royce, how can we break up when we're not even going together yet? So let's get this started, but first we have to make time by managing it," she said.

"But I have no time to manage; between classes and traveling—"

"—That's *exactly* what I mean," said Taylor. "You do your homework whenever you have a few extra minutes, like during the car ride to practice. You'd be surprised how much you can get done just riding in a car—especially in the crazy city traffic around here. Dominique and I do it all the time. We take turns driving. We take our books with us to tournaments, between matches, waiting for the bus or whenever there's down time—even if we can knock off only one sentence or math problem. It all adds up, and before we know it we're done!"

"It must be really boring at your tournaments," Royce remarked.

"If it is, we don't even notice because we're busy either playing or getting our assignments done. When we get home we have some time left for our scant, social lives."

"What do you mean *scant?* You and Dominique are popular at school. I see you with lots of friends. You definitely have a social life."

"At school, sure. But after school we're back on the volleyball court, running drills and getting tired. Like you, we practice everyday. Volleyball is pretty much our social life outside of school."

"Yeah," admitted Royce. "That's two things we have in common—we both love anchovies and barely have social lives."

Taylor giggled just before the morning bell rang. As if on cue, more students filled the hallways. Taylor checked the time on her cellphone but missed Dominique's urgent message.

"Oops, where did the time go? Guess I have to get going," Taylor said.

"Thanks for listening and for all the advice," said Royce. "I'd love to talk with you again about it." Then he smiled down at her. She pulled him down even lower and offered a kiss. He turned his cheek to her, but she kissed him squarely on the lips. He shuddered with surprise. *She said she'd kiss on the first date, but this isn't a date*, he thought. She steadied him by wrapping her arms around the back of his head. A few whistles came from some freshmen boys who were heading to the gym.

Upon hearing them, Taylor pulled away. "I'd love to talk again with you as well." She then turned and lost her balance. She started to fall, but Royce hooked under her arms and caught her.

"Whoa, Taylor, are you OK?"

She smiled up at him. "I am now," she said. "Your kiss must have made me woozy."

"Yeah," Royce admitted. "I got woozy, too."

"This must be good karma." Then she shook off the feeling. "OK. I've got to go," she said, turning back towards her locker. "I'll call you when I can." She then disappeared down the hall.

As if in a daze, Royce froze in place. Taylor's kiss made him feel funny in a way he never felt before. Then his daze was interrupted by calls from the gymnasium doors, and he ran to join his classmates.

Meanwhile, Taylor wandered aimlessly down the hall towards her locker, stopping first at the water fountain. She pulled out her water bottle, but it was already full. The wall clock glared in fiery red numbers that she had five minutes before class.

Seemingly out of nowhere, a sea of students flowed towards her like a tidal wave. Dominique, riding on the crest of flesh and schoolbooks, barged her way to the water fountain.

"Check your messages lately?" she asked Taylor.

"No, I was with Royce," Taylor answered. "We kissed, and now I'm a blissful wreck! I don't even know where my locker is."

Dominique grabbed Taylor's forearms and stared into her turbid eyes.

"OK, Taylor, time to snap out of it. You need to tuck Royce away for now," Dominique said.

Taylor blinked a few times then refocused on her captain. "OK, he's tucked away. What's up?"

"Check your phone messages," Dominique said, brushing her black hair away from her beaded face. She then blotted her forehead with the sleeve of her sweatshirt. Taylor reached for her phone and flipped it open. Dominique then pulled out her water bottle to fill it. Taylor bent over her phone to better see her message screen while avoiding other students who were rushing past.

"Gillian's phone number is urgent?" Taylor asked.

"Afraid so," replied Dominique as she took a quick sip from her bottle and capped it. Her breathing slowed back to normal. "She heard about your fact-finding mission with Roeser. She wants you to do it for the newspaper."

Taylor gasped. "No freaking way!"

"Freaking way, partner! Not only does Gillian want facts, but she also wants you to write a first-hand account," Dominique said.

"But my interview with Mr. Roeser was just a ruse. I can't really report for the Searchlight," said Taylor.

She turned away, gazing down the hall. For a moment she pictured herself wearing a visor with a large *Press* badge plastered on its brim. She clung to a notebook while scaling down a vertical cliff high above the Colorado River with screams of floundering students resonating from the rapids below.

"No. I can't do it; I can't climb—I mean, I can't write." Then she heard Dominique repelling the sheer rock face downward, resting on a nearby ledge. She climbed over to Taylor patting her on the shoulder.

"Look, Taylor, it's not that hard," she said while attaching another rope onto her buddy's harness. "Actually it's a lot easier than writing a book review. You report the facts. No opinions, no analysis. Besides, Mrs. McNair is the faculty adviser for the Searchlight, and she likes you, right?" Taylor nodded, and Dominique continued. "So, she'll help you out. Hey, she did give you a *B+* on your book review, right? So, you'll be OK." They both slowly descended together, repelling off the vertical wall a few feet at a time until lightly touching down to the river's silted and soft bank.

"Yeah, but *you* got the better grade, right?" Taylor reminded her as she disconnected her line and climbed out of her harness. "And we're a *team*, right?" Her mind then returned to the school hallway as she continued. "So Mrs. McNair won't be helping me as much as *you* will, buddy."

Knowing Taylor's impeccable logic, Dominique sighed then nodded. "Right, but you'll have to include me on your byline."

"Sure," Taylor answered. "—Whatever *that* is."

"I can see this is going to be another educational moment," Dominique remarked as she further explained the term *byline*, and they both dissolved into the student flow of the hall.

Taylor arrived at her first period geology class and sat in the first seat—closest to the door. She pulled out her notebook and textbook. Most students passed her without notice except for one, who quickly sat in the seat behind her.

"Taylor Mayer, right?" whispered a boy's voice. She turned partially around but didn't look directly at him.

"Who wants to know?" Taylor asked.

"Bryce Lyght, Gillian's brother," he replied.

Taylor then turned completely around and saw a young, round-faced boy with red, curly hair and freckles. "Hey, you don't belong in this class," she replied, sounding annoyed.

"Shh, keep it down; the seniors in this class are savages," he said, nervously scanning a much older group of students entering the classroom. "I'm risking my life being here. But my sister wanted to make sure you got her message."

"How do you know who I am?" Taylor asked.

"I'm sort of Royce's friend. We're in the same homeroom."

181

"A freshman—yuck!"

"Shh!" Bryce sounded sharply, looking around again and ducking his head. "Funny, you don't feel that way about Royce," he retorted.

"Well, he's different, and how would you know?"

"I saw the two of you sucking face in the sports' shrine earlier. Anyway, my sister says none of the seniors on the Searchlight staff are going on this field trip, and she wants a first-hand account." At this time Mr. Roeser entered the class with his lecture notes and laptop.

"How did she find out?" Taylor asked. Bryce looked around again and hid his head with a notebook.

"People talk, ya hear things, and word gets around. Anyway, she wants you to meet her at third period, study hall. She'll meet you at the cafeteria doors."

Mr. Roeser powered up the projector and connected his laptop. Bryce got up and slid out of class, but not before being detected by a few seniors who launched paper wads at him.

"Hey, that's no way to treat a junior member of the Searchlight staff," Mr. Roeser said. "Alright now, settle down." He watched Bryce escape unharmed. "Please take notes on this lecture because I didn't have time to print out the handouts..."

He went on to introduce his lecture as Taylor opened her notebook and jotted inside the margin: *Gillian, third period, cafe doors.* She then slumped in her chair and tapped her pen on the desk, mulling over her new job as newspaper reporter.

Mr. Roeser heard the tapping and came over to her desk. "Miss Mayer, you look and sound troubled; do you have a question?"

Taylor then realized the distraction she was causing. She put away her pencil and sat up in her seat. "Oh, I'm sorry, I was reading the chapter and got stuck on the term, *confluence*. Is it like a fork in the road?"

"More like a fork in a waterway only backwards," he replied with his eyes gleaming from her interesting question. "It's where the two join together—not separate. For example, the point where the Little Colorado River flows into the main Colorado River is called the confluence. The dynamics of the confluence actually forms a delta." He displayed a map on the screen and pointed at a small land mass right where the two rivers met.

"Isn't that like the Mississippi Delta?" Martina asked from the back row.

"Good question, Martina. By the way, I need to see you after class to get an emergency contact number for your permission slip." Martina nodded as he continued. "But to answer your question…well, it's sort of like the Mississippi Delta, but not as big. The Mississippi Delta is formed from the silt carried by a massive water flow. The silt is deposited at its confluence with the Gulf of Mexico, which has less current than the river does, so there's a huge delta that keeps growing with the silt deposit. The Little Colorado deposits silt but its bigger sister carries off most of it. The result is a small delta that can change with flow fluctuations."

"Can you walk on the Colorado River's delta?" asked Sayuri, an exchange student from Japan.

"You sure can, Sayuri," he answered. "River runners park their watercraft on it for rest, lunch, picture taking—all sorts of fun. But it can flood or shift with the flow change, so the park rangers won't allow any overnight camping. They don't want park visitors floating away in the middle of the night."

Seeing all attentive faces of his class encouraged him to stay on the subject. He continued lecturing about the Grand Canyon and fielded several questions.

Just when he was describing the canyon's Inner Gorge, the bell sounded for class change. Taylor, being closest to the door, slipped out first. However, several students behind her stopped at his desk, asking about the field trip. She felt good about spawning class interest.

By third period, Gillian stood at the double doors of the cafeteria. She was a poised and self-confident upperclassman. Her poker-straight, sandy-brown hair hung down over her shoulders and covered the top of her large portfolio binder that she was carrying. A freshly sharpened pencil twisted her bangs back from her face, anchoring them on top of her head. She wore a green plaid three-piece skirt suit—one of many outfits having the school colors.

She was the epitome of school spirit and information. She joined the Searchlight staff as a freshman, writing articles, essays and editorial opinions. Her quest for information and ability to transform it into interesting articles moved her quickly up the ranks of the staff. Many of her writings won state honors for originality or creativity. She was the first sophomore ever to become editor-in-chief of the Searchlight. Her dream is to become editor for a national news magazine.

She smiled at familiar faces that filed through the double doors. This study hall was by far the largest period for the senior class to assemble, catch up with homework, tutor or even perpetuate juicy rumors. Her eyes searched intently for Taylor from the sea of heads that bobbed up and down. Gillian finally caught sight of Taylor and waved. Dominique followed Taylor closely.

"Are you two together on this?" Gillian asked. She was very good at guessing, and her instincts were correct this time, too.

"Yes, we're a team—always and everywhere," Taylor cheerfully replied, hooking her arm around Dominique's.

"That's even better," Gillian replied. "Please follow me." She led the two towards the Searchlight staff room. It was located at the intersection of two hallways and had glass windows as walls. One side had a bulletin board that obscured the upper two-thirds of the glass, so that only the feet of the office's occupants could be seen. On the bulletin board were oversized pages of the most recent Searchlight issue. The pages were mounted on thick, neon-colored paper shaped like broad light beams coming from an even larger lighthouse on the lower left side of the bulletin board. The other glass wall had vertical blinds that were partially opened revealing slits of light that fluctuated by every passing student.

Gillian opened the glass door for the volleyball duo. They entered and saw most of the staff members seated at a long table with a light-colored laminated surface. All heads turned to the editor.

"Does everyone know Taylor and Dominique?" Gillian asked as she turned on the voice recorder, which was at the end of the table. Her staff acknowledged the girls including Bryce, who winked at Taylor. "They may just be our eyes and ears in the Grand Canyon for this year's geology field trip." A few excited comments launched like torpedoes from the table.

"Cool! I've been there, but my family never took me down to the Colorado River," said Katie, one of the sports' reporters.

"Bummer," commented Bryce.

"Yeah, we got as far as Indian Gardens and had to climb out because of the rain, but not before we ran into Kathy, the wild turkey."

"You're kidding, right?" Taylor asked.

"No! Anybody who's hiked that trail knows Kathy," answered Katie.

"We should get both audio and video accounts," suggested Kevin, the photojournalist. "I can get you recorders, video cameras, and a great, single-reflex camera with tripod for still shots—"

"—Wait, we haven't agreed yet," Dominique said. She turned to Taylor. "Have we, partner?"

"*You're* the one who was trying to convince *me*," she replied.

Dominique whispered to her partner, "I know, but let's see if we can get them to sweeten the deal a little more."

She then turned to Kevin. "Look, we can't carry all that equipment; we hike with everything on our backs—clothes, food, water and sleeping bags. The extra weight of recorders and tripods would kill us. I don't think we should take this job."

"OK, OK, no bulky equipment," said Kevin. "How about one digital camera that takes stills and video and can fit in your pocket?" he asked holding up a thin, lightweight camera.

Dominique began her haggling. "How about two—you can get two perspectives if each of us had one."

"Only if you promise to get a picture of Kathy," Kevin said.

Dominique turned to Taylor. "Now this job is starting to sound more appealing." Then she turned back to Kevin. "OK, we'll even get two pictures of Kathy," Dominique said, accepting the first camera then winking at Taylor.

"Deal!" Kevin cried. He quickly jumped up to get another camera for Taylor.

"Can you also record your daily accounts?" Bryce asked them.

Now it was Taylor's turn to negotiate. "Oh, I don't know; that involves a lot of time not to mention a lot of extra weight to carry." Taylor nudged Dominique with her knee, and both giggled.

Bryce jumped out of his seat and walked over to a gunmetal gray storage cabinet. He opened its double doors and searched the top shelf. He finally pulled out what looked like a thin leather-covered book. He walked it over to Taylor.

"I was saving this for a very important assignment, but I guess yours qualifies." He then handed it to her. "It's a travel journal, but not just any travel journal…"

He went on to describe the journal's features, including the richly textured cover, the lightweight paper and pen pocket, to name a few.

Taylor lightly ran a hand across the leather cover then fanned the pages. She whispered to Dominique. "Wow, this feels very expensive and professional—not like the cheap, vinyl covered diaries I always used." Then she noticed that the strap that bound the journal had a metal clasp but no lock. "Hey, wait a minute, Bryce; you can't lock up this journal!"

"Of course you can't," Bryce answered. "This journal is completely accessible to the public." Then he snickered. "So you may not want to describe your fantasies about Royce in it, unless you want the whole school to know." He winked again and she cringed.

Dominique also inspected the journal and was impressed by the paper's rich feel. "Hey, these pages feel like sketching paper," she remarked.

"Sure, you can use it for sketching in case your camera accidentally drops off a cliff," Bryce said.

Dominique whispered to Taylor. "Lock or no lock; I like this journal." Then she looked over to Bryce. "Do you have anymore of these?"

Bryce walked back to the cabinet, closing both doors. "Maybe, but you have to fill up that one, first."

Dominique and Taylor looked at each other and decided that the reporting job was well worth the tools that were supplied.

"OK," they both said at the same time.

"Super awesome rockness!" He quickly returned to his seat and jotted in his notebook, *travel journal by Taylor*.

"You got that right," Taylor said with a smile giving Bryce a thumbs-up. Then she saw a flash. Kevin had taken her picture. He changed out the memory chip and handed the camera to Taylor. Other staffers soon barraged the two with more questions.

"Can you get Skype down there?" asked Tatum, one of the staff's online researchers.

"Maybe, but we're not bringing laptops—they're too heavy to carry," answered Dominique, "and neither of us own smart phones."

"Gee, I wish I could go, but I have a family reunion down in Cabo San Lucas," Tatum replied, glowering.

"Going to Cabo sounds like fun, Tatum," replied Dominique.

"Yeah, but hanging out with my preschool cousins can't be half as exciting as a field trip with hunks in hiking shorts and danger lurking all around," she said.

"No frigate ship," Bryce remarked, watching the legs of female students walking past the window.

Gillian realized that the chaotic conditions in her staff room had gone on long enough. She stepped onto an empty chair and waved her hand. "If I can have your attention, please." She then waited a few seconds for silence.

"Now that we have Dominique and Taylor officially on our staff we need to better define their job. Let's start fact-finding. We'll go around the table, one at a time, asking what they already know." She then turned to Savannah. "Let's get this clearly recorded."

Savannah, the staff secretary, moved the table microphone closer to Dominique and Taylor just as Gillian stepped down from the chair.

"We'll start the questions with Savannah. Then we'll move to Kevin, going around the table clockwise. Only pertinent comments or questions would be helpful." Gillian then slowly circled behind the seated students and let her staff proceed.

"What's your mission?" asked Savannah.

"To study the geological features of the canyons: rocks, sand, sediment, fossils, petroglyphs, whatever," answered Dominique.

"The entire week?" asked Kevin, the photojournalist, who sat to the right of Savannah.

"No, only three days and three nights," said Taylor, counting out three fingers on her hand.

"Location of study?" Bryce asked.

"Not sure yet. Based on past trips we're guessing some smaller canyons within the Phantom Ranch area."

"We'll find out," replied Gillian as she pointed to Bryce. "That's your job to find out. OK, who's next with a question?"

Katie raised her hand and then proceeded. "How many students?"

"Not sure—whoever turned in a permission slip. Maybe fifteen out of both classes."

"We'll find out," and again Gillian pointed this time to Katie to find the answer.

Gillian smiled, her eyes widening as the interview progressed. She continued her slow orbit around the table and looked over to the next staff member.

"Just Mr. Roeser—or are other teachers coming?" asked Jeremy, another freshman staffer.

"Not sure. We're guessing a guide or two to keep all of us out of trouble."

"I know; I'll find out," Jeremy replied, jotting down his task.

"Communications?"

"Mr. R. said that cell phones have limited use and not to count on them. He'll have radio contact with the park rangers if necessary."

"Hammocks?"

"No, tents."

"That is so cool! I wish I could go," commented Katie.

"Yeah, that sounds more fun than my spring break to Grandma's in Nebraska," added Kevin.

"Ahem, just the pertinent stuff," Gillian sternly reminded them. "We don't have much time here." She motioned for the next staff member's question.

"Food?"

"We're supposed to bring water bottles, energy bars and non-perishable foods, although Mr. R. mentioned a hot meal for dinner each day. He's bringing a bunch of provisions down by mule or boat—we're not sure which."

"I'm on it," and, of course, that particular staff member wrote it down. The questions then circled back to Savannah.

"That's what I was going to ask—about the food," she said. Gillian motioned to Kevin who shrugged off his turn.

"Anyone else?" She looked around the entire table, and was met with shaking heads. "Well, if there are no further questions, I guess we're done for now." She walked over to Savannah. "Please transcribe this and save it as a document file," Savannah nodded then grabbed the recorder and walked over to her desk to start her task.

Gillian then stood behind Dominique and Taylor while addressing the rest of the staff. "If anybody here comes up with other questions for our new stringers you can text me or just forward them to Savannah." She then tapped the backs of the girls' chairs, as if to dismiss them. "I'll get these action items over to you as soon as they are typed. Thanks for your valuable time and information."

"That's all? That's not much," commented Taylor.

"That's all for now," answered Gillian. "We're just getting this party started. This will turn into a great article. Here's how I see it." She walked away from the table towards the wall with the vertical blinds. She then turned around and faced them. "There have been books, movies, and documentaries about the Grand Canyon. But none have had the guts and glory of Sunnyslope High's finest geology students as they go against all odds of Mother Nature."

"What are you talking about?" asked Dominique. "This is just a trip to study formations and look at rocks. It's not like a journey to the center of the Earth."

Gillian smiled as if to disagree. Then she took slow steps down the narrow aisle of the Searchlight office and stopped in front of the large, framed photos of Arizona's red rocks, pine dotted cliffs, and canyon creeks which hung on the wall.

"Maybe just a field trip to you, Dominique, but not to our student body. They are going to read about a group of fearless junior geologists, who, against all odds, took on the forces of our own Grand Canyon, to discover its darkest secrets…"

"And to discover Sunnyslope's resident cuckoo bird," Taylor whispered into Dominique's ear. They both giggled as they watched Gillian continue her pitch. The rest of the staff rendered undivided attention with an occasional nod.

"Look," Gillian said, "We can turn an ordinary, uneventful field trip into a fantastic one by including the *wow factor*. By using said factor we'll make this field trip sound like the greatest adventure in the history of Sunnyslope!" The staff burst into spontaneous applause. Gillian smiled and bowed to her staff.

Then her jubilant face dropped to a more serious one. "Now, let's get started." Each staff grabbed a pencil and started jotting notes. "We'll start with a teaser that introduces the upcoming field trip. We'll use the transcription from today's interview and construct five paragraphs of information, and it needs to be finished by this afternoon's deadline. We'll include past trips and locations, any local alumni's accounts—the works."

"Should I show her the notes from my interview with Mr. R.?" Taylor whispered to Dominique.

"Sure," said her partner. "That's why you got it in the first place, right? We gotta make this legit so Mr. R. doesn't get suspicious." Taylor then showed Gillian her notebook containing Mr. Roeser's information.

Gillian quickly scanned Taylor's notes. "Stop the presses! This is it! I believe we have our first teaser!" She then turned to Taylor. "May I photocopy these?"

"Sure, as long as I'm on the byline," Taylor said while lightly punching Dominique in the arm.

"That-a-girl," Dominique whispered back to her partner.

"No, not *on the byline*," Gillian said, "but *in the story*. This article will feature *you*."

"Me?" Taylor asked tentatively. She looked at Dominique who gave her a reassuring nod. "Well, then OK."

Savannah returned from the copy machine and handed back Taylor's notebook. The new Searchlight stringers gathered their books and headed for the door.

Gillian ran ahead and opened it for them. "One of my staff will run that transcription to you later today. We know where to find you. We'll be in touch."

"Bye," said Dominique as she and Taylor exited the staffroom. As they walked along the windows, they saw Gillian's legs through the glass, scurrying towards the copy machine. Then they saw her and Savannah's legs together, obviously reading the copy of Taylor's notes. All of a sudden Gillian's high-heeled shoes went airborne a few times before scurrying back to the table. Soon two chairs were pulled out from the table then scooted back in quickly.

"Boy, the Searchlight staff is pretty intense," Dominique remarked.

"You got that right," said Taylor, agreeing with her captain.

# Chapter IX

**The Searchlight**

**...Coming in Soon...**
The Grandest Adventure of All!
By Gillian Lyght

*In three short weeks the brains and guts of Mr. Roeser's geology students will be tested as they brave the forces within the Grand Canyon. With no phone contact or electricity they'll spend three days learning how Mother Nature beat up on this bad boy to make him one of the Seven Natural Wonders of the World.*

"We will?"

*Eleven bodacious seniors will hike down with only three days' worth of provisions. Included in the expedition is none other than our own Taylor*

*Mayer, fearless co-captain of the women's volleyball team. When asked if she was prepared for the historical trip she emphatically replied in the traditional Sunnyslope spirit, "You got that right!"*

"She didn't ask me that?"

*This is the eleventh year for Mr. Roeser's trip to an area once dubbed "The Great Unknown." Our geology students will carry on the spirit of the famous 1869 Expedition led by Major John Wesley Powell. If the Major were alive today he would most certainly be proud of our budding geologists, who will be facing potentially brutal conditions. When asked about the possible dangers that could compromise life and limb, Miss Mayer's comment was remarkably casual: "You're kidding, right?" She sounds ready to face any challenge that the Great Unknown can throw at her.*

"Those pencil-eared geeks quoted me out of context!"

*Previous geology classes have hiked the Bright Angel Trail, just over nine miles, down to the Colorado River leading them to study areas near Lava Rapids, along Pipe Creek, over to Burro Springs, and upon Ribbon Falls. Past trips recorded harrowing experiences such as rafts turtling in the rapids, escaping flash floods...*

195

Taylor showed Dominique the current issue of the Searchlight, thrashing the long thin pages together. "Did you read this trash? It's like a supermarket tabloid! For one thing none of Roeser's field trips escaped flash floods," she complained.

Dominique took the paper from Taylor and quickly scanned the article that Gillian featured on the front page of the Searchlight. Next to the print was a century-old photo of early hikers scaling a cliff wall in the Grand Canyon. The photo of Taylor giving the thumbs-up gesture was inserted in the corner next to the hikers, making her look like part of the expedition!

"Well, technically the group that camped along Phantom Creek did escape a flood by a few months," answered Dominique. "Remember their trip was in May, and the creek flooded in August. So, of course, they escaped the flood. But the article is not going to mention the time factor."

By this time the whole school was reading the latest edition of the Searchlight. As Dominique and Taylor walked down the hall towards the cafeteria, several students, who already read the Searchlight article, asked Taylor to autograph their issues. She politely declined and resumed her gripe with Dominique.

"How can they print this—it's not exactly the truth," she said, cramming her issue into a side pocket of her backpack.

"That's the idea," Dominique replied. "The story sounds better when it's *embellished* a tad."

"That's a huge tad," interrupted Royce, who caught up to them while heading for lunch. He had a copy of the Searchlight in his hand. "This sounds like the trip of the century. No, maybe the millennium!" He then detected Taylor's anger and walked behind them. "Are you guys really gonna do all that guts and glory stuff?"

"Ugh, don't even get me started," grumbled Taylor as she brushed past several ninth-graders, who stared at her with admiration. She smiled back politely then resumed her angered march.

"This story is falsely painting us as some kind of modern-day Lewis and Clark Expedition!" she cried.

Royce tried to sympathize with her, but at the same time he wanted to impress her. "Not really, Taylor; Lewis and Clark charted unknown territory in a canoe down a waterway. You'll be observing canyons on foot, so technically it's more like a Hayden Expedition," he proudly stated, recalling famous American expeditions.

"Thanks for the clarification, Royce," said Taylor trying to control her temper, "but it's still not right."

Dominique stopped Taylor and yanked her inside of a doorway. Royce, not being quick enough to follow, got caught up in the flow of students and had to walk a few extra yards before weaving his way back to them.

"Look, Taylor, we'll just write the facts, see?" Dominique said. "That's all we can do. And we'll do our best to keep the Searchlight honest." Taylor paused, trying to absorb Dominique's words.

Royce finally rejoined them in the doorway. "I know you'll do the right thing." In the spirit of the moment he wrapped them both in a tight embrace causing the girls to exhale forcibly.

"Aagh! Thanks, Royce. Can we breathe now?" asked Dominique gasping for air. He then quickly released his hold, and the girls caught their breaths.

"Sorry, about that," he said. "Sometimes I don't know my own strength, especially when I hug girls. I'm usually hugging my Mom or the guys on the swim team, but you didn't really need to know that. Uh, what I really meant to say was—"

"—Thanks, again, Royce, for whatever," said Taylor.

Royce recollected his thoughts. It wasn't easy acting sophisticated, especially when he's only a freshman dog. "Well, Taylor, if Gillian Lyght doesn't write it accurately, you could always start your own travel blog," he said.

The girls looked indecisively at each other, pondering his idea. Finally Dominique answered him. "Royce, although your idea sounds tempting, it's not nice to undercut the school's exclusive rights to our story, especially since they supplied us with digital cameras and a professional journal," she said.

"We won't post anything unless we have to," said Taylor still incensed about the article. "But for now, let's just cross that creek before we get there." Royce agreed, although he wasn't sure what Taylor really meant. Dominique laughed at Taylor's mixed-up adage.

# Chapter X

*Bay-beh, yer just no good for me, Mamma sez you ain't reality...*

Desiree answered her phone. "Hey, Mom...Mom?"

*Hey, sweetie! Sorry I'm sending a voice message, but I have to prepare a lesson plan for the kids' farming class. So here's my message: the collision shop called. Your car is ready, and you can pick it up anytime. It figures—now that you're gone, ha ha! I'll see if your dad can drive me to the collision shop to pick it up. He's really been helpful lately. Hey, Royce wants you to tell Taylor that he's thinking about her. He says that the time management thing is working out great—whatever that means. Oh, and he's going up to Flagstaff for a swim meet at Northern Arizona University this weekend, so he won't be that far from her heart—isn't that romantic? OK, take care. Really. Keep your eyes on*

*the trail and your hands out of your pockets; I don't
wanna see you on the evening news. I love you. Bye.*

Desiree laughed and closed her phone. *Mom is such a
worrywart*, she thought while tucking away her phone.

This morning Desiree was tired. Being so excited about the
trip, she barely slept the night before. She spent most of it in her
room checking and double-checking her camp gear, even though it
was packed for over a week. She finally fell asleep after midnight
fully dressed in her hiking outfit.

The bus ride out of Phoenix rudely presented itself as an
ice-cold seat and a dark view through the bus window. The skies
had lightened, but the landscape was still shrouded by night.
Desiree had hoped to see the rocky cactus-dotted desert transform
into pine-covered plateaus covered with pines. But the sun still had
another hour's climb over the vast Mogollon Rim that shielded the
eastern horizon. Desiree slumped back in her seat and decided to
catch up on some sleep.

Across the aisle, Taylor, armed with her pen, book light and
school-issued journal, began writing her first entry.

*Left school at five a.m.—sheesh! Can't believe I'm
up this early. Hope to catch some zs on bus ride to
Grand Canyon.*

"Is that it?" Dominique asked, reading it from the seat right
behind her. "Aren't you gonna write anything else?"

"Nothing worth writing," answered Taylor. "But I will
when the action starts."

"Taylor, journal entries aren't always about action. You can write opinions, thoughts and analysis—like you do in your personal diary."

Taylor vehemently objected, snapping the journal closed. "Are you kidding? Personal diaries are personal, and, most importantly, they have locks. This one doesn't, remember? I'm not writing anything personal, knowing damn well that Bryce Lyght's sleazy eyeballs will be drooling all over it. Yuck, just thinking about it weirds me out."

"Then leave the color commentary to me," susggested Dominique. "We're a team, right?"

Taylor thought about her captain's offer. "OK, but make sure you sign your entry, so that everyone knows it's yours—not mine," she said, handing journal to Dominique.

"Deal," agreed her captain, taking it. "By the way, buddy, how do sleazy eyeballs drool, anyway?"

Taylor blew a raspberry before answering, "Come on, you know what I mean!"

Dominique laughed then pulled the pencil out of the journal's holder. "Hmm, how should I start this off?"

Meanwhile, Aaron and Wes were sitting in the rear-most seats across the aisle from each other. Aaron was trying to sleep on his pack, but he slipped off when the bus rolled over some uneven pavement. In aggravation he sat up, dropped his backpack to the floor and leaned across the aisle to watch Wes, who was viewing his hiking map using a flashlight.

"Dude, still looking for a pattern?" he asked in a quiet voice, not wanting Mr. Roeser, who sat in the front, to hear.

Wes sighed, and then turned to his friend. "I've looked at these stars at least a hundred times. They're all at confluences, and they're on both sides of the Colorado River. I ordered them by

201

dates, sorted by number of students—I even changed the color of the stars, and I still can't see a pattern."

Aaron got up and sat next to Wes for a better view of the map, which was tattered from all of Wes' analyses. "Hmm. Well, maybe Mr. Roeser is more systematic but in a random sort of way," said Aaron.

Confused by Aaron's comment, Wes slumped back in his seat. "Aaron, what do you mean?"

"We keep looking at the campsites as if they formed some complicated pattern," Aaron began to explain. "What if it's something stupidly simple?" He pulled the map closer. "Let's not sort by anything and just look at the big picture. The west-most point is Trinity Creek on the river's north side and Horn Creek on the south. The east-most point is Boulder Creek on the south side. With all the other stars falling in the middle of these boundaries, it looks like Mr. R. is forming a rectangular search area—with a north corner missing. I'm guessing that this corner would be farthest east on the river's north side."

Wes leaned forward to inspect the map again. "So if we were to assume that Mr. R. is forming a rectangle and the campsite has to be near a confluence…" Wes then he traced his finger from the Boulder Creek corner upward, "…then the northeast corner might just be here—Clear Creek." His finger stopped where the hiking trail ended at Clear Creek.

"That'd be my guess, too," said Aaron. "We're hiking the Clear Creek Trail and we'll camp at the confluence of Clear Creek and this other nameless drainage."

Wes quickly circled the area then popped up from his seat. "You're butt-freaking amazing, Aaron! Why couldn't I think of it before?"

"Because, you butt-hole," Aaron said, grabbing the map from Wes and throwing it across the aisle onto his own seat, "you're in love."

Wes shined his flashlight into his buddy's face. "Now where the hell did that come from?"

"From what I've seen this whole year with you and Desiree." He then grabbed Wes' flashlight and turned it off.

"Was it that obvious?" Wes asked.

"Pretty much—have you told her yet?"

"I was gonna tell her before this trip, but I didn't have the guts."

"You wuss," Aaron replied as his voice grew louder. "What do you need guts for?"

"Cause I'm butt-freakin' scared."

"You—big man on campus, Mr. All-State Varsity Swimmer—scared?"

"Yep," he admitted coolly, peering out the window. "I'd rather swim in a sea of sharks than smear my heart all over my sleeve.

Aaron wrapped an arm around his buddy's neck. "Come on, Wes, who needs guts when you're in love."

Feeling uncomfortable with the topic, Wes slipped out of his best friend's hold. "Look, I'll tell her at the end of the trip. If I tell her now, and she doesn't feel the same way, then the whole trip will be butt-awkward for me."

"You're already a butt-*head* for not telling her sooner," Aaron accidentally shouted, causing a few sleeping students to stir.

Wes tried to stifle his friend's exuberance. "Shh, Aaron, you're waking up the bus!"

Mr. Roeser suddenly appeared standing in the aisle at their seat. "Sounds like there's a whole lot of *butting* going on back here," he said.

"Aaron called me a butt-head," said Wes, as if snitching on his friend.

"I said butt-head, but I meant *blithering* butt-head," replied Aaron.

"Aaron, now that's really mean," Mr. Roeser remarked sarcastically. Then he noticed the map on Aaron seat and picked it up. The two guys watched in terror as Mr. Roeser shined his flashlight on the stickered areas of the map. The stars immediately bounced the light back on their teacher's face.

"Hey, that's mine," claimed Aaron, trying to yank it back, but his teacher held on tightly.

"Well just looky here," said Mr. Roeser, pointing to the stars. "You marked all my past trips. And over here you circled an area by Clear Creek—what's that all about?" Wes and Aaron looked at each other not knowing what to say.

"Busted," Wes mumbled to Aaron.

Aaron gulped hard while confessing to his teacher, "You never said where we were camping after Phantom Ranch. So we gathered all the info about the past trips you mentioned in class, thereby coming up with this stompin' guess. So, how'd we do?" Aaron asked.

Mr. Roeser smiled as he scratched underneath the ski cap he was wearing.

"You know, every year I try to make this field trip a mystery, and every year a student or group tries to solve it. This is the first time someone actually figured it out before we even got there."

Wes and Aaron grinned with accomplishment.

"So why the big mystery every year?" Wes asked.

"Because I'm butt-roguish," Mr. Roeser answered, chuckling at his newly created term. Then he further explained, "Most of my classes never cared where we went, while others— like yours—did. So for you I made the location a mystery, letting you have some fun trying to solve it. Makes my class more interesting, and I get more student participation." He smiled and handed back the hiking map.

"Butt-roguish," Wes remarked, using his teacher's term.

"Stompin' butt-roguish," Aaron added.

A few rows up from them, Dominique finished jotting her thoughts down in Taylor's journal.

*Our bus chugged out of the desert valley and up the steep grade to Table Mesa. Now why would somebody name a mesa—which means "table" in Spanish—Table Mesa? That means they're calling it "Table Table." Whatever!*

*Ooh, we just passed another exit sign—Bloody Basin Road. Don't think I want find out the reason for that moniker.*

*Yay for Wes and Aaron; they just discovered the location of Roeser's mysterious destination: Clear Creek! – Dominique*

# Chapter XI

*One, blue.*
*Ten, blue.*
*Ten, yellow.*
*Three, yellow.*
*Yellow, reverse.*
*Five, yellow.*
*Wild...*

"Green!"

*Seven, green.*
*Green, take two.*

"You creep!"

*Ten, green.*
*One, green.*
*Green, skip.*

"Ugh!"

*Red, skip.*
*One, red.*
*One, yellow…*

"I'm out—I win."

"What?" Candice shrieked.

"You cheated," declared Wes as he collected his losing hand and tossed it into the middle of the table.

"How did I cheat?" asked Aaron.

"You must have cheated because I was supposed to win."

"And why is that?"

"Because *I cheat*, that's why I'm supposed to win—but you didn't have to know that." The other players moaned, tossing in their cards.

"Alright. Give me the cards and I'll shuffle this time," said Candice. She stood on the bench and gathered the cards.

"Fine, but I'll deal," said Dominique. Just then the sound of shuffling feet came from behind the table.

Everyone turned to see Mr. Roeser standing behind Wes with his face glaring in the fluorescent light emitted by his large flashlight. "Guys, shouldn't you be hitting the sack?"

"Oh! Hey, Mr. R., we were just playing a friendly game of *Uno*," Aaron replied.

Mr. Roeser pointed his light at Aaron. "Friendly, huh? Sounds like it was getting downright ugly."

"Mr. R., we take our *Uno* games very seriously," said Dominique as she quickly uncapped her water bottle and sucked down a mouthful of water. She then wiped the drips from her chin and lip while forcefully slamming the bottle on the table, causing water to splash out.

Wes agreed with Dominique. "Yeah, Mr. R., sometimes our game can escalate to a full contact sport. Hey, would you like to join us?"

"No thanks," their teacher replied. "Although the offer sounds tempting. But, really, can this be the last hand, please? Tomorrow is going to be a long day, and you'll need your rest."

"Sure, boss—I mean—professor," said Taylor.

Mr. Roeser rolled back his eyes in disgust. "Miss Mayer, I am neither your boss nor your professor. I am your teacher, and regarding me as anything else only knocks points off your grade." Then he turned to the rest of the group. "Now please finish the game quietly; the other students are trying to sleep." He then headed back to his tent.

Dominique dealt this hand, and the game began.

*One, green.*
 *Green, skip.*
"Yikes!"

*Five, green.*
*Red, five.*
*Draw four, red.*

Aaron gasped. "Why, you son of a stinking slimy frog!" he cried.

"What kind of cussing is that?" Candice asked.

"The kind my Lithuanian grandma always used 'cept I can't remember the actual Lithuanian words," he answered.

"I'll bet they sounded nasty," Dominique guessed.

"Did they ever! I remember once she accidentally dropped a box on her foot and cussed like hell broke loose," Aaron replied. "I swear I saw fire spitting from her lips. You wouldn't want her playing *Uno* at this table." Everyone laughed as the hand played out a few minutes more.

Other students not in the card game were already asleep except for Sayuri. Her mind raced while her sore legs pleaded for repose. The hike down the Bright Angel Trail wasn't difficult, but her legs were now complaining from the long descent. Her thigh muscles started aching after the first couple of miles, and wearing crampons on the snow-encrusted trail only added to the discomfort.

In the past Sayuri camped often with her family, but this time she felt uneasy about doing it alone. Right now she wanted to talk with someone but was too tired and sore to join the card game. The unfamiliar sounds of the camp area pierced her tent walls like sharp arrows. The whooshing wind, the gurgling creek, and the squeaky crickets distorted the voices of her classmates. Troubled by the sounds, she wrapped her pillow completely around her head to cover both ears.

Suddenly a yell followed by the sound of thrashing bushes startled her. She held her breath, tensed her muscles and waited. The thrashing stopped, and she exhaled. She waited longer. Her body began to surrender from the overwhelming exhaustion of the day, and her mind started to purge all her troubled thoughts. She relaxed her grip on the pillow.

Then she heard a high-pitched scream followed by low-pitched moans. Her mind automatically dissected the sounds and processed them in her head for several minutes. Maybe the scream came from a girl, and the moans came from the rest of the group. She decided it wasn't worth losing sleep over and rolled to her other side. Soon just the wind, water, and cricket sounds dominated her surroundings again. Again the pillow slid off her ears.

But seconds later yells and screams simultaneously impaled her tent like a jolting shock wave. Her mind automatically analyzed the sounds as being those of pain. She waited, hoping that they, too, would go away. With the pillow she again covered her ears, then covering it with her sleeping bag. Now safely wrapped in her double-insulated cocoon, all she could hear was her pounding heart. It eventually diminished to gentle thumping and she again relaxed.

But not for long. A host of screams, this time of variable pitches, sheared through her tent. In exasperation, she refused to dissect the sounds anymore and threw off her pillow.

Sayuri sat up and fumbled for her flashlight. She crawled out of her sleeping bag and past Martina, who was sound asleep. Sayuri then pulled on her boots and grabbed her jacket. She heard several more moans as she unzipped the tent flap and crawled out. With sore muscles and disrupted sleep cycles she stumbled down the path towards the picnic table.

The card game finished with Aaron winning again. Candice again collected the cards, but this time she leaned over too far and lost her balance. She toppled over the table's corner while everyone else laughed. Candice rolled onto the ground, stopping at Sayuri's feet.

"Hey, Sayuri, what are you doing here?" Candice asked. Desiree then pointed the large lantern at Sayuri so that all could see her better.

Sayuri's face appeared pronounced and animated. Her teeth were bared and her eyes bulged. Her short black hair extended from her head in single strands, as if they were electrostatically charged.

"Aagh!" Sayuri screamed. She stared at every card player, breathing forcefully through her flaring nostrils. "Aagh!" She then extended her arms causing her otherwise petite, Japanese frame to expand like a huge bird about to take flight.

Sayuri's actions startled the card players. Candice dropped her cards. Taylor gasped, and Dominique knocked over her water bottle. The guys stood up and stared at her. The card players held their breath while waiting for Sayuri's next action.

Her charged hair jostled in the gentle evening breeze. Then she blurted, "That's all I hear! All the screams make me think horrible things are happening! I think you all get attacked or eaten by wild animals!"

Just then Martina, still wrapped in her blanket, came up from behind her tent mate. "Sayuri, why are you out here—did you have a bad dream?" she asked. Sayuri didn't respond; her eyes were still glued on the students at the table.

Candice scrambled to her feet and examined Sayuri's face, whose cheekbones, forehead and chin were brightly highlighted, leaving her eye sockets and nostrils darkly shaded.

"Wow! Her face looks like a zombie out of the *Scream* movie—except hers is so much cuter."

Desiree, who was standing next to Candice, also saw Sayuri's expression. "Poor thing; she's either having a night terror, or she heard our *Uno* game," said Desiree.

The rest of the group gathered behind Candice, who was gently holding the exchange student. "Hey, Sayuri, it's Candice. Can you hear me?"

"Sayuri, we're sorry; we didn't mean to awaken you," said Desiree, who was also trying to calm her down. "We must have sounded pretty scary from your tent." The rest of the group agreed and nodded.

Sayuri's animated face slowly lost its zombie-like character. She blinked and again, looking at each student. Her loose hair was still statically charged, but this time she was grinning.

"Well, your noises were pretty scary. And I was really hoping that wild animals ate everyone, so I could get some sleep," she confessed.

The group laughed then made rude comments about who got eaten. Wes joked about a python eating Aaron only to puke him out because of his smelly feet. Aaron was about to return another insult when Mr. Roeser again emerged from the dark. The hood of his sweat suit was tightly tied around his round, wrinkled face. He also could have passed for a zombie.

"I can see that the card game is over, but the party hasn't broken up," he said, looking at all the students. "In fact it appears to have gotten bigger."

Dominique grabbed Taylor. "We're going to make it smaller, so goodnight everybody!"

Mr. Roeser looked at the remaining ensemble. "Sayuri, you don't belong in this cut-throat group," he remarked. "Why are you and Martina out here?"

Sayuri did not want to get anyone in trouble, so she offered a clever excuse. "Ah, well, we wanted to know who won the game?" Then she and Martina gave him a contrived smile.

But Mr. Roeser wasn't buying her explanation. "I'm sure there's more to this, but it's way too late to even bother."

Sayuri turned to Martina and giggled. Then they both retreated to their tent. He watched them walk away then turned back to the rest of the group. "The rest of you folks need to clean up and retire to your tents—NOW!"

Wes saluted his teacher then hurriedly cleared the snack foods from the table. Candice collected and stacked the playing cards. Desiree walked in reconnaissance around the table, picking playing cards. A few minutes later Candice motioned to Desiree that it was time to head back to their tent.

Desiree carried the large, fluorescent lamp back to her teacher. "Guess we're all done with this," she said. But he refused it and pulled out his mini-flashlight, jamming it between his hood and neck.

"Better leave it lit on the table in case someone decides to sleepwalk, Miss Sumner," he replied. "They may want to see the creek before they stumble into it."

Desiree giggled as she replaced the lamp on the table. "Yeah, I read a book about some accidents that happened down here—like someone falling down a cliff while trying to pee in the dead of night. That and other crazy stuff that seemed too ridiculous to be true."

"Crazy stuff happens out here all the time, Miss Sumner. That's why I keep this area lit. And I make sure you're in your tents. My rules are simple but strict—for your safety. I don't want anyone getting hurt—or worse—getting in trouble with the park rangers." Then he chuckled. "You don't want to feel their wrath."

Desiree chuckled with him. "I understand," she said, switching on her flashlight and pointing it on the path. "Goodnight, Mr. Roeser."

She turned and walked back to her tent. She passed Dominique and Taylor's tent, which was still lit. Taylor was still awake, updating her journal:

*An awesome, four-hour hike down the Bright Angel Trail! So much canyon and sky! I slipped on the icy trail only three times. Well, the first one doesn't really count because it was actually before the*

*trailhead in the parking lot over a curb, that I didn't*
*see because I was watching a squirrel lick a melting*
*ice cream cone that some kid dropped...*

Mr. Roeser remained seated at the table for a few more minutes. He heard a few, muffled voices of students in the confining, two-person tents. But soon all lights went out, and the only sounds he heard were from the creek and the crickets. He knew that the students' spirits would eventually succumb to exhaustion. He then left the table and returned to his tent.

Desiree was the first to awaken the next morning. Her nostrils felt the pinch of the cool morning air as well as a slight scent of hot cocoa. It instantly took her mind back to the late-winter campouts with her folks up on the Mogollon Rim. She laid back and closed her eyes, imagining the large log cabins. They had heat and electricity but no bathroom or kitchen. Getting to those facilities involved a hike along an unpaved path that was sometimes snow-covered and other times muddy. But she tackled the challenging journey every morning as soon as she smelled the thick, chocolate aroma that permeated the thin, frosty air. The journey soon became an adventure as she learned to scale rocks, jump across potholes, and walk the logs that lay along the path.

She unzipped her sleeping bag and sat up to stretch. Her purple and pink plaid flannel pajamas still felt warm and cozy. She looked over to Candice who was still in deep slumber. Her wavy, red hair had framed her face, and the ends were tucked under her chin. Her head was tilted back, and her mouth was open, resembling a singing choir angel. Desiree giggled at the sight.

She then crawled over to the vestibule to pull on her boots. The previous day's hike left a few patches of mud in the treads, but the dry air reduced them to loose dirt balls that easily fell off when she gently tapped them together. She tucked her pants inside the boots but was in too big a hurry to tie the laces.

The aroma of cocoa grew stronger as she pulled on her jacket and cap and crawled out of the tent. She then walked to the table that had an insulated, hot beverage dispenser upon it. Mr. Roeser was sitting at the table studying his trail map. He was still wearing the same hooded sweatshirt and sweatpants from the night before, so he hadn't yet dressed for the day.

He looked up from his map when he heard her approaching. "Good morning, Miss Sumner! Did you bring your beverage cup?"

She held up her index finger as if to hit a pause button. "Oh! Oops—no, I didn't," replied Desiree, "I'll be right back." She turned and ran back to her tent. He heard her open and close a zippered bag before she reappeared on the path towards the table. "Got it right here. You explicitly told us to bring one, but I somehow assumed that the Grand Canyon provided everything, including disposable cups."

He smiled at her then looked back down at the map. "No, it does not, Miss Sumner. Getting out of the disposable mindset will take time, but after a while it will become automatic. Lucky for you we've got the Phantom Cantina this morning. They provided the hot cocoa for us this time. They even have real food we can enjoy before toughing-it out on the trail."

Desiree dispensed a steamy cup of cocoa into her insulated polycarbonate cup. "Yeah, lucky this cantina is here. So, how far is it to Clear Creek?" she asked before sipping her hot cocoa.

Mr. Roeser grunted while sipping from his cup. "I take it you were part of the solve-the-mystery location team," he said. She nodded. "Good for you. But, to answer your question, Clear Creek is not more than a half-day's hike, but just so's you know, there are no facilities there. It'll be just canyons, creeks, skies, and whatever else Mother Nature provides."

"What—no Clear Creek Cantina?" Desiree kidded.

But he thought she was serious. "Oh, come on, Miss Sumner; there's over ten thousand square miles of canyons beyond the Phantom Ranch. You don't expect a coffee shop at the turn of every trail, do you?"

Desiree sipped again from her cup while looking out at the Phantom Cantina. It was an old, but well-maintained building that was comfortably nestled within several cottonwood and box elder trees. She watched smoke waft from the chimney. Then she answered her teacher, "No, Mr. Roeser, I don't expect a coffee shop at every turn of the trail, but my mom sure does."

Mr. Roeser laughed. "You wouldn't believe how many other parents do, too. Some have even asked about automatic teller machines and laundromats. They obviously don't realize how vast and desolate this park is."

A few more students came down the path sniffing the chocolate aroma. He held up his cup, signaling the students to go get theirs. Every single student stopped and returned to their tents.

He laughed and shook his head. "But don't worry, Miss Sumner, most of the main trails are well-traveled and patrolled. We won't be as far from civilization as I'd like." He took another sip from his cup and looked down at the map. "But that's another field trip for me—not you."

The other students returned with cups and sat at Mr. Roeser's table while Desiree went back to her tent to see if Candice was awake.

When she got there, she heard some fumbling along with some grunting. "Candice, are you dressed yet?" she asked.

"Yep, just pulling on my boots," Candice replied. Then she stuck her head out of the vestibule. The dry air made her just-brushed hair burst out of the opening like licks of flames from a burning house. "Did I smell hot cocoa?"

"That you did," she answered while laughing at the sight of her tent mate's hair.

Candice tried puffing the wisps of wavy hair from her face, but to no avail. She finally pulled it all back behind her ears. "Now I can really smell the cocoa; so glad they invented the stuff for these chilly mornings." She finally climbed out and tied back her hair before joining Desiree on the path towards the liquid decadence.

Suddenly Desiree stopped her best friend. "Wait, Candice, you need your beverage cup," she said.

"Oh, yeah. That's right—no disposable cups in the Grand Canyon," said Candice, and she ran back to retrieve her cup. She pulled out a large, stainless steel commuter cup with double-action sip holes. One sipper had a small opening for fluids and the other had a large opening for chunky soups and stews.

"Wow! That's one, serious camping cup," Desiree remarked.

Candice held it up proudly for show. "My mom got this for me. She thought that having a multi-purpose cup would save space in my pack."

"But what if you want a beverage along with the stew that's in your cup?"

"No problem," Candice replied, popping off the lid and pulling out a smaller cup. "And watch this." She pulled out collapsible silverware that was rolled up in a pliable, silicone plate. "How's this for space saving?"

"Looks like something NASA developed for the International Space Station," Desiree replied, giggling. Candice then packed away her extra tableware and joined her best friend for hot cocoa.

By the time they reached the table, all eleven students had gathered. Some were sitting at the table while others sat on rocks. Desiree and Candice joined Wes and Aaron, who were seated on a log looking out at the creek. Mr. Roeser was talking with two older hikers while inspecting a trail map.

Wes pointed them out to the girls. "Those two are the trail guides, although I suspect they'll be more like prison guards," said Wes, laughing.

"We may need a few extra guards," replied Candice. "Ya never know—some of us may be stupid enough to jump off a cliff or take a dip in the river."

"I wouldn't mind dipping in the river," said Wes. "I'm sure it's cold, but I swam in some open water races before and got used to the cold."

"A cold, calm ocean—yes, but not a cold river flowing at seventy-five thousand cubic feet per second," Aaron remarked.

"That sounds massively fast," Desiree guessed.

"More like butt-furious," answered Aaron. "I read about the flow rates of the Colorado River. During the flood season it can tumble army tanks like pebbles on a shore. You don't want to swim in that."

"That sounds awesome!" exclaimed Wes.

"Sure—if it's just you and the water. Not so awesome if you're joined by tons of debris. Your soft, squishy body has no chance surviving with stuff tumbling with you. I'm talking crush, kill and destroy!"

"Oh," Wes replied meekly, picturing himself tumbling with logs and rocks. "OK, maybe not so awesome."

Just then Mr. Roeser blew his whistle. All the students migrated to his table.

Dominique remarked to Taylor. "I *so* want that whistle!"

"Ugh," Taylor replied as she rolled up her eyes. She opened her travel journal and wrote a brief passage:

*Woke up to cold morning and achy muscles. Hot cocoa made it feel better. My tent mate is already showing kleptomaniac tendencies—Taylor*

Mr. Roeser tucked the whistle back inside his hoodie and addressed the students. "Mr. Tom and Mrs. Bessie Clyde will be joining us as trail guides. They've worked the Grand Canyon for many years and can make this expedition more enjoyable. They'll be happy to answer any questions you have about the local flora and fauna as well as the park rules."

The middle-aged couple smiled at the group before checking provisions strapped to the mules. Mr. Roeser pulled up his sleeve to check his wristwatch. "You have one hour to finish breakfast, get dressed and break down camp. Then meet me right here. We will hike the Clear Creek Trail and head east towards our next camp area."

Some students mulled around the area while munching on granola bars and sipping hot cocoa. Others went to the cantina for better offerings or a chance to phone home. Candice and Desiree walked back to their tent, as did Wes and Aaron.

Desiree finished dressing while Candice packed her gear. "I like these tents; they're so beautifully simplistic," she commented to Desiree.

Aaron overheard the girls' conversation. "Yeah, once you figure out how they work," he said while dressing inside his tent.

"What—you had problems with the set-up?" Candice asked.

"A little," he admitted, stepping out of his tent. "But who didn't?"

"Well, *we* didn't," she replied.

Desiree heard the verbal jousting and came out of her tent. She knew that a challenge was to follow. Aaron tapped Wes and they both approached the girls' tent.

"Well, Miss Tent Expert, do you think you can take it down just as easily?" Aaron asked.

Desiree stood a few inches away from Wes, threw back her shoulders, tossing back her hair. "Not only can we take it down easily," poking his chest with her index finger, "but way *faster* than you two."

"Really," said Aaron standing next to Wes. "I've got a can of *Pringles* that says we're faster than you," he said, placing it on a nearby boulder.

Candice stepped up to Aaron and pushed him in the ribs with a bright orange bag. "And my bag of *Cheetos* says you aren't!" She held the snack bag up to his face then placed it next to the can of *Pringles*.

Martina and Sayuri heard the commotion and walked over to join the group.

Candice saw them approaching. "Martina, would you and Sayuri care to referee?" They both accepted the task and sat down on a nearby log between both tents. More students gathered to witness the impending competition.

Several yards away Taylor and Dominique shared a table just outside the cantina, enjoying some fresh melon. The morning sun lit up a few canyon walls with burning, red-orange hues.

"This color reminds me of the monsoon sky in late afternoon," Taylor said as she opened her journal. "I should enter that in my journal."

"I thought you wanted to write just action," said Dominique.

"Yeah, I did," Taylor admitted. "But I've been reading all my entries so far, and they're kind of boring. They need some jazz."

Dominique smiled. "Now you're starting to sound like Gillian Lyght," she remarked.

"Oh, no, I could never get that extreme," Taylor replied. She looked up at the canyon walls then over to the Phantom Cantina. "But this trip so far has so much—oh, I don't know—splendor and beauty, I guess." Then she started writing. "Who couldn't help getting emotionally pumped by all this visual stimulation?"

Dominique looked down at the current entry in Taylor's journal. Taylor was outlining the building. It was one-story with a vaulted ceiling. The walls were paved with various granite and river rocks native to the area. Taylor's pencil raced over the journal's page, outlining the structure with quick, straight lines. Then she started to scribble and scratch the texture of the roof. Finally she detailed the walls' masonry with heavy, bold curves.

"Hey, Taylor, that's pretty good," commented Dominique. "I didn't know you were good at sketching."

Suddenly a raven, looking for scraps, swooped by and perched onto the porch railing. Taylor began to sketch the large black bird. After a few minutes she colored in its body and feathers, but when she got to its eyes she stopped.

"What's wrong?" Dominique asked.

Taylor signed. "The raven's eyes have a yellow sheen, and I don't have a yellow pencil."

"Would you care to borrow mine?" a voice asked from behind them.

Both girls turned around to see a man in his early forties with a tan face and short, spiky hair. Rimless glasses framed his brown eyes. The edges of his lenses reflected the red and green hot sauce bottles that dotted his tropical shirt. His outfit suggested that he was not a hardcore hiker. He was clutching a leather pack that held various colored pencils and was offering a yellow one to Taylor.

"Do you work here?" Taylor asked.

The man paused as he searched for a humorous reply. "Only when I can't pay the check," he answered chuckling. Taylor took his pencil and continued drawing.

"Are you an artist?" Dominique asked.

"Oh, I draw a little here and there," he replied vaguely.

Just then a young couple ran up to him and interrupted the conversation. "Mr. Ybarra, I can't believe you're here!" exclaimed the man as he offered a handshake. "I'm Steve and this is my wife, Jill." The artist shook hands with both. "Your works are amazing! We have several of them at home."

His wife held out her trail map. "Can you please autograph this for us?" she asked. The artist winked back at the girls. Then he smiled and signed Jill's map. The couple thanked him and ran back to their table, ecstatic about their encounter. Mr. Ybarra laughed and introduced himself to the girls.

"OK, so maybe I am a somewhat known artist—Frank Ybarra from Phoenix," he said as he shook each girl's hand. "But I'm not here working—just on vacation with my family. Still, I never go anywhere without some of my tools. Do you mind if I watch you?"

Taylor nodded. "Not at all, Mr. Ybarra," she said, "I'd also appreciate any tips you have."

He stood behind her, watching over her shoulder as she colored in the raven's eyes. She used short strokes to outline the eyes depicting the end of the bird's short, fine facial feathers. Then she looked back at him for critique.

"No, don't stop—please continue. It looks good so far," Frank said, encouraging her. She continued, now coloring in the bird's eye, alternating the gray and the yellow pencil strokes to give the raven's eyes more depth. The artist leaned in closer, watching with fascination. His dark brown eyes intently followed every stroke she made.

"That's an interesting way to get different shades and textures with just two colors," he said. "You really gave that raven some deep-piercing eyes."

Taylor looked back at him and smiled. "Thank you, Mr. Ybarra, I wanted the raven to look, uh, ravenous," she said, giggling at her own pun.

He chuckled as he walked away. "Glad I was able to help you," he said.

"Wait, Mr. Ybarra, your pencil!" Taylor called out, holding it up.

But he refused it and waved back. "No, you keep it, and good luck with the rest of your drawings," he said, walking up the steps and through the door of the cantina. The two girls stared at him until he disappeared inside the building.

"Wow!" Dominique exclaimed as she leaned over to Taylor. "We just met a real, live artist!"

"Yeah, and I got a souvenir, too," said Taylor as she held it up as if it were a trophy. Just then they heard a whistle blast coming from their camp area.

Dominique immediately checked her watch. "Uh-oh, we've only got thirty minutes. We still need to get dressed and packed."

Taylor tucked both pencils in the journal and closed it. They both got up and ran back to the camp area, where most of the students had already finished packing.

Mr. Roeser and the tour guides were collecting tent rolls and loading them onto the mules. He then saw the two girls and motioned for them to hurry. They went to their tent and scurried in to change out of their sleeping clothes. Then they started throwing all their provisions out of the vestibule.

Candice walked by and saw the bundles tumbling out of the girls' tent. She called for Desiree, and they both came over to help.

"Get your other stuff packed," Candice instructed, munching on chips from her can of *Pringles* that she won from Aaron. "Desiree and I will break down your tent. We can do it in less than a minute."

"Yeah," said Desiree, glancing over at Wes and Aaron who were still not completely finished with their tent. "We got this down to a science."

"Thanks, you guys," said Dominique gratefully as she and Taylor quickly rolled up their sleeping bags and assembled their backpacks.

By the time Mr. Roeser blew his final whistle, all students were at the table, ready for the next leg of their journey. "We're running a little late, so let's get moving." He pointed his walking stick towards the creek. "I will take the lead and the Clydes will be follow up the rear with the mules. I hope you all used the restrooms here because there are none on the trail."

Sayuri seemed confused and whispered into Martina's ear.

Martina then raised her hand. "What if we have an emergency?" she asked. The other students laughed.

But Mr. Roeser understood her concern. "That's a good question, Martina, glad you brought it up. I'm sure other students would like to know, too. I packed a few shovels for latrine-digging," he said. "And if you need further help, please ask me or either of the Clydes. We will be happy to assist you as discreetly as possible." The students laughed again, this time including Sayuri.

Aaron walked over, wanting to help clarify the procedure. "Technically, Sayuri, there is a correct way to handle that type of emergency while on the trail," said Aaron. "It's described on the bottom of our trail map—see?" He pointed at the text on his map. "It says right here—you're supposed to dig a, well, a potty. Then you have to carry out all your—"

"—Aaron," Candice interrupted as she tapped on Aaron's shoulder, "I think the girls have the same map and can read the potty procedure."

Aaron looked up from his map, realizing that his discussion with the girls had gotten a tad gauche. "Oh, sorry. Just trying to help," he said flashing an awkward smile and rolling up his map.

Candice politely pulled him away from the girls. "But thanks for pointing out that important park procedure," she replied. She then picked up her pack and pulled her ponytail back away from her face. "Look, Aaron," she said trying to quickly change the subject, "this posse is finally moving." He responded to her hint and walked ahead of the girls.

Their teacher, carrying only his walking stick, led the group up the wide, well-trodden path leading north from the camp area. The students followed, walking in double-file as they pointed and gazed in awe at the majestic and brilliant canyon features. Some had never seen the Grand Canyon at the river level.

The sun had lit up the south- and east-facing walls, warming the entire area. Students started shedding their vests or sweaters and packed them away. Several other hiking groups were on the same path and had stopped to take in the views of the creek and bridge.

Taylor turned back and saw Frank Ybarra with his family crossing the bridge back towards the River Trail. "Will you look at the lucky stiff," she commented to Dominique. "He's just carrying a daypack. He probably stayed in one of the cabins. We should be so lucky—but no, we got all this other stuff to carry."

"We *are* lucky," said Wes. "We have the mules carrying the tents, the tools and most of the food. Our loads would be way worse without the mules."

"Yeah, but they're carrying Roeser's pack, too. That's not fair," complained Dominique.

"Look, Dominique, unless you're a geology teacher, or you have a broken leg, you'll just have to carry your own stuff." said Wes. The students nearby laughed. Dominique continued walking, muttering to herself.

Meanwhile Candice's eyes were fixed on the bright orange and red colors off the east-facing cliffs. "Hey, Aaron, any idea where we're going?" Candice asked.

"Yeah, wherever you're going," he answered.

"Great, so where is that?"

He pulled out his map. Then he pulled up his compass that was hanging from his belt. "We're heading north from the creek at a five-degree incline. This could only mean we're on the North Kaibab Trail heading towards, uh, towards—"

"—Sumner Butte," interrupted Desiree.

"No Vishnu Schist!" Wes exclaimed, taking the name of a basement rock layer in vain. He turned to Desiree. "That thing's named after you?"

Desiree laughed. "Probably not," she answered. "*Sumner* is a fairly common last name."

"They named it after John Colton Sumner, one of the guys on the first Powell Expedition," Aaron said. "But, Desiree, how did you know it was Sumner Butte?"

"From my grandpa's journal—right here, see?" She held up her grandpa's journal to show everyone behind her. A half-page sketch depicted a tall and wide butte resembling the one just off to the right of the trail. Most of the features were exactly as he drew them except the shadowing was more pronounced. "He must have drawn it earlier in the morning."

"Probably because he broke camp earlier and was not held up by clueless students," Candice commented contemptuously.

"Surely you don't mean me," said Wes, and he acted out the part of a disconsolate, little boy who just lost his kite in a tree. "Boo, hoo, hoo, woe is me! I feel like the little red engine that couldn't." He then grabbed the bottom of Aaron's T-shirt and faked a nose blow into it. Martina saw Wes' theatrics and turned away in disgust. Candice stared at Desiree with her typical, *there-he-goes-again* look.

Sayuri was curious about Wes' theatrical display. "He is kidding, yes?" she asked. Candice and Desiree both nodded. Then Sayuri turned to Martina, who was her partner on the path. "American men have no shame showing emotions."

"Apparently not," said Martina.

Just then their leader stopped the caravan and called out to the students. "You folks don't want to miss this spectacular creature." He pointed up in the sky. "See what looks like a black bird with a red head soaring way up along the cliff? It's a California condor, an endangered bird that's trying to make a comeback in these parts. It's actually quite large and can have a wing span up to nine feet." The group looked up and saw the condor circling with outstretched wings. It swooped over some of the rocks jutting out from the cliff.

Sayuri cried, "That is a beautiful bird!"

"Actually it's pretty ugly when you see it up close," replied Bessie Clyde from behind. "But we won't be scaling any cliffs to get close enough to find out." Then she smiled. "Unless, of course, you happen to be its dinner."

Sayuri turned to Martina with a worried look. "I do not want to be an ugly bird's dinner," she said.

Martina agreed. "Nor a beautiful bird's dinner," she added.

# Chapter XII

"Most of the western U.S. is enjoying a ridge of high pressure that has settled in the *Four Corners Region*," said the meteorologist, standing in front of a huge high-definition screen that displayed the boundaries of Utah, Arizona, Colorado, and New Mexico. "But with an El Niño pattern in place, we have an additional jet stream from the tropics, pumping up warm, moist air. If this collides with the cooler air, we could get some much-needed rain in this area. Unfortunately this would not be good for the skiers since it will raise the snow levels way up to nine thousand feet..."

"Uh-oh, the folks up at Snowbowl aren't gonna be happy about that," said Janelle just before she sipped some coffee. She turned away from the TV screen and walked into the kitchen. She and her son were enjoying a late, lazy Friday morning at home. Royce was still in his pajamas, sitting at the counter and eating cereal out of a large, salad bowl.

"Wish I could ski instead of swim in Flagstaff," he complained. His mom stood next to him and ran her fingers over his short hair.

"Sweetie, you don't wanna ski in the rain," she advised. "I did once when I was young. Got really wet and miserable." She then went to refill her coffee cup.

"Mom, I would already be wet and miserable in a swimming pool, knowing that I can't ski. I'd *rather* be wet and miserable while skiing. That would be so cool."

She filled her cup then stood across the counter facing him. "Cool ain't the word, honey," his mom said and further explained. "*Freezing* is a better term. It's OK being dry and cold, but when you're wet and cold your body loses heat quicker. Your circulation starts shunting blood away from your arms and legs. Your joints stiffen. Your feet and hands go numb. Heck, you can't ski anymore let alone think clearly. You get hypothermia much faster when you're wet."

Royce's eyes were glued onto the TV screen the whole time his mom was lecturing. Finally he asked, "Hey, Mom, can I get a half-day pass at Snowbowl if I get my events done early?"

She walked around the counter and noticed his focus on the TV. "You haven't heard a word I said!" She gave a sigh of frustration and refilled his orange juice glass. Then she sat at the stool next to him.

"Tell you what," she said, "you cut time in any of your morning swim events, and we'll see about driving up the hill to Snowbowl—that is, if it's not raining too badly and the lifts are still running. I can't promise they'll stay open. They will close when lightning's in the area."

"Deal!" Royce cried. Then he swung around in his stool and gave her a big, tight hug. "You're the best mom in the world!" But he accidentally pushed his juice glass into his breakfast bowl. He caught it but splashed some of the milk on his face. He shrugged his shoulders while milk dripped down his smiling lips. She rolled back her eyes and grabbed a few napkins from the dispenser.

"Just one day without a mess would be a major victory to me," she said, handing them to Royce.

"Hey, do ya think the rain will mess up Dizzy's field trip?" Royce asked as he sopped up the milky mess.

"Maybe," his mom answered, "They'll certainly have to wear rain gear. But the weather report said that the rain will be warm, so they shouldn't be too uncomfortable."

"Hope they packed a portable clothes dryer," he said.

"Sure, Royce, along with a diesel-powered generator to run the thing," she joked.

* * *

*Hiked a switchback trail up to Phantom Overlook. Steep climb, but not too tough. Took a water break as the Clydes talked about deer, squirrels and the California condor. Mr. R. talked about geology of area. —Taylor*

*The different rock layers exploded with a brilliance of red stone, limestone and blue-grey sandstone. Sure could use more of Mr. Ybarra's colored pencils! —Dominique*

"That's what the camera's for," said Taylor while reading Dominique's entry.

"Oh, yeah—the camera—I almost forgot," Dominique replied, closing the journal. Taylor was already taking photos of the

231

canyon walls including a nearby squirrel that was looking for food scraps.

Sayuri also saw the squirrel and broke off a piece of her snack bar to feed it, but Bessie Clyde quickly stopped her. "Sayuri, there's a park rule against feeding the animals," she warned.

"But he looks hungry, and this food is all-natural," argued Sayuri, pointing at the wrapper's label.

Bessie heard this argument a million times and was poised for her million-and-first explanation. "Sayuri, there are two good reasons why *Mr. Squirrel* has to get food from nature and not from visitors," she began. "The first reason, he and his friends get aggressive towards people who offer food. The second, your *all-natural* foods aren't all that natural for him, and can disrupt his digestive system. The no-feeding rule is in place to protect both you and *Mr. Squirrel*."

Bessie's explanation may have been more suitable for elementary school children, but for a foreign student still learning the culture and language, the explanation was perfectly suitable. Sayuri nodded, and then tightly wrapped up her snack.

"Thank you, Mrs. Clyde; I will keep my all-natural food and leave *Mr. Squirrel* to find his own," she replied, tucking it back into her pack. She then ran to rejoin the group, which was gathering to take in the views.

"What do you think about this spot, overlooking the Phantom Ranch?" Dominique asked Taylor. She agreed and Dominique blew her whistle.

Taylor then held up her camera. "Can we get a photo for the school newspaper?"

Mr. Roeser immediately directed the students away from any potentially dangerous edges. Wes and Aaron, being the class clowns chose to walk on their hands in front of the group.

One student from the back row noticed them. "Hey, you guys are pretty good at that." Then the student also pressed into a handstand and joined them. He was as tall as Aaron, but much more compact and muscular. The three guys circled in front of the group just in time for the photo. Then they walked off together while still on their hands. "Are you guys gymnasts or something?" the student asked.

"No, I'm just a swimmer," answered Wes, "and swimmers do this as part of our land exercises to strengthen our upper bodies. But my friend, Aaron, is not a swimmer. He does it, hoping to get buff—like me." Aaron grunted in protest and pulled Wes to the ground.

"Why you little, chitin' grit!" Wes cursed as he fell. He sat in the loose dirt and watched the shorter student. "Hey, have we ever met? Are you in first period geology?"

"No, we have never met, and *sí,* I am in first period geology. My name is Teodoro, but my friends call me *Perro de José.*" Aaron then dropped his feet to the ground, obviously confused by the student's introduction.

"*Joe's Dog?*" Aaron asked. Teodoro nodded.

"That's an interesting nickname," said Wes. "Usually nicknames are shorter."

"How did you become *Joe's Dog?*" Aaron asked.

"Well, my uncle used to have a chihuahua also called Teodoro. My little sister confused me with the dog, especially when *Tío José* would call it for dinner or a walk. I used to tease her about that. After a few years she started calling me *Perro de José* whenever she got angry with me, and the name just stuck." He then dropped his feet over his head, and with a strong push kicked back up to his feet. Aaron and Wes were amazed at Perro's agility.

"Hey, you're pretty good, Perro—can I just call you Perro?" Wes asked.

"Sure, that's what people ended up calling me anyway," he answered, clapping the dirt off his hands. Wes and Aaron then got more acquainted with Perro.

Soon after, Mr. Roeser blew his whistle and stepped upon a knee-high rock as the students gathered in front of him. "Make sure you pick up all your trash. We're moving onto the next amazing geological feature of this canyon," he announced.

Desiree stood at the scenic viewpoint while paging through her grandpa's journal. He wrote a brief entry at this point of the trail with a sketching of the river, the camp area and both bridges:

*Nice view, no artifacts worth the trouble of bending over.*

She laughed at his candor. She ran her fingers over the page and closed her eyes. She tried to picture her grandpa's writing this entry. He was obviously disappointed from not getting any *stuff* here, but at the same time he had to have been enjoying the clear sky above him, the clean air in his lungs and the magnificent features all around him. With her eyes still shut she slowly closed the journal and took a deep breath. Not since before his death had she felt so close to him. He was practically standing out in front of her. She reached out with her hand as if to touch him.

But Candice, who was standing a few yards away, thought her best friend was leaning too dangerously close to the edge. "No, Desiree, don't go any farther!" she yelled.

Dominique also noticed. "Please step back from the edge, Desiree," she pleaded.

Desiree opened her eyes and realized that she was, indeed, standing dangerously close to the edge of the cliff. "Oh, I didn't realize that I—"

"—Have lots of friends who care about you," interrupted Taylor, who stood alongside her captain. "Please, Desiree, take my hand." The rest of the students heard the pleading and walked back over to the overlook area to see Desiree being coaxed back from the edge by her friends.

"C'mon, you guys," said Desiree. "It's not what you think."

"No, Desiree, don't jump!" Candice cried reaching out for Desiree.

Wes barged through the group of girls. "No, Desiree, don't jump—let me push you," he said while wrapping his long arms around Candice and Desiree. They shrieked as he leaned them towards the edge then pulled them back. He fell to the ground with both girls falling on top of him, kicking up trail dust. Desiree dropped her journal as she tried to catch her fall. Other students laughed at the melodrama pathetically fizzling out.

Taylor framed up the three dust-ridden entangled bodies as other park visitors stepped over them without losing stride. "This is too funny, you guys," she remarked, taking pictures of the body pile.

Mr. Roeser heard the commotion and walked back to reprimand them. "All right, students, time to cut the theatrics. Wes, you and your harem are blocking the trail and holding up traffic. Move aside and let the other hikers through," he commanded.

"Sorry, Mr. Roeser," replied Wes as he pulled off the girls. "This is our first adventure together."

"And it could be your last," warned his teacher. "Most casualties here start with innocent horseplay. You have a better chance surviving a fire in the movie theatre than you do clowning around near the cliff's edge."

"Sorry, Mr. Roeser, it won't happen again," said Wes. He and the girls got up and dusted off their clothes.

Desiree then went to pick up her journal, but Mr. Roeser got to it first. "This must be yours," he said, brushing off the loose gravel. Then he inspected the front cover. "*Stuff*? Now that's an interesting title for a journal."

Desiree felt jittery about his having the journal, and she snatched it back. She then realized her rude gesture. "Oh, sorry, Mr. Roeser; you know how we girls like to protect our private stuff, especially diaries," she replied. She clutched it in her arms and managed a nervous smile.

"No problem, Miss Sumner," he replied, smiling. "I hope you didn't write too many nasty nice things about me."

"No, just nasty stuff about my so-called friends," she replied, glaring back at Wes.

Candice scrambled over to Desiree as their teacher headed to the front of the group. Both girls waited until he was out of earshot. "Wow, that was close," said Candice, holding onto her best friend while watching Mr. Roeser. "He had your grandpa's secrets in his wretched little hands."

"Don't worry, Candice, he didn't open it," assured Desiree as she turned to get her pack. "Nor did he ask much about it."

"Good thing," Candice replied, going for her own pack.

Wes got to Desiree's pack first and held it up for her. "Here, let me load you up," he offered.

"Thanks, my rough-housing prince who almost got us all killed back there," she answered, backing into the pack.

Wes adjusted her straps while softly apologizing into her ear. "Sorry; didn't mean to roll you in the dirt. But you did look like you were in a trance. The way you were reaching out made Candice think you wanted to jump. I told her you were just kidding, but she didn't believe me. When she and Dominique got involved, I thought I'd better save us all a trip to the park service psycho-ward and conjure up a theatrical scene." Then he smiled and turned her towards him. "Worked pretty well, didn't it?"

"Wes, I wasn't in a trance," she insisted while straightening her wide-brimmed hat. She reached back for her braided ponytail and pulled it over the front of her shoulder. "I was just reading my grandpa's journal. Wes, he was here on the same trail, and look," she showed him the sketch. "He was on this very spot. It's like he's with us right now!"

Wes saw the drawing then read his entry. "Well, he sure wasn't all that impressed by this spot," he said, chuckling. Then he pulled up her chin and peered into her eyes. "But *I'm impressed* by the trail dirt bringing out the color of your eyes." She promptly smacked him in the arm with her journal and let out a contrived laugh.

Aaron watched the couple together then approached Wes after they separated. "Wes, did you tell her?"

"Tell her what?" Wes asked.

"You know, what we talked about in the bus?"

Wes blew a raspberry, belittling Aaron's advice. "No, Aaron, I didn't," he replied.

"Come on, Wes, it was the perfect time, especially after your brush-with-death experience."

"We didn't brush with death—give me a break," Wes argued.

"The sooner the better," his best friend advised. "You don't want to lose her."

"I'm not going to lose her—don't be a jerk," Wes replied.

"Just saying," Aaron said.

Then Mr. Roeser's blew his whistle. Dominique blurted out a blissful moan while the rest of the group muttered random responses as they again formed a double-file line, ascending onto the Tonto Platform.

After another hour of hiking, the group stopped at a gray-colored rock layer. Mr. Roeser called out to the students; "We can take a break here while I explain to you where we are in geological time." He pointed at the path and the surrounding walls with his walking stick. "This is the Tapeats Sandstone Layer of the canyon. It's just above the Vishnu Schist, which has fascinated geologists for decades. These two layers comprise what's known as the Great Unconformity."

Aaron raised his hand to speak. "Wait, Mr. R., this is the part on our test I got a little confused."

"That you did, Aaron," Mr. Roeser said. "Your answer was about as muddy as that river down there, but perhaps you can redeem yourself now for extra points."

Aaron tried to collect his thoughts. "Really? Well, OK. Uh—"

"—Perhaps, Mr. Howard," his teacher interrupted, trying to help him, "you can start by defining the term."

Aaron nodded and continued. "Sure, I memorized the definition. The Great Unconformity is a gap in time between two rock layers—almost like more layers should have been between them. But the missing layers may have eroded away or gotten buried, hence the unconformity."

"Not bad, Aaron. That's sounds much clearer this time around," Mr. Roeser said as the other students applauded. "Does anyone remember the age of the bottom rock layer here?"

"Vishnu Schist is purported to be one-point-seven billion years," answered Dominique without hesitation. She aced this question on the test.

"Correct," said their teacher. "And who knows the age of the Tapeats Sandstone Layer?"

Perro raised his hand. "Five hundred and fifty million— give or take a few," he shouted. A few students laughed at his humorous estimation.

Pleased with the correct answers, Mr. Roeser decided to challenge them. "So—and I know this is going to take some thinking—what is the time gap between the Vishnu Schist and the Tapeats Sandstone Layer?"

Although it was a simple subtraction problem, many students weren't prepared for one involving such huge numbers. Several groans came from the students as they tried to float their decimal places.

An elderly couple, hiking from the opposite direction, heard Mr. Roeser's question. The elderly woman whispered the correct answer to Taylor, who was tracing numbers in the dirt. Taylor then blurted out the answer, repeating the woman's exact words. "One thousand, one hundred and fifty million, *honey*!" She then realized that she included the *honey* part and quickly covered her mouth.

Boisterous laughter rose from the group as well as from the mules.

"Your answer is correct Miss Mayer," said her teacher. "But tagging on words of affection doesn't get you extra points. If anything it'll get both of us in trouble with the principal."

Taylor's face turned beet-red as all the students again laughed at their teacher's comment. She laughed with them this time, and then opened her journal to sketch the Tapeats Sandstone overlaying the Vishnu Schist.

Mr. Roeser discussed more about the Great Unconformity while moving the students swiftly across the Tonto Platform. It was a great day for learning as they hiked the vast geological lab.

But the weather progressed with the day. The sunny skies gave way to high clouds offering some veiled relief to the group. They journeyed for another hour then rested for lunch at Demaray Point, where some students snacked while others practiced digging small latrines.

Just before they resumed the trek, Dominique tried getting more photos of her classmates. "Come on, Wes, smile for the camera," she pleaded, centering him in the foreground of the majestic formation—the Zoroaster Temple. "This photo would look much better if you were smiling."

"I thought I was smiling," Wes answered. He was not as concerned about the photo as he was about the skies. He looked up and saw three long clouds having the shape of flattened lenses stacked upon each other. "Looks like the weather is changing fast," he said. Then the wind suddenly shifted direction.

"Change is good," said Candice, "As long as we adjust."

"Yes, I agree," said Desiree. "We may want to keep our ponchos handy."

Everyone within earshot agreed and pulled out rain gear. Mr. Roeser, aware of the weather change, went to the back of the line and conferred with the Clydes while viewing a map.

"We're past the point of no return," Mr. Roeser informed them.

Bessie Clyde agreed. "We have to get to Clear Creek before the rain starts. We could camp in the Zoroaster Wash—just a mile ahead."

Tom Clyde paused to listen to the weather forecast on his radio. "The rain is not expected for a few more hours, so we've got time. If we hurry to the creek's descending trail, we'll have some shelter from the wind and rain."

"Camping is forbidden on this trail, so we can avoid trouble by getting there as soon as possible."

Taylor overheard their conversation and turned to Dominique. "She said trouble. I heard Mrs. Clyde say *trouble*," she said nervously.

"Trouble can mean anything," Dominique said, "like rain, flash flooding—"

"—Or, even worse, angry park rangers," Desiree said, remembering Mr. Roeser's joke back at Phantom Ranch. Then she turned to Taylor. "But don't worry; we should be OK as long as we camp in designated areas and higher than the waterways."

Taylor moved her poncho to an outside pocket of her pack. "Well, at least I'm ready for the rain," she replied. "But I'm not sure about the floods or the park rangers." Both Dominique and Desiree laughed at Taylor's unintentional joke.

The group pushed onward at a much quicker pace. The high clouds thickened, and the winds continued whipping across the plateau. Any dirt dislodged from the students' boots immediately swirled up in the air like tiny dust devils. Chinstraps were tightened and sunglasses were worn to protect against the blowing dust. Suddenly the sound of flapping wings was heard overhead.

"Look at those birds," remarked Sayuri pointing. "They try hard to fly but get nowhere."

"They're up against some pretty stiff wind," Martina replied. "They may be trying to get to their roost."

"I hope that is where we are going, too," Sayuri remarked.

The group made it down to Zoroaster Canyon and took another water break. Mr. Roeser discussed camp plans with the Clydes again before proceeding.

"So glad we got out of that wind; it was really getting annoying," he commented to the Clydes. "Hey, did any of you notice that there's no more hikers coming out of Clear Creek?"

Bessie giggled. "That's because they found out that high school seniors were coming." The three of them laughed.

Wes, who was standing nearby, walked up to his teacher. "Hey, Mr. R., is that Clear Creek?" he asked while pointing down a nearby ravine.

"Well, Mr. Ward, yes and no," answered his teacher. "It's an arm of the creek, but not the one that we want."

"Awh," Wes whined in disappointment.

Mr. Roeser chuckled. "Don't worry, Wes," he replied, "we only need to follow this ridge just a little while longer; then we'll see the creek we want. It won't be long now—I promise."

Wes relayed the information to the rest of the group, who responded cheerfully. The veiled sun disappeared behind the canyon wall giving the group a sun and wind break. This helped raise their spirits as they trudged on, following the ridge then turning north. After a few minutes they saw a creek below and to their right.

"Hey Mr. R., is that it?" Aaron asked, pointing down the canyon.

"That it is, Aaron," his teacher answered. Almost on cue the entire group let out a collective hooray, and conversations got livelier.

"Look—it's bigger and more beautiful than ever!" Wes exclaimed.

Candice moaned. "Wesley, we're not skipping to Emerald City in *The Wizard of Oz*." Desiree smiled at Candice, and the two laughed. It seemed like a long journey, but both felt better knowing it would end soon. Wes started whistling *We're off to see the Wizard,* and soon other students joined him.

The group finally made it down to the creek. It was clear but running swiftly from the recent snowmelt. The students raced down to its edge—like it was the finish line of a race.

Dominique dropped her pack and jumped upon a large snag along the water's edge. She pulled out her camera, framed up the group and called out to them. "How about a victory pose for the newspaper?"

Feeling jubilant, the group hooked up with each other. Wanting to further stand out in the pack, Candice jumped on a nearby rock. Perro saw her and likewise found a boulder on which to handstand.

"This is going to be my signature pose," he remarked. Aaron and Wes, of course had to do the same. The Clydes hitched the mules onto a tree by the water and then offered to take the group picture. Several more cameras ended up in the Clydes' hands from other students. This was the group's best photo-op ever!

Mr. Roeser let them savor the momentous occasion—but only briefly. "Alright, students, no celebrating yet; we need to find good spots to pitch tents. The weather forecast calls for rain, and we don't want to be near the creek when it rises. This area is just a little too close to the creek, and there's not enough room for all of our tents. So don't drop your proverbial anchors yet. We should hike back up the trail and look for another large clearing.

Upon hearing this, Desiree opened her grandpa's journal and quickly paged to his entries of the Clear Creek Trail. She saw a sketch of his camp area having several tree clusters growing along a flat area gently sloping down to the creek. In the background tall boulders partially obscured the descending trail.

"Hey, Mr. R.," she called out. "There could be a better spot a little farther downstream."

Mr. Roeser stopped upon hearing a useful suggestion from one of his students. "Miss Sumner, how do you know—are you sure?" The Clydes checked their own hiking map and then conferred with Mr. Roeser. They showed him the topographical features on their map.

"It's possible that there's a more level camp area about a quarter-mile downstream," said Tom Clyde, concurring with Desiree.

Mr. Roeser accepted her suggestion. "Guess we'll hike downstream and find out. If you're right, Miss Sumner, you got your *A* for the semester," he said and then blew his whistle. "Let's all head downstream!" he announced.

The Clydes untied the mules as the students filed by and proceeded downstream. In a few minutes they came upon a much larger clearing that inclined slightly from the creek. Mr. Roeser walked up the embankment and scanned the area. The ground was a mix of pebble and sand with a few larger rocks dotting the area. Inside a circle of knee-high rocks were the charred remains of a campfire—illegally built. This area was obviously used recently by other campers, who had no regard for park rules.

"Tsk, tsk," Mr. Roeser commented, looking disgustedly at the charred remains of an old campfire, "Good thing those campers are gone. They were violating park rules, giving all campers a bad name. Then he walked back to the group. "This looks like a good spot to camp. Pitch your tents up the embankment as high up as possible."

The students started unloading tents from the mules and climbed up the embankment. Candice and Desiree each grabbed an edge of their tent and looked for a level spot.

"Hey, look—there's some caves!" Candice cried as she pointed upward at several recesses in the canyon wall. "That would be a nice place to go in case it rains."

Desiree also looked up at the caves. "Yeah, but I'll bet a lot of wild animals think so, too," she said.

Candice gave an exaggerated shiver. "Ooh, not to mention spiders, mosquitoes and fleas. I keep forgetting we're in the wilderness," she said.

"And all those critters got here first, so invading their turf would not be good," replied Desiree. They circled the area directly under the caves then stopped at a level area. "OK, this looks as good a spot as any." Then both began setting up their tent.

Suddenly a gust of wind whistled through the trees and swept over the embankment. Everyone stopped to listen. A few birds flying overhead chirped their alarm of the approaching weather. The girls felt a few spits of rain. Candice looked at Desiree, and immediately both dropped to their knees to anchor their tent.

"Let's see if we can get this up faster than we did last night," said Candice.

Several more tents went up while Mr. Roeser and the Clydes were building the mules' shelter.

"Did you see the caves above our camp area?" Tom Clyde asked the geology teacher.

"Yes, I did," he replied. "We'll have to take the kids up there for a study. Maybe we'll find something interesting."

"—Like your missing ancient tribe?" Bessie Clyde asked.

"Maybe I could get lucky this year."

"Bradley, you've been searching for ten years with no luck. Do you know exactly what you're looking for?" Tom asked.

"Of course I do; a tribe wearing buckskin and fur using stone-age tools and weapons. So if I find chards of pottery, bones or even rock art, I may be on the path to finding them."

"But thousands of hikers have crawled over this area. Any evidence of your tribe may have already been destroyed or removed."

"That's why I want to search in places that are hidden from the general hiking public. Rocks shift and creeks change direction. This place is dynamic. A natural event such as a flood or rockslide could expose a cave or tunnel that houses this tribe."

"Will you ever reveal your secret mission to your students?"

"Hell no; I don't want them to think I'm a crazy old man," Bradley Roeser replied before chuckling. "Although some already think that." Then he spied two students approach and abruptly changed the subject. "No, Mr. and Mrs. Clyde, this will not be an archeological study—strictly a geological one." Then he greeted his students. "Ah, hello, girls!"

Desiree and Candice stopped in front of the group leaders. "We got our tent pitched and want to help with your shelter," said Candice.

"Great, grab a pole," said their teacher. "By the way, Desiree, thanks for the helpful advice back there." He was holding up a pole for the Clydes to secure. "We would have wasted time hiking back up the trail and would have never gotten our tents up before the rain."

Candice grabbed another pole while Desiree unrolled the tarp.

"Glad to be of help," Desiree replied. "Hey we're a class and—"

"—As a class we have to support each other!" Candice cheerfully added.

"But how did you know to hike downstream?" Bessie Clyde asked Desiree.

The student's face went blank. She frantically searched for an answer while looking at Candice for help.

Candice came up with a clever answer. "Well, you see, we both learned basic orienteering from Girl Scouts," she replied. "We saw this flatter area on the trail map and figured it was level enough for a campsite."

"Sure, but the map doesn't have that much detail. It's only a rough estimate of the elevation," argued their teacher.

"Then it must have been a lucky guess," Candice answered as she fed a nylon cord through the tarp grommet before securing it to a corner pole. "Desiree is good at lucky guesses."

Just as Candice finished speaking, Wes, Aaron and Perro ran down to the shelter. "Hey, Mr. R.," said Wes, "we're done pitching our tents. Can we help you with anything?"

Mr. Roeser smiled as he secured the last corner of the shelter with a few extra tugs of the line. "Well, we're just about done with this—thanks to your *compadres*," he answered as Desiree and Candice waved from behind him. "But you can help us with the dining shelter."

Candice tapped Desiree's shoulder. "That should be interesting," she said, then addressed her teacher again. "Ahem! Well, if there's no other use for us, then we'll just return to our tent."

The girls started walking away when Mr. Roeser called out to them. "As the matter of fact, girls, there is something else," he replied. He unstrapped a large pot from one of the mules. The girls stopped and returned to their teacher. "I'd appreciate if you two

247

could fill this pot with water from the creek. We'll need to boil more drinking water for everyone."

"Sure," said Desiree, grabbing one of the metal handles.

"Our feet are like wings," replied Candice as she grabbed the other handle. Together they ran the pot down to the creek's edge.

Meanwhile the Clydes showed the guys what to do while Mr. Roeser started assembling his camp stove.

Martina and Sayuri finished pitching their tent and ran down to help their teacher. "Can we help with something?" Sayuri asked.

"Absolutely, Sayuri, we'll need some wood to set up a wind break for the mules," he said. Then he clambered onto a rock and sniffed the air. "And right now it smells like more rain is coming, so we'd better hurry."

Two other students saw the girls gathering wood and joined them. "I'm Jeremy and this is my twin brother, Jace. Can we help you get wood?"

"Yes, please," replied Sayuri. Then she closely examined the boys' faces. "You are both in my music theory class."

"Yep," affirmed Jeremy. "And we're in band, too. We play percussion—"

"—And we've heard you play one *mother* of a cello," said Jace, finishing the sentence.

But she didn't know what they meant. "Excuse me, please, what is a *mother* cello?" Sayuri asked.

Martina laughed. "It's colloquial English—actually American descriptive—meaning that you play cello very well."

"Oh," Sayuri said to Martina then turned to the twins. "Thank you very much. You play one mother percussion, too."

They laughed at her funny-sounding compliment then got more acquainted as they walked along the creek, finding a *mother lode* of driftwood for the mule shelter.

By late afternoon a heavier cloud deck crawled across the sky. The sun dropped well behind the canyon cliffs, but intermittent cloud breaks allowed for a few yellow-orange rays to stream across the purple and blue sky.

"The sky looks so weird," commented Dominique as she and Taylor leaned over a large boulder taking in the views of their campsite. "The light seems to come from everywhere. You can't tell if it's sunrise or sunset." Taylor pulled out her journal and began to write.

> *Finally made it to Clear Creek. Took just over four hours but had several breaks for water, rest and geology. Winds shifting, and rain falling. Got our tents up, and stove lit. Sure hope there's more to eat for dinner than nuts and twigs. Hell, a bowl of hot soup would taste mighty fine right now!*

Dominique laughed while reading Taylor's entry. "Now you're giving this journal some character," she said patting Taylor on the shoulder with approval. "I knew you could do it."

Taylor then started to sketch the cliff walls. She used several geometric shapes imbedded in her long strokes to give the rock layers a faceted texture. Finally she sketched the cloudy sky using Mr. Ybarra's yellow pencil to line the sunrays.

"Too bad no artists are around to loan me a red pencil," she grumbled.

Her team captain offered some advice. "Taylor, you gotta be resourceful here," said Dominique. "Ya gotta look around and find stuff that has the colors you want." She pointed to the creek. "Look at the silt in the creek. You can probably use that to get a nice red pigment."

"Sure, but it won't stay on my page. As soon as it dries it'll crumble away."

"Then you find a resin or something really sticky," her partner answered. "Gosh, do I have to think of everything? I'm sure there's stuff like that around here, too, like pine sap or hairspray."

Taylor frowned at her partner. "Dominique, why do you always have solutions?" she complained. "Can't I ever have a problem you can't solve?"

"OK, next time—I promise," Dominique answered with a grin.

Desiree and Candice came over to the rock to join them. "There will be some clean, drinking water for you guys as soon as the pot cools down," Candice announced. Then she looked down at Taylor's drawing. "Ooh, can I see?"

"Sure," said Taylor, sliding her journal across the rock for both to see. Dominique slipped away to find her teammate some resin.

"Hey—that's pretty good!" Candice exclaimed. "I love how you got the sunrays to come from everywhere. It keeps you guessing about the time of day. Except the sky's missing something." She looked up and scanned the skies then looked down at Taylor's drawing. "Yeah, another color. Can't quite decide which one."

"I can," replied Taylor. "Red."

Desiree agreed, "Yeah, red. That would be a perfect color."

"Got any red?" Taylor asked the girls.

"No, but I have a bunch of colored pencils at home," Candice answered. Just then they heard the pebble-crunching sound of boots running towards them. They looked up and saw Dominique stopping at the boulder and pouring out a small pile of red silt from her hand.

"I scooped it from the creek's bank," said Dominique, clapping the residual dirt from her hands. Then she pulled out a small bottle of hair spritz and placed it next to the pile. "And here's your resin. Just mix and apply."

Taylor's hugged her captain. "Thanks, buddy, you're the greatest."

"Don't I always take care of my team?" Dominique asked.

The girls then watched as Taylor sprayed a small amount of hair spritz into the palm of her hand. Then she took a pinch of the red silt and placed it on top of the liquid. Using the tip of her index finger she mixed the concoction of color and dabbed a small pea-sized drop onto the drawing. Then she scrunched her face as the rest stuck on her finger.

"Ew! This is worse than bloody nose snot," Taylor remarked. She flicked her finger a few times before the rest landed on the paper. Then she tried spreading the lumpy gob.

"Now parts of your sky look like bloody-nose snot," Candice joked.

"Boy, this is gonna be tricky," said Taylor as she kept spreading the color. "Maybe I should thin it out a bit. Hey, Desiree, can you hit this with a little more spritz?" Just then a huge drop landed on her page. "Great—perfect," she said as she mixed it.

"That wasn't me," Desiree said, looking at the spray knob. "I'm still trying to figure out how to open the nozzle." She then looked up at the sky just as another big raindrop landed in one of her eyes, causing a temporary blur. "Uh-oh, the rain's here. Taylor, you'd better quit because the sky's about to unload," she warned while blinking away the blur. "Hope you got a waterproof cover for that journal."

Taylor immediately pulled out a large, gallon-sized plastic bag. "Sure do," she said, tucking the journal inside and sealing it. The journal was still open to the page she was working on, but the clear, plastic bag was big enough to accommodate the expanded size. "I brought a bunch of these from home. My parents sail on Lake Pleasant, and they swear by these bags for keeping money, phones and cameras dry." She pulled out an extra one for Desiree. "Want one for your grandpa's journal?"

Desiree gratefully accepted it. "Thanks, Taylor, that's a great idea," she said as she tucked her journal inside it. "This is wide enough to keep my journal open, too." She kept the journal open to the page about this campsite, although the area her grandpa described was slightly different:

*Wide-open area with useful trees. Almost too much driftwood to clear for my tent, but at least I don't have to hunt for firewood. The large boulder just a few yards from the water is a great place to hang clothes out to dry. The trickling waterfall higher up the bank is comforting to the ears and eyes.*

Desiree couldn't believe what she just read. "Waterfall?" Her friends heard and stopped chatting.

"There's a waterfall here?" Candice asked. "What are you talking about?" A few more heavy raindrops fell on the girls.

"We need our raingear now," Desiree advised while running to the tent. Candice ran with her still wanting to know about the waterfall.

"I'll tell you all about it when we get to our tent," Desiree answered. When they reached it she looked up at the caves, which were directly above their tents. "Candice, we had better move our tent away from here."

"But don't we want to be closer to the caves in case we need better shelter?" Candice asked. By this time the other girls arrived at their tents and were asking the same thing.

"Trust me on this," she told them. "These aren't the kind of caves we want to use when it rains."

Candice watched the guys run for rain gear. "We should tell them, too."

The girls walked over to advise the guys to move away from the caves. Word spread about a waterfall mentioned in Desiree's journal. All the students gathered by Desiree's tent. She pulled out her grandpa's journal from the front pouch of her poncho.

It was getting much darker as the heavier cloud deck creeped across the sky. Desiree reached for her flashlight and stooped down in the middle of the student huddle. More large drops of rain plopped on their raingear.

"Look," she said holding up her grandpa's journal for everyone to see. A few more flashlights lit up the page. "My grandpa described this camp area as being a shoulder-ripping stone's throw downstream from the trail's end. He also described all the same features we've got here: the trees, the driftwood—even the big boulder. But look at his sketch of this waterfall flowing from the caves."

Candice pointed to several small columns of water running down in cascades from the cave opening. "Hmm, maybe these caves drain the upper plateau during monsoon season," she guessed.

"Yeah, maybe," answered Desiree. "But he wasn't here during monsoon season. That's closer to July. Look at the date of his entry," she said pointing to the top corner of the page. "April fifteenth; that's not monsoon season."

"It's more like snowmelt season," Aaron interjected, pulling out his waterproof hiking map. "And those caves could be draining all the snowmelt from upstairs." He folded it back to the North Rim area. His eyes quickly scanned the topography and nearby trails. He turned Candice around, pushing aside her thick ponytail. He then placed his map right on her shoulder blades.

"Thanks for being the perfect-sized presentation board, Candice," he told her. She smiled back at him as he flattened the map down along her back. He then pointed to a few areas. "Look, everyone, this place is a watershed for several areas. As the matter of fact Clear Creek starts way up at the North Rim—here, and it runs several miles down to us—here," he said as his finger stopped at the end of the Clear Creek Trail. "That makes this creek a drainage for all those peaks. If they're snow-covered now then all the snow upstream from us..."

# Chapter XIII

"...Could melt considerably with warm rains," said the long-legged, blond-haired meteorologist as she passed her hand over a map of Northern Arizona. Her graphic depicted a cluster of arrows moving from the southwest colliding with a dotted line over the Utah-Arizona border. "This could result in small stream flooding as well as…"

"Don't say canyons," Janelle said to the meteorologist on the TV screen. She was sitting on a bench at a heavily varnished, hardwood table near a wooden-framed window. She sipped some coffee and swung around in her seat, looking out at the patio, which was lined with weathered picnic tables that were dripping from the rain. Down the steps of the patio she could barely see the chair lift through the drizzly fog. A tall skier wearing a dark-green parka propped up his skis against the patio railing before clunking noisily up the wooden steps.

Janelle walked to the entrance door and opened it as the skier approached. "So, how's the skiing, Royce?"

He pulled off his hood and raised his ski goggles up to his forehead. "Kind of mixed," he replied as a few drops of water ran down the sides of his face. "It's snowing on top, so the skiing is great. But as I skied down it turned into rain, and I was plowing through heavy slush."

"Sounds like real fun," his mom replied sarcastically. "Hey, do you have time to warm up with a cup of hot cocoa?"

He pulled off his gloves and unzipped his parka. "Actually I'm not that cold, but hot cocoa would still work. Let me just loosen my ski boots so I can walk better." Royce bent down, and with a few high-pitched *pings,* he popped open the top buckles of his ski boots. "There, that feels much better." He straightened up and followed his mom back to her table. He hung his wet parka on the back of his chair and laid his gloves down on the bench while his mom walked to the beverage counter for a cup of cocoa.

Royce looked around the sparsely occupied lodge. The rainy weather sent most of the local skiers home. The only ones remaining were the out-of-towners, wanting to maximize their ski time before the long drive home.

Janelle heard a young child complaining about skiing one last time with his dad. The child then smelled Janelle's cocoa and began negotiating with his dad for a cup of hot cocoa in exchange for one more ski run.

"Guess kids never grow out of the bargaining phase," she said placing the steamy hot beverage in front of Royce. "After all, that's how you got here."

"Thanks, Mom, you're the greatest," he said before taking a small sip. A dollop of whipped cream stuck to his upper lip and tip of his nose. His mom immediately grabbed her cell phone and snapped a picture before he knew what happened. She quickly closed her phone and slipped it into her fanny pack. "Hey!" he cried, "Why did you take a picture?"

"Oh, I couldn't help capturing the moment," she confessed. "Especially after your fantastic swim this morning."

Royce smiled and licked the cream from his lips. "Yeah, my coach was pretty happy, too. He didn't expect anyone to perform so well at the higher altitude."

His mom grabbed her coffee cup. "Too bad none of your swim buddies wanted to join you," she remarked then sipped some coffee. "But maybe they couldn't handle the higher altitudes."

Royce didn't hear her. His attention was on the local weather channel on TV. "Mom, they're predicting flash floods in the Grand Canyon."

Janelle looked up at the screen. A local meteorologist dressed in a long, hooded rain parka was standing at Mather Point at the Grand Canyon, pointing out at the snow-covered tops at the distant North Rim.

"Wow, even in the rain that place sure looks pretty," she commented.

The meteorologist continued, "...If this warm rain continues, it can hasten the snowmelt to possibly record-setting runoff. The National Park Service has been alerting hikers to stay away from the washes and creeks. No new backcountry permits will be issued, and hikers at all campsites have been asked to return to the South Rim as soon as possible..."

"Sure hope Taylor's not in any kind of trouble," said Royce.

"What about your sister—aren't you worried about her?" Janelle asked.

"No, she can take care of herself," he said after taking another sip of his cocoa. "She's got outdoor smarts, Ma, probably from all the stuff grandpa used to tell her." His eyes were still glued on the rain-soaked reporter. "Nope, I'm more worried about Taylor, who's never camped outdoors."

257

His mom leaned across the table towards him. "And you know all this about Taylor because—?" She wanted to know more about her baby boy, who suddenly grew up and got a girlfriend.

"Mom, we hardly see each other at school, so we text each other instead."

His mom leaned back in her seat and let out a deep sigh. "Relationships are getting so complicated these days," she remarked.

"If that's what you call it," said her son. He looked outside the window and saw the steady, relentless rain falling onto the patio. He then looked out at the empty lift line and sighed. "Dizzy told me that seniors are past primal infatuation and into sophisticated romance, but I'm too young for that stuff."

His mom smiled and reached across the table to hold her son's hands. Through his cool and damp skin she could feel a strong pulse. He managed a slight smile then held her hands tightly. She seldom gets to talk to him about life's experiences involving the opposite sex, but now she's ready.

"If you're still interested in Taylor despite your hormonal frustrations, then maybe you're already at the sophistication level," she said.

"But my hormones aren't," he admitted. "Mom, she kissed me only once, and I think I hugged her twice. We're hardly alone for more than a couple of seconds. What kind of relationship is that?"

"Well, what kind do you want?" asked his mom.

He leaned back away from the table and stared at the burning fireplace at the opposite wall. "I want more time, more flesh, more body heat, more sweat, and more passion." Then he looked back at his mom. "Just thinking of her I feel like a runaway eighteen-wheeler down a steep, mountain highway. When I'm with her I feel like an exploding pyroclastic cloud from a volcano."

His mom stared at him, amazed by his techno-Shakespearian descriptions. "Honey, your hormones may not be sophisticated but your similes certainly are."

"Similes? Huh—what?" He didn't really understand what she meant.

Then she looked soulfully into his eyes. The windows, which were streaked with condensation, pulled in the light from the snowy slope and gave her deep blue eyes a shiny glow against her tanned face. She wanted to impart some advice, but she wasn't sure it was any good. It couldn't be any better than her husband's advice because of their separation. Still, Royce needed a masculine pair of ears for listening. She laughed at her resolve, which wasn't very encouraging. She blinked her eyes a few times and finally spoke.

"Oh, never mind," she said as she tenderly patted his hands on the table. She then reached for her cell phone. "What do you say we call your dad and ask him to join us on an extended vacation here?"

"Sweet!" he cried, thumping both his hands on the edge like a pair of bongo drums. "Tell him to bring his skis!"

Just then the sound of thunder cracked right above them. One employee immediately posted a sign on the ticket office window. Royce got up to read it then dropped his head and slowly walked back to the table. His mom looked up at him for an explanation.

"The Agassiz chairlift is closed due to lightning," he said. "The weather must be getting worse." His mom got up and walked to the windowpane. With her napkin she wiped away the condensation just in time to see some lightning flashes up the mountain.

"With this storm intensifying, maybe your dad should bring his water skis instead," she said.

* * *

"Water skis? More like surfboards," said Aaron. The field trip group had gathered under the kitchen shelter and was chowing down on hot chicken soup and biscuits—compliments of their teacher—as they watched the creek flow faster. The rising water pulled several pieces of driftwood along causing them to twist and tangle forming a cataract. The once, hard-driven rain reduced to a steady drizzle that gently tapped on the vinyl roof allowing the students to converse in low voices. They were huddled around the camp stove.

"Well, one thing's for sure," said Wes after slurping up some soup. "The creek is a lot more interesting to watch than before."

"Good thing we got our tents and shelters up before things really got wet," Martina commented.

"And higher than the flooding creek," added Sayuri.

Mr. Roeser and the Clydes were huddled closely under one corner of the dinner shelter discussing possible consequences of the changing weather. Desiree and Candice listened in.

"What do you think they're planning to do?" Candice whispered as she nibbled around the crusty edge of her biscuit.

"My guess is we stay put tonight," her best friend answered. "They were smart to have us pitch our tents high above the creek's edge, and we were smart to stay clear of the caves."

Aaron was scraping noodles from the bottom of his cup. "Yeah, but they may have to move the mules' shelter up a bit— look," he said, pointing at it with his spoon. The water level was up to within a few feet of the mules, causing them to stir nervously.

Hearing the mules Mr. Roeser hurried over to the students.

"Anyone strong enough to help us move the mule shelter higher up the embankment?" he asked while putting on his wide brimmed hat.

Wes immediately set down his cup, pulled on the hood of his bright yellow poncho and followed his teacher. "He must mean me," he said, flexing his arm muscles over his head like a body builder. The other guys watched Wes then followed him to the shelter. Wes winked back at the girls who then giggled. The Clydes each guided a mule while the boys helped Mr. Roeser pull out the tie lines and carry the shelter higher towards a cluster of trees. They strapped the shelter under the branches and tied the mules loosely around the tree trunks. The rain stopped, but a gentle breeze remained.

"Thanks, guys," Mr. Roeser said as he and Mr. Clyde threw a wool blanket over each of the mules. "You each get five bonus points added to your next exam score."

After dinner Mr. Roeser discussed the day's lectures as well as night plans. It rained off and on during the course of the early evening.

"We're camped high enough from the creek for tonight, but just to be sure, keep your bags packed in case we need to make a hasty escape. The Clydes have already surveyed the area up these cliffs as well as downstream and found some even higher retreats if we need them. Stay close to your tents, and don't even think about a night stroll. If we have to move, we'll alert you with three whistle blasts."

The students were then dismissed to their tents. A full moon peeked through a foggy, cloud layer that seemed to race across the sky. It was just before twilight, but the overcast sky made it appear later.

261

As Desiree and Candice walked to their tent Mr. Roeser caught up with them. "I noticed that you folks moved your tents away from the caves," he said. "Any reason?"

"Well, ah, yes," said Desiree as she frantically searched for a reason without divulging her true source. "You see—"

"—There may be bats or other rabid creatures in there," Candice answered quickly, trying to help out Desiree with the explanation.

"You girls seem to know a great deal about this area. Are you sure you haven't been here before?" Both Desiree and Candice began to feel uneasy about his pressing questions.

"Well, my grandpa used to tell me stories about his canyon trips," Desiree confessed. "He told me about water trickling from the caves, so I'm guessing that having tents parked below them was probably a bad idea."

Mr. Roeser thought for a second before punching himself lightly in the forehead. "Why, yes, of course," he replied. "The cave could be the outlet of an underground spring! I should have thought of that." Then he looked directly at Desiree. "Your grandfather was Joe Sumner, right? Didn't he die a few years back?"

Desiree nodded, although she was struck by what her teacher knew. "How did you know my Grandpa Sumner?"

The low rain cloud thinned slightly revealing more of the full moon. It lit the top of their teacher's hat but his face remained in the shadow. "Your grandpa Joe and I go way back. We used to hike the canyons together. I went for the geology and he went for the junk."

"You're kidding!" Desiree cried. She couldn't believe what she was hearing.

"Don't get me wrong, Miss Sumner; he collected junk in a good way," he said with a chuckle. "Your grandfather was actually a collector of canyon antiquities—at least that was how he described it. He was hoping to find something historical like John Wesley Powell's sunken barometer, or Teddy Roosevelt's lost cuff link. He'd hike with me carrying an oversized backpack in case he found anything. Sometimes his backpack was full. I thought he was crazy for trying to carry out such a heavy load."

"He always brought back souvenirs for me," she said. "When I was five, he gave me a complete set of tin dinnerware. I used it for tea parties with my dolls."

"That set was probably used by campers way back in the sixties. Guess that's why your grandpa considered that stuff valuable." Out of respect he removed his hat, and Desiree could see the moonlight cast upon the sincerity of his face. "I never realized that he brought stuff back for you. I am truly sorry for your loss."

She smiled at her teacher while Candice leaned onto her arm. "Thank you for your kind words," said Desiree. She felt much better about Mr. Roeser now. *He can't be that devious if he says nice things about Grandpa,* she thought.

"Well, my tent is on the other side of the cave, so I'll part with you here," he said.

"Good night, Mr. Roeser," said both girls.

He looked up at the sky. More dark clouds appeared, stretching like fingers across the moon. "Let's hope it stays both safe and dry," he said, putting on his hat while walking away.

Candice watched him until he disappeared in the canyon shadows then turned to her best friend. "He sounded worried," she said.

"He'd be crazy if he wasn't," replied Desiree. "It makes me feel better knowing that he is."

"Not me," disagreed Candice. "I'd feel less worried if he sounded less worried."

"Yeah, but this is one worried teacher who seems to really care about us. We are lucky to have him and the Clydes with us on this trip."

All the girls' tents were arranged like the spokes of a bike with their openings together in the middle like a hub. Candice went inside her tent and lay on top of her sleeping bag. After getting her toiletry bag, Desiree stepped out briefly to brush her teeth and use the latrine.

At this time the rain wasn't steadily falling; only a few drops would occasionally tap on the tent tops. However, the rushing water of the creek now drowned out any campsite sounds. Candice was feeling a little nervous while lying on her back and staring up at the roof. She took a deep breath and exhaled loudly.

Martina heard Candice's uneasiness and called out, "Are you OK, Candice?"

Candice stammered her reply, "I-I'm fine. Why?"

"You don't sound fine. Are you worried about the weather?"

"A l-little. Aren't y-you?"

Just then a voice came from the adjacent tent. "We all are, Candice," said Dominique. "But maybe you can busy yourself with playing cards or reading."

"What are you guys doing?" Candice asked.

"Well, I'm reading one of my favorite Agatha Christie books, *The Mystery of the Blue Train*," answered Dominique.

"One of your favorites? So that means you already read it, right?" Candice asked.

"Of course," Dominique answered.

"So you know who done it, right?"

"Sure do, but the first time I read it I didn't know until the end."

"Then why do you keep reading it over and over again?"

"Because, Candice, it's a masterpiece! I love when I can enjoy a masterpiece slowly—page by page. It's like looking at a painting inch by inch. Lets me appreciate it longer."

"Same reason why I read *Great Expectations* by Charles Dickens over and over again," said Taylor, cutting into the conversation.

"Me too, Candice," said Desiree, who suddenly appeared at the vestibule. "I can read Shakespeare's plays over and over again." She crawled in and explained further. "I get immersed almost like I'm a character in one of his plays. Reading Shakespeare slows my heart rate and calms me when I'm sad or upset." She pulled off her boots, tucked away her toothbrush, got her book and crawled onto her sleeping bag.

Taylor thought it was a great time to coax her classmates into some friendly competition. "OK, so we've all got our favorite books, and we've read them enough to have them practically memorized, right?"

Dominique and Desiree both agreed.

"So, how about we play a game of literary banter using the books we've got right now?"

"Literary banter?" Candice asked.

"Yes, it's a game where every player tries to make sensible conversation by quoting from their favorite book," explained Taylor. "Desiree, did you bring a book?"

"Of course—I have *Macbeth*," she replied.

"Great! Dominique has her *Mystery of the Blue Train*, and I've got *Great Expectations*."

"Awh," Candice whined. "I don't have a book."

"That's OK, Candice, you can read from mine," Desiree said, sliding it closer to her tent mate.

"But I don't know that much about Shakespeare—"

"—But I do. I'll find the passage and you can read it," said Desiree. "Besides, reading the lines is the most fun part anyway."

"OK," agreed Candice.

"All right then," said Taylor clicking on her flashlight and grabbing her book, "we'll start this little game with Desiree, and whatever order you start in you have to remain. No quoting out of turn."

All agreed, and Desiree began. *"Is this a dagger I see before me, the handle toward my hand?"*

Taylor turned a few pages in her Dickens' book and giggled before her reply. *"Oh, don't cut my throat, Sir...pray, don't do it, sir!"*

Candice laughed. "That's funny—it sounds like Dickens was talking to Shakespeare."

"That's the point, Candice," said Taylor, who then addressed her tent partner, "You're turn, Captain."

Dominique fanned the pages of her Agatha Christie book and found a response. *"Have no fears, I will discover the truth."*

It was Desiree's turn again, but this time she let Candice quote Shakespeare. *"I have done the deed. Didst thou not hear the noise?"*

Then it was Taylor turn again. *"Hold that noise...or I'll knock your head off!"* Loud laughter came from all three tents because the banter between characters humorously made sense!

Dominique's turn came up again. *"You agree, Monsieur, with this view?"*

Then Desiree replied, *"I dare do all that may become a man; who dares do more is none."*

266

*"What's in the bottle, boy?"*

*"No gentleman is happy unless he drinks something with his meal."*

*"What three things does drink especially provoke?"* asked Candice, quoting from Desiree's book.

*"The heartaches, the despairs, the jealousies,"* answered Dominique.

But Desiree interrupted. "Wait, Dominique, you're out of order; it's supposed to be Taylor's turn."

"But mine is a perfect reply to *Macbeth*'s question," Dominique contested.

"Rules are rules; we don't go out of order," Desiree replied. "OK, Taylor, what is Dickens' reply?"

Taylor madly flipped the pages of her book and accidentally ripped one of them. "Just give me a second," she said. "Oh, I got one. OK, read your question again."

Candice repeated her *Macbeth* question, *"What three things does drink especially provoke?"*

Taylor giggled before answering, *"...Ooze, and slime and other dregs of tide."* She clapped loudly and cheered. The others— including Martina and Sayuri—also laughed.

Candice felt better because the game took her mind off the rain. "Hey, this is fun! We should do this more often," she said.

"Sure, Candice, who's your favorite author?" Dominique asked.

Before Candice could answer, a loud splash of water hit the rocks seemingly just outside the tents.

Candice quickly jumped to her knees, accidentally knocking *Macbeth* off Desiree's pillow. "Did you guys hear that?" Everyone paused and listened.

Finally Taylor answered, "It sounds like someone is either taking a shower or pissing like a racehorse."

"I hear it too, Candice," Martina called out from her tent. "Do you think the water is rising from the creek?"

Desiree returned *Macbeth* to her pillow, crawled over to the vestibule and pulled on her boots. "I sure hope not," she said. "I'm going to find out."

"Not without me; I'm going with you," said Candice. They both pulled on their rain ponchos and crawled out of their tent.

"Be extra-mother careful," cautioned Sayuri.

Candice and Desiree giggled at Sayuri's remark but reassured their Japanese friend.

"Don't worry, Sayuri; we will," Candice replied as she and Desiree stepped slowly down the embankment. They shined their flashlights just a few yards ahead of their feet, anticipating the rising water. They passed the dinner tarp, which was still illuminated by Mr. Roeser's large lantern.

Some long thin clouds striped the moon, but the girls could see most of the trees and cliffs as well as the glistening of the creek. They proceeded cautiously down to the water's edge.

"Look at the area where they first tied the mules," said Desiree, shining her light onto a cluster of trees. Water was already flowing over the trees' roots.

"The creek level sure rose fast," said Candice. "But that's not the sound I heard up by our tent." Then she turned around and looked up towards the caves. "Look, Desiree!"

"I see it," replied Desiree, turning around and looking upward.

The clouds suddenly parted like a stage curtain allowing the moon to fully shine onto the precipice tops. Then their eyes scanned down the cave walls. They saw flickering specks of light falling like tiny diamonds onto the pebbles.

"It's your grandpa's waterfall!" Candice exclaimed, turning to Desiree for confirmation. But Desiree just stood gazing in awe at the sight. She pulled her Grandpa's journal out and shined her flashlight on the page opened to his sketch.

"My grandpa sure helped us out tonight," she said. "He saved us from one terribly soaked slumber."

"At least we don't have to walk too far for a shower," said Candice. They pointed their flashlights down the waterfall to the embankment where it split at the large boulder and rippled around it. "Well, isn't that's just great; the waterfall split our camp right down the middle."

Soon they heard footsteps approaching. Candice spotted Wes and Aaron on the other side of the streaming water.

"OK, who left the faucet running?" Wes asked. "Mr. Roeser will be so pissed."

"And he'll take away all our bonus points," Aaron said, laughing. He then started to step into the stream of water.

"Careful, Aaron," warned Candice. "You don't know how strong the current is."

"So, Candice, you really do care about me, huh? Well, don't you worry your pretty little head," said Aaron. He kept his weight on his back foot while carefully stepping into the stream. It was only a few inches deep and a few yards wide, but the incline of the embankment made it flow rapidly.

Wes followed Aaron closely, ready to retrieve him if necessary. The small river rocks made each of his steps shaky, but Aaron changed weight slowly onto the forward foot until he regained his balance. The water curled and rolled over his rubber-topped boots as the girls aimed their flashlight beams on each one.

Wes backed off and let Aaron proceed unaccompanied. Then after another slow step he unexpectedly lurched sideways as if caught by the flow.

Both Candice and Desiree shrieked as they reached for him. He straightened up then dashed across and dove into Candice's arms. His force tilted her backwards, but he pulled her upright and held onto her. Her wavy, red hair flew forward over both their heads. He laughed as he pulled her hair back behind her shoulders.

"Just kidding, it wasn't that bad," he said.

Candice caught her breath, stepped back and patted down her hair. "Aaron, don't you ever do that again," she sternly warned. "You *so* had me scared."

He smiled as he pulled her in his arms again. "I love the look on your face when you're both mad and scared at the same time," he said.

Desiree laughed while watching Wes cross the creek. He tried the same theatrics, but no one fell for it. As Desiree reached out for him, her journal dropped into the water.

She immediately shrieked. "Wes, my journal!"

He was still midstream when he turned to follow the plastic bag flowing down towards the creek. Being just out of reach he started to run after it but splashed water up his pant legs.

"Ugh, now I'm all wet. Geez, that water's cold!" He stepped back towards dry land on the opposite side. "I'll try to catch it from this end. Desiree, you follow it at your end in case it drifts your way." She agreed and ran after it.

The flow pushed the journal down the embankment in surges. A few times it momentarily washed upon the pebbles only to get picked up into the current again. It reached the boulder and flowed around Desiree's side of it then swirled into the creek. Desiree followed it for what seemed a few yards downstream. She lunged into the water and plucked out the journal. She shook the excess water from its plastic jacket and pulled it in close to her heart.

"It's so good to have you back, Grandpa," she cried with relief. Then she turned back towards Wes and yelled, "I got it! It started swimming away, but I got it."

Wes didn't answer. Instead she saw a tall, dark figure parallel the creek and continue downstream. She followed it, calling out again.

"Wes, you can stop looking now...Wes?"

The dark figure disappeared into the trees. Desiree stopped and looked upstream. She could hear voices calling, but the exact words were swallowed up in the splashes and whooshes of the water.

She yelled back at the dark figure. "Wes, you can stop screwing around now. Everyone is looking for us. The game is over." She walked along the bank towards the cluster of trees. She tucked her journal in her poncho pocket and took a deep breath before stepping into the wooded area. She pointed her flashlight to the ground ahead of her and carefully walked past some branches. One branch from an old snag scratched her left arm just below the shoulder, tearing the sleeve of her poncho.

"Ow—you little unchin-snouted nut-hook," she cried while rubbing her arm. She then felt wetness on her fingers. She pointed her flashlight at them and saw blood. "This so sucks! C'mon, Wes, let's go back!" Then she heard the branches shake a few yards ahead.

She figured Wes was playing hide-and-seek, and wasn't going to quit until she found him. She played along, but instead of paralleling the creek, she turned and hiked up the bank, hoping to intercept him in an end-around pattern. She soon emerged from the trees and came upon several large boulders, which she climbed.

The moon lit the evening sky enough for her to see all of the surfaces she had to reach. After jumping across the tops of a few more boulders, she then saw the creek and headed back downstream. She could see a clearing ahead, and at the same time a lurking figure that kept looking back for her. She smiled and jumped off the rock, landing on a softer surface.

*This should make my approach to Wes quieter*, she thought peering out from the rock. She saw the dark figure walking up from the creek. She followed, keeping cover behind the rocks. He walked at a slower pace towards the cliff. This was her chance to catch him while he was still out in the open. She slipped out of the last rock about ten yards away from him and jumped out behind him. She was just about to tag him when he turned around. She startled him, and he jumped while grunting loudly. She laughed and shined her flashlight on his face.

"The game is over, Wes. You lose!" she cried victoriously. But it wasn't Wes. "Oh!" Desiree cried, her smile dropping onto the silt along with her flashlight.

The stranger stood a bit taller than Wes and had much longer hair that hung wildly in dreadlocks. The man was wearing a dark wool poncho; not the bright yellow rain poncho that Wes wore.

She quickly picked up her flashlight and again shined it in his face. It appeared more weathered and wrinkled like that of someone ten years older than Wes. She then shined her flashlight at the bow and quiver that was strapped over his shoulder. He growled at her and she shrieked.

"You're not Wes; he doesn't carry hunting weapons," she said as she kept backing away while rubbing her injured arm. She felt it starting to burn but managed a quick apology to the stranger before turning and running back towards the creek.

He followed her, keeping a short distance between them.

She ran along the swollen creek back to the trees. She glanced back to see if the stranger was following. The burning in her arm radiated to her neck. Before reaching the trees she stepped into water. Its level was higher than before! She sidestepped it and climbed higher up the bank, but it was also underwater! She decided to run through the wet, wooded area.

She started to panic. Her breathing quickened, and her side muscles spasmed. She stopped at a tree and held on to catch her breath. She now felt the cold water flowing into her boots. The creek was still rising!

*Keep moving, Desiree, you've been in situations worse than this,* she thought. Her mind flashed back to the *I Love Lucy* television show. *It sure would be nice to have firemen rescue me like they did Lucy and Ethel,* she thought. Then she heard water splashing. She tried to look back, but her neck muscles cramped. She couldn't hold onto the tree anymore, and her grip of the tree trunk loosened.

\* \* \*

"Where did you lose sight of her?" Mr. Roeser asked the students, who were huddled together under the dining tarp.

"Where the waterfall flowed into the creek," answered Wes.

"You mean *confluence* don't you?" Aaron whispered to Wes.

"Ugh, Aaron, not now," Wes replied in frustration.

"Any idea which way she went?" Mr. Roeser asked.

"She was chasing her journal, that fell in the water—thanks to Wes," said Candice, glaring at him. Mr. Roeser huddled with the Clydes to discuss the situation. Wes looked back at Candice then slowly walked towards the creek.

Sayuri pulled Candice aside. "Candice, he does not need guilt with his grief right now."

Candice agreed and ran down to Wes. "I'm sorry, Wes, I was angry and didn't mean to say those stupid words."

He held her hands firmly. "But Candice, you're right; it is my fault. I was clowning around and shouldn't have been."

Candice got on her tiptoes and grabbed his poncho at the neckline. "It's not entirely your fault, Wes," she said. "I talked her into coming with me to the creek, so it's my fault, too. But, you know, finger pointing isn't going to bring her back. We need to be a team again. We need your leadership and your wits."

She was right.

He took a deep breath and slowly paced a few steps in front of her. "I have a confession to make, Candice. I've really enjoyed being with Desiree this past year. But now it's turning into more than fun and laughs." He turned back to her. "I love her, and I never got a chance to tell her."

Aaron came up alongside Candice and took her hand. Candice smiled at Aaron but then turned back to Wes. "I'm sure she already knows that, Wes."

Aaron, knowing exactly what was being discussed, nodded in agreement. "Wes, remember what we talked about on the bus and on the trail—about how you were going to wait until the end of the trip? Big mistake."

Wes looked at them both. He thought about what each had said. He then thought about Desiree. Her images passed through his mind like a digital picture frame—her smiling face, her long brown hair, the doughnut jelly on her nose, her face and his together in the mirror. All these thoughts and feelings overwhelmed him. He fell to his knees in the sand. With his fists clenched he yelled at the top of his voice, which echoed off the canyon walls. He put his hands on his thighs and leaned over as if the pit of his stomach imploded. Aaron and Candice both kneeled on either side of Wes and embraced him. Wes pulled out his long arms and hooked onto their shoulders. It was a sad and frustrating moment for Wes.

Finally Candice spoke up. "So, Wes, what do you think? Is your love for her strong enough to set up a rescue mission?"

Candice made sense.

A tear ran down one of his cheeks. He quickly wiped it away, knowing that he needed to focus on getting Desiree back. He grabbed Candice's head and kissed it.

"Yeah, you're right. I think it's time we save Dizzy from the wrath of the canyon," he decided.

Feeling Wes' spirit Candice jumped energetically to her feet. "Now that's the Wes I know and love!"

He slowly got up, and pulled Aaron up with him. "You were right, Aaron, I lost her before I got a chance to tell her," Wes said, sniffling slightly.

As the two guys walked back to the group, Aaron scolded his best friend. "So, Wes, next time I give you good advice, please act on it right away." Wes laughed and jokingly pushed him away. They joined the other students who were waiting under the shelter.

"You OK, Wes?" Taylor asked.

Wes paused briefly before answering her and the rest of the group. "Candice is right—it's my fault Desiree is missing. So I take full responsibility for her disappearance."

Aaron stepped forward. "Wes, it was my fault, too. I started the whole cross-the-stream-adventure."

Perro then stepped forward from the group. "Well, I had nothing to do with anything, but I'm part of the group, so I have to share the blame."

Martina and Sayuri both stepped forward grabbing Jeremy and Jace. "We do, too," they declared.

Dominique and Taylor both looked at each other, wondering what to say. Then they finally stepped forward. "We don't want to share blame, but we do want to help with the rescue," said Dominique as she put her arm around Taylor.

"You got that right," agreed Taylor.

Mr. Roeser and the Clydes then gathered the students under the tarp. The Clydes open their map on top of the table, and the students encircled it, illuminating the map with their flashlights.

Mr. Roeser pointed to the area they were currently located then ran his finger southward. "There are some wide embankments farther downstream, but with the rising creek the path to them may already be underwater," he explained.

"We will definitely be wading past this first escarpment," Tom Clyde advised.

"Maybe you can bridge it or place some stepping rocks into the water," suggested Dominique. Just then one of the mules from the shelter brayed seemingly in response to her suggestion.

Mr. Roeser looked at the mules then got an idea. "Of course—the mules, that's it!" Then he addressed the Clydes. "We can use the mules to wade the students across the water."

"What—you want us to ride on *those* things?" asked Taylor.

Aaron laughed at her. "That's their job, Taylor. They're beasts of burden," he said.

"Yeah, they were born to carry heavy loads—*chicas* included," added Perro. Everyone else laughed. Taylor then blushed with embarrassment.

276

"Miss Mayer, if you won't ride on a mule then you'll either have to swim past the escarpment or stay here at the campsite," replied Mr. Roeser.

"Sorry, Mr. R., as you can tell, I don't get out much," she admitted.

Dominique laughed and lightly punched her teammate in the arm.

Mr. Roeser also laughed, but then became very somber. "We'll use the mules to carry everyone past the first escarpment, and then once on the other side, we'll break into three search groups. Miss Sumner may simply be stuck on the other side waiting for the water level to drop. She couldn't have gone too far away if she's still on foot."

"That's what worries me," Dominique said to Taylor.

"What's worries you?" Taylor asked.

"*If* she's still on foot," Dominique answered.

# Chapter XIV

The stranger caught Desiree under her arms just before she fell into the water. He easily scooped her up into his strong arms. Her chest muscles cramped, forcing her to exhale loudly. He felt her body tremble as he waded quickly downstream, kicking the cold water ahead of him like the bow waves of a motorboat. He was fairly tall, so the water barely came up to his knees.

Carefully avoiding any long branches, he dodged and ducked the trees until he reached the embankment. After carrying her a few yards up from the creek, he then stooped and carefully lowered her to the ground. She groaned as he sat on his heels and positioned her head gently onto his thighs just above his knees.

He saw a faint trail of blood mixed with water running down her left arm and over her wristwatch. He pulled away the poncho sleeve and saw a long scratch between her shoulder and elbow that was smeared with coagulated blood. He lightly ran his fingers across the scratch, assessing that it was not bleeding badly. Puzzled by her condition, he then brushed the hair from her face and felt her forehead, jaw and neck. She was not burning with fever.

Desiree closed her eyes. The stranger's hand felt rough as it brushed across her skin. But it reminded her of the time she had the flu in fourth grade. She remembered lying in her bed and feeling woozy from a high fever until she felt her dad's hand stroking her forehead. He also had rough hands from working outdoors in the dry, desert climate. But his touch somehow drained her wooziness like a magical, healing wand. Then she remembered looking at his smiling face. His crystal blue eyes would shrink to slits by his grinning eyelids. Only then did she know that everything would be all right. How she wished to be sick at home with him at her bedside!

Desiree then opened her eyes. She was not at home in bed but on the bank of a flooding creek with her head propped up by the knees of a stranger. She looked up to see a silhouetted face hanging upside down with moonlight streaking through the stranger's knotted hair.

"If you're not my dad then you must be Wes wearing a Jamaican wig," she mumbled. Realizing that neither was the case, she gasped in fear. He covered her mouth gently with his hand and spoke to her in a soft, deep voice.

"As a great and ruthless hunter of this canyon, I see no honor in capturing prey that was not wounded by my hand."

His words at first confused her. They seemed threatening yet merciful. They reminded her of the last chess game she had against Candice. Still trembling, she pulled his hand from her mouth, telling him the same thing she told Candice after losing the chess match.

"You may, indeed, be a great and ruthless hunter, but I admire your integrity," she said, then turned away, cramping and losing her breath. A few wisps of her long hair fell back over her face.

The stranger accepted her compliment with a grunt of pleasure. She will not be his captured prize tonight. Instead she was his grateful but injured responsibility. He brushed back the wisps from her face. She again felt his gentleness, but unlike her dad's magical touch, her symptoms remained.

"Maybe I should not be so ruthless right now," he said. "What is your name?"

She sensed more benignity from him this time. Maybe he was not trying to be threatening at all. "My name is Desiree—but my friends call me Dizzy," she said through her clenched teeth. "And does my captor have a name?"

"Enrique is my birth name, but around here I am known as Naturale."

Now feeling less fearful, Desiree searched for his eyes. "To me Enrique sounds more honorable than Naturale," she said, then turned away to retch.

Two more hunters approached Naturale and teased him. "We saw her surprise you from behind," said the first hunter.

"Guess the prey caught the hunter this time," chuckled the second.

Feeling irritated, Naturale grunted. "Maybe so, but now is not the time to poke fun. This woman is not breathing well and trembles from a strange sickness. We must get her to the cave for medical help," he said.

The first hunter disagreed. "Medical help perhaps, but not in the cave—you know the rules."

Naturale showed them Desiree's wound. "She cannot stay here," he argued. "She has an illness that makes her legs weak. Her muscles have no control, and she cannot breathe well. The rising creek has cut her off from her group. It may take them hours to find her. She may not survive that long."

The second hunter acted as an arbitrator. "We can always carry her back to her campsite," he proposed.

"But our medicine is much better than theirs," Naturale argued further.

"If you decide to take her to the cave, Naturale, then she is your responsibility," the second hunter decided.

"So it shall be, but you must help me," Naturale said.

The other two agreed then dispersed to find branches for a carrier. They found a few long ones and weaved them together, forming a crude stretcher. Naturale removed his bow and quiver then pulled off his poncho and laid it across the stretcher. The hunters then placed Desiree on it.

They carried her up a narrow switchback to a crag that jutted partially out over the creek. Water sprang from a group of rocks just above the trail and trickled over the rocks.

The hunters ducked behind it and entered a narrow passageway. Desiree twisted and squirmed in the stretcher as the hunters bounded over several, knee-high rocks. Then suddenly some of the branches cracked under her weight.

Naturale commanded them to stop. "I will carry her myself," he said. They stopped and lowered Desiree to the ground. The first hunter proceeded ahead towards a dimly lit passageway. The second hunter pulled Desiree off the stretcher while Naturale retrieved his poncho. After slipping it back on, he scooped Desiree up in his arms and followed the first hunter. With one of the branches of the stretcher the second hunter moved a large stone across the entrance.

They proceeded down a narrow passageway that was lit by two small torches mounted on the wall. The first hunter grabbed one and descended with Naturale following closely behind. The

281

second hunter grabbed the last torch and followed Naturale. The flames dimly flickered against the high walls.

While cradled in Naturale's arms she tried to look past his face for a ceiling. But all she could see were the walls reaching endlessly into the dark. *We must be traveling along the bottom of a deep crevasse*, she thought. She could see the shimmer of water seeping through some of the cracks and streaming down both walls eventually being collected in waist-high gutters that appeared to be chipped out of the wall. She could hear the water dripping and flowing over the irregular bottom.

Suddenly another strong back spasm caused Desiree to arch backward. Naturale lost his grip, and she fell headfirst towards the rocky ground. With quick reflexes he managed to hook onto one of her elbows, slowing her fall. She ended up lying on the rocks relatively unharmed.

She tried to explain her difficulty. "S-sorry—"

"—You can't help it. I know," Naturale said, interrupting her. "I realize that your spasms are uncontrollable."

He picked her back up and adjusted his grip. As they continued through the crevasse Desiree could feel Naturale's rib and arm muscles contract and relax with each of her sudden jerks as he tried to maintain a firm hold. He could feel her breaths getting more shallow as if a snake were constricting her rib cage tighter with each exhale. Naturale motioned for a torch from the first hunter, who held it close to her face. She was panting so rapidly through her mouth, that the saliva was thickening into threads between her lips.

"Her breathing is getting worse; we must hurry," he said. They quickened their pace, hurdling rocks and dodging low ledges. Soon they entered a larger area of the crevasse, and the second hunter ran ahead to announce their entrance.

Desiree could see a few small fires; some with seating around them while others with tall wooden racks set up alongside them. Two smaller figures—appearing to be youngsters were seated at the closest fire. When they saw Desiree they ran over, inspecting her face closely.

Naturale showed them Desiree's wounded arm. One of the youngsters then pointed to a wooden pallet, which stood about four feet from the floor. Stretched across and secured to its frame was a large animal hide.

The other youngster unfolded a wool blanket over the hide just before Naturale laid Desiree upon it. Despite her tremors Desiree could feel warmth and softness of the pallet as well as its rich, earthy aroma.

Soon a petite, elderly lady with wavy silver and auburn hair walked up to the pallet. She was dressed like a typical hiker, wearing faded jeans and a light-colored sweatshirt with the words, **I love I ❤ shirts**, across the front. Around her neck was a long beaded necklace, which rattled with her every step. She came up alongside the pallet, looking concerned.

"What's your name, dear?" she asked.

Desiree squinted her eyes to focus on the beads of the woman's necklace. They were small, flat, and mostly deep blue in color. Some had tinges of turquoise while others had streaks of cream and gold. They reminded her of the chess pieces she got from her grandpa.

"Can you hear me—what's your name?"

Desiree tried to answer, but the spasms were now severely affecting her speech. "D-d, D-des, D-des," she stuttered, looking frantically into the lady's eyes.

Naturale spoke for her. "Desiree is her name. I pulled her out of the flooded creek. She has a strange affliction that makes her twitch and jerk uncontrollably. If she cannot speak now, then she must be getting worse."

The woman held Desiree's hand and smiled. "It's OK, Desiree; we'll take care of you. My name is Evaline, and I'm the closest thing to a nurse around here. Please let me remove your poncho, so I can figure out why you're so twitchy."

Desiree tried to sit up, but another spasm caused her to drop back onto the pallet.

"Don't worry," Evaline said, trying to calm her down, "I'll do it for you." She pulled the vinyl poncho out from under Desiree's back and slipped the front panel over her head. "There, that wasn't so bad." Desiree then shivered, and Evaline looked down at her wet boots. "Guess we'd better remove those soaking-wet boots, too." She motioned for Naturale to help, and they both pulled off the wet boots as well as her fleece socks. Evaline then quickly covered her with a second wool blanket. "I'll bet you feel a little warmer now." She and Naturale then hung the socks and boots on one of the wooden racks.

For a moment Desiree imagined Evaline as being her own mother, providing care with so much tenderness. How Desiree wished to be back home with her mom!

"Naturale, I think our medicine man got lost," said Evaline. "Do you mind finding him?" He grunted and left the area.

Evaline returned to Desiree and examined her wounded left arm, which was still twitching. The bleeding from the scratch had slowed, but the area was thickly smudged with coagulated blood.

"Well, Desiree, your scratch isn't as bad as it looks and certainly not as bad as your other symptoms," she said. She then took Desiree's wrist, feeling for a pulse while watching her chest for respirations. "Were you sick before this or taking any kind of medicine?"

Desiree shook her head while trying to breath between her spasms. The entire pallet quivered with Desiree's movements.

Evaline continued with her examination. "I realize your muscles are going crazy, but if you feel any specific pain where I poke or squeeze, let me know." Desiree nodded. Evaline then palpated Desiree's arm all the way to her the shoulder. "Well, so far I don't feel any broken bones, but I'm not the best x-ray machine," she said with a slight smile.

She then examined Desiree's head, face and neck area. "Still no pain?" Desiree shook her head. Evaline checked for, but didn't find, any apparent wounds along her back and ribs. Perplexed by the presented symptoms, Evaline covered Desiree back up with the blanket and heaved a deep sigh.

"Well, you got me beat; I can't figure out what's ailing you, but maybe our medicine man can," she said, gently stroking the side of Desiree's face. "In the meantime let me clean up your arm."

Desiree tried to take a deep breath of relief. But her back muscles again spasmed, causing her to cough. Evaline turned to get a bowl and cloth from a flat rock by the fire. When she rinsed the cloth in the water Desiree caught a fresh aroma and closed her eyes.

"Mm," she slowly moaned, enjoying the aroma.

"What, you like this stuff?" Evaline asked, holding up the bowl. "It's snowmelt infused with desert oregano and dried yucca root." She began washing the area around Desiree's wound. "It works like a soap that helps remove dirt and dried blood. Not the best stuff to put directly on a wound, though; it stings like hell!"

She started cleaning above the wound and removed the dried blood that had dirt and debris embedded in it. "Boy, you sure saw a lot of action tonight!" Then she rinsed her cloth and cleaned below the wound towards Desiree's wrist. She rinsed her cloth a few more times before returning it to the bowl.

The more Evaline cleaned, the more aroma filled the air. It reminded Desiree of an herbal tea that her mom once brought home from the farmers' market. The aroma filled the kitchen when her mom brewed it. It reminded her of a desert rain. She remembered tasting the tea, but it was so bitter that she spit it back in the cup. Her mom laughed and said the taste had to be acquired over time. How Desiree cherished that memory!

Just then Desiree heard footsteps approaching. She saw Naturale and another man walk up to a nearby fire. Naturale sat at the fire while the other man remained standing. He was wearing a sand-colored, camouflaged parka. She squinted, trying to make out his features. His face looked tanned and weathered, appearing much older than Naturale. His rounded face, high cheekbones and broad nose reminded her of some Native American students that attended her school.

When he turned to remove his jacket, she saw his long, straight black hair wrapped several times by a thin, brown leather strap. He hung his jacket on the drying rack then walked up to the foot of Desiree's pallet. He wore blue jeans that were faded at his thighs and calves, hinting of well-developed leg muscles. His black sweatshirt stretched tightly across his upper body revealing broad neck and shoulder muscles. His eyes were almond-shaped and dark brown in color. Thick, black eyebrows canopied them.

He scanned over her trembling body then focused on her injured arm. Evaline continued to clean it while reporting her findings as he stood by her side. Desiree then noticed his incredible height. Evaline's head barely reached his elbows. His massive stature alarmed Desiree, and she looked away in fear.

"Taqa, glad you're here," Evaline said, greeting him. "I can't figure out what's bugging her."

"What have you learned so far?" Taqa asked. He grabbed a campstool and sat next to Evaline. Desiree wasn't comfortable at all with his close proximity to her.

Evaline began her report. "I found just this one superficial scrape on her left arm. Doesn't really explain her muscle spasms. No fever. Shallow pulse but normal rate. Respirations quick and irregular. No tenderness in the chest, back or diaphragm area, which might have explained her breathing problems. No prior illness and not currently on medication."

Taqa leaned forward to better inspect Desiree's arm, but she jerked it away, glaring at him with the eyes of a wounded animal. *I never felt so sick and helpless in my life, but it's my life and my arm*, she thought.

Realizing her condition, Taqa backed off. "OK, I guess she doesn't want my help." Then he turned to his nurse. "Evaline, maybe she trusts you more than me."

Evaline agreed and gently stroked Desiree's cheek, trying to comfort her. "It's all right, Desiree, Taqa is here to make you better. He's a medicine man—not a witch doctor."

Taqa's facial expressions immediately froze. His dark brown eyes gazed aimlessly into the distance while pondering Evaline's half-derogatory comment. He then nudged her arm.

"Thanks, Evaline, for your help—I think," he said. Then he got up and looked his patient in the eyes. "Desiree, I don't blame you for not trusting strangers. But I really am the good part of whatever Evaline just said."

Desiree's eyes darted around, trying to avoid his. Despite her cramps and twitches, she managed to avoid him by folding her arms and rolling to the other side of the pallet. But then she caught another whiff of the herbal solution and relaxed, letting her mind drift back to a memory of her kitchen.

Meanwhile, the medicine man was not one to give up so easily. He walked over to the other side of the pallet, and squatted down to the level of her face.

"Desire, you're in pretty bad shape right now. I may be able to help you, but you have to trust me," he explained. "Please, let me see your arm—I promise not to hurt you."

She didn't reply right away. For a moment she pictured Taqa as her own dad, who once pleaded to clean her scraped knee she once suffered from falling off her swing. Back then she didn't trust him either, but he didn't give her a choice. Luckily his first aid wasn't too painful, especially after he applied a bright, smiley-faced adhesive bandage.

Desiree then opened her eyes, seeing Taqa's own eyes sparkling from the flames of the nearby fire. "Come on, Desiree, *pretty-please*," he said emphasizing his words with a high, falsetto voice.

That caught Desiree by surprise. She would have never guessed that a dark and scary wilderness man would resort to *pretty-please* for a favor. He even said it like her dad. *I guess I have to trust him if I'm going to get better*, she thought. She finally nodded, consenting to Taqa's help.

"That-a-girl," he replied with a reassuring smile. Evaline brought over the campstool for him. "Thank you, oh nurse, of bitter compliments," he said, still joking about her previous comment. Then he sat down and gently held Desiree's arm.

While he was examining the wound, Desiree noticed a thin, leather strap around his neck holding an oblong-shaped stone pendant roughly the size of a quarter. The stone was similar in color and texture to the smaller ones in Evaline's necklace.

Desiree continued staring at Taqa's stone as if she was trying to peer through its surface. But her eyelids twitched, impairing her vision.

Taqa noticed her half-drooped eyelids and further quizzed his nurse, "Was there debris around the wound?"

"All kinds," Evaline replied. "Wood and silt mostly. It was mixed in with her dried blood, but I removed it."

Taqa then turned to Evaline. "May I see your rinse bowl?"

Evaline passed it to him. He looked inside and stirred the cloth using his long index finger, trying to loosen all the debris from the cloth's fibers. Then he wrung it out and handed it back to Evaline. From his belt he pulled out a long, broad knife and used it to stir the liquid. The blood clots had dissolved, leaving behind only dirt and debris.

"Naturale, can you please bring me a torch?" Taqa asked. Naturale, who was drying his pant legs by the fire, got up and brought the torch to Taqa. "Here, hold it right there," the medicine man instructed as he trapped some of the debris onto his knife blade. Then he raised the blade up to his eyes.

"What do you see, Taqa?" Evaline asked.

Taqa inspected the particles that lay on the smooth shiny blade. He muttered something to himself before taking Desiree's arm and closely examining the area just below the wound.

"Ah-ha," he finally remarked. "There—fang marks of a spider. Most probably a black widow, which would explain the muscle spasms. See the marks, Evaline?"

She looked closely at the area right at the tip of his knife and saw two tiny punctures in the middle of a reddened patch of skin just below the cut. Desiree also tried to look but couldn't steady her shaking head and shoulders.

"Well, I'll be damned!" Evaline exclaimed. "The venom caused the poor child's spasms. How did you know to look for a spider bite, Taqa?"

Taqa was still examining the puncture site when he answered her. "A wise old medicine man once told me, *when you hear the sound of hoofs look for bighorn sheep—not mules.*"

Evaline laughed at the misconstrued saying. "Taqa the saying goes, *when you hear the sound of hoofs look for horses—not zebras.*"

He gently lowered Desiree's arm. "Now Evaline, where around here are there horses and zebras?"

"Good point," Evaline replied, chuckling.

Desiree also lightened up and giggled. *This big and scary wilderness guy is actually kind of funny*, she thought.

Taqa then explained his findings. "The debris in the bowl was not just silt and pieces of bark. It was also fragments of a black widow spider. Look," he said holding the knife blade for Evaline to see. "Here is a leg and the abdomen with the classic, hourglass marking. Maybe I can piece together what happened. While this woman was frolicking with Naturale in the woods…"

Naturale growled, not happy about Taqa's choice of words.

"…She brushed up against a dead tree branch ripping her sleeve and exposing her skin to the spider, which must have been on the same branch. It jumped on her arm and bit her but probably got crushed later when she rubbed her arm. The smeared and clotted blood entrapped the spider's remains only to be washed away by your cleaning cloth."

"Holy cheese and crackers, tsk, tsk," Evaline remarked after viewing the spider pieces on Taqa's knife blade. "A black widow spider bite! Poor child—she's in for a rocky night."

"She's not a child," he disputed, tilting his head to size up Desiree while cleaning his blade with Evaline's cloth. "She looks to be about eighteen years old, roughly five feet ten inches tall, and maybe one hundred and fifty pounds."

Desiree confirmed by nodding.

"She's tall and, judging from her muscle mass, strong. She's probably an athlete—no, maybe more like a dancer."

Amazed by his correct assessment, Desiree nodded again. *This guy is freaking psychic*, she thought.

Taqa continued. "So, her body mass can help dilute the concentration of the venom. She'll be uncomfortable for the next three or four hours, but that's all. For now we should clean her wound and maybe chill down the puncture site." He then handed Naturale the torch before rising from his chair. "Now, are there any other illnesses or injuries that need my attention?"

Evaline chuckled. "Maybe Naturale's bruised ego," she said. "The other hunters claimed that Desiree surprised him in the dark. It had to be quite humbling for a hunter to be surprised by his prey."

Naturale growled at her remark while Desiree giggled. Taqa smiled, taking his jacket from the drying rack. He walked past Naturale, firmly patting the hunter's shoulder. Naturale grunted in response as Taqa headed towards the cavern's exit. Evaline followed Taqa helping slip on his jacket.

"I can't see how it's humbling," he said to her softly. "He rescued her cramping body from the cold, rising waters. Got her here relatively safe and dry. Probably saved her life tonight."

"Amen!" Evaline remarked, and they both smiled back at Naturale. He knew they were talking about him and walked away in disgust.

Taqa then whispered to Evaline. "You know that I have to report Desiree's case to the tribe counsel."

"Yes, I know; Tsk, what a shame."

# Chapter XV

"OK, let's move out," Mr. Roeser commanded the students as he walked from the dinner tarp down to the creek. The Clydes untied the mules and followed him down the embankment. Dominique and Taylor were the first to follow the Clydes. Then two-by-two the other students followed.

"This is scary but so cool," said Dominique. "I've never had to search—"

"—On a night so dark," added Taylor.

"—In a Canyon so Grand," added Candice.

"—While raining so hard," added Wes.

"—On the rocks and sand," added Aaron.

"—With two mules to ride," added Perro.

"—And students so few," added Martina.

"—With no mother a clue," added Sayuri.

"—How to search and rescue!" Jeremy and Jace said simultaneously. All the students laughed and applauded each other, but deep in their hearts they realized the gravity of the situation.

The group walked along the bank of the creek downstream. Some flashlights beamed upon the waters and some on the other side. Still others shined at the massive escarpment ahead of them that seemed to rise out of the waters like a giant sentinel.

Mr. Roeser motioned for the group to stop, and the Clydes brought the mules to the water's edge. They pointed to Dominique and Taylor to mount the first mule while Bessie Clyde mounted the second. Dominique stood at the side of the mule and got a foothold from Tom Clyde before springing upward and swinging her leg over the mule's back. Then she raised both arms over her head in victory. The other students cheered.

"C'mon," Dominique called to Taylor. "We can do this!"

Taylor hesitated, looking worried, but Wes held her shoulders and pushed her forward. "The mule doesn't know how scared you are," he said. "So keep fooling him for as long as you can."

She took a deep breath and stood at the mule's side. She signaled to Wes that she was ready. He then lifted her onto the mule's back. She panicked for just a second as the mule steadied his footing to adjust for her weight. She quickly grabbed Dominique's waist but eventually straightened up, feeling more secure. They rode behind Bessie's mule in the water around the escarpment.

"This isn't so bad," Taylor said to Dominique as they traveled another twenty-five or so yards before heading up the embankment.

"Here's our stop," said Dominique. The two dismounted and watched Bessie Clyde lead the mule back to the other students.

"That was actually fun!" Taylor exclaimed. "Next time we visit here, remind me to inquire about those mule rides down the Bright Angel Trail."

Jeremy and Jace were the next two students to be dropped off. After dismounting they huddled with Dominique and Taylor until the others joined them.

"I hope Desiree didn't fall into the creek," Dominique said as she squatted down at the creeks' edge and poked her finger in the water. "Man, this stuff is ice-cold."

Jace also felt the water. "It's like, frozen solid—only liquid," he said.

His brother did the same, but rapidly shook the water off his finger. "Man, I hope Desiree is no where near this water," he said.

The night air was much warmer than the water and the moon was still peaking in and out of the clouds. All were silent except for the running creek and the splashing of the wading mules. Finally Mr. Roeser and the Clydes arrived and secured the mules at the trees farther up the embankment. The group then huddled around their teacher.

"We still have the light of the moon to help us, so use your flashlight sparingly," he said.

"What's your plan?" asked Wes.

"We spread out and look for Miss Sumner or a trail that she may have taken," he replied. "If you find any trace of her—a piece of clothing, flashlight or even a footprint—let your team leader know. They have a whistle and a radio."

Bessie, suddenly checking the pockets of her jacket and pants, interrupted his announcement. "Bradley, I think I left my whistle back in the tent. It'll just take me a few extra minutes to go back to get it," she said and started walking towards her mule.

But Dominique proudly stepped forward. "You don't have to do that, Mrs. Clyde; *I* have a whistle," she said, pulling out the bright, orange-colored plastic whistle, which hung around her neck.

"I never travel without it." Her friends cheered as she bowed and was quickly assigned to Bessie's group.

The groups split up and searched the entire embankment, calling out Desiree's name. This particular area was long and narrow with most of the trees in the swollen creek. The three groups systematically combed the area, which included a few caverns in the crag. In less than twenty minutes Dominique's whistle blew when her group found a trail up the crag. They regrouped and climbed it about fifty vertical feet until they reached a waterfall. All flashlights shined randomly on the rocks around it.

"This looks like a dead end for now," said Mr. Roeser as he beamed his flashlight on the gushing water, which ran off the cliff and onto the jagged rocks below. "We'd better head back to our tents and resume our search tomorrow."

Feeling despondent, Candice spoke up as she stepped out of the line. "But Mr. R., we can't desert Desiree now; she could be in trouble."

Mr. Roeser shined his flashlight on her face. She didn't have the look of a fiery, competitive athlete. Instead he saw worry and concern drawing her cheeks down over the sides of her frowning lips. He saw her eyes well up with tears ready to overflow. He felt her emotions briefly then turned towards the group, looking gravely concerned.

"Look, I don't want to leave her either. But right now the safety of this group is my priority. Darkness and flooding are two major factors working against us. We can't search for her if we're blind or floundering in the waters. We shouldn't even be on this trail at night—too many chances for accidents."

Wes walked up to Candice and held her by the shoulders. "Mr. R. is right," he said. "As much as we all care for her, we still need to keep our composure. We can't afford to lose more than one friend tonight." Candice agreed with tears flowing down her face. She hugged Wes and sobbed. He rubbed her back and likewise shed a few tears. Everyone else tried to surround them but the trail was too narrow, so they all bunched up in a single-file line each holding the student in front of them.

Mr. Roeser then spoke. "Alright, Sunnyslope seniors, keep your flashlights and eyes on the trail. We'll carefully descend and return to the campsite. We'll get a fresh start at daybreak tomorrow. The canyon may have won the battle tonight but she hasn't won the war."

They descended the switchback returning to creek level, and then rode the mules back to their campsite.

Returning to their tents, Martina walked alongside Candice. "If you'd like you can sleep in our tent tonight," she offered.

Candice smiled back at her. "Thanks, but there's hardly any room for you and Sayuri."

"Well, then, we'll keep you company and talk through the tents with you for as long as you'd like," Martina replied.

Dominique, who was walking with them added, "I think we all could use a little girl talk before going to sleep. After all, it's tough trying to sleep on all this excess baggage."

"But wouldn't that be kind of lumpy?" Sayuri asked. Martina then explained to Sayuri the term *excess baggage* in Dominique's context. Sayuri held her head as if in pain. "All your English metaphors give me a headache," she complained.

The girls stayed up for a while, discussing many worries and concerns about their missing classmate. One by one the number of voices dwindled until only Candice's remained.

With no light she lay still on her back, staring upward. "Hello," she called out, "is anyone still up?" Apparently the rest had fallen asleep. Feeling unsettled she turned on her flashlight and pointed it at Desiree's sleeping bag. *Macbeth* was still lying on the pillow. She reached over for it, opened it and started reading.

About an hour later Taylor crawled out of her tent to use her latrine. When she returned she saw Candice's tent still lit up. Taylor poked her head inside. *Macbeth* was lying on Candice's chest, but her head was tilted back and her mouth wide open. Taylor giggled quietly, closed the book and returned it to Desiree's pillow. She then turned off the Candice's flashlight, crawled out and returned to her own tent.

Dominique heard Taylor's rustling and clicked on her flashlight. "How's Candice doing?"

"She's sound asleep," whispered Taylor. "Thanks to a little quiet time with *Macbeth*. I found her asleep with it."

"That's good," said Dominique as she turned off her flashlight. "I guess reading William Shakespeare can be pretty therapeutic."

Taylor crawled back into her sleeping bag and turned off her light. "Yeah, Desiree was right when she said it's calming. It apparently worked well tonight for Candice. I think I should give ol' Bill another try," she said.

Dominique yawned and rolled onto her side. "Yeah, me, too," she said. "Right after we find his number-one fan."

# Chapter XVI

"Rain is always welcome in the deserts of Arizona, but not so much in the state's snow country," said the grungy, snowboarder-looking meteorologist from the local weather station. "Snowmelt from the White Mountains is causing record-high water levels at the Roosevelt Dam. So much so, that the spillover is threatening to wash out the nearby roadways. Geologists have been called to assess this potentially dangerous situation. Meanwhile, the Colorado River has exceeded fifty-year high levels. The flow at the Park Service Station near the Phantom Ranch area was estimated at over eighty thousand cubic feet per second. The park rangers have been busy evacuating hikers out of popular campsites, but there's no telling how many others have been stranded due to rising waters in the remote canyons and drainages..."

"Sure hope she's not in one of those areas," said Janelle as she poured herself a glass of wine. She set the bottle in an ice bucket on the dining room table next to another empty glass. Her son, who was sitting on a firm, rust-colored couch in front of the TV, jumped up to the snack bowl and grabbed a handful of mixed crackers and nuts. Just as he sat back down, her cell phone rang. She opened it and, seeing it was her husband, greeted him.

"Babe, you better be close. My guts are splittin' with worry," she said.

"Just passed the park entrance," he replied. "Where are you staying?"

"We're at the Bright Angel Lodge."

"Be there in a few."

Janelle closed her phone. She sighed, brushed the loose hair from her face and sipped some wine.

"Come sit with me, Ma," offered Royce. Janelle looked at the digital clock on the microwave. It was already ten o'clock, and they were both still wide-awake.

"OK, but just for a few minutes more, then you need to get to bed."

"Can I at least stay up until Dad gets here?" Royce pleaded.

She placed her wine glass on the counter and walked over to the couch. "Yeah, sure, baby. He shouldn't be too long." She then sat next to him, putting her arm around his neck and resting her head against his shoulder.

They both watched the local weather forecast. The current temperature at the South Rim was sixty degrees Fahrenheit.

"Man, it's still pretty warm outside," said Royce. "Usually the nights here fall to around freezing."

"That explains the rain, the rising waters and my blood pressure," said his mom.

After a few minutes a knock came on the door. Royce ran over to open it. His dad stood in the doorway and immediately hugged his son before rushing to his wife. Janelle sprang off the couch and ran into her husband's arms. She held him so tight that her voice muffled through his buckskin jacket.

"I am so glad you're here," she said. "Desiree is down in the canyon with her friends, and the creeks are flooding."

"Then let's hope she's above the creeks," he said, gently pulling away from her. He removed his jacket and hung it on a nearby chair. She led him to the dining room table and poured him some wine. They sat opposite each other at the table. With deep concern she looked at him while he calmly sipped some wine. Sensing her worry, he leaned across the table and reached for both her hands.

"Sorry I took so long; I came as fast as I could. I canceled my last tour at Roosevelt Lake because of the spillover issues. But I would have canceled anyway; you and the kids are way more important right now."

"Wish Desiree could hear that."

"Aw, she will—soon."

"You sound so sure."

"I am, honey," he said and explained further, "Bradley Roeser is a seasoned hiker. He's been hiking before they started damning Glen Canyon back in '63. He knows all the safety procedures. He follows the rules and registers with the Back Country Office before every trip, so they know where he is. If the group camped low, Bradley Roeser is smart enough to get 'em high. I have great faith in him."

"How do you know all this?"

"He and my dad hiked together a lot. Dad was kind of reckless, but Bradley always played it safe. Kind of pissed Dad off sometimes, but that's how Bradley was. Maybe that's why the high school lets him have a field trip every year."

"OK, I feel a little better now." She leaned back against her chair and let out a big sigh.

"Then, of course there's his kryptonite," Walter added.

301

She quickly sat up again. "His what?"

"His kryptonite. He has an obsession with ancient cultures. He goes down year after year in search of an ancient civilization that he believes still exists. He thinks they're a ubiquitous tribe that eludes the park rangers while hiding in the canyons.

"You mean like the Havasupai once did?" asked Royce, who was still on the couch watching TV. "Didn't they live there full-time?" he asked.

"Well, in the beginning—before we showed up, son," his dad answered. "A great deal of the Havasupai lived in the Indian Gardens, a beautifully lush farming area along the Bright Angel Trail below the South Rim. But then they had to relocate farther west. Kind of a shame for a peaceful and resourceful tribe, that lived in the same area for hundreds of years and thrived in the harsh elements. Not only were they peaceful, but they also networked with the neighboring tribes—even helped them out in times of trouble. But President Teddy Roosevelt felt that the Havasupai should not live in a national monument set aside for tourists."

"Maybe some of the Havasupai still live down there," Royce guessed.

"Maybe so," he agreed. "And maybe non-natives, too. Bradley Roeser believed that hikers wanting to escape from civilization melded with this surreptitious group. I was just a kid when he told your grandpa what he believed. I thought it was a cool story. Now that I'm older I think Bradley could be right. After all, history has documented hundreds of explorers who hiked the trails or ran the river but never returned. They could have survived and became part of this subculture."

# Chapter XVII

Desiree's muscle cramps finally subsided shortly after midnight. She called for Evaline, who was rolled in a blanket and sitting near the fire.

"Can I please have some water?" Desiree asked before letting out a dry cough.

"Why, sure!" Evaline cheerfully answered as she rose to her feet. "It's nice to hear you talk. Can you sit up?"

"I think so," replied Desiree. But before doing so, she noticed several penny-sized, blue stones lining the entire frame of her pallet. She raised her head saw a slightly larger one lying squarely on the middle of her chest.

Evaline noticed Desiree's hesitation and hurried to the pallet. "Oops, forgot about the healing stones," she said, hastily collecting them. "I should have gathered these sooner." Evaline placed the stones on a ledge by the trough then handed her patient an old metal canteen filled with water.

"Sip it slowly, dear," Evaline advised. "If you swallow too much, you'll throw up." Desiree cautiously sat up and tipped the canteen a little at a time, letting a small amount of water roll across her tongue. It was the best water she had ever tasted!

"Thanks, Ms. Evaline, that was refreshing. Did you have any medicinal herbs in there?" Desiree asked while returning the canteen to Evaline.

"Well, maybe there's a little Rayweed tea leftover from yesterday. But it's also good for calming your stomach." She then set the canteen on the ledge by the first trough. "So, how are you feeling?"

Desiree stretched her arms and shoulders. "Well, I *have seen better days,*" she answered, quoting Shakespeare. She then did a few side stretches. "My abs ache like I just did three thousand crunches."

Evaline didn't understand her. "Abs? Crunches?"

"Abs are abdominal muscles," said Taqa, who suddenly appeared on the other side of the pallet. "And crunches are like partial sit-ups; way after your time, Evaline."

The wilderness nurse was still hazy with the terms. "Taqa, next time you find a fitness magazine, please save it for me, so I can catch up on these new-fangled fitness terms," she said, turning away and walking back to tend the fire. Desiree giggled.

Taqa, however, remained at Desiree's side. "You must be feeling better now," he said.

"Oh, I am *as merry as the day is long,*" she said, again quoting Shakespeare. She was feeling better but was still uncomfortable in a strange place with strangers. Taqa sensed this and tried to ease her worries.

"Shakespeare, huh?" Taqa asked.

"You know Shakespeare?" Desiree asked, becoming less uneasy and more intrigued.

"Yes, my dad read his works to me often when I was a child," he answered. "My favorite quote is: *The miserable have no other medicine but only hope.* It's my motto as a medicine man— gets me off the hook when treating patients who are miserable," he said, chuckling. "My next favorite one is: *The first thing we do, let's kill all the lawyers.* But that's pretty evil-spirited since I don't have to worry about malpractice down here." They both laughed together. She appreciated the medicine man's humor—it was just like her dad's.

Taqa then reached for her arm. "Can I please check your wounds," he asked. "Or are you going to make me say *pretty-please* again?"

Desiree laughed hysterically. "No, not this time," she replied, holding out her arm. "My arm is already starting to feel better."

Sitting in the camp chair again Taqa unrolled the soft bandage and removed the flat river rock—about the size of a hamburger patty—that had covered the puncture site.

"Hmm," he remarked while rolling her arm to inspect the entire area. "There's still some redness and swelling, but that's to be expected. We'll keep the area chilled for a while longer." He took the rock over to a second trough of running water, which was connected to the first one by a gutter. He placed it in the trough and pull out another one. "Ooh, that water is cold!" He then hurried back to her while calling out to his assistant. "Evaline, this whole area will need some healing tea."

Evaline grabbed a glass cruet of liquid from the same trough that the stones were kept and carefully drizzled the tea over Desiree's wounds. It felt icy-cold, but Desiree didn't flinch. Instead she deeply inhaled the tea's aroma.

"Ah, that smells sweet, but it's not as pungent as the cleaning tea," she remarked.

Evaline held up the cruet for Desiree to see. "This tea is made with prickly poppy," she said. "Gotta be careful with it, though. It can make you pretty sleepy—like the poppies did to Dorothy in *The Wizard of Oz*."

Then Taqa gently held the replacement rock directly on the puncture site while Evaline slowly wrapped the bandage around it. He stepped back to let his nurse finish. He was still trying to gain Desiree's trust, so he continued talking with her.

"When it comes to wound management Evaline is the best, don't you think?" Taqa asked Desiree, who then nodded. Evaline smiled at the medicine man and returned the cruet to the water trough.

Taqa stepped closer to inspect Evaline's work. "How does it feel—not too tight?"

"It's comfortably snug," Desiree replied while eyeing his stone pendant once again. "Hey, Mr. Taqa, what kind of stone is that?"

"Please, Desiree, call me Taqa—just plain Taqa," he replied, trying to dissolve any formalities that may be forming between them.

"Oh, sorry, Taqa," Desiree replied, "it's just that you remind me of my dad, but I can't really call you *Dad*, so out of respect for people like you who are older than me..."

Evaline started laughing as she watched Taqa raise one of his bushy, dark eyebrows, trying to figure out if his patient was insulting or complimenting him.

"...And I won't hesitate using Mister, or Misses, or Miss, or Mizz, or whatever your social status may be."

Taqa walked over to the second trough to rinse his face, secretly hoping to dissolve away any obvious signs of old age. Then he grabbed a towel from his bag and dried his face. "Really, Desiree, just call me Taqa—it would make me feel less old and a lot better."

"Whatever," she said. "So anyway, as I was asking before, what kind of stone is that?"

He thought she was asking about the river rocks, which were in the trough. "Well, it's just one of the countless river rocks that line our creeks," he answered. "They have amazing heat capacity or, in your case, *chill* capacity."

Desiree needed to clarify her question. "No, Taqa, not the stones in your sink—that blue one around your neck."

"Oh, this?" he asked holding it away from his neck. "It's called azurite, want to see?" She nodded, and he went over to show her. Keeping it around his neck, he bent over so that she could inspect it more closely.

This time she wasn't troubled by his close proximity. She felt warmth radiating from his broad chest and smelled the musky odor of his shirt. It reminded her of how her grandpa's clothes smelled upon returning from a Grand Canyon trip.

Taqa was pleased with Desiree's developing comfort with him.

"This is really beautiful," she said while rolling the stone in her fingers. The golden flecks within the blue matrix captured the fire's radiance and reflected back into her eyes. She was bedazzled just like the first time she received her grandpa's chess pieces. "Are the stones that Evaline used on me also azurite?"

"Yes, they are," he said. "We believe azurite has healing powers. We can't explain how, but we've had some good luck with it."

Desiree's mind immediately flashed back to her most recent visit at a day spa, and she blurted out a laugh.

Taqa didn't understand her reaction. He plucked his pendant from her fingers and backed away. "Are you mocking our beliefs?"

Desiree immediately retracted. "No, I'm sorry—I didn't mean to laugh. What you said reminded me of a memory. You see—my mom and I once visited a day spa in Sedona—the city where some say magical vortices exist. Anyway, at this spa we sat in a steam room, then showered and then rolled up in towels. Then the spa attendants placed several warm stones on our spine and down our legs. They explained that the whole process was supposed to magically detoxify both our body and spirit."

This time Taqa blurted out a laugh.

"What?" Desiree asked. "Wasn't it the same kind of healing therapy as your azurite stones?"

"Well, sort of," he replied. "They got the sweating and the rinsing part right. But lining warm stones all down your body— that's just ridiculous," he said, shaking his head and fanning away the idea like he was shooing a fly. "A linear arrangement won't focus the healing powers as well as a radial one. And I'm guessing they didn't use azurite, either, because it's not that common a stone."

"Can you get azurite stones around here?"

He turned and walked to the foot of her pallet. "There are a few veins of azurite within some hidden canyons," he admitted, then quickly spun back towards her, "but if I told you I would have to kill you," and he pulled out his bear knife.

Suddenly Desiree's comfort zone vanished. "Oh!" she shrieked in terror while staring at his knife.

"Just kidding, Desiree—sorry," he said calmly, using the knife to scrape some dried herbs off his jacket sleeve. "Look, I may appear to you as a huge and scary creature of the wilderness, but I'm actually a *fun-loving*, huge and scary creature of the wilderness." He returned the knife to his belt and Desiree sighed with relief. *OK, he's got a weird sense of humor, but he's still huge and scary*, she thought.

Then Taqa paced back and forth while describing the composition of azurite. He sounded a bit like her geology teacher with all the technical terms he used. He seemed to go on forever.

Desiree did her best to listen attentively. But the physical stress of the evening overcame her, or maybe it was the prickly poppy tea. She stretched both arms over her head. Then she laced her fingers and slipped them underneath her head. She relaxed all her muscles and drifted into sleep, breathing slowly and spasm-free.

Evaline checked on her then walked over to Taqa. "Well, wilderness man of many facts, you didn't hold her attention for very long," she said, teasing him.

"Never said I was a captivating speaker," Taqa admitted, while pulling Desiree's blanket up to her chin and tucking in the loose ends.

"Speaking of captivating," Evaline began as she led Taqa over to the fire, "did you talk with the tribal counsel yet?" They both sat down at the fire with their backs to Desiree.

"No, not yet," he whispered back to her. "I was busy making a cold, creosote infusion for Nanu's cough. But I will see the counsel tomorrow at dusk."

Evaline leaned closer to him. "Taqa, you know in your heart we shouldn't keep her here. Naturale and the others told me that her group is camped in the very next cove upstream."

He looked into the small fire dominated by glowing embers. "The secrecy of this tribe must be maintained," he said, grabbing a stick and stoking the fire. He then turned to her. "As an elder, you know that—more than anyone. Naturale told me he could have left Desiree out on the bank of the creek, but he felt her injury was serious. He also told me that she was conscious when they carried her through the crevasse's entrance, so she knows its location. If we let her go she'll tell others—whether purposely or by accident—and we will be discovered. We can't afford risking all that has been established over centuries of time."

Evaline got up from her seat and fed the fire with more wood. "You forget, Taqa, that I was rescued, nursed back to health and set free. The rules of this tribe are not engraved in stone."

Taqa answered her while rearranging the wood. "My father told me you returned to the tribe on your own volition. He said you were desperate and suicidal."

Evaline circled the fire, which had grown brighter. "Did your father also tell you that I was a stupid, misguided teenager? Instead of understanding my problems, my parents rejected me. When I left home they slammed the door behind me. They wrote me off as a runaway child of the streets."

She began to whimper and stepped away from the fire. "Of course I came back—to a place where I felt loved and cared for— where no one judged me by my past. In gratitude, I have always been faithful to your tribe." With her sleeve she wiped her runny nose.

He walked around to the front of her. She did not look up but instead gazed upon the ground. He pulled up her chin and saw her tearful eyes.

"Yes, you have been faithful to our tribe, Evaline," he said and offered his handkerchief. "My father used to say that you followed the code of laws better than any of the native members. But, tell me, why do you feel it does not apply to Desiree?"

She took his handkerchief and began to dab her tears. "Because, Taqa, she didn't come here by choice, and she wasn't mortally wounded," his nurse replied. "Besides, Naturale found her trembling and confused in the dark. Now we both know that rock formations don't look the same in the dark as they do in the light. She may recognize the trail up the crag but not the exact location of our entrance."

Taqa wasn't entirely convinced by Evaline's explanation. He walked over to Desiree's pallet and watched her sleep. Both her arms were still bent comfortably behind her head. The corners of her mouth were turned slightly upward as if she was smiling.

"Look at her sleeping so peacefully," he remarked.

Evaline joined him at the pallet. "Most do when they sleep free of anxiety and pain."

"She was a feisty little patient—reminds me of you," he said, nudging her arm.

Evaline smiled, returning his handkerchief. "And you really don't want more than one of us in this tribe," she said.

He chuckled at her then led her away from Desiree. "Ugh, it would have been so much easier if she didn't see the entrance to our shelter."

"Taqa, rocks shift, water flows and landscapes change with time and weather. The entrance may not look the same in daylight. With the rains it may not look the same tomorrow." She then walked over to hang Desiree's poncho on the rack by the other fire, which was already beginning to burn out.

Taqa followed her and likewise hung his handkerchief on the drying rack. "Maybe, but we can't take the risk. There is too much at stake." His voice grew louder with his increasing

311

frustration. "And you have to remember that Naturale and the others also know she's here. They know what I must do."

Their voices caused Desiree to stir. They both returned to the pallet to see if she had awakened. But she didn't; she merely rolled onto her side without awakening.

The two caretakers returned to the first fire as Taqa continued whispering. "Well, we can't just let her go." Evaline looked up into Taqa's dark-brown eyes that peered through his scowling, thick eyebrows. She thought about what he said, and then slowly smiled mischievously. Fire-sparkled jewels replaced her tear-swollen eyes.

"Of course we can't *just let her go*," she whispered back. He saw her grinning face, and understood what she meant. His heavily puckered brows then lifted to inquisitive ones.

"Evaline, are your thoughts more cunning than your smile?" He then turned to grab a sleeping cot that was leaning against wall.

Evaline cleared away the area from the first fire, so that Taqa could place the cot near it. "Taqa, I didn't realize your psychic powers were so strong," she said with an even wider grin. She then walked over to a dowel of blankets that were hanging from the wall. She kept one blanket and handed the rest to Taqa.

"No, Evaline, my psychic powers are not that strong; I just know my Evalines really well," he replied while unrolling a thin, foam mattress at the foot of the cot. He was too large for the cot, so he had to sleep on the mattress. He laid out his blankets and crawled inside them.

Evaline then reclined onto the cot, covering herself with her own blanket. "Well, Taqa, I'm going to sleep on this problem, and I'd appreciate your staying out of my dreams," she said closing her eyes and shifting to a comfortable position.

Taqa chuckled before reaching for more wood to place into the fire. It crackled with new life as he then covered himself up and rolled into a comfortable position. The two caretakers soon fell sleep after an exhausting night.

Sometime during the night, the journal fell out of Desiree's poncho and onto the cavern floor.

# Chapter XVIII

*The early morning sun danced across the clear skies above our campsite and thrusting its rays into the orifices of the majestic canyon cliffs, resulting in a spectral orgy of red, purple and yellow. The exhilarating views of the canyon and creek could arouse the senses of even the most frigid visitor.*

*The rustling leaves of the nearby trees sound like the crackling of long organza prom gowns being tossed and flittered by anxious senior girls anticipating their first—*

"Dominique, what are you writing?" Taylor cried. "Give me that!" She snatched the journal from Dominique before the entry was completed. Taylor's eyes raced across it. "*Thrusting into orifices?*"

"Sounds pretty racy, huh?"

"*Spectral orgy?*"

"Sure, it was pretty easy getting my creative juices started," Dominique said, smirking.

"And what's with comparing tree leaves to a prom dress?" Taylor then pulled out an eraser from her pocket.

"Wait—don't erase that," Dominique pleaded.

"This junk is not staying in my journal," Taylor replied angrily. "It sounds like a slutty nature book."

"But you said I could help you, and you said your entries needed a little more pizzazz."

"Dominique, I said *jazz*—not *pizzazz*. Your bizarre, suggestive descriptions make this read like a Salvatore Dali romance novel—and a steamy one at that!"

Dominique grabbed Taylor's eraser. "That's what makes it perfect for the Searchlight! Gillian and her editing staff won't have to embellish this story one tiny bit. They'll like it so much, they'll publish it verbatim."

Taylor sighed and put away her eraser. "Yeah, it does sound like their writing." She then gave the journal back to Dominique. "I hate when you're right," she admitted. "Oh, you may want to finish your sentence."

"Thanks, partner," Dominique said gratefully as she finished her sentence:

*—dance.*

She then smiled, feeling pleased, and closed Taylor's journal.

Mr. Roeser and the Clydes were firing up the stove to heat water for coffee and hot chocolate. At the same time they were discussing search plans for Desiree.

"I need to re-establish radio contact, so I'll hike up to the plateau and contact park service," said Mr. Clyde.

315

"While you do that, we'll resume our search down here. If she's anything like her grandfather, Miss Sumner found shelter somewhere on the other side of the escarpment." Mr. Roeser said.

Perro was the first to awaken and walked down to the shelter, wearing his pajamas and hiking boots. The air was cool and crisp, but Perro was comfortable without a jacket.

"*Buenos días*," he said to the adults.

"*Buenos días*," they replied.

"*No tienes frío?*" Mr. Roeser asked.

"*No, porque mi corazón está en llamás*," Perro replied.

"Your heart is on fire?" Mr. Roeser asked.

"Yes. Desiree was on my mind all night, and my blood boils with desire for her rescue."

"Oh, that is so romantic!" Bessie Clyde commented as she looked out at the creek. Then she turned to him. "Do you have feelings for her?" she asked.

"Feelings of a hero with the passion for rescue. But as for *amor, realmente no.*"

"Too bad," she said as she reached for the coffee pot on the stove.

Perro grabbed the pot first and poured some coffee for her. "But don't you see, señora, that's an advantage for me. My emotions are not based on love, so I am not distracted by all the craziness that love causes. I have a clear head and will do all the right things needed to find her. *Mi cabeza está por encima del corozón.*"

"I'm glad to hear that," said Mr. Roeser.

"What are you glad to hear?" asked Sayuri standing just behind Perro.

"That Perro's head is above his heart," answered Mr. Roeser.

"That is a good place for his head to be," she said then changed the subject quickly and turned to Tom Clyde. "Is the hot cocoa ready yet?"

"Just a couple of minutes more," he answered and then chuckled while stirring the large pot of water on the stove.

Other students filed down to the dining shelter. Some were already dressed for the day while others were still in sleep clothes. Candice was not only fully dressed but also loaded with gadgets.

"I've got my shovel, my pickaxe, my Swiss Army knife, and my telescopic fencing foil," she proudly declared, pointing out each tool that was hanging from her belt.

"A fencing foil?" Jace asked before he bit into his granola bar. Candice opened her foil to full length and sliced the air with a coupé then lunged.

"What do you need that for?" Jeremy asked.

"To defend myself, of course," she said snootily.

Perro chuckled then continued the fun poking, "Planning any fencing matches down here, Candice?"

"No, but you just never know when you might need it," she said, closing it down to the length of a pencil and returning it to her belt. "Besides, they don't allow guns in the National Park, and a girl's got to protect herself."

Just then Aaron came up and surprised her from behind. "Sure, Candice, you'll never know when Zorro's gonna show up," he said grabbing her at the ribs while laughing.

Candice was startled by his sudden appearance, but then turned to giving him an annoyed look. "Very funny, ha, ha, ha," she replied.

"Well, at least it shows your assailant that you have culture," said Perro. Just then they looked past Candice and saw Taylor marching towards them.

She sounded ready and armed. "You can pack away your foils and your pickaxes because they are no match for my secret weapon," she declared, stopping just a few yards short of the shelter.

"And what is that?" Wes asked just before he stuffed a handful of raisins into his mouth.

"Silly, if I told you, then it wouldn't be a secret," she said slightly sneering.

"Then give us a clue. Will it blow us to smithereens if you detonate it?" Wes asked, accidentally spitting out some raisins.

"No."

"Will it burn us all to a crisp?" asked Aaron.

"No."

"Will it vaporize everything within a twenty mile radius?" asked Jace.

"No."

"Then what good is your secret weapon?" asked Jeremy.

"Better than you think."

"We give up. What is it?" Dominique asked. Taylor went into her back pocket and pulled out a small bottle.

"I found this next to Desiree's pack. It's her infamous shower gel!" She shook the bottle of thick light-blue liquid for everyone to see. "This stuff's pretty potent, ya know."

"Great, let's just hope there's a hive of bees nearby when you use it," said Dominique.

"That stuff attracts bees?" Jeremy asked.

"Sure does," Dominique replied, "Taylor's boyfriend used it as cologne after swim practice one morning, and it turned on a bunch of bees. They found him before Taylor did.

Taylor wasn't ready for a catchy comeback. She pictured Royce in her mind, wearing his swimsuit. "*Bzz!*" was her only response.

* * *

"Hmm, let's see now; we'll need a tent, poncho, water, food, flashlights, radio and maybe an extra set of clothes," said Walter from behind the lift gate of his truck as he packed supplies in a large nylon duffle bag. He then looked down at Royce who was wearing sandals. "Do you have boots?"

"Yep, wore 'em at Snowbowl, but they got pretty wet in the slush. Had to dry 'em in front of the fireplace for a few hours; they should be toasty by now."

"Super, but you'll also need crampons for them. Let's see…now where did I store those little stinkers." He pushed a few loaded boxes around the back of his truck and emptied one out on the ground. "Ah, here they are," he said, pulling them out. "Here, put these in your bag." Royce packed them away in his bag while his dad returned all the gear back in the box.

"Boy, Dad, you sure keep a lot of stuff in your truck."

His dad tossed all his supplies back into the box and slid it back into the truck. "Better to be over-equipped, son," he said as he pulled out some ropes and harnesses. "There, I think I got everything. Too bad your mom isn't coming with us, I got enough for her, too."

"No, you know she'd rather be here, holding down the fort by keeping the parents informed of any news from the Park Service. She's got her cell phone and laptop set up in the hotel room in case anyone calls or emails."

Walter smiled, closed his tailgate and wrapped an arm around his son. "That's your mom; always the communications specialist."

As they returned to the lobby, Royce defended his mom. "Being in touch has always been important to her, Dad. She says that's why she likes her job so much. Her farm group always has meetings to discuss different parts of the business," he said.

They reached the lobby doors, and his dad opened one for a Japanese couple who nodded with gratitude and hurried inside. He motioned for his son to go through next. Royce had to pull the gear bag in front of him in order to slip through cleanly.

"Well, sometimes it's hard to stay in touch because of other things," his dad said. "I still have to work to pay the bills."

"Maybe that's what Mom didn't like about you," said Royce. His dad stopped and dropped his bag in front of the concierge's desk before turning to his son.

"What didn't she like?" his dad asked.

"I shouldn't tell you, Dad."

"Why not?"

"Because Grandma said that if you can't say anything nice, then don't say it at all."

While the Japanese couple was questioning the clerk at the registration desk a few feet away, Walter was pressing his son for more information.

"You can tell me," he said but then tartly added, "If you're man enough."

The registration clerk pointed the Japanese couple to Royce, but he didn't notice because he was facing a verbal showdown with his father. He was damned if he told his dad the truth, but he was really damned if he remained silent.

"Well…" Royce began, glancing at the hotel bar area. An old western movie was airing on the TV. For a moment he pictured himself as the fair but timid sheriff on the main street in an old Western town trying to avoid a gunfight with a bold and dangerous outlaw.

"I'm listening," his dad said as he leaned forward, staring directly into his son's eyes. Royce could almost see hot magma building pressure in his dad's pupils. Royce took a deep breath, swallowed hard and returned the glare. He was as tall as his dad, but his athletic build made him look more dominant. It was time for a showdown.

"She said that you talk to your fish cooler more than you talk to her," Royce said as he squinted his eyes extra hard to punctuate his statement. He was hoping that his dad wouldn't pull out a six-shooter and plug him full of lead like the outlaw was about to do to the poor sheriff on TV. Instead his dad stumbled back a step, surprised by Royce's words.

"She really said that?" Walter asked.

"That's what I heard her tell Grandma," his son replied.

Walter paused for a moment, and then decided that the battle was just getting started. "Well, at least my fish cooler doesn't argue and yell at me," Walter replied leaning more into Royce's chest. Royce wasn't prepared for this kind of discussion and didn't know what to say. He was digging himself into a deep hole and had to come up with something clever to save his own neck. He relaxed his squinting eyes and raised his eyebrows.

"Well, she did admit that a minute of arguing with you was better than a year of sweet talk from anyone else."

Suddenly the heat in his dad's eyes was quenched like hot lava rolling into the cold sea. "She really said that?" he asked in disbelief.

321

"Yup," his son answered with conviction.

"She really said that," Walter said again, stepping back and blinking his eyes a few times.

"Pretty much those exact words," insisted his son with even deeper conviction. Whether it was really true or not didn't matter to Royce right now. Just stunning his dad was all that mattered.

"Well, now," his dad exclaimed, looking away and rubbing his chin. "I just never realized that even bad communication is better than none at all." He then turned to his son, affectionately mussing up his hair. "Glad you told me son. Glad we had this conversation, but, ah, don't tell your mom."

Royce was thoroughly relieved. "Nope, we never had this talk, and I'll deny everything if she asks," he said, glancing over at the TV. On the screen, the outlaw was chased out of town by the sheriff, who then rode off with his sweetheart into the sunset. It was a happy ending for both the sheriff and the Sumner youth.

The Japanese couple, which politely waited for Royce and his dad to finish their verbal exchange, finally addressed them.

"Excuse us, please, are you part of the Sumner Family?"

Both father and son smiled at each other then turned to the couple. "Yes, now more than ever," said Royce proudly.

"And how can we help you?" Walter asked in his usual tourist-greeting voice.

"I am Kenji and this is my wife, Seiko," he said. We are looking for Janelle Sumner. Our daughter, Sayuri, is with the geology group and Janelle said she would have information about them."

"She's upstairs. Follow us," said Royce. Father and son led them up the darkly stained, wooden stairway to the second floor. They passed a few rooms before stopping in front of their door only to find it opened with several parents already inside conversing. Sayuri's parents quickly entered the room.

Janelle was sitting at the dining table, talking on her cell phone and scratching down some notes on a notepad. "OK...OK. That's all you got... Thanks. Call me if you hear anything else...Yes, I'm at the Bright Angel Lodge...Bye-bye." She scribbled a little more before closing her phone. Then she stood up and waved for attention from all the parents in the room. They quieted down and gathered around her.

Walter whispered in his son's ear. "I sure hope all these parents have their own rooms, or this place is gonna be real cozy at bedtime," he said.

Janelle then addressed the parents. "Thanks for coming. I thought it'd be better if just one of us got all the information from the Park Service and passed it to you." She placed a yellow, legal pad on the table with a pen. "Please sign in and include your phone number, so we know who's here and how best to reach you."

Janelle's management of the situation impressed Walter. "Your mom sure keeps a cool head during a state of crisis," he told his son.

# Chapter XIX

"Taqa, wake up; this is an emergency," Evaline whispered while firmly shaking his shoulder. It was early morning, and Evaline was the first to awaken in the cavern. She had already rekindled both fires and was heating a kettle of water. The flames lit up the entire area including Desiree, who was still sleeping.

Evaline's wavy hair was not yet brushed, and she still had puffy eyes from a hard sleep. Taqa opened his eyes, blinked a few times then focused on Evaline's distressed face, which was practically touching his.

"Evaline, the sight of your face right now could wake the dead," he said bluntly.

Evaline let out a snorting laugh. "Sorry you caught my raving beauty so early in the morning, but you have to see this," she said, showing him Desiree's journal.

"In a minute," Taqa replied. "Let me put on *my* morning face first." Taqa slowly got up and walked over to the first trough to sip some water. Then he pulled off his sweatshirt and walked to the second trough. He rinsed his face and neck a few times then tossed his shirt into a third trough, that was just a few feet farther down the gutter. He got a new shirt from his gear bag and pulled it on. He then stretched, arching his broad back while extending his arms over his head. He punctuated this whole routine with a low-pitched, growling yawn before rejoining Evaline at the fire.

"OK, now I'm awake. What is your emergency?" Taqa asked as he pulled the journal out of the plastic bag.

"I found that on the ground next to Desire's poncho, so I started reading it," replied Evaline. "It has sketches of our crevasse, and—look," she said turning the page. At the top was a sketch of the switchback trail up to the entrance of the crevasse.

Taqa looked at the sketches and read the scribbled passages. "This can't be Desiree's journal. The sketches were made many years ago—see the date?" He pointed to the date on the upper, right-hand corner. "No, this belongs to someone else—someone much older than Desiree," Taqa concluded.

Desiree called out to the wilderness caretakers, "It belonged to my grandpa. It contains all his travels through the Grand Canyon." She pulled off her blanket, sat up and stretched.

"Well, look who's come back to life!" Evaline cried. She snatched the journal out of Taqa's hands and walked it over to Desiree. "We didn't mean to be nosey about your journal. Actually I found it on the ground next to your poncho but didn't know whose it was, especially since the scouts are always bringing in stuff."

"Oh, that's OK," replied Desiree. "My grandma always said that anything found on the ground is automatically a universal possession."

Taqa returned the plastic bag to Desiree and rejoined the conversation. "Desiree, you have an astute but wise grandma," he said. "By the way, how are you feeling?" he asked.

"Just achy—like I got over the flu. My bandage loosened and the river rock fell out. But my arm's not that sore anymore," she said, hopping off the pallet and slipping her journal back inside the bag.

"Can I take a peek at your arm?" asked Taqa, who walked over to her. Desiree, who was considerably taller than most of her girlfriends, barely reached Taqa's shoulders.

"Festering clot-pole!" Desiree exclaimed, looking up at him. "You've got to be at least seven feet tall!"

"Perhaps in my younger years," he said, "But now I think I'm down to six-foot, ten." He then took her arm and bent over to inspect her wounds, but the lighting was dim. "Here, let's step closer to the fire."

When they did, Desiree noticed Taqa's new T-shirt, which was olive-green and had a picture of the San Francisco Peaks with the words *SNOWBOWL 11,500 ft. High, how are you?* It was apparently a souvenir shirt from the Snowbowl Ski Resort outside Flagstaff, Arizona. But, like the previous shirt he wore, it was a little tight for his massive upper body.

"Ugh, I still can't see," he complained.

"How about if I raise my arm?" She jumped up on the nearby rock and held it up for him, but he shook his head.

"Nope, now it's too far from the light." Then he chuckled, "Guess we're both too tall for a small fire built by my much shorter assistant.

Both looked out at Evaline, who was at the other fire, brewing herself some tea. They quietly chuckled, not wanting to be heard.

Then Taqa found a way to examine his patient's arm. "Guess we both better get a little shorter," he said and directed her to sit on the rock. Then he went into a deep squat, sitting on his heels while inspecting her arm. He slowly rolled it in order to view both the spider bite and the scratch.

She watched as he moved about in his squat. *Geez, this guy is incredibly limber for his size*, she thought then told him, "My scratch still hurts but not as bad as last night."

Taqa gently pressed on the skin around puncture site. "Like most scratches, it will hurt for a while. And, like most scratches, it will itch as the scab forms. We may as well remove the bandage and let the air do the healing." He then rose out of his squat, towering over her.

Desiree stood up and stepped back from him while smiling nervously. "Awesome—so, can I leave?" She then went to get her journal and tucked it back into the pocket of her poncho. "I really have to get back to my friends who, no doubt, are worried about me."

Evaline walked towards Taqa, giving him a frantic look. The caretakers hadn't yet decided what to do with Desiree.

Taqa improvised a generic answer. "Sure, Desiree, you can leave as soon as we find the best way to get you out of here," he said.

"How about the way we came?" asked Desiree, confused by his hazy answer.

"You can't," Taqa answered, conjuring up an explanation as he spoke. "The waterfall pushed mud and debris across the entrance. We'll have to find another way out for you."

"Out of where—where are we anyway?" she asked. Taqa got up and circled the fire in silence while Evaline answered Desiree.

"We're in a cavern within a larger crevasse. It protects us against the rain and cold, but unfortunately the entrance is blocked right now," she said.

Desiree was beginning to suspect a fabricated story by her caretakers. "I've seen several people coming and going. Even if the way I came is blocked, you obviously have other ways to get out," she said. As grateful as she was about their aid, she was now feeling more like a prisoner. "And who exactly are you people anyway?"

Evaline wanted to answer, but she relinquished to Taqa. But before he said anything, a scout suddenly appeared, carrying a bundle of clothes.

"What do you got, Vance?" Taqa asked the scout.

"Someone left these at the mouth of Clear Creek," Vance replied. "No one has come back for them, so I brought them here for us."

The sight of Vance's bundle delighted Taqa. His face lit up like that of a child viewing a stack of birthday presents. "Oh, good! Maybe some oversized river runner left some oversized clothes for me," he said cheerfully. Vance opened the bundle of clothes on the top of a wide rock by the fire. Both men immediately rummaged through the pile.

Evaline chuckled before explaining to Desiree what was happening. "Lots of clothes are left in the canyon, so we try to recycle them; it helps minimize litter." While she was speaking Vance found a black T-shirt with a picture of Michael Jackson on the front.

"Aw, cool!" Vance exclaimed, "The King of Pop, and he's all mine." He tucked the shirt into his belt and ran off.

Taqa also found a T-shirt and held it up. It looked like his size, but not really his color.

"Oh, great—bright pink," he grumbled. On the back was an iron-on photo of a knobby-kneed, three-year old ballet student. He

328

flipped to the front and saw words printed in fancy scroll across the chest:

*Happy Father's Day from your little princess!*

"I can't wear this," he said, dropping it back onto the pile. "Why can't someone leave a *normal shirt* that's my size?" Both Evaline and Desiree laughed.

He then shrugged his broad shoulders and walked back to Desiree. "So, Desiree, you wanted to know who we really are, right?"

Desiree nodded.

"Well, how can I explain this—we're members of a group called *Friends of the Canyon,* who patrol the park to learn of its mystery while enjoying its splendor," said Taqa, winking at Evaline. "In fact, we get free access to the park in exchange for services to lost or injured hikers. We help the park service in remote areas where they can't always patrol."

To Desiree his explanation was plausible, and she felt somewhat satisfied but at the same time more fascinated. "Do they pay you for your service?" she asked.

"No, they don't have to," answered Evaline.

"Then how do you get money for all your provisions?"

"We don't need money," argued Taqa. "Mother Nature provides us with most everything." Then he pointed at the clothes pile. "And, as you can see, so do some forgetful visitors. The Grand Canyon is the largest lost-and-found in the world. We have everything we need: clothing, water, shelter—even entertainment."

"Really—you get cable TV down here?" Desiree asked.

"No, better than that; twenty-four hours of the Natural Wonder Channel," answered Taqa.

"Then you *don't* get cable TV."

"We don't need it; we do a great deal of people-watching, and I'll tell you that's more than enough entertainment for us."

"But how do you stay in touch with the outside world?"

Evaline just had to get back into this conversation. "Child, the Grand Canyon is the largest newsstand in the world," she said. "We read all your discarded newspapers, magazines, and books. We even have a few of those tiny music players. Thank goodness you don't use those boom boxes anymore. They were so bulky, loud and just plain annoying."

"Desiree, we even know how your stocks are doing—well, maybe just a day behind," Taqa added.

Suddenly two younger cave dwellers ran inside the cavern. Desiree recognized them from the night before. To her they looked about ten years old until she heard them talk with younger dialect.

"Nana, we hear voices from outside the chimney," said the shorter one, pointing upward.

Evaline looked up and listened. "Shideezhi, it must be hikers off-trail," she answered. "Quietly keep vigilance until they go away."

The taller girl then showed one of her fingers to Evaline. "Nana, I hurt my finger on the rocks. Can you please make it better?"

Evaline examined it, lightly running her fingers over it. "Oh dear, Shedi, you really scraped it up this time. Let me clean it for you."

Both youngsters then noticed Desiree and smiled at her.

"She looks a lot better than she did last night, Nana," said Shideezhi.

"Is she our new sister, now?" Shedi asked.

"No, she's from a different tribe," Evaline answered. "Why don't you two introduce yourselves to Desiree?"

The younger girl stepped forward and extended her hand. "Hello, Desiree. My name is Shideezhi, and I'm five years old."

Desiree gazed in astonishment as she shook the girl's hand. Shideezhi stood about five feet tall and had the physique of a gymnast. Her well-developed neck and shoulder muscles could be seen from the jeweled neck of her T-shirt, which was partially exposed from her half-zipped hoodie.

"You're only five?" Desiree asked. Before she could say anything else, the other girl proudly stood forward and extended her hand.

"Pleased to meet you, Desiree. I'm Shedi, and I'm six."

Desiree's jaw dropped as she shook the older sister's hand. She was maybe an inch or two taller than her sister with a similar physique. Desiree couldn't help noticing how her well-developed calf muscles resembled small tree trunks.

"You certainly are tall and strong for someone six years old," Desiree remarked.

"Thank you," Shedi replied, "I soon hope to be a great hunter like Naturale."

"And I want to be a scout, scaling the cliffs, like Nanu and Vance," Shideezhi added with enthusiasm.

Evaline then guided them to the second trough. "Alright you two, I'll get Shedi's scratch cleaned then you could help get more wood for the fire—how does that sound?" The two jumped up and down eagerly. Shideezhi then leaped like a frog upon a nearby rock that was at least three-feet off the ground.

While watching them Desiree whispered to Taqa, "Are they Evaline's granddaughters?"

"Yes," he replied. "Aren't they great—so ambitious and smart."

"They are so developed for their ages," she remarked. They're so tall and nimble; they look like they could slam dunk a basketball."

"Evaline must have passed down some good genes," replied Taqa.

Desiree disagreed. "Maybe her good nature but none of her physical qualities. I have cousins their age that are much smaller and can barely jump half that high."

"Then it must be the clean air and water," he answered.

"More like supernatural air and water, Taqa. All your people seem far more developed in size and strength. Naturale carried me out of a raging creek and through the crevasse like I was a sack lunch. Then I saw the other hunters bound up vertical cliffs like monkeys up a tree. They all showed incredible strength and agility."

"—Because they work out daily in the world's biggest fitness gym," Taqa answered, trying his best to convince her.

But she wasn't convinced. She approached him, stopping a few yards short. "Even you, Taqa," she said holding her hand up to block her view of his body. "From the neck up you look like someone my dad's age." Then she blocked her view of his head. "But from the shoulders down, you look like a cross between an oak tree and a Mack Truck—fully loaded with options."

Taqa was stunned by her acute yet candid description of his personal appearance. Evaline gasped, then covered her mouth, trying to suppress her laughter.

Taqa smiled. "Now you're making me blush," he said crossing his long, muscular arms as if hiding his physique.

But Desiree was becoming more suspicious. "So really, who are you and how do you all get so healthy?"

Taqa paused for a few seconds before answering her with a question of his own. "Well, Desiree, who do we appear to be?"

She walked from the fire to the pallet then back to him. "Except for Evaline, your people appear to be a tribe of super humans. I can't explain Evaline; maybe she started out as an outsider and joined up later. As for the rest of you, maybe living off the land has made you super humans. But I suspect there's more to it."

"Very interesting so far," said Taqa. "Please continue."

She then turned to the first trough, and slowly ran her fingers along its edge. "You're not visitors of the park. Judging by the limited provisions and these water troughs you seem more like full-time residents. And I'll bet the park rangers don't even know you're down here. Am I right so far?"

Taqa's eyes widened, amazed at her correct suppositions. At the same time he feared that she knew too much to be released. With his arms still crossed, he slowly paced to the fire then turned back to her.

"Yes, you seem to be—as they say—batting one thousand. Our ancestors have lived in these canyons for centuries. We hunt, gather, grow and thrive in this area. Some of us stayed with the old ways, wearing buckskin and fur. That pallet you slept on is over one hundred years old. It was originally made with bark and hide, but we upgraded it a bit. Like that pallet most of us have modernized. We wear the same clothes as you—although no one seems to leave around anything my size."

Desiree couldn't help giggling at his joke. "So, you're a hidden tribe of the canyons, huh?"

He nodded. "To everyone else in this park we look just like them. And just like them we roam the trails and enjoy the sites. But we also offer aid to the lost or injured. If they sprain an ankle, then we wrap it, and make sure they get out OK. If they have more grave conditions we take care of them for the rest of their lives."

"What do you mean, *grave conditions*?" Desiree asked.

Taqa walked towards her while brushing the crevasse wall with one of his large, broad hands. "Desiree, some visitors are mortally wounded from a serious fall, heart attack or severe exposure. If they're alone, we stay with them and try to keep them comfortable before they expire. We believe no one should be alone when they pass to the next life. After they do, we make sure their bodies are discovered, so that they can be returned to their loved ones."

Evaline finished cleaning Shedi's scratch and sent both grandchildren off for firewood. She then rejoined Desiree and Taqa by the trough. "Then, Desiree, there are others who feel destitute, desperate or even suicidal—like me. I came here over forty years ago looking for a quiet and quick death after feeling neglected by my parents. Taqa's father found me ready to jump over the edge of a hundred foot cliff. He pulled me back and took me into his family. He and his people lifted me out of my depression. He gave me a second chance on life. I've been here ever since."

"What about your family—didn't they look for you?" Desiree asked.

She shook her head. "They probably thought I ran away to prostitution and drugs. I'm sure they were glad I left," said Evaline, looking down at the ground.

"Didn't you ever miss them?"

"I never missed the hate and rejection I felt at home. Here I am with the people who love me. They've become my family. I found my soul mate, raised my children, and now enjoy watching their children." She looked out where her grandchildren left the main cavern area. Then she looked back at Desiree. "The canyon has been my home for over forty years, and I don't regret a minute of it," she said smiling. Desiree returned Evaline's smile upon hearing such a happy ending.

But then Desiree's smile fell, thinking about her own family. She ran her fingers through the cold water then took a quick sip. "Well, it has only been two days for me, but I already miss my family. I'll admit we're not perfect; we've had our ups and downs. My parents separated a few years ago, and it really floored me. I lost interest in my hobbies and studies. I didn't even care about failing in school. My mom wanted me to get counseling."

Evaline leaned towards Desiree to hold one of her hands. "Do you know why your parents separated, dear?" she asked.

Desiree looked down at her bare feet then walked to the drying rack by the fire. She felt her socks. They were already dry, so she pulled them onto her feet. Then she turned to answer the wilderness nurse.

"Mom and Dad separated soon after my grandpa died about four years ago," she said while flexing and pointing her toes in her socks.

"The same grandpa who wrote in that journal?"

"Yes," Desiree answered. "He got some sort of blood disease from a rose thorn. Can you believe it? A rose thorn! Stupid plant."

Her voice rose with her anger. She grabbed a half-burned twig from the fire and crammed it deeper into the fire. The twig cracked and folded, causing the flames to burn brighter.

Both caretakers acknowledged Desiree's frustration. They continued to listen intently as Desiree vented her feelings. She needed healing far beyond her physical wounds.

She continued. "So, anyway, my dad felt he could have prevented grandpa's death. He had so much guilt that he withdrew from us and got absorbed more in his work. We wouldn't see him for days. He eventually moved out but only to a nearby town. He would phone my brother and me every now and then, but never once did he phone my mom. I don't know…it just wasn't the same as living together. Even though Mom said he was an emotional wreck, I still love him. I love them both very much." She began to sniffle.

Evaline's eyes began to water, and Taqa once again handed her his handkerchief. She took it, dabbing her eyes and sniffling. Desiree returned to the trough and watched the water flow down to a wide and shallow ditch that ran back through the rest of the cavern.

Then she began to smile. "But, you know, things are looking brighter," she said, turning back to them. "Dad has been coming around the house lately, and he's starting to work things out with Mom." She giggled. "They even went out on a date! So I think they may get back together soon. It keeps me hopeful— wanting to be back with them more than ever."

Evaline was overwhelmed with emotion and started sobbing. She wanted to cry on Taqa's shoulder, but it was too high for her, so she jumped up on a nearby ledge…

\* \* \*

"Come on, Aaron, hold still!" Candice cried while on top of his shoulder. They were trying to ascend the rocky cliff upstream of the waterfalls. The precipice had irregular edges but was reachable for everyone taller than Candice.

"I'm doing the best I can," Aaron yelled up to her. "You're not exactly a lightweight, especially with your hard boots—ow! That was my ear!"

"Sorry, I thought it was your nose," she said, laughing as she boosted herself up to the next ledge. "When you're pint-sized like me, you got to find as many footholds as you can—even if it's a classmate's head." She got to her feet then watched Aaron from below. "Being resourceful can help overcome your deficiencies," she commented.

Aaron pulled himself up to her ledge effortlessly. "Deficiencies? Don't know anything about having deficiencies," he said brushing the loose gravel from his denim jacket and jeans.

Meanwhile Dominique and Perro were on the very next rock above them. "Just a few more feet, and we can get over to the next cove," Dominique yelled down to the others.

Perro was jumping in place like a boxer waiting for his fighting bout to start. "Man, I'm so full of energy for this mission; I want to get to the top right now—before anyone else," he said.

"Now, Perro," Dominique advised him sternly, "there's greater strength in numbers, but you have to wait for the numbers to catch up," she said. "We're already in trouble with Mr. R. for going on this unauthorized search party."

"Yeah, but as an unauthorized search party all the rules go out the window," he replied. He then crossed over to a wider, ledge and stood on his hands.

Dominique shrieked. "Perro, what are you doing?"

"Ugh," he groaned, pushing his arms straight and stabilizing his balance. "I'm practicing patience. You should try it sometime."

"No way! It's too dangerous here," she said.

"Then maybe you should come over to this ledge where there's more room."

"I don't know—will you hold me so I don't fall?" she asked.

"*Prometo*," he said, "I promise." Perro dropped to his feet to help her. Dominique jumped over to his ledge, which was wide enough for both of them. She did a handstand as Perro supported her legs.

"Hey, this wasn't too hard," she said. "Wow! Perro, you have to see the canyon wall across the creek from upside down; it really looks cool." Perro walked Dominique over to the cliff face and propped her legs up against it.

"Stay right there while I join you," he instructed as he got back into his handstand.

Taylor, who was at the same elevation but a few yards away, grabbed her camera. "Wait, you two. Hold that pose!"

"*¡No problemo!*" Dominique yelled as she and Perro smiled for the photo. Dominique could feel the blood rushing to her head, and Perro noticed.

"You look cute—being all red in the face like that," he commented.

"Thanks, *amigo*," she replied. " By the way, what kind of car do you drive?"

"Oh, it's a hundred year-old Toyota from *mi Tío José*. But I take good care of it and wash it every Saturday," he answered.

That was the answer Dominique was hoping to hear. "Really—you wash it every week?"

"*Sí*, a clean car is important," he said.

Dominique dropped her feet and sat on the ground. "I can't agree with you more!" She then tried to stand up quickly, but she lost her balance when the blood rushed from her head. She stumbled towards the edge. "Whoa, the ground is tilting a bit."

Taylor saw Dominique's difficulty but was too far away to help her partner. "Dominique, watch it—you're too close to the edge," she warned.

But Dominique couldn't keep her balance. Her one foot slipped over the edge. She fell onto her seat and slid off the rock feet-first down a crumbly slope, trying to catch a firm edge with her feet.

"Dominique!" Taylor shouted then gasped in terror. Perro scrambled over and tried to grab Dominique, but she already slid beyond his reach.

"OK, this is *not* where I want to go," Dominique said, terrified at the sight of the steep drop ahead of her. "Somebody help me!" She screamed her lungs out as she rolled onto her stomach and slid thirty more feet. Trying to slow down, she clawed at the rocky surface, but the crumbling stones slipped through her fingers.

She accelerated down to the last edge, still clawing for any kind of hold, but she ultimately dropped twenty feet to the ground. She landed on her feet, but her knees buckled instantly as she fell to her hands and knees. Taylor, Perro, Candice and Aaron hurried down to where Dominique landed and joined everyone else who were already there.

Dominique groaned as she rolled to a sitting position, grabbing her leg from behind the knee.

Upon hearing the screams, Mr. Roeser ran from the kitchen tarp in time to see Dominique adjusting into a less painful position.

"Hey, Mr. R.," Dominique groaned while looking up at him. "Thought I'd drop in—ouch."

Mr. Roeser inspected Dominique's shinbone, which was pale and maligned. He lightly ran his fingers over it, and she winced in pain. "Sorry, Dominique. Can you move it at all?"

Dominique lay back onto the ground and closed her eyes tightly. "No, it hurts really bad."

Mr. Roeser ran to get some blankets while the rest of the students huddled around Dominique.

With her scraped and dirtied hands, Dominique reached out to Taylor. "Don't think I'll be spiking a volleyball anytime soon with these hands," she said.

Taylor smiled at her captain. "That's OK. You couldn't really spike a volleyball all that well, anyway."

"Ooh, ouch—Taylor, now that really cuts me," Dominique remarked.

"Here, let me clean them for you," Taylor said, squirting some water from her bottle over Dominique's palms and fingertips. Taylor then pulled out a cleansing wipe from a plastic bag she kept in her pocket. Moistening it with more water, she wiped the grit and dust from Dominique's face.

Dominique smiled at her teammate. "Thanks for the first aid, Taylor. Glad you're on my team," she said. "Sure wish your water bottle could rinse away the pain in my leg."

The other students, who were stunned from the whole incident, just watched Dominique—not knowing what to do. When Mr. Roeser returned, he instructed the students to move Dominique onto one of the blankets. He then rolled up another blanket and placed it under her leg to cushion it from the hard ground.

"Miss Cruseaux needs medical help right away, so I'll need a few of you to catch up with Clydes and inform them of our emergency. We've got to get Dominique out of here as soon as possible…"

* * *

"Taqa, someone is injured just upstream," reported a scout, who seemed to appear out of nowhere.

Taqa greeted the messenger with a firm arm shake. "Good to see you, again, Nanu," he said, as if the scout were a bigger concern than the news he reported.

But Desiree was more concerned about the injury. "Did you see who it was?" she asked, interrupting the tribal men.

Nanu didn't answer her right away. He coughed a little and walked over to the first trough to sip some water. His height and build was similar to Naturale's, although his face looked more Polynesian. He wore a green, camouflaged sweatshirt and green-colored cargo pants. His hair was brownish-red and braided in one, long rope down his back. From his appearance Desiree guessed that he was one of the scouts that Shideezhi had mentioned.

After drinking some water, he waited for Taqa's permission to answer Desiree. Taqa nodded, allowing the scout to report.

"It was a short woman with olive skin and long dark hair," he said. "She was about halfway up the cliff before losing her footing."

Naturale, who also seemed to appear out of nowhere, joined Nanu at the trough. "She lost her footing because she was careless on a dangerous ledge."

Desiree gasped. "That's got to be Dominique," she said and ran to Taqa, grabbing his sand-colored jacket along the way. "Please help her—she's one of my friends."

Taqa took his jacket. "Of course I will help your friend, Desiree." He slipped it on and went to grab his medical bag, a

341

nylon gym bag with an *Iowa State Cyclones* emblem on the side panel that was hanging from the wall.

Desiree wanted to bolt for the entrance, but she knew that the tribesman would catch her in a heartbeat.

For the moment Taqa's attention was on the scout. "By the way, Nanu, how's your cough?"

Nanu cleared his throat before answering. "Much better—almost gone—thanks to your medicine."

"Good to hear," said Taqa, who then held onto the scout's shoulders. "Can you take a few deep breaths for me, please?"

Desiree watched as Taqa pressed one ear onto Nanu's chest, listening to the scout's breathing.

But she was getting impatient. "Taqa, come on—you've got to help Dominique," she said, stressing her own urgency.

Taqa ignored her, his attention still on Nanu. "Yes, your breathing does sound better, but keep my infusion in a bowl close to your mouth and nose when you sleep; it should clear your breathing passages..." The two continued conversing with each other as if they were catching up on old times.

"Ugh!" Desiree cried out in exasperation.

Just then Evaline gently pulled her aside. "Dear, all medical cases are important to Taqa. You just have to be patient," she said.

Desiree then remembered the lecture her dad gave about patience and acknowledged the wilderness nurse. "You're right, Evaline; Nanu's health must be very important to your tribe—I just keep forgetting that other people have needs besides me."

Taqa ignored the women's conversation, but finally inquired about the falling accident. "So, Nanu, about the injury—did you see how she fell?"

"She landed feet-first," Nanu replied. "But her legs buckled, possibly from an injury."

Taqa opened his bag and added a few more rolls of cloth strips.

"OK, I think I've got what I need," Taqa said, zipping the bag shut. "Evaline, I think you should come with me in case I need to splint the leg."

Evaline nodded and grabbed her vest. Nanu coughed again before heading for the cavern's exit. Taqa began to follow, but Desiree darted in front of him. "Please, you have to let me go, too—Dominique is my friend," she begged him.

The tribal elder was not prepared to deal with her at the moment. He dropped his bag and held her firmly by the shoulders, motioning for Naturale. The tribal hunter came up from behind to seize her, and she immediately struggled. But his grip on her was too strong.

Taqa transformed from a jovial caretaker to an agitated oppressor. "No, Desiree, you absolutely cannot leave right now," he harshly replied. "Naturale will keep you here until we return," he said then turned from her, zipping up his jacket and getting his bag.

Desiree knew she couldn't break free from Naturale, so she grunted in frustration. "Taqa," she called out to him. "I sense that you're not planning to let me go."

He wished for more time to figure out what to do with her, but the injury took precedence. "You are amazingly perceptive, Desiree, but I'm sorry; you'll have to stay."

Naturale grunted in delight, knowing his prey was permanently captive.

Desiree pleaded further with the medicine man. "Although your life here is fascinating, Taqa, I do not wish to be part of it. My family and friends are more important, and I would not be happy living without them," she said, walking cooperatively with Naturale to the seats by the fire.

Evaline did not feel comfortable with Taqa's decision. She felt that Taqa was so locked into tribal code that it blinded him from any clever thought.

Then suddenly an idea came to her, and she tugged on Taqa's sleeve. He looked down and saw her crafty smile. He also saw mischief twinkling in her eyes—the same kind she had the night before. He sensed that she had devised a plan for Desiree, and he nodded to her. Then he smiled and turned back to Desiree.

"Oops, I forgot to tell you, Desiree, Naturale is a skilled and *honorable* hunter, and you are just a *meager* challenge to him."

Evaline also added, "But meager is a relative term, Desiree, if *you have resources*," she said and winked.

As the scout and tribal elders turned to walk away, Evaline shouted back a few more parting comments. "By the way, Desiree, did I ever mention that Naturale *taught my grandkids cliff climbing*? They're getting pretty good at it." Then they disappeared from sight.

Desiree stared into the fire, thinking about what Evaline and Taqa said. They apparently left some sort of cryptic message for her, but she was so flustered and couldn't think clearly.

She looked all around the cavern. Far off she could hear the happy voices of Evaline's grandchildren at play, but, for the worst part, she and Naturale were alone together. This unnerved her.

"I thought that the entrance was blocked by debris from the waterfall," she said to him.

"It is blocked for you and no one else," Naturale replied, smiling smugly.

Not appreciating his explanation, Desiree stomped her stocking feet and glared back at him. "Ugh! I don't know what to believe. Everyone here talks in lies or riddles. This whole place is filled with deceit and trickery. There is no honor here."

Her words angered him. "How can you say that!" He pounded the base of his spear on the ground, making a sharp, cracking sound that echoed through the cavern. "Last night you said you admired my integrity. That means I have *honor*!"

"Yeah, for *not* hunting prey that is wounded," she replied. "Well, I'm still wounded, and you stand there, poised like a lion, ready to pounce on me if I try to flee."

"If you flee, then you are not wounded," he stated in a calmer voice. "And if you *are not* wounded, then you will be hunted like prey."

Desiree thought about the strategy of chess: to exploit the opponent's weakness. She then recalled Taqa's statement about Naturale's honor as a hunter, and that she was just a meager challenger. But *meager* was a relative term. Could it mean she was considered meager by only Naturale's standards? Did Taqa and Evaline think she was more than meager? And what about the resources Evaline mentioned? Maybe there are resources around to help Desiree.

She guessed that one of Naturale's weaknesses was his faulty logic. She got up and casually circled the fire, eyeing her hiking boots on the drying rack. She needed them as much as she needed to plan her strategy against her opponent—the honorable Naturale.

"So, if I stay, I'm wounded, and you *will not* hunt me, right?"

"Correct."

"But if I leave, then I must *not be* wounded, and you *will* hunt me, right?"

"Yes, like fair game."

Now that the rules of Naturale's game were established, Desiree needed to challenge him. She got up and walked to the trough where he was sipping some water. She stopped a few feet short of him and, with hands on her hips, poised to taunt him.

"How can a great hunter like you get caught by prey like me?" she asked, "It must have been humiliating."

He turned towards her and growled. She looked up into his large, brown eyes that were growing more intense with her biting words. She then watched his chest heave inside of the flowered Hawaiian shirt that he wore.

*But I could never embarrass you the way that tacky tropical shirt does*, she thought to herself.

His angered breath displaced the dreadlocks that draped over the flowered print. "Yes, you did humiliate me," he said, seething.

"So, you probably don't want me here as a reminder of this humiliation," she said watching his eyes grow wider and chest heave more deeply. "I must be a thorn in your side, the pith on your orange and the sock scrunch in your boot."

"Yes, you are that pesky to me," he admitted then started sharpening the edge of his spear by the trough.

"Wouldn't you like to get rid of me?"

"What do you mean?" he asked.

"How would you like another chance to hunt me down and rid yourself of the embarrassment I caused?"

Naturale tested the now sharper edge of his spear with his fingers. Then he refocused on Desiree. "I could think of nothing better right now," he answered.

Desiree was now set to strike a deal with her captor. She stepped upon a rock by the fire, took a deep breath, and posed her challenge.

"Then turn me loose and give me time to escape before you hunt for me. If you catch me, then I'm your captured prize. You win and I lose because I'll be your trophy—a testimony of your greatness. If you don't capture me, and I escape, then I will not be around as a reminder of the humiliation I caused you. You could tell your tribe that I fell in the deep crevasse or drowned in the swift-running creek. I win because I'm gone, and you win because I will no longer be the thorn in your side."

Naturale approached her at the rock. "But I am bigger, stronger and more skilled. There is no glory in capturing meager prey like you."

Desiree held the top of his shoulders for balance and rose onto her toes, so that she could appear more dominant. She wanted to tap into his honorable soul with her tempting prowess.

"It is true you are big and strong…but skilled? How can meager prey like me surprise a skilled hunter like you? Obviously I am more cunning and adept than you think. Your size and strength mean nothing if you can be outwitted." She stepped off the rock, walked a few feet away and turned back to him. "And therein lies the challenge," she said.

A crafty smile began turning up the corners of his lips as he considered the winning outcomes. His smile grew larger and the fire in his eyes flickered with delight.

"You realize that the capture process may injure or even kill you," he advised, stroking his spear's sharp tip. "As a hunter I never had to worry about the safety of my prey because I always killed it."

"Oh, yeah," she mumbled. That was, indeed, a dangerously significant glitch that Desiree hadn't considered. The stakes were indeed high. But she was desperate, and this challenge at least gave her a chance—an extremely small one—to gain her freedom.

She took a deep breath. *"Fair is foul and foul is fair,"* she declared, borrowing a line from Shakespeare. "My drive for freedom overruns any danger from this hunt." She then pulled the pointed end of Naturale's spear towards her. "In fact, I laugh in danger's face," and she laughed directly at the sharpened point, "Ha!" She couldn't believe what she was saying, but it certainly sounded convincing to her opponent. *It's a good thing I took theatre for four years,* she thought.

The smile on the hunter's face was brighter than any of the tropical flowers on his shirt. "I like the rules of this hunt," he said.

Her virtual chessboard was opened and her pieces set. She pushed the spear's point back at him. "So, what do you say, Enrique?"

\* \* \*

"Hello, this is Wally-Ray. How can I help you?" Walter asked the caller on his cell phone while sipping a cup of coffee at the dining table in the hotel room. "No, I have suspended all bookings for this week due to a family emergency. Your concierge will provide you with another tour service. Sorry for the inconvenience. Good luck and have fun."

He closed his phone and looked beyond the hiking map, phone directory, legal pad and coffee cup that lay in front of his wife. Her hair was tucked back behind the ears, exposing long sterling silver earrings that were lined with tiny turquoise stones.

"Honey, can I get you some more coffee?" Walter asked, getting up from his seat. She looked up from her paperwork and smiled at him.

"Sure thing, babe," she replied. He walked over to get her cup, bending over and brushing back her graying hair to better view the earrings she wore.

"I love how silver sparkles up your face—are these new?"

She swiveled in her seat towards him. "No, you gave me these for our tenth wedding anniversary, and they've always been my favorite pair."

He smiled, holding her face in his hands and looking all around it before finding her deep-blue eyes, which seemed to mirror the early morning canyon skies.

"They look better on you now than they ever did," he said and kissed her ear lobe. She smiled as he grabbed her cup and walked to the coffee pot.

It was a thermally insulated, having a fifty-cup capacity—compliments of guest services. On the lower tier of the coffee cart was a large tray of fresh fruit, bagels and muffins. Several parents were gathered around the cart, enjoying the breakfast offerings while waiting for any news updates about their children from Janelle.

As Walter finished pouring his wife's coffee, his cell phone went off again. He quickly delivered his wife's coffee while listening to the caller, but the noisy room caused him to head towards the hallway.

"I'm sorry; I didn't hear you very well. I'm in a room full of worried parents." The caller at the other end repeated his identity and Walter's voice rose with intensity. "Pete, good to hear from you! How's your helicopter business doing?"

"Really busy now—thanks to all your referrals," Pete answered. "Hey, I heard on the news about the flash floods in the canyon. Might your daughter be with that Phoenix group that's still down there?"

"Yeah, she and her class were studying geology," answered Walter, "but I guess Mother Nature changed it to hydrology."

Pete first laughed at Walter's joke but then realized the potentially grave situation.

"Sorry to hear that," Pete said, then asked, "Hey, any idea where they camped?"

"According to park service, the school's permit listed the end of Clear Creek Trail," Walter answered. Then he heard the sound of a map unfolding over the phone.

"Just a minute, here...OK, I found it," said Pete. "It's right on the north side of the Colorado River and runs few miles east of the North Kaibab Trail. How about I drop you down there to see if the kids are OK?"

Walter jumped at Pete's offer. "Really? Hell, Pete, that would be great!" Walter ran back into the room, waving to get his wife's attention. She saw him and rose from her chair as he called to her. "It's Pete Piper on the phone. He wants to fly me into the canyon and search for the kids."

Janelle tried to get to her husband, but couldn't get past all the parents, who were lined up at the coffee cart. Instead she yelled back to him, "That's great, honey! Tell him we'd be forever grateful."

Walter got back on his phone. "Pete, my wife and I would be forever grateful."

"Are you kidding me—it's the least I can do for a great friend and business associate. I'll just need another hour to file my flight plan and get clearance. I can pick you up at the helipad, OK?"

"We're already packed, so we'll see you there," replied Walter.

"Someone else joining you?" Pete asked.

"Yes, Royce will be with me," Walter answered while pushing past the parents and meeting up with Janelle.

"Royce? Wow! I haven't seen him since he was knee high. I hope he isn't as ugly as you," Pete joked.

Walter initially laughed but then answered more earnestly. "Nope, he has the best of Janelle and me," Walter said, wrapping one arm around his wife.

"I'm sure he does," Pete agreed. "Can't wait to see how he's grown."

"See you in a bit. Thanks again, Pete," said Walter. He closed his phone and gave Janelle an energetic hug. "You can't imagine how excited I feel right now—especially with you in my arms."

She squeezed him back and closed her eyes. "You can't believe how long I've ached to be in your arms again." She then pulled away while running her hands up and down his arms. "I always loved you, Wally-Ray, and I ain't just saying it 'cause of now."

Walter smiled and held her at the hips. "I know, babe, I feel the same way. I just had to kick a few stupid obstacles out of the way, first. When I think back about how unimportant they really were, I just wanna kick myself instead. I realize now that nothing is more important than you and the kids." He then pulled her back into his arms. "I wanna be the same husband, lover, and best friend like I was before."

Royce was watching the news on TV, and suddenly jumped up from the couch. "Mom, Dad, there's a news chopper hovering over a flooded creek!" Everyone migrated towards the TV screen and saw the Bright Angel Creek flooding its banks. "I wonder if we could see Dizzy down there."

The camera zoomed in on a group leaving a nearby campground and heading for the bridge. Most appeared to be young boys lead by a few adults. Walter and Janelle walked hand-in-hand towards the TV.

Walter pointed to the boys, one of whom was carrying a flag. "No, they look more like boy scouts, not high school seniors," said his dad. "Come on, son, we have to go."

"Are we hiking down the trail to find Dizzy?" Royce asked.

"Better 'n' that, son. We're gonna fly down there in a chopper!"

"Better still!" Royce cried as he headed to his bedroom. He politely nudged aside some of the parents. "Give me a minute, Dad; I gotta change and get my gear."

Some of the parents heard Walter and spread the news. In no time the room was filled with excitement. Janelle walked over to the dining table. She stepped onto a dining room chairs with help from her husband.

"Thank you, my handsome, buckskinned hero," she said as he held her steady. She then called to the parents. "Can I have everyone's attention, please?" They all turned to her and moved closer. "Some of you have already heard the good news, but I'll make it official. My husband and son are joining a helicopter search for the geology group. They will be leaving shortly for the Clear Creek Trail."

The group stirred and began to murmur. One parent asked, "Will they be able to evacuate our kids?" Janelle looked down at Walter, prompting him for an answer.

"Not all at once," he said. He was tall enough to speak out to the others while standing on the floor. "Pete's helicopter is not equipped for large-scale evacuations. Last I heard his chopper could carry only four people beside himself. But I'm sure if there are any medical emergencies he'll fly them out first."

The parents again muttered with more concern. Janelle sensed it and asked her husband to reassure them. Walter then proceeded to jump on another chair. The fringes on his buckskin jacket, which were curled and twisted from years of use, swayed with his every movement.

"Now, hold on just a minute, folks; you've got to understand something. My friend, Pete Piper, operates a helicopter touring service and has limited transport capabilities." His sun-tanned face scanned the room like a radar transmitter, meeting every parent's face as he continued speaking. "But he is certainly another critically-needed eye in the sky. The priority right now is to locate your—*our*—children. And when we do, we'll first assess their situation; they may not need immediate evacuation. We'll radio back their position and status from the chopper." He looked back at his wife and spoke with a softer voice. "How did that sound, honey?"

She smiled back at him. "Pretty damn convincing. Even I feel better now," she said.

Just then Royce came out from the bedroom dressed in cargo pants, safari jacket and boots. A daypack was strapped to his back, and he was sporting a wide-brimmed hat that his mom got him at the camping store.

"I'm ready, Dad," he said. "Being part of a rescue operation is so cool!" Both Janelle and Walter gazed at their grown-up son in his entire outdoor-looking splendor.

"He actually looks handsome in that get-up, don't he?" Janelle asked. Walter grinned and puffed up his chest.

"Yep, just like his old man," he said. Then he turned to kiss her.

She kissed him back while holding him tightly. "I love you, Wally-Ray, be careful," she said.

He gave her an extra squeeze then turned to grab his duffle bag from the kitchen counter. He pulled out an empty daypack and filled it with vital provisions before slipping it on his back.

"I promise we'll stay in touch, honey," he said to his wife and smiled, "I know you like when people do that." He and Royce then headed for the doorway. They both turned to wave at the parents, who cheered and waved back. Then the Sumner men descended down the stairs and left the hotel.

Outside they passed two more hotels before turning south to cross the railroad tracks. A silver helicopter passed from overhead.

"That's not Pete's," Walter told his son. "He's got a neon-yellow one. I'm sure there's a whole mess of choppers involved with rescue operations."

They hurried to the helipad and saw several people moving in and out of the control office. Some were dressed as pilots, wearing aviator glasses and flight jackets. Others were dressed as hikers, wearing several layers of clothes to accommodate the changing weather. Still others were dressed as concerned family members, holding cellphones up against their ears.

"That's got to be the busiest place on Earth," Royce commented.

"That's nothing; wait till you see the corridor trails," his dad replied. "They'll be jam-packed with mules and hikers trying to get out."

The silver helicopter landed at the next available pad just as another one took off. Royce watched it as it rose, turned towards the canyon and sped away.

He and his dad stopped at the steps of the control office and slipped off their packs. Walter checked his watch and sat on a bench on the other side of the porch.

"This is where we wait," he said. "Pete should be here soon."

Royce looked around at all the people coming and going from this area. His pulse was racing from all the commotion, including another chopper that zoomed overhead and hovered briefly before landing. It was neon-yellow with the words *Pete Piper's Heli-Tours* painted in black on the bottom of the fuselage.

"That's him," said Walter. "Always keeping a subtle image."

Royce watched the helicopter land, and his jaw dropped. "That is the coolest chopper I ever saw," he remarked.

* * *

"You're not gonna chop off my leg are you?" Dominique asked the oversized wilderness medic while spying the bear knife he had in his hand.

Taqa chuckled before answering her, "No, I just need to cut away your pant leg a little, so that I can better assess your injury. After that I'll know if I need to chop off your leg."

Dominique's eyes widened with apprehension as she watched Taqa carefully slice her pant leg along the seam a few inches up from her knee.

Several minutes before, Nanu had directed the wilderness medics to the geology class campsite, where they found the students huddled around Dominique, who was still on the blanket with her leg propped up. Mr. Roeser saw their approach and welcomed their offer of assistance.

"Just kidding about chopping off your leg," said Taqa as he pulled away the material from her knee. He then inspected the alignment of her leg and started muttering to himself.

Dominique could not understand him, nor could she read his expressions. "So, if you're not going to chop it off, what are you gonna do?"

With his eyes still fixed on her leg he answered, "Ah, not sure yet. Hmm, would it be OK if I take off your boot and sock?"

"Only if you promise to massage my foot," she said while winking at Taylor, who giggled.

"OK, I promise," said Taqa, not sure why she had such a strange request. He then stabilized her leg while Evaline loosened the laces and carefully removed the boot.

"Hey, you're pretty good at that," Dominique said to the wilderness nurse. "That didn't hurt at all."

Evaline smiled, accepting the compliment. Taqa likewise complimented his nurse. "Aunt Evie is certified in painless boot removal," he said.

All this time Sayuri was carefully inspecting Taqa's physical size and features. Then she did the same with Evaline. "Is that small lady really your aunt? You two don't look alike at all," she remarked.

Taqa and Evaline exchanged looks before the medicine man replied, "My parents adopted Evaline many years ago," he said. "I look like all my other sisters and brothers—"

"—But I don't, so you could say I'm the *runt* of the litter," Evaline said, finishing his sentence. Some of the students laughed at her humor.

Martina then pointed to Taqa's muddy jeans. "What happened to your pants?"

"Well, we, ah, crossed the creek by jumping rocks," Taqa answered, lying through his tribal teeth. "My aunt is a nimble fox and I'm a clumsy oaf." Evaline giggled at his humorous explanation.

Then Taqa grabbed the top of Dominique's sock and slowly rolled it back before pulling it completely off her foot. He checked the color of her toenails and took a pulse at the top of her instep.

"Hmm," he said, and mumbled a little more.

This time Dominique sensed his diagnosis. "I don't like the tone of your *hmm*," replied Dominique, "My leg's pretty bad isn't it?"

Taqa didn't answer her directly because he didn't want to alarm her. "Well, your color and pulse could be better," he said, looking at her foot and running his fingertips lightly along the shinbone. Then he turned to her. "But that's the painless part. The next part won't be."

Dominique's worry intensified. "The next part—what do you mean?"

"Well, in order to improve your leg circulation, I need to straighten your leg," Taqa replied, but then added, "Don't worry; the intense, pain of realignment will only last a few seconds."

Evaline lightly punched him in the arm. "Taqa, take it easy; you're scaring the bejeebers out of her," she whispered.

"Oops, guess I left my bedside manner back at home," he whispered back to her. Then he turned to Dominique. "Sorry, didn't mean to scare the bejeebers out of you."

But Dominique appreciated his honesty. "You're not scaring me any more than I already am. I actually feel better— knowing what to expect. Thanks for not sugar-coating this."

"You're welcome," Taqa replied. He then poked Evaline in the arm. "See? The brutal truth sometimes works better."

Evaline huffed at him before crawling to Taqa's medical bag for the leg-splinting materials.

Taqa then continued explaining the rest of his procedure to Dominique. "Anyway, after I realign your leg, Aunt Evie and I will splint it, and that should make everything better."

"Wait," said Dominique, having second thoughts while guarding her injured leg with both hands. "Have you done this alignment thing before?"

Some of the other students started backing away. "Come on, Wes," said Aaron. "We'd better leave. I think this is the gory part."

Wes agreed. "Good idea—I faint at any and all bone-setting procedures," he said. They slowly backed away from the group, heading towards the rocky cliff. Perro followed them, picking up a long piece of driftwood before he ascended.

Dominique noticed the guys' retreat, "Now there's a bunch of real he-men. Thanks, guys—love you, too!"

Taqa also watched them leave then turned back to Taylor, who was at Dominique's side the whole time. "You sure *you* want to stay? This could get ugly," he advised.

Taylor emphatically nodded. "I stay with my captain through thick and thin," she declared proudly while holding Dominique's hand tightly.

Taqa was impressed and remarked, "Yours is *no act of common passage, but a strain of rareness*."

Taylor's face lit up. "Hey, that sounds a lot like Shakespeare," she remarked.

"Right you are," answered Taqa, "I love quoting Shakespeare—makes me sound tastefully literate."

"No kidding," said Taylor. "I have a friend who likes quoting Shakespeare, too." Then she hung her head. "But she's missing from our group right now. Hey, maybe you saw her. She went downstream last night, chasing after her journal that she dropped in the creek."

"She has long, brown hair and was wearing a light-blue rain poncho," added Dominique.

The two caretakers hesitated, looking at each other before Taqa answered, "Nope—didn't see anyone matching that description," he said, lying to them again.

As much as she didn't want to, Evaline had to agree with him. "I didn't see her either, but she couldn't have gone too far. From what we've seen, most of the creek paths are flooded and impassible. She can't be more than a cove or two away. But if we do see her, we'll direct her back to your campsite," she said.

"Thanks," replied Taylor, obviously satisfied with Evaline's answer. "We hope her disappearance is only temporary." Taylor then pointed to her classmates, who were already climbing the rocks. "You see—our search and rescue group is forming at this very moment."

Taqa watched as the search party climbed higher before turning back to Dominique. "But of course, *Mademoiselle,* you are going nowhere," he said using a thick, European accent.

His voice sounded familiar to Dominique. "Hey, you sound like detective *Hercule Poirot* right out of the Agatha Christie Mysteries! Do you know her stuff?"

Taqa thought for a moment about the thousands of books he has read. Lately, however, he has leaned more towards fictional adventures and not murder mysteries.

"Agatha Christie? Um, don't think I'm familiar with her stuff," he replied. "But I have read a bit of Anne Rice, and didn't she used to live near French Quarter, Louisiana?"

Dominique nodded, and Evaline chuckled at his answer, knowing that the medicine man fancies Anne Rice novels more than U.S. geography.

Taqa then stabilized himself, sitting on his heels and planting his shins firmly in the loose ground. "Getting back to your injured leg—yes, I've done this bone-realignment procedure several times when I was on the Snowbowl Ski Patrol."

"Oh, yes, you wouldn't believe how many times," said Evaline, collaborating with the medicine man's half-truth. He did, indeed, perform the procedure many times, but not on the ski patrol and nowhere near the Snowbowl Ski Resort.

Dominique smiled at them both, although she was still a little jittery about the procedure.

Taqa clapped his hands once and rubbed them together—just like a magician before the last, show-stopping trick.

"OK, Dominique, here we go. I am going to grab your foot at the heel and instep, then give it one strong jerk towards me. You'll definitely feel it, and hopefully you'll feel less pain afterward. Then we'll quickly splint the whole leg and make it feel much better."

Dominique looked over at Taylor, who gave her partner a reassuring thumbs-up. Dominique then looked back at Taqa, who was waiting with his large, broad hands resting flat on his thighs and his long fingers spread apart. His hands looked way too powerful to perform this type of operation on her painfully tender and delicate leg.

"Wait, can I have a bullet or something to clench down on?" Dominique asked.

Evaline checked the front pockets of her vest. "I'm fresh out of bullets, but I do have some gum," she said, pulling out a stick.

Taqa, looking puzzled, asked his nurse, "Why would anyone want to bite a bullet?"

Evaline explained, "Bullet-biting was what folks did in the old western movies. Back then they'd chomp on it during a painful procedure, taking their mind off the pain. But nowadays it's a bad idea—it can crack your teeth," she said while handing the gum to Dominique. "It can also give you lead-poisoning."

"I always bit on a strip of wood or animal hide," said Taqa.

"Sure, that stuff works, too," agreed Evaline. "But gum tastes much better and keeps your breath minty-fresh." Dominique started to put the gum in her mouth with Evaline's guidance. "Dear, the trick is not to dissolve the gum right away," she explained. "If you soften it up too soon, it won't cushion your teeth when you're clenching them."

Dominique thanked her and folded the dry gum stick a few times between her teeth. "OK, all set," she mumbled.

"OK, I'll count to three," said Taqa, holding Dominique's foot. "Ready? One, two..." Then he quickly jerked Dominique's leg. "Unh!"

"Ouch!"

"Three!"

Dominique practically choked on her gum. "Mr. Taqa, you tricked me. You said you'd pull on *three*—not two. I wasn't ready on two."

Taqa and Evaline quickly applied the splint, tying it snugly to her leg. Taqa smiled and explained his rationale to Dominique while he worked. "Dominique, I said I'd *count* to three. I didn't say I'd *pull* on three," he said. The medics had her leg splinted in less than a minute, and Dominique was already feeling better.

"Ooh, *I see* what you did there, and I like your style," she said smiling as she softened the gum wad and chewed happily.

"How does your leg feel now?" Evaline asked as she crawled towards Dominique's head.

"Much better," answered Dominique, wiggling her toes. "But now your nephew owes me a foot massage."

Taqa rolled his eyes upward. "OK, a deal is a deal."

He gently stabilized her foot with both hands while starting to massage her toes. He worked his fingertips between them, moving the blood from each joint to the base of her toes. Then with the same strokes he massaged along each tendon towards her instep. He then took her pulse again.

"There, that's better," he said. "Pulse is much stronger now, but probably due to the realignment and not the complimentary foot massage."

"Whatever—you're amazing!" Dominique exclaimed. "Where did you learn how to do that?"

"From my service on Ski Patrol," he said. "Most of my patients were women who, like you, wanted a foot massage. No guys I treated ever asked for one. It must be a female thing, huh?"

"Guess so," answered Dominique, giggling.

"But while massaging your foot I felt calloused skin. Your feet are in athletic shoes a lot. See how your toenails dig into the skin of the adjacent toe? You're probably a basketball player—no, wait…" He looked at her knee then rolled up the other pant leg and checked that one. "You must play volleyball," he concluded.

Dominique yanked Taylor's arm, astonished by Taqa's correct deduction. "OMG, you're absolutely right—how did you know that?" Dominique asked.

Taqa pointed at her knees. "You have old bruises on both your knees. You obviously drop down on them a lot. You must play libero."

"Shriveling sheet skirts—you're right again!"

362

Taqa then ran his fingers around both kneecaps and shook his head. "You really ought to wear knee pads," he said, sounding like a scolding parent.

Taylor tried to explain Dominique's bad habit. "Well, she sort of wears them, but keeps them down at her ankles. I try to remind her to pull them over her knees, but she doesn't always do it," she said.

"Knee pads are so constricting," Dominique argued, "I feel like they slow me down."

Taqa crawled over to his bag to repack his bandages while arguing Dominique's point. "So, Dominique, what's more constricting; your knee pads or all the injuries from not wearing them?"

Dominique gazed up at the cliffs while pondering his question. Then she lightly punched herself on the side of the head. "Ugh, you're *so* right," she decided. "I should take better care of my knees, especially if I want to get that volleyball scholarship from Stanford."

Taylor nodded, agreeing with her captain. "You mean the both of us, girlfriend," she said, reaching out her fist out to Dominique who tapped it with her own.

Taqa checked the tightness of the splint, and then turned to Mr. Roeser. "Her leg is safely immobilized now," he said. "But she needs to stay off it. Can we help move her to the shelter?" He looked up at the towering cliffs above him. "You never know who else may want to tumble on top of her."

Mr. Roeser laughed at the medic's humor. "You've done more than enough, and I've got a few able-bodied guys who can help me…" He turned to look for them, but they were gone. "Uh, what the hell?" Then he looked up the cliff and saw them climbing.

They had already reached the ledge where Dominique had slipped. He yelled up to them, "What the hell are you doing!"

Taylor gave Dominique's hand a squeeze. "That's my cue, captain, gotta go," she whispered, then ran to join the rescue party.

"Be brave and powerful," Dominique called out, sending off her friend. "Remember, there's greater strength in numbers!" Taylor saluted and began climbing the first set of rocks.

Wes, already halfway up the cliff, cupped his mouth while yelling down to his teacher.

"We heard voices up here, Mr. Roeser, so we're going to see if it's Desiree!"

Mr. Roeser jumped to his feet and walked towards the rocks while yelling, "You'll do no such thing. I don't want anymore casualties!"

"Don't worry," said Perro, reassuring his teacher. "We won't be walking on our hands this time," he said while waving his hiking stick. Mr. Roeser surveyed all the ascending students, who appeared as earthly-colored pearls strung out on several elevations as they climbed to the top of the cliff.

Mr. Roeser threw his hands up in exasperation then turned back to Taqa and Evaline. "What am I gonna do with these bozos?" But the medics were gone; it was just he and Dominique at the campsite. "Hey! Where did our heroes go?"

Dominique answered her teacher while pointing at the ascending students. "Mr. R., *there* are your heroes now." She then blew Perro a kiss and waved.

Taylor, who was the last to join the rescue party, scurried like a spider monkey up the rocks. Mr. Roeser watched as the students climbed up to the top ledge before traversing southward to the crag. Soon they disappeared behind it. He shook his head and walked towards the dinner tarp.

364

Dominique called to her teacher, "Hey, Mr. Roeser, can you do me a favor?"

He stopped and turned back. "What's that, Miss Cruseaux—do you need to be moved?"

"No, I'm fine right here. But can you please get me Taylor's journal? It's just inside our tent. Since I'm not in the rescue party, I may as well update this adventure in our travel journal," she said, scooting towards a nearby rock.

Mr. Roeser soon returned with the journal and a pencil. "This pencil was all I could find. I hope it'll suffice," he said.

"Oh, it will more than suffice," she answered, opening the journal on the flat surface of a nearby rock. "It's perfect for documenting the adventure of a lifetime!"

# Chapter XX

Naturale removed Desiree's boots from the drying rack and dropped them at her feet.

"Put them on," he commanded harshly. She slipped them on quickly, and tied up the laces. Just before she finished, he grabbed her wrist that had the digital watch. He pulled it next to his large, black-faced watch, which had several functions and was waterproof up to three hundred feet—no doubt another article lost or forgotten by a park visitor.

"Set your timer for ten minutes. That is your head start. Then I will hunt you." He waited for her to set it, so that the two watches were synchronized.

Desiree gasped at the short head start he allotted. "Only ten minutes? Naturale, I will need more time—"

"—That is plenty of time for someone who is more cunning and adept than I," Naturale angrily replied. "Or do you wish to stay here for the rest of your life?"

*I wouldn't wish that on anyone,* Desiree thought. She swallowed hard then answered him, "No, I don't wish to stay. I guess ten minutes will have to do, but you can't see which path I take."

"Very well," he replied, "I will close my eyes and block my ears. But it will not matter—I can track your scent even after you are gone." He reached for a wool ski hat from his pocket and pulled it over his ears and eyes. "I will even lay under a blanket in the corner while you escape. Now go." He walked to a small recess in the wall and sat down facing the wall while covering his head.

She looked around quickly then ran deeper into the cavern towards the grandchildren's voices. After running about twenty or so yards, she looked upward. Shedi and her sister were scaling a rock wall.

"Hey, you two, what are you doing?" Desiree asked.

"Oh, hi, Desiree," said Shedi. "After we got firewood for Nana, she let us play on the rock wall. We're racing to the top."

Desiree looked up and saw above them a blue sky peeking through the top of the crevasse. Freedom!

"That's up pretty high," Desiree remarked. "Aren't you scared of falling?"

"Not at all," answered Shideezhi. "There are plenty of rocks and ledges to grab. Besides we've been doing this before we learned to walk."

"I believe you," said Desiree, who also began to climb. "I remember your Nana saying that Naturale taught you."

"Yes, then he began racing us after we got good at it," said Shedi. "Hey, Desiree, do you want to race us?"

"Oh, I don't know. I'm probably not as good a climber as Naturale," Desiree answered as she kept ascending towards them. She was still about fifty feet below them but at least a hundred feet from freedom.

"You never know, Desiree; you could be better than Naturale," said Shideezhi. "The nooks and ledges get smaller as you go higher. It's an advantage if you have smaller feet. Naturale's feet are really big, so he can't get good footholds at the top. Come on, we can start the race up here at the big ledge."

Desiree glanced down and estimated that she was already about thirty feet off the ground. "Sure, racing could be fun," she said nervously as she continued her ascent. She checked her watch and noticed that five minutes had elapsed since Naturale released her. She finally reached their ledge and glanced upwards. The fissure was a little wider, so the area was more illuminated. She could see small puffy clouds floating by. "Hey, girls, what does it look like on the outside?"

"We're not sure; Nana told us never to go up that high," said Shedi.

"But we think it's the plateau where the trail connects because we hear voices all the time," said Shideezhi.

"Well, I don't want you to disobey your nana, so where should we finish our race?"

"Oh, that's easy," answered Shedi. "Right at the end of the azurite vein."

"It's the shiny blue part of the stone with the gold streak that goes all the way across the chimney. You can't miss it. We use it as a finish line all the time," said Shideezhi.

"OK, we race to the azurite vein," Desiree said with a large dose of doubt. She wasn't very confident in her climbing skills, but she had to what was necessary to escape. She checked her watch again and had four more minutes before Naturale started his hunt. She took a deep breath. *Come on, Desiree, you've been in worse situations*, she thought. *Are you kidding? The only escape from a raging, über hunter is a one hundred and fifty-foot cliff with no net, no ropes, and no life after you fall. No, you have never been in a worse situation—not even Lucy and Ethel on TV. God, I'd give a million bucks to have their rescue ladder and firemen right now!*

The tribal children each picked her favorite starting spot. "Desiree, you can have the easy path in the middle since this is your first race," said Shedi. "Naturale always told us to make it easy for beginners, so that they will feel confident enough to want to race again."

Desiree looked at the middle path and then the rest of the wall. To her none of the paths looked easy. "Thanks, Shedi, that is so sportsmanlike of you," she replied.

"You can start the race, Desiree," said Shideezhi as she got a grip on one rock while both her feet were still on the ledge.

"Yes, we will give you that advantage, too," added Shedi as she grabbed a rock just above her head.

Desiree surveyed the wall above her. The angle of the chimney was not as vertical anymore. It angled forward and the natural light gave it two distinct hues—dark black immediately in front of her, but deep blue and creamy white just above. *So I aim for the blue-white finish line,* she decided.

"Come on, Desiree—what are you waiting for?" Shedi cried.

Desiree blinked her eyes, returning her focus to the area immediately in front of her. "OK, all you tribal rock climbers— ready, set, go!"

The grandchildren sprang upward, grabbing and pulling with eagerness. Desiree watched them start then took a deep breath and ascended. The surfaces felt moist from the rains, but luckily her boots had excellent traction, and she moved up the chimney easily. *Good thing Dad insisted on getting me these hiking boots,* she thought.

Desiree found several small ledges jutting out from the wall, and she soon realized how easy the climb was. "Lookout, Shedi, I'm catching up to you."

Shedi had stopped. "That's because I climbed to an area with no nooks."

"No problem," replied Desiree. "Traverse over to my path for some."

"That is very sporting of you, Desiree," Shedi replied. "Thank you."

"You're welcome, and please call me Dizzy, it's my nickname," she replied.

Shideezhi suddenly stopped. "Where did you get that nickname?"

"Well, my little brother made it up," Desiree replied, pulling herself up to the next small ledge. "When he was little he couldn't say Desiree very well, so he just called me Dizzy. Even after he was old enough to say my real name correctly, he still called me Dizzy."

Both sisters laughed.

"When I was younger, I used to call my sister, She-she, because I couldn't pronounce Shideezhi very well," said Shedi. "But I don't call her that now because it sounds so silly."

"That's why nicknames are fun," Desiree replied. "When they're silly or fun to say, you remember them better. They become special names for friends or loved ones—like your nana. She's your grandmother, but Nana is a lot easier to say."

"I like Dizzy as your nickname," Shedi decided.

"Me, too," agreed Shideezhi.

"Me, three," said a much deeper voice from below. Desiree gasped. Her ten minutes were up, and Naturale was coming for her.

Taqa and Evaline hurried back downstream to their cave entrance. Evaline was riding on his back while carrying the gym bag. Taqa waded through fast-moving, knee-deep water, and he was grunting with each long stride.

"The students said they heard voices from atop the cliff," said Evaline. "Do you think Desiree was up there?"

"Unh, with all the clues we gave her, unh, I hope she was up there, unh." Soon he reached the other side of the escarpment and stooped down to let Evaline hop off his back. Together they quickly ascended the switchback trail up to the crevasse's entrance. The waterfall, which was previously torrential, was now trickling.

"Ugh, this is going to be one, wet passage," he warned Evaline. He pulled out a poncho for her.

She put it on as Taqa pulled out a large trash bag and sliced open a hole along the bottom seam. He then pulled it over his head and punched out two armholes, creating an instant poncho for himself.

"Desiree seems like a pretty sharp kid," Evaline commented, "I hope she figured out a way to escape."

"Me, too—for everyone's sake. But it'll be tough escaping from Naturale. I hope that her friends find her before he does," said Taqa, as they both ducked under the trickling water. He then grabbed a large branch nearby and pried a boulder away from the cave's entrance. They both slipped inside the entrance. Taqa then rolled the rock in front of the entrance before they continued through the fissure.

The torches that usually illuminate the passageway were already extinguished since light from the mid-morning sun flooded down through the crevasse.

They descended back down to the cavern and saw only embers glowing in the fireplace. Evaline walked to the drying rack and noticed Desiree's boots gone, but her poncho remained. Taqa checked the poncho's pocket for the diary. It was still safely inside.

Evaline quickly checked the other areas of the cavern, and then reported back to Taqa. "Both Naturale and Desiree are gone," she said.

"That's good news," Taqa replied, feeding the fire embers with more wood. "It appears Desiree figured out a way to escape, but she forgot her poncho."

"Just like all forgetful canyon visitors do," replied Evaline.

"Yes, but she may still need it, especially if it rains again."

"Since when did you start returning forgotten articles, Taqa?"

"Let's just call it preventative maintenance," he said, turning back towards the exit. "Desiree could get wet then cold and end up back here again. And like you said, I really don't want more than one of you in this tribe."

\* \* \*

"Hey, look, it's Naturale," said Shideezhi, alerting the other wall climbers. Then she yelled down to him, "Hey, Naturale, you want to be in our race?"

"Sure. But this time I will race Dizzy," he replied and started his ascent. He was still wearing his tropical shirt but now a spear was strapped over it. "

"Well, she's got a big head start on you," Shedi replied. "I think she'll make it to the top first."

"The top is not my goal," he said, moving up the wall so rapidly that he already reached the ledge where the race started.

372

Much farther above him, Desiree stopped to catch her breath. She saw the opening just a few yards up. Her throat was parched from breathing rapidly through her mouth, and her fingers started cramping from exertion. But fear of capture kept her climbing. The nooks were, indeed, getting smaller and more difficult to hold. Her one foot slipped, but she held on, gasping loudly.

Naturale heard her difficulty and rolled the deepest, most wicked chuckle in the back of his throat. She shuddered at its sound. He then called to her, "It will not be long now before this race is over," he said.

Desiree stabilized her position and checked on Naturale's progress. He was now only about thirty feet away from her!

She decided to take Evaline's advice and tap some resources. "Hey, kids, Naturale needs more of a challenge. How about cutting him off?"

"OK," said Shedi. "We do this all the time. Come on, Shideezhi!"

The two traversed towards the middle and ended up just above Naturale. He growled in displeasure. He now had to traverse to the outside of Shedi and climb around her. But it gave Shideezhi time to traverse even farther, cutting off Naturale's path again.

Frustrated by their tactics, Naturale growled then called out to the tribal climbers, "Children, I hear your nana calling you from below," he said.

The girls held their positions, and Shedi answered him, "Aw, you're just making up that story."

"Yeah, Naturale, you can't fool us," agreed Shideezhi. Both girls turned to each other and laughed. Then they both looked up and saw Desiree reach a wider ledge about ten feet from the top.

"Hey, Desiree, you reached the finish line—you win!"

Desiree saw the blue and cream-colored vein just above the ledge she reached. It was indeed the azurite vein! She immediately flashed back to her grandpa's story of finding the chess pieces. *He did not chip out the nuggets; they were lying on the ground across from the canyon wall. Maybe those nuggets came from this very wall,* she thought.

"Thanks for the race!" she called to the girls. "Maybe we can do it again sometime."

At this point Naturale caught up to Shedi, who turned and smiled at him. "This was the best race ever!" she remarked.

"And you did a nice job cutting me off," Naturale said, "I am proud of your skills. Now you should both go back down to your Nana." He then looked up in time to see Desiree disappear over the top. He growled and continued his ascent. His footholds were getting more difficult at this level, and he had to traverse across the ledge to a rope that was hidden in a large fissure.

The stall tactic on Naturale gave Desiree enough time to reach the opening. She climbed out, crawling several yards across the sandy ground and collapsed, exhaling loudly. She rolled onto her back and closed her eyes, so that she could feel the full effect of her freedom. The ground felt cool and moist on her warm, sweaty skin. But sun's warm rays, carried by the gentle breezes never felt better on her face.

While still on her back, she heard shouts and rolled towards their source. She squinted hard and saw her friends hopping across rocks and scrambling towards her. She smiled and rose to her knees.

She waved to them, but, before she could get to her feet, was knocked back to the ground. She grunted as air forcefully left her lungs. She rolled onto her back just as Naturale straddled her body, pinning her wrists to the ground! His face was silhouetted

374

against the bright blue sky, but it was not the same face as the one that pulled her from creek. This time it had angry protruding eyes and heavily panting breath.

"I've got you, Dizzy, fair and square!" Naturale declared. If not for his deep voice, he could have sounded like a bragging first-grader after winning a schoolyard game.

Desiree trembled at his words and threatening posture, but managed a flash of wit. "Hey, Enrique, wanna go two out of three?"

He lowered himself to just inches from her eyes. His body heat radiated from his sweaty face and the huge veins in his neck were bulging. "No more hunts. You have lost, and I have won. You posed the challenge and the rules. I accepted, and I won. You are now my trophy and will return with me to the cavern."

Desiree closed her eyes and turned her head in an attempt to avoid sweat, odor and breath that reeked from her captor. In desperation she fell back on a Shakespearean quote: "*Sweet mercy is nobility's true badge.*"

Suddenly she heard thudding sounds of several hiking boots rapidly approaching.

"Desiree, roll right!" Wes yelled as he and Aaron tackled Naturale. Desiree rolled away from her captor, who fell over but swiftly returned to his feet. He grabbed both guys by the arms and threw them a few feet away. They kept rolling, trying to get away. He charged after them, but Desiree cut him off, grabbing one of his arms.

"You are correct, Naturale, you indeed have won," she began to say while catching her own breath. "But I wouldn't be a good trophy for you. What you really need is a woman more your size, with dreadlocks—artfully anchored with some brightly colored beads, and maybe a better sense of personal hygiene."

Naturale was confused by her words, but Wes and Aaron weren't and both laughed from her humorous insult.

Desiree's distraction was all Candice needed to sneak up behind the tribal hunter. She quickly scrambled atop a nearby rock and launched from it, landing on his back. She wrapped both her arms around his head, covering his eyes. Then Taylor ran in front of him and rubbed a large dollop of Desiree's shower gel on the lapels and pocket of his tropical shirt.

"There you go—now your foul-smelling pheromones will smell foul no more," Taylor said then laughed at him.

Candice took a deep whiff. "Hmm, definitely smelling fowl no more," she said.

Naturale reached behind to pull Candice off, and then he grabbed the spear from his shoulder.

"You obviously have a death wish to battle me," he said, taking a threatening step towards her. She tucked, summersaulted then sprang to her feet.

"Not really," she said while fixing her hair, "I just love a good fight when I have a few friends at my side." Candice then felt along her utility belt for her fencing foil.

"Having a few *hundred* friends couldn't help you now!" he angrily shouted.

She quickly pulled the foil from her belt. By this time Perro, who caught up to see the battle, joined Wes and Aaron in a wide perimeter around the unfolding duel. Candice opened her foil to full length and claimed her ground with a fencer's stance.

Naturale laughed at her weapon, and with his spear knocked it from her grip. The foil flew several feet before rolling down the crevasse. Candice gasped, but Perro tossed his climbing stick on the ground in front of her.

"Candice, try using that," he shouted to her. She reached for it, but Naturale thrust his spear between her and the stick.

Aaron and Perro immediately rushed over to tackle Naturale.

"What's the matter, big man, scared to duel against a *girl*?" Aaron asked, teasing him. Naturale growled as both guys pushed him off balance just enough for Candice to snatch up the branch.

"OK, now this match up isn't so one-sided," she said although not too confident about battling with a tree branch.

Naturale's spear was over six feet long. Candice's branch was much shorter—maybe five feet, affording Naturale an obvious advantage.

Knowing this, the hunter laughed then made an advance. Candice held her new dueling weapon with both hands and posed defensively as if holding a medieval sword. She trembled as he stepped closer. Naturale then turned his right hip towards her and readied his spear for attack.

Aaron noticed his stance and yelled to Candice. "Look, Candice, your opponent is right-handed!"

Candice's trembling immediately stopped. *A righty! Now I have the advantage*, she thought and went into attack mode. Like lightning, she quickly faked a lunge and retreated onto her back leg.

Naturale parried, but with his spear off to the side, she jabbed the branch's tip into his abdomen. Caught by surprise, Naturale grunted from the blow. She quickly positioned her weapon underneath his chin. Then, yanking the branch straight up, she caught him squarely on the jaw.

"Ooh," said Wes, wincing. "That hurt me just watching it hurt him."

Aaron rolled next to Wes and cheered. "Candice, that was an awesome combo!"

Meanwhile, Taylor spied a sage bush nearby, having small, purple blossoms fully opened from the recent rains. She then grabbed Desiree by the arm, leading her over to the bush. Taylor showed her the bees busily extracting nectar from the blossoms.

"Listen," said Taylor, "I smeared a bunch of your shower gel on Godzilla's tropical shirt. If we can lure him over here, maybe the bees will jump on him like they did on Royce." She opened shower gel bottle and passed it across the bush. A few bees had flown onto the bottle.

"It's worth a try," said Desiree.

"Candice, get over to this bush!" Taylor yelled to the battling redhead.

Candice glanced over and acknowledged with a nod before looking back at her opponent. Naturale resumed his battle stance while rubbing his injured jaw. She faked another jab then dashed towards the sage bush. He swung at her feet, but she quickly jumped it. She made it to the bush with Naturale in hot pursuit.

"If this guy ever lands a solid hit on me, I'm toast!" she cried.

"Just float like a butterfly and sting like a bee," Desiree replied. "Get it, Candice—*sting like a bee?*"

The duelers both circled the sage bush. Candice was quick enough to keep it between her and Naturale. It was only about five feet tall and just as wide but enough to keep his powerful swings ineffective.

In frustration he leaned into the bush and swung at her head. She ducked, but when she straightened back up the shaft of his spear caught the right sleeve of her sweatshirt. At this point some bees left the blossoms and flew towards Naturale. Candice quickly checked her arm, but felt that it was barely scratched.

"This is why wearing baggy clothes can save your life," she remarked. With the bees buzzing around him he backed off, trying to avoid them.

"I will finish this fiery little varmint and then tear the rest of you apart," he said. Desiree and Taylor hid behind Candice who held up her guard against Naturale. The bees came after him, some landing on his shirt. He tried to bat them away, while still threatening the students. "You weak pathetic little people will not even make this victory glorious—"

Before he could finish his threat, several more bees swarmed around him. He tried shooing them away but his movements seemed to attract them even more. He yelped in pain as some started stinging.

"Look, Desiree, the shower gel is working!" Taylor cried.

Now overwhelmed by the bees, Naturale retreated to the crevasse. He descended while grunting in pain.

Desiree jubilantly hugged Taylor, almost knocking her down. "Taylor, you're brilliant!"

Upon regaining her balance, Taylor replied, "Thanks. Like they say, there's greater strength in numbers, especially when they have stingers," she said.

"But how did you think to use my shower gel?" Desiree asked.

"Oh, let's just say thinking about *my new boyfriend* had something to do with it," she said, giggling.

At the same time Candice was completely overjoyed from her apparent victory. "I can't believe I won my first claymore sword match," she said swooshing her weapon a few times through the air. "This begins a new chapter in my sword-fighting experience."

Aaron walked over to Candice. "Congratulations," he said. "You stomped that battle!"

She then dropped her weapon to fix her hair. "You know, Aaron, even without the bees I would have had him on style points," she said. Then she checked her arm, running her fingers over the scratch. "Thanks for your help, too. I was pretty scared. If you hadn't mentioned that he was right-handed I probably would have ended up like a shish kabob."

Aaron also inspected her scratch before softly kissing it. "Hope this makes it feel better," he said.

She smiled and pulled him closer. "No, not really. But this might—" and she kissed his lips. Aaron wrapped his arms around her and kissed back. She tried to talk with her lips still sealed over his. "Yeff, Aar'n, de'f'n''ly be''er."

A few yards away, Desiree picked up her shower gel bottle just before Taylor handed her the cap.

"Hey, Desiree, you may want to get more of this shower gel the next time you visit the Grand Canyon," Taylor quipped. "After all, a girl's got to defend herself." Both girls laughed.

Wes and Perro brushed off their clothes and rejoined the girls.

"Where did Godzilla come from, anyway?" Wes asked.

Desiree did not want to divulge Naturale's identity, so she fabricated an answer. "Well, I'm not sure. I met him last night when I ducked in a cave. He told me he was from a circus group, vacationing in the park. He was trying to hit me up for my phone number. Maybe he just broke up with the bearded lady or something. Anyway, I turned him down, and he went ballistic."

They held hands while walking back to the campsite. "Yeah, I can understand his reaction," he said. "I can't handle rejection either, which was why I never asked you to go steady with me."

"What?" Desiree asked, suddenly stopping. "I always thought you didn't want a serious relationship."

Candice and Aaron walked a short distance ahead—giving Wes and Desiree some privacy. But soon Candice became impatient and started kicking the loose gravel.

Wes didn't notice Candice and continued his discussion with Desiree. "I *did* want a serious relationship, but I was not very good at hinting, nor was I good with the direct approach. Ugh, it doesn't matter now." He put her hands together then raised them to his lips and kissed them. "I'm just glad you're back with me. When you disappeared last night my heart sunk into my boots. It made me realize my strong feelings for you—well, maybe not as strong as Godzilla's, but—"

Desiree had enough of his monologue and placed her index finger on his lips. "Shh—you had me at *I'm just glad you're back*," she said and wrapped her arms around him. They embraced long and hard. Then their faces gravitated towards each other as if to kiss.

But Candice grunted again. "You guys want to get out of here, or shall I call Godzilla back for a rematch?"

Taylor heard Candice and joined the group. "Relax, Miss Swordfighter, he won't come back; he's got too many stingers to deal with first," she said.

"Well then, Miss Burro Rider, maybe we should get back down to the campsite before Mr. Roeser fails us in geology," advised Perro as he and Candice ran ahead and climbed down the rocks. Wes and Desiree smiled before followed them back down the rocks.

When they finally arrived at the campsite, the twins, Martina and Sayuri were already breaking down their tents. The Clydes had also returned and started packing the mules. Dominique was still sitting by the same rock she was before, but now in a more comfortable position with her splinted leg propped up by the blanket roll. She greeted each member of the rescue party as they descended.

"Hey, guys, what took you so long? We were going to leave without you." Then she saw Desiree. "Holy mountain sheep—you're back!" Dominique threw aside the journal and tried standing, but Perro saw her difficulty and ran over to help. He picked her up and carried her towards Desiree.

Desiree couldn't help making light of Dominique's injury. "Oh, no! Let me guess—you were looking for your lucky break, right?" she joked.

Dominique laughed, remembering the conversation they had at the library a month before. "Nope, it's more like my *unlucky break*; I was definitely in the wrong place at the wrong time. But it would sure make a great bedtime story for my kids."

Desiree stroked her friend's leg splint. "Dominique, I'm so sorry you got hurt because of me," she said, feeling remorseful.

"Don't sweat it," Dominique said, patting her splint proudly. "It was my own, stupid fault. Luckily a huge, mysterious but witty hiker showed up along with his cute little aunt, and they fixed my leg."

Desiree smiled, knowing that Taqa and Evaline were the first-aiders. "A huge, mysterious but witty hiker and his cute little aunt, huh? Sounds like they may have been your fairy godparents," she guessed.

But Dominique disagreed. "No, I think their being here was just dumb luck," she said.

Desiree smiled, knowing it wasn't dumb luck at all.

Candice suddenly appeared jumping down from the last rock. "Hey, Dominique, want to see what happened to me?" She extended her arm, showing off her ripped sleeve and wound. "I got this during my duel of the century."

"Duel—you mean you used your telescopic foil on a formidable foe?" Dominique asked.

Candice shook her head. "Not quite." Then she held out her weapon, "My opponent, who was as tall as a tree and strong as a bull, knocked it down a deep crevasse, so I used this instead." She demonstrated some offensive maneuvers. "It's kind of heavy and cumbersome, but I learned how to grip it with two hands. I landed a couple good strikes on him."

"Well," began Dominique, "I'm just going to have to get all this recorded in our official travel journal."

Just then Desiree gasped, "Journal!" She turned towards the creek "My grandpa's journal—I left it in one of the caves on the other side!" She ran down the embankment towards the stream, which was still running swiftly and looked muddier by the minute.

Candice ran after her. "Wait; you can't, Desiree!"

Taylor, Wes and Aaron saw Desiree running and likewise followed.

"But Candice, I have to," Desiree yelled back to Candice while still running. "That journal is very important to me."

Taylor and the others caught up with her. They all stood between Desiree and the creek's edge.

"You can't go back—it's too dangerous," said Aaron.

"Yeah, you'll get swept away by the muddy creek," said Candice.

"Godzilla may still be lurking around," said Wes.

"And this time we're all out of shower gel," added Taylor.

Desiree looked into each of her friends' pleading faces. They were right. Going back now was dicey at best. As much as she wanted, she couldn't risk running into Naturale again. She looked out at the creek and let out a sigh of futility.

"Guys, you're right," she said to them. "You have done enough rescuing for today." Then she smiled, thinking about her past twelve hours. It was her adventure of a lifetime, and now more than ever she was glad to be with her friends. "I think I'll go get my stuff packed."

She hooked onto Candice and Wes, and they walked together back to the campsite in time to hear Mr. Roeser's sharp whistle blast.

"Mr. R. probably wants to evacuate while we still can," said Wes. Aaron and Taylor ran ahead to get their packs.

Suddenly a helicopter flew overhead. It hovered above the creek for a moment and then slowly descended until it was about fifty feet above the embankment. Instinctively everyone looked up and waved. Desiree saw the camp's attention diverted and quickly ran to her pack. She pulled out her bag of chess pieces and returned to the escarpment at the edge of the creek.

\* \* \*

"Dad, it's them!" Royce cried, pointing at an area just below helicopter. "I can see Wes next to a couple of mules. Uh-oh, looks like he's helping a girl whose leg is splinted."

His dad leaned into the side-view window and saw a bunch of students jumping and waving. Then he saw his daughter walking towards the creek.

"Well, at least it's not your sister in the splint." Then he turned to Pete. "Can we land down there?"

"Sure, if I wanted us all killed," Pete answered over the headset. "I'm not comfortable landing around the rocky terrain inside this narrow canyon. It'll be safer to land on the flat plateau, and then you guys can hoof it down," he advised. He climbed a few hundred feet, rising out of the canyon, and flew to a flat area by the trail. "I'll drop you off here and radio back your position. Maybe I can get more help, too."

Walter and his son removed their headsets, grabbed their gear and stepped out of the helicopter. Ducking low, they ran from the helicopter and towards the trail. Pete waited a few minutes before heading back to the village helipad.

\* \* \*

"Hello, this is Janelle...Wait—what? Hold on." She rose from her chair and waved, trying to get the parents' attention. It was already noon, and several parents were noshing on croissant sandwiches served from a huge tray—again, compliments of guest services. There was little room to accommodate the large gathering, so guest services added several folding chairs in the dining and kitchen area. Most parents, however, moved them closer to TV screen.

Not everyone saw Janelle's waving, so she buried the phone in her cleavage and whistled loudly. The high, shrill tone surprised a few parents, and some glasses of lemonade accidentally spilled.

"Hey, everyone," she announced. "It's my husband's call from the chopper!" The parents immediately hushed as Janelle continued speaking into the phone. She repeated Pete's words loudly, so that everyone could get the information first-hand.

385

"Uh-huh…you found them…Wally and Royce are heading down…one student is in a leg splint…back for more help…OK, thanks for the info. Call me when you know more. Bye."

She closed her phone and tried to climb onto the chair. Wes' dad saw her difficulty and held out his arm for support. She smiled and grabbed it as she climbed. "Much obliged," she said. He then held onto her thickly woven belt for extra support.

"Hey, we're all on the same team," he said, smiling back.

She then looked out at the parents. "OK, folks, you just heard Pete Piper calling from his chopper. He dropped off my guys, who are now hiking down to Clear Creek. They're gonna see how the students are. It looks like there's one injury so far, but hopefully it ain't that serious…"

# Chapter XXI

Walter and his son quickly descended down the trail to Clear Creek. From their vantage point they could see the rapidly moving muddy water carrying wood and ice chunks.

"That water's sure runnin' angry," said Walter. "Hope no one's decided to go for a swim."

His son agreed. "This wouldn't be *my first choice* for spring break," he remarked. "So, what's our plan, Dad?"

"We'll assess the situation and extricate the injured," said Walter, who was walking ahead of his son with his eyes focused on the wet, gravelly trail. "Good thing Brad's got a couple of mules; we can use them to transport the casualties up to the plateau, so Pete can fly 'em out," he said.

"What about Dizzy?" Royce asked, just as he stumbled on a loose rock. It turned his ankle enough to upset his balance, and he stumbled forward onto his knees. "Oops…I'm OK, I'm OK."

Walter turned back quickly to check on his son. "Careful there, buddy." Then he chuckled. "Son, if you don't watch where you're going you'll be one of the first injured passengers on that chopper."

Royce laughed with him. "Sorry, Dad. I'll try to be more careful. I was just thinking about Dizzy. Well, Dizzy and her friend, Taylor."

"I'll bet you're more worried about Taylor than your sister, but we'll soon find out."

The two continued for another twenty minutes or so down the trail until they reached the creek. They still couldn't see the campsite but knew it wasn't too much farther.

"We just need to get downstream a little more. They should be just around that rock and those trees," Walter told Royce while pointing to the flooded woods just downstream.

\* \* \*

Desiree returned to the creek's edge, which was more muddy and foamy than the night before. She headed for the escarpment, but the higher water level cut off her path downstream. She looked through the flooded wood area, hoping to find a dry path, but the waves were washing over all the logs and rocks with tremendous force.

She really wanted to get her grandpa's journal, but there was no easy way. In frustration she dropped to her knees and started crying. She felt like she had lost her grandpa permanently. She then got up and stepped out a foot or so into the creek. The muddy water immediately flowed over the toes of her boot. She took a second step farther into the creek, and the water ran over the top of her boot. She felt the icy-cold sensation rapidly spread inside her sock—it was too deep for travel!

Feeling defeated, she looked down at her boots and sobbed uncontrollably. She then turned around and began to step out when suddenly a pair of strong hands grabbed her firmly around the ribs and lifted her out of the water. Before she could see who it was she was whisked towards dry ground.

"Tsk, tsk, it takes all night to dry your boots—and then you go and get them wet again," a voice scolded.

She spun around to see Taqa's scowling eyes glaring down at her. In fear she jumped back and scanned the cliff, looking for other tribal members.

"Taqa, you'd better not be trying to recapture me," she said, threatening him. "Because my many classmates are just up the bank, and—"

She then patted the back pocket of her jeans.

"—And I have a whistle."

She really didn't have a whistle in her pocket; she was bluffing.

Taqa somehow sensed it and chuckled. "Whistle? Pfft! What are you going to do with your whistle—knock me out with it? If so, you better have a *really big* whistle."

"Well, I—I could blow my whistle, and everyone would hear it and come running to my rescue," she said backing away from him even farther.

"OK," said Taqa, stepping closer. "Go ahead and blow your whistle—I'll just wait here."

She nervously looked back at her friends, but they were all distracted by the helicopter, which by this time was veering off, ready to land atop the nearest plateau.

"Eh, forget them; they wouldn't even hear my whistle—if I really had one," she confessed.

He laughed at her again then walked back to the crag leaning against it. He held his hands out—as a gesture of no harm to her. "No, Desiree, I'm not trying to recapture you; you escaped from Naturale—fair and square."

"Really?"

He pushed off from the crag and cautiously stepped towards her. "Yes, really. Both Evaline and I were relieved that you successfully escaped. We figured you were smart enough to pick up all our hints. At the time we were more concerned about your friend's injury and had to improvise a plan to get you out without breaking the most important rule of our tribe."

"What's your most important rule?" Desiree asked.

He held her by the top of her shoulders. "Once you enter our world, Desiree, you can't leave," he answered.

She stepped back, choking on her badly timed gulp. "Yikes, *ahem*, that's kind-of permanent!" She then cleared her throat.

"Yes, it kind-of is," he said, chuckling at her reaction. He then explained further, "When Naturale found you last night he thought you were dying. The other hunters didn't think so, but Naturale insisted on bringing you to our cave. He felt that your group wouldn't find you in time, and you would either die from spider envenomation or from drowning in the creek."

This stunned Desiree. Naturale wasn't *hunting* her—he was *rescuing* her!

"Son of a pig spit! All this time I thought he was a mean and cold-blooded hunter."

Taqa chuckled again. "No, that's a façade he uses on strangers. He's actually very cute and cuddly once you get to know him. He's quite skilled with the bow and arrow, and you should see him spearfish! He provides much needed fresh meat for our tribe during the winter months. He can also track wounded or lost hikers like a bloodhound. He's the best of the best. That's why we thought his hunt for you—or rather your escape from him—would get us all out of this pickle. And you did quite well. You used all your available resources, especially that perfume to attract the bees."

Desiree laughed. "Actually it was shower gel, but whatever. How is Enrique—is he in a lot of pain?"

Taqa was surprised that she knew his real name. "Enrique? Oh, he's fine. Evaline is pulling out the stingers as we speak. He didn't get that many; he's more upset about your escape, but he'll get over it. Your escape got him off the hook with tribal violations, too."

Desiree smiled and pulled out her chess bag from the pocket that supposedly contained the whistle. "Then please ask Enrique to accept a token of my appreciation," she said, handing it to him, "for saving my life *and* letting me escape."

Taqa accepted the sack and pulled out a chess piece.

"Well, now, this is the funniest looking whistle I ever saw," he joked. But as he further examined the piece, his eyes lit up with surprise. "Do my eyes deceive me? These are pieces made from azurite!"

She smiled and nodded. "I didn't know that until I saw Evaline's healing stones, your pendant and the blue-colored vein in the chimney."

Taqa inspected a few more pieces. "Where did you get these?"

"Oh, my grandpa found them in a secret canyon," she said, then recalled his threat the night before. "But if I tell you exactly where, then I'd have to kill you."

Taqa laughed with her while holding up the queen piece in the sunlight. "You know, Enrique had a chess set when he was young. I chipped them from the vein in the chimney. They weren't as formed and polished as these, but the colors were amazingly similar."

"Enrique plays chess—how weird!" she exclaimed.

"Why is that?" he wondered.

391

"I just can't picture someone loud and physical like him, playing such a quiet and cerebral game," she replied.

"Why, Enrique loves chess," he assured her. "He and my dad used to play for hours. Unfortunately he—like a lot of forgetful kids his age—left them on the bank of the creek one day. When he finally remembered and came back, they were gone. I remember that he cried for days."

At that moment, Desiree realized that these might have been the very same pieces her grandpa found! She chose not to mention it to Taqa. If they were the very same pieces, then they're back to their rightful owners.

"Well, now Enrique can play chess again without spearing anyone," she said. Taqa returned the pieces to the bag. Then he reached into his jacket pocket and pulled out her poncho.

"I believe *you* forgot *this*," he said, handing the neatly folded poncho back to her. "You'll find your grandpa's journal tucked inside," he added with a wink.

"But what about the sketches of your waterfalls—aren't you worried about my knowing your secret entrance?"

Taqa's happy expression dropped. "Yes, I am worried, and by taking this journal back you'll be shouldering a huge responsibility of keeping our world a secret…"

She listened intently—his whole tribe was, indeed, depending on her.

Then he blurted out a laugh. "Ha—I'm just kidding, Desiree. To quote Shakespeare: *This is the long and short of it*; rocks shift, water flows, and landscapes change with time and weather," he explained, also borrowing Evaline's words. "In time the crevasse will widen, and expose itself as either a recreational climbing wall for hikers or as a final resting place for idiots who aren't careful. We'll move on—we've done so for centuries. If you haven't guessed by now we've re-invented the term, *resourceful*. We'll find other shelters, although it will take some time to rebuild our crafty indoor plumbing system. Wasn't that the coolest?"

Desiree nodded then looked at his jeans, which were soaked up to his knees with mud. "Hope your indoor plumbing includes a clothes washer," she kidded.

"As the matter of fact, it does," he answered. "Remember the water troughs in the cavern? The third one farthest downstream is loaded with small stones which tumble in the current and clean our clothes. Sometimes we have to add dried yucca root as soap for those hard-to-get-out stains. It's sort of a stone-age washing machine—get it—*stone*-age?" He then poked her in the arm.

But it was her sore arm. "Ow! Yes, Taqa I get it," she said gently rubbing her injured arm.

"Ooh, sorry. Forgot about your wounds," he said, gently cradling her arm in his huge hands.

She looked down at them and took one into her hands, running her fingertips over his large, rough knuckles. She did the same across the ropelike veins on the back of his hand. *It's so hard to believe that this big and tough wilderness guy has such a gentle touch. He is truly a great medicine man,* she thought.

Then she looked up at him and smiled. "Taqa, if it weren't for you and your tribe, I probably wouldn't even be here complaining about my arm. But it's much better now. And don't worry about your secret entrance; I promise to keep it and your stone-age washing machine a secret. It's the least I could do for your taking such good care of me," she said gratefully.

She then held open her arms, offering him an embrace. He bent down and wrapped his long, muscular arms around her. She was completely enveloped by his massive upper body. She inhaled deeply through her nostrils, taking in all the herbal aromas from his shirt. She also felt the slightly chilled azurite pendant pressing against her cheek.

"It was a pleasure treating your injuries, Desiree," he said while resting his chin on the top of her head. "Although that does sound a little strange. But I speak for Evaline, her grandkids and even Enrique when I say: if I ever had a daughter, I would have wish her to be as perceptive, cunning and resourceful as you."

Puzzled, she stepped back from him, "Ever had a daughter—you mean you don't have a family?"

"Of course I do—no daughters, but six magnificent sons. Some you've already met. You can probably guess which one is my oldest," he said, quizzing her.

Desiree didn't have to ponder that for long. "It has to be Enrique, right?"

Taqa turned away, throwing his hands up in amazement. "See how perceptive you are? Not very many people could find the resemblance," he said, turning back towards her. "Most of his good looks, though, come from his mother."

"Does she wear dreadlocks, too?" Desiree asked while grinning.

"Oh, good heavens, no!" he exclaimed. "That's all Enrique. His mother blessed him with thick wavy hair. He thinks it looks too girly. That's why he keeps it knotted."

"I'll bet she's beautiful. Is she here with you?" Desiree asked.

Taqa shook his head. "Yes, she is beautiful, and no, she's not here. She also serves our tribe as medicine man—I mean, medicine woman—but in another area of the canyon. Our tribe has many members in many places, so my wife and I travel a lot to ensure good health coverage—it keeps us young and fit." He then chuckled. "Unlike most of your doctors, *we* still make house calls."

Suddenly another helicopter flew overhead. Taqa glanced up at it.

"Well, it looks like the cavalry finally showed," he said. "And that's my cue to leave." He then pulled off his necklace. "Here," he said, placing it around her neck. "My people believe that wearing azurite can heal the damaged soul. Please wear it as a souvenir of our encounter. And don't be a stranger to the canyon. Please, come visit again, but next time be more careful; don't go wading through flooded creeks in the dark where there's dead tree branches—*pretty-please*?"

Desiree giggled. "OK, Taqa, I promise to be more careful, but only if you promise to stop saying *pretty-please*; it just doesn't sound right coming from a big and scary wilderness guy like you."

Taqa laughed, turned and waded into the creek. Desiree, however, was more interested in the souvenir he left. She held out the pendant and examined it in the early afternoon sun. The deep-blue colors seemed to tumble with the white ones—resembling two cats at play. The gold flickers danced throughout the inner lattices like tiny fireflies. All the colors seemed to portray a happy and carefree world within its spatial lattice.

When she finally turned back at the creek, Taqa was gone. She smiled again thinking about her encounter with his tribe. Then she let go of the pendant, tucked the poncho under her arm and rejoined her classmates.

* * *

*This is KCliff-TV reporting from the skies over the Clear Creek drainage of the Grand Canyon. Clear Creek has been running rampant from recent warm rains. So much so, that Cheyava Falls, which is normally a majestic and beautiful icefall—just a few miles north of here—has started to melt, generating a potentially hazardous flow of mud and ice. Right now we're hovering above a camp group getting ready to evacuate from a flooded area. There appears to be around sixteen people and two mules down there. One person seems to be wearing a leg splint. We'll stay over this area and report back any developments...*

"Hey, get that peanut can out of my air space, you festered sack of scum!" Pete Piper yelled over his radio microphone. The news chopper disrupted his airspace. Both pilots faced each other while hovering over the plateau.

The other pilot quickly responded using polite sarcasm. "Oh, uh, sorry Mr. Piper, we didn't think you'd be flying tours while the canyons were flooding."

Pete continued transmitting his anger over the airwaves, "I'm on a rescue mission here! I filed my flight plan at the village and got clearance," he replied then snootily asked, "Did you?"

The other pilot paused because he didn't get clearance. "OK, OK, cool your rotors. We'll move to the other side of the creek. Maybe we can get some tight shots of your rescue. Hope you shaved this morning, ha, ha." Pete gave him a one-fingered salute as the news chopper veered off. Pete then maneuvered to his spot on the plateau, landed, and powered down.

* * *

"Dad!" Desiree yelled, running through the trees towards him. Walter and Royce heard her voice, and likewise sprinted towards her. The flooded creek had left a narrow passageway between them. Some debris, however, was getting pushed ashore, becoming extra obstacles. Walter and Royce dodged and jumped a few of them while hurrying towards Desiree.

Mr. Roeser saw the reunion scene playing out and stopped packing. "Hey, look," he announced to the other students. "We have company!" They cheered as Desiree ran into her dad's arms.

Desiree then grabbed her brother and hugged him tightly. "I can't believe how glad I am to see you, Baby-bro," she said.

"I hate to admit it, Dizzy, but I'm just as glad to see you," he said. "You had me scared when I saw all the canyons flooding on TV."

"Flooding wasn't the worst of our troubles," she said while pulling up her sweatshirt sleeve. "Look," she said, showing off her arm.

"Wicked scratch," Royce remarked.

"And check this out," she said, pointing to the tiny punctures in the center of a reddened patch of skin.

Walter took Desiree's arm and held it in the sunlight for better inspection. "Hmm...looks like a spider bite," he guessed.

"A *black widow* spider bite," she said emphatically. "It happened last night in the dark while I was wading through the flooded woods."

"Now, why were you doing something foolish like that?" Walter asked.

"Well..."

Desiree didn't want to divulge too much more about her extraordinary adventure, but at the same time her dad needed some kind of explanation.

"... I accidentally dropped Grandpa's journal in the running creek and went after it. I had to—I promised you I'd take care of it, and I didn't want you to get mad if I lost it."

397

Her dad knew there had to be more to this story, especially how the journal accidentally fell in the water. "Oh? Well, if that's your best excuse, then it'll have to do for now."

But Royce was still curious. "Hey, doesn't black widow venom make you really sick?"

Desiree tried to explain, again keeping the details sketchy. "I *was* sick, Baby-bro; I was cramping most of last night, but I'm much better now."

Her dad was still inspecting Desiree's arm, and took a whiff of the area. "Hmm, your arm smells a lot like prickly poppy." Then he lowered her arm, staring at her suspiciously. "I don't think Bradley Roeser knows about using prickly poppy as an antibacterial wash. Are there some details you're leaving out?"

Desiree, now busted by her dad, had to satisfy her brother's curiosity. "OK, yes, I was chasing Grandpa's journal in the dark through the flooded creek. And yes, I got the spider bite while brushing up against an old tree branch. And I would have drown right then and there if it weren't for some tribal hunters nearby who pulled me from the waters and took care of me in their secret cave using medicinal herbs."

Both her dad and brother stared at her in disbelief. Then Royce laughed. "Ha, ha, Dizzy, that's a good one!"

Desiree knew that neither would believe her fantastic story. She just smiled while fingering the azurite pendant.

Her dad noticed the necklace and leaned in for a closer look. "Is that azurite?" She showed him, and he held it in his hand while passing his thumb over its surface. "That's quite a specimen! I've seen a lot of azurite stones, but never one with so many infusions of color—where'd you get this?"

Desiree didn't want to divulge anymore about her encounter with Taqa's tribe, but she wanted to be very accurate about her necklace's origin. "I got it as a souvenir from the canyon," she said smiling.

Her dad gently released it. "Well, one thing's for sure; the souvenir around your neck is much better than the ones on your arm," he said.

The three joined the rest of the group and helped with packing. Dominique was already mounted on one of the mules. The other mule carried its normal load of provisions, but each student had to carry the equipment that Dominique's mule wasn't.

"Thanks a lot for breaking your leg and making us carry the extra baggage," Perro complained half-jokingly as he strapped a tent to his pack.

"Sorry, my bad," Dominique replied without any hint of remorse. Then she giggled. "Tell you what—how about if I repay you by washing your car as soon as my leg heals."

Perro dropped his pack. "¿Estás bromeándo?"

"I kid you not; it's the least I can do," she replied.

"You have a deal, *amiga!*" They hugged each other to seal the deal.

At the same time Taylor met up with Royce who was standing at the large boulder. "What's a cute frosh like you doing in such a mucky place like this?" she asked.

Royce slowly pulled her into his arms. "Well, to be honest, Taylor, I was looking for you," he replied. He then peered into her eyes. "I was worried sick about you."

"About me?" she asked in disbelief. "Are you kidding? I was an integral part of Desiree's search and rescue team. I saved her from a raging lunatic who was trying to hit on her."

"Wait a minute," said Royce, who was now perplexed. "Desiree said it was a tribal hunter who saved her from the flooded creek."

"Lunatic...hunter—what difference does it make? You should have seen it! Candice jumped on his back while I spread Desiree's shower gel all over his shirt. Then the bees went after him and he disappeared down a deep dark crevasse."

Royce scratched his head, more confused than ever. He decided that the story was going to sound more fantastic as more people told it. "You guys must have been drinking some bad water or something." Then he paused to think. "Or maybe it was good water. *Really good water*! Hope there's some left when it's my turn for this field trip," he said.

Walter, meanwhile, continued helping Mr. Roeser pack the camp equipment. The day's excitement was taking its toll on the geology teacher.

"Thanks for coming down, Wally," said Mr. Roeser. "I appreciate the help more than you can imagine."

"Hey, you've got more help than just me and my son," said Walter. "We got a chopper upstairs, standing by to carry out your injured student, so you can get your mule back for hauling the rest of the supplies."

"That's even better," he said. He looked out at the campsite, and at all his students before letting out a big sigh. "Well, this field trip was a complete wash. Other than the lectures on the trail, we didn't get much geology done."

"Or hidden civilizations discovered?" Walter asked.

Bradley was surprised. "So, you know about that, too, huh? Yeah, I had hopes of finding them. I had so many clues from your dad's artifacts that he found over the years. I thought maybe this would be my lucky year. But I wasn't counting on the rains, and I wasn't counting on your daughter's disappearance. Kind of wrecked my whole mission." He then threw his hands up into the air. "Oh, hell, there's always next year."

Walter chuckled while patting the geology teacher's shoulder. "Yep, Bradley, there's always next year. Who knows—maybe next year you may just make your long, sought-after discovery."

Walter had a sneaking suspicion that Bradley's hidden civilization was very close by—given the fantastic story he just heard from his daughter and the smell of herbal medicine on her arm.

"Maybe you're right," Bradley cheerfully replied. "It's why I teach these kids year after year. I can't think of a better adventure for them and me."

"I would be more than happy to chaperone Royce's trip when he's a senior," Walter offered.

Bradley briefly turned to check his students' progress in packing. Candice had stacked so much equipment on her backpack, that as soon as she strapped it on, she fell over backwards. The geology teacher laughed along with the other students then turned to answer Walter, "I may just take you up on that chaperoning offer."

Walter then walked over to his daughter. "Hey, baby cakes, got all your stuff packed?"

"Yes, I'm all set to go," she said. She then pointed at Taylor. "But not before one last group photo, I fear."

Taylor backed away from the group while holding up her camera. "Hey, we need to get a shot of everyone before we leave the campsite from hell!"

A couple of students laughed while she stood with her back to the creek and directed everyone to bunch together with the mules in the center of her frame.

"Can we get in a little tighter, please?"

The students tried squeezing closer together. They started to turn one shoulder, just so they can compress even more, but the mule carrying Dominique was taking too much room.

Taylor stepped back a few feet. "I almost got everyone in the frame. Hey, Mrs. Clyde, do you mind moving Dominique's mule to the edge of the group?"

"Great, Taylor, I thought we were friends," complained Dominique as she moved from the center to the very edge of the group.

"Of course we're friends, Dominique, but your mule isn't," Taylor replied, stepping back a few more feet.

Walter and Bradley opted out of the picture while continuing to pack the other mule. By this time, Taylor was getting fairly close to the creek's edge and didn't notice the water running up her heels.

Wes did notice and warned her. "Taylor, ah, you may want to be careful. You're getting a little too close to the water. Maybe we could move to a better spot."

Taylor looked behind her and saw the water just a few inches from her heels. "Oh, I'm OK. I can risk some wet boots for this all-important Kodak moment," she said. She looked back into the viewer. "OK, keep those smiles…Hold it!"

Mr. Roeser left the mule and walked over to the edge of the group. He noticed creek debris colliding with a large crust of soil just upstream of where Taylor was standing. The crust then crumbled into the water.

"Glad you can join us, Mr. R., now can you smile?" Taylor asked.

He stepped towards her. "Taylor you're standing on unstable ground. You have to move," he warned.

Before she could react, more of the bank crumbled, throwing Taylor off-balance. She screamed, tossing the camera towards the group as she tumbled backwards into the water.

The water was only shin-deep, so she was able to climb back to her feet. But the swift current pushed her a few more feet downstream. She tried to wade back to the embankment, but an ice chunk bumped her, knocking her over. She was now soaked up to her neck in cold, muddy water. The other students ran down to the water's edge to help. They encouraged her with out-stretched arms, but she could not steady herself long enough to reach them. Royce saw her difficulty and immediately pulled off his boots.

Desiree sensed his intentions and ran to him. "Royce, what are you doing?" He glanced at her and proceeded to pull his pants down. But instead of his usual boxer shorts, he was wearing his team swimsuit.

"Dizzy, I'm going in for Taylor. I know the water is cold and full of mud. The less clothes I have on, the less I'll get dragged down." He then pulled off his jacket and shirt. "Besides, these were clean when I put them on today," he said smiling. "And I promised Mom I'd keep 'em that way." Then he tossed his clothes in a pile a few yards from the water.

But Desiree was not amused by his joke. "No, Royce, you can't go in there, you'll be swept up in the current."

"OK, I'll stay here and *you* go rescue Taylor," he said cynically.

She looked down at her boots with no reply.

"No, Dizzy, you won't because you're more sophisticated than I." He tightened the drawstring on his suit. "Look, Taylor needs our help right now, and no one else seems to have any better ideas. Her clock is ticking. She's losing body heat by the second. The longer she's in the water the weaker she becomes. We have to

403

get her out—now." He looked at all the able-bodied students standing along the waterline. "We'll form a chain and I'll be the hook. What do you say?" He then took up her hand. "Can a freshman dog and a sophisticated senior work as a team?"

Desiree felt proud of her brother's bold plan and she smiled at him. "Yes, Baby-bro, we can!" She squeezed his hand tightly as they both rushed towards Taylor, who had drifted even farther downstream. Royce waded in first while Desiree followed an arm's length behind him in ankle-deep water.

"Wes, grab my hand!" Desiree yelled. "Then somebody grab his!"

Wes jumped forward to take her hand, but instead he switched places with her, taking Royce's hand. "Let me be his wing man this time," he said.

She nodded, grabbing his other hand. "With pleasure, my courageous hero," she said taking the third spot in the human chain. She then waved for Candice, who ran up to her and joined as the fourth person.

Aaron anchored Candice by holding her by the waist right at the creek's edge. "Now why didn't I think of this?" Aaron asked Candice in her ear as he held her tightly.

She turned slightly back towards him. "Oh, I'm sure you would have if it was *me* out there," she said smiling. Aaron squeezed her waist a little tighter then kissed her neck.

The other students remained at the bank shouting encouraging words to the team. Walter and Mr. Roeser had grabbed a few blankets from the mule and ran down to the students who were waiting on the creek's edge.

Dominique was still on the other mule, several yards away, but she cheered while snapping pictures with her school-issued digital camera. "This is way better than a group photo," she commented.

* * *

*This is K-Cliff News Chopper. We've been watching a group of campers evacuate the Clear Creek area about three miles upstream from the Colorado River. We learned from a rescue pilot that they are a geology class from Sunnyslope High School in Phoenix. They look to be grouping for a photo. Uh-oh, now it appears that photographer has fallen into the muddy creek. As you can see it's full of debris, so the student could be in big trouble. Hold on a minute...there's a guy down there...it looks like he's peeling off his clothes...yes, that's what he's doing...and he's stripped down to a...what looks like one of those fancy competition swim trunks...now he's running into the water...*

* * *

Back at the Bright Angel Hotel, Janelle on her cell phone while viewing the TV broadcast of another flooding canyon area.

"So, Pete, you're waiting for my guys who hiked down to the creek...Hey, wait a minute...I can see your chopper on TV. Wow, that bright yellow paint is intense; couldn't miss that thing in a midnight snowstorm, hee, hee. The camera is now panning out and showing the trail down to the creek. It's now zooming in on the creek...wow, that thing looks Sid Vicious...yeah, like the punk rocker only more brutal. Wait... I can see the kids. What the flying fork are they doing?"

405

Some of the parents were already pulling their chairs into the living room and watching the live telecast. Several voices rose with excitement.

"Hold on. I'll tell you what I see. The camera is zooming in closer on the water. There's a girl getting washed downstream. God, I hope it's not Desiree. Wait...a boy is going after her. Oh no...he's wearing just his swim suit...it's...no it can't be...ROYCE! Pete, I'll call ya back."

She sidestepped past all the seated parents, brushing against their knees along the way until she made it to the front of the TV screen. She pointed at the boy in the green and black swimsuit then wagged her finger at him as he ran into the water reaching for the girl.

"Royce, I thought I told you that your competition suit was *only to be worn at swim meets*! Why couldn't you have worn one of your practice suits?"

Some parents laughed at Janelle. Others cheered as they watched Royce grab the struggling girl. Then when both fell back in the water the parents groaned. They watched the next boy in the towline lean forward to help Royce.

Mr. Ward then jumped with excitement. "Hey, that's my son next to Royce!" He pointed to the screen just as Wes pulled Royce back onto his feet. Wes was fully clothed but getting muddier each time the water lapped against him. "Geez, what a mess he's become!" Then, like Janelle, he started wagging his finger at the screen. "Wes, why aren't *you* in *your* swimsuit?" The other parents laughed. He then turned to Janelle. "Your son is very brave."

She smiled back at him. "And I'm glad your son is at his side."

Bryce Lyght was at home, sitting on the couch and watching *The Weather Channel*. He had a large bowl of popcorn nestled between his knees and had just popped a small handful into his mouth. Just then the local forecast was pre-empted by live transmission of the Clear Creek rescue. He recognized Royce right away, trying to pull Taylor out of the creek.

"What the—!" he cried, spitting out the popcorn. Some of it landed back in his bowl while the rest flew onto the floor in front of him. "Hey, Sis, get over here—you gotta see this!"

Gillian came out of the kitchen with a tall can of iced tea and stood next to the couch. She noticed the popcorn scattered on the floor.

"Bryce, you're not doing a very good job finding your mouth," she said stepping over his mess and walking towards the TV screen. "Look at that—a rescue in the Grand Canyon! Finally we have some national coverage of a local event. Hey, wait a minute… That looks like Royce Sumner on TV pulling…Oh my god…pulling Taylor Mayer out of the mucky creek. Boy, look at her hair and clothes! She'll be in the shower for days getting out all that mud."

With her eyes still fixed on the screen she walked closer to it, crushing Bryce's fallen kernels with each step. "Hey, check out Royce's bod!" She stepped closer, watching his back and shoulder muscles as he pulled Taylor towards the shore. "This high definition television really shows a lot of detail." The camera refocused several times on Royce's muddy muscles. "Even covered with mud, he's so *ripped*!"

* * *

Back at the Heritage Farm, Janelle's parents were also watching the rescue on TV. Her dad was finishing his lunch at the kitchen counter. "Honey, doesn't that look like Royce and Desiree down there in the creek?" he asked his wife, who was viewing it from the family room sofa.

She got up and walked closer to the screen. "Yes, it certainly does!" she exclaimed. "Look at how they formed a chain to rescue that poor girl."

He walked over to the sofa, while pointing his chocolate chip cookie at the screen. "Remember when Janelle said that our grandkids couldn't work as a team, and how they're always at each other's throats? Sure doesn't look that way right now," he remarked.

"I'm so proud of them," she said. "The only thing they're fighting against now is that muddy creek."

* * *

"Taylor, hold on—I've got you!" Royce shouted, once again pulling her towards him. He contracted his bicep muscles hard as he tried to lift Taylor and her wet, silt-laden clothes. He turned back to Wes, "Man, I can't handle all this heavy muck!"

Wes hooked his elbow around Royce's for a stronger grip. "Come on, Royce, this isn't any tougher than that swim drill where we tow a ten-gallon bucket across the pool," he yelled back as the water lapped up against his knees. "And right now it feels like I've only got about two gallons of mud in each pant leg."

Royce laughed. "After this I'll be ready for a hundred-gallon bucket!"

But Taylor was getting colder by the second, and the mud in her clothes was constricting her movements. "Royce I'm s-so c-cold. I c-can't f-feel m-my f-feet." She then tried to wrap both arms around him but accidentally poked his ribs.

Royce instinctively flinched backward. Luckily he kept hold of her waist. "Taylor, cut it out; I can't help if you're tickling me," he cautioned. He stepped towards her again, but this time she lunged for his ribs again.

The tickling sensation caused him to jumped back with so much power that he pulled Wes and Taylor with him out of the creek and onto the bank.

"Whoa—lookout!" Royce yelled as he lost his footing and stumbled backwards. Wes lost Desiree's grip and fell right next to Royce still hooked at the elbows.

"Hopping humpback chub, Royce, that's one freaking reflex you got!" Wes cried. Both managed to laugh while gasping for air.

"Yeah, I got it from years of my sister's tickling me," Royce replied. "Whew! Never thought it would come in handy for a water rescue."

Wes pushed off Royce's chest then rolled to his knees and stood up looking for a towel.

Aaron tossed one to him along with a puzzled look. "Hopping humpback chub?"

"It's a fish from around these parts," said Wes. "Oh, and thanks for the towel." He then shook Aaron's hand, leaving a gob of mud in it.

"Yeah—whatever," said Aaron, trying to fling the mud off his hand.

All the other students were offering towels to Desiree and Royce. Taylor was still lying next to Royce, holding his ribs and shivering uncontrollably. Royce felt her cold body through his bare skin. He immediately yelled for his sister, who was toweling the mud off her hands.

"Dizzy, Taylor is going hypothermic," he said, remembering his mom's lecture in the ski lodge. He got to his feet and picked up Taylor. "We need to get her rewarmed quickly."

"Should we start a fire?" Desiree asked.

"There's no time," he replied, his arms still wrapped around Taylor. "We have to act quickly. This is going to sound like I'm a freshman dog, but I need to rip off her wet clothes. Can you blanket her when I do?"

Desiree nodded and grabbed a blanket from Aaron. "Just tell me when," she said, unfolding the blanket and holding it just above Taylor's shoulders.

Royce then looked down at his shivering girlfriend. "Taylor," he said, stroking her muddy hair, "Please trust me."

Her mud-splattered eyelashes blinked back at him. "I d-do, with all m-my heart," she said, her teeth chattering.

Wes grabbed another blanket, holding it as a screen in front of Royce. With his torso pressed tightly against Taylor's, Royce reached behind her back and firmly grabbed the neckline of her sweatshirt.

"Man, this shirt feels as stiff as a floor mat," he commented to his sister. With his strong fingers he yanked at the neck seam. After several attempts the material finally ripped vertically down her back. He pulled it down to her feet, freeing her arms from the sleeves.

"Taylor, I was hoping our first interlude would be more romantic than this," he said, "But, perhaps another time." He then signaled his sister to cover Taylor's shoulders before ripping open Taylor's jeans, and pushing the pant legs down to her ankles.

Desiree finished wrapping Taylor with the blanket as Royce pulled the muddy clothes away in one big, wadded ball.

"Just think, Taylor," Desiree said as she held the blanket tightly around Taylor while rubbing her back. "You won't need another mud pack from the day spa for at least a year." Taylor agreed with a nod and even managed to giggle.

Candice ran to Taylor and put a ski hat on her head. "Taylor, this should help," Candice said while tying together the chinstraps. "My mom always said *if your feet are cold put your hat on*, so this should at least help warm up your feet."

"Thanks, I'm already feeling warmer," said Taylor. She then watched Royce scurrying about with no towel or blanket for warming. "Royce, aren't you c-cold?"

He finally grabbed a towel from Wes. "Yeah, I'm cold," he admitted as he wiped his face, neck and hair. "But I can't feel anything because of all the testosterone that's flowing through my veins." He then laughed and winked at his sister. "We freshman dogs seem to have this problem a lot."

Desiree smiled back, recalling their discussion about sex and sophistication. "Royce, you can't be a freshman dog once you've morphed into a superhero," she contended.

Wes hung a blanket around Royce's neck just before he placed Taylor's clothes on top of a nearby rock. He then grabbed the top corners of his blanket and stretched it across his broad back. Then he extended the blanket across his long arms, resembling a large soaring condor. Taylor couldn't help gazing at his sculpted pectoral muscles, that were dripping with mud and cascading over his rippled abs.

She swooned in bliss. "I must have died and went to heaven," she said. "I finally got to see you in a bathing suit."

He looked down at Taylor's mud-encrusted face and gently wiped away more mud with a corner of his blanket.

"You're wrong, Dizzy," he told her. "I'm still a freshman dog. But now I have only one primal drive." He pulled Taylor inside his blanket, "And that's to be with one cold and muddy, senior girl—"

Before he could finish his sentence the other students stepped forward, one at a time and did it for him:

"—Who's fallen in water," said Candice.

"—Of muck and mess," said Aaron.

"—Rocks and logs," said Perro.

"—And ice, no less," said Martina.

"—Against the flow," said Sayuri.

"—No oars in hand," said Jeremy.

"—To row a creek," said Jace.

"—In a Canyon so Grand," finished Wes.

They bowed together then congratulated each other.

Mr. Roeser shook his head in distaste and complained to Walter, "Maybe this *should* be my last year with this field trip; I don't think I can handle another poem recited with such defective meter."

\* \* \*

*This is K-Cliff News Chopper reporting the latest on the rescue at Clear Creek. It looks like the female victim has been pulled ashore and immediately uh... well... I really can't see what's happening next. The whole group seems to be...let's just say they are wrapping her in a blanket. Some of the rescuers are also warming up in blankets. Quite cozily indeed! So, it looks like everyone is*

*OK—a happy ending. We'll see if we can find other campers up a creek—I mean, near this creek..."*

Back at the lodge Janelle bounced joyously off several other parents in celebration. Hugs and kisses went around the room. Two hotel attendants entered the room rolling in carts that contained ice buckets of champagne. The parents pulled chairs away to clear the path for Janelle as she walked up to the first cart and grabbed the first champagne glass. One attendant popped the cork of the first bottle and poured it into her glass. She did not drink from it, but instead motioned for all the parents to get some champagne. She waited until all the glasses were filled.

"Please raise your glasses with me in a toast," she said. Everyone obliged. "I would first like to toast the Grand Canyon National Park for being such a wonderful, uh, wonder of the world!"

Everyone laughed at her trip-up.

"Secondly, I would like to toast the Lodge's Guest Services for their gracious hospitality. And thirdly, I would like to toast all you parents for being the best supportive group that helped me get through the most difficult time of my life. You kept me focused on a task here, so that I wouldn't be at home drowning my troubles in alcohol—oh—I guess I'm already doing that here."

All the parents laughed and sipped champagne. Mr. Ward swallowed his first sip but then held up his glass and proposed another toast.

"And here's to Janelle Sumner, who commanded this information center with radio, cell phone, and a really nice high definition TV. This experience was more entertaining than *Monday Night Football!*"

"Here, here!" the parents cheerfully yelled.

413

Sayuri's parents walked over to a cooler and pulled out several trays of freshly rolled sushi. "Please enjoy with us," Seiko offered graciously. Her husband carried a tray to the parents in the living room. Seiko held a tray in front of Janelle, who chose the raw eel.

"You'd better have some wasabi paste in that cooler," Janelle said. "I need a good smear of it on my tongue when eating raw fish."

"Yes, of course," Seiko replied as she went back to the cooler and pulled out three small bowls of sauces. "As for me," she said, "I need it swimming in soy sauce."

"Speaking of swimming," Mr. Ward said, interrupting them as he was enjoying a California roll, "Janelle, how fortuitous it was that Royce happened to be wearing his swimsuit for the rescue."

Janelle answered him just after she dredged her eel in the wasabi paste. "I'm not sure about fortuitous, Mr. Ward, I just know that Royce loves his swimsuit. You wouldn't believe how many times I've told him to change out of it. He'd wear it everywhere if I didn't catch him first. Wouldn't surprise me if he wore it to bed," she said laughing before popping the raw eel into her mouth.

* * *

"Eeyuuw!" Royce exclaimed, squirming in his seat. He, Taylor and Dominique were the first ones getting air-lifted out of Clear Creek in Pete Piper's chopper.

"What's wrong, Royce?" Taylor asked from the back seat.

"Well, uh, the creek mud is squirming in my bathing suit, and it feels kind of funky. I won't tell you exactly where—and you probably didn't even need to know that," he said feeling more

414

uncomfortable by the minute. "Anyway, I can't wait to take a long hot and soapy shower."

Taylor laughed. "Too bad we ran out of your sister's shower gel, but maybe the general store has some," she said.

Royce looked back at her. "No thanks. As good as that stuff smells I think I'll use my *Forever Evergreen* and a scrub brush," he said.

"Hey, you guys! Isn't this helicopter ride the best!" cried Dominique as she laid her splint across the middle-back seat of the helicopter. "Too bad I can only see the sky and the buttes. I'll bet the canyons look really cool."

Taylor was sitting in the other window seat behind Pete, still wrapped in a blanket. "I think I've seen enough of the canyons for a while," she said, looking straight out at the horizon.

"Check that out," Royce said pointing his muddy finger down at Clear Creek. "That creek is really tiny compared to the Colorado River," he said. "And there's the—uh, the place where the two join, the uh—"

"—Confluence," both girls answered simultaneously before laughing.

Pete heard their conversation through his headphones and laughed along with them. "Guess you'll learn all about that when you take geology in a few years, Royce," he said.

Royce's eyes were fixed out the window. "I can't wait, Mr. Piper," Royce replied. "It'll be so cool."

"As long as you stay out of the icy creek," Taylor replied.

\* \* \*

An ambulance transported Dominique to the village's emergency clinic, where her leg was immediately x-rayed. The radiologist and attending physician marveled at the results.

"Will you look at this," said the radiologist pointing at an area of Dominique's leg on the x-ray film. "It's a good tib-fib fracture reduction."

The physician agreed. "All I have to do now is replace the field splint with a fiberglass cast," he said. "Someone made my job easier. You know, I asked our patient who splinted her leg, and she said it was another hiker and his aunt who just happened to be in the area."

"We sure could use more hikers like them," the radiologist commented.

"Yeah," agreed the doctor. "She also said the guy gave her the best foot massage ever. Maybe he and his aunt are on a ski patrol somewhere." They both laughed together.

Afterward, the doctor went to report the results to Dominique and her mom. "Good news," he announced, pulling open the curtain and standing at the foot of her bed. But before he could continue, he was interrupted by a short woman wearing a pastel-pink pill hat and carrying a matching-colored purse, who rushed past him and over to the side of Dominique's bed. The woman had a hand-knit hat and caftan slung over her other arm.

"There you are, *bella*," the woman said softly wearing a pink-lipsticked smile as wide as the Grand Canyon. She immediately placed her purse on the side table, took off her gloves and unfolded the afghan. It was thick but loosely knit with geometric patterns of dark green, blue and purple. Rich, golden chenille yarn fringed all the edges.

"Aunt Toni, I can't believe you're here!" Dominique cried as she held out her arms for a hug. Her aunt embraced her.

416

"Your mother told me about your accident, and I came as fast as I could," she said, and then covered Dominique with the afghan. "Luckily I didn't have far to drive." She looked at the splint. "*Poopa-dolla,* are you in pain?"

Dominique felt the soft fibers of the afghan and ran an edge of it along her cheek. "No, Aunt Toni," she said. "Not while I'm covered with this. It's so soft and beautiful."

Aunt Toni tugged on all the corners of the afghan to make sure that her niece was completely covered. "It's made with fine, Italian chenille. I got the yarn at a knit shop in Scottsdale the last time I was visiting with your mom. Never had a good excuse to knit anything with it until now."

Dominique's mom smiled. "Antoinette, you are always so good to my kids," her mom said while walking around the other side of the bed to hug her sister. "You're the best godmother my Dominique could ever have."

Dominique smiled, remembering the fairy godmother discussion she had with Desiree and Taylor in the library a month ago. *OK, I guess my story can have a real godmother,* too, she thought.

The doctor, who never finished his report, stood back and let Dominique's mom pass in front of him. The two sisters kissed each other's cheeks and hugged tightly.

"Well, I guess I'll come back at a better time," the doctor said, slightly annoyed by their apparent neglect of him.

Antoinette then realized her discourtesy. "No, doctor, please stay. I am so sorry to have interrupted you," she replied. She went to her purse and pulled out a square, plastic container and handed it to him. "This is for you—in appreciation for your wonderful care of my precious niece."

417

The doctor took the container and opened the lid. He immediately caught the aroma of oven-baked pizza dough as well as the garlic in the tomato sauce. "Mm—that's smells good; I think I can accept your apology."

"I made it this morning. I hope you like garlic and basil." He graciously accepted it then happily reported the results from radiology.

# Chapter XXII

## THE SEARCHLIGHT

### Vikings Conquer the Canyon!
By Taylor Mayer and Dominique Cruseaux
(Barely) edited by Gillian R. Lyght

### Sunnyslope High School 1, Grand Canyon 0
Arizona's Wonder of the World relinquished to Sunnyslope's geology class this past weekend. Led by expert geologist, Mr. Bradley Roeser, eleven courageous seniors trekked down to the Colorado River from the South Rim and began their three-day expose of the Canyon's deepest secrets. Unbeknownst to them, Mother Nature planned torrential rains and record snowmelt. She also threw in some extra punches that tested our heroes' guts, wits and talents.
### Spiders...

*One senior succumbed to the venom of a black widow spider. Desiree Sumner thought she was playing late-night, hide-and-seek with fellow classmate Wesley Ward when she brushed against an old log in the darkened woods. Turns out Ms. Widow, who was perched on said log, bit Ms. Sumner in the arm. After several agonizing hours of cramps, twitches and retches, Desiree emerged with just a scratch and two fang marks. When asked about the experience, she replied, "I can't remember. I was busy running from an oversized and crazed hunter."*

**...And hunters,**

*Other seniors could attest to Desiree's ordeal. According to Candice Carter the too-tall lunatic battled her for dinner—the loser being skewered and roasted over an open pit. Luckily several honeybees in the area were lured by Taylor Mayer's shower gel towards the hunter, so that both Desiree and Candice could escape. Candice commented on the ordeal, "It's a good thing those bees were out there, or else I would have been the hunter's main entrée!"*

**...And floods,**

*After the battle, Ms. Mayer ran into trouble when she fell into the frigid and ferocious clutches of Clear Creek. It sent her tumbling downstream to the horror of her classmates. Thanks to the quick thinking of freshman Royce Sumner, a human towline was spontaneously assembled. He, Wesley Ward, and several other classmates waded out to*

420

*Taylor and plucked her from the silt-laden and debris-carrying waterway. Millions on national TV witnessed this amazing feat.*

***...Oh my!***

*Dominique Cruseaux's absence from said rescue was due to a broken leg caused by a rapid descent down the Inner Gorge. No one told her that part of the descent involved a twenty-foot drop to the canyon floor. She found out the hard way and suffered a tibia-fibula fracture of her leg. She later assured this reporter that she is looking forward to rehab and should be back on the volleyball court shortly.*

*In summary, Mr. Roeser managed to keep everyone's head above water despite the hazards. When asked about his success of the trip he was quoted as saying, "The odds were stacked against us, but it seemed like luck was literally oozing out of the canyon walls." Can you bottle some of that oozing stuff for the rest of us Mr. Roeser?*

Desiree laughed at the article's seemingly Hollywood-like account. *Dominique and Taylor definitely gave that story a large dose of wow,* she thought. Only Desiree knew that the accounts were really true, even though everyone else regarded them as fantasy.

Desiree read the article while sitting at the kitchen counter, waiting for her friends to arrive for a barbeque. She had invited them over to recount the events and exchange pictures of the field trip that ended just a few days before.

421

On this particular evening she wore her favorite denim jeans that still had traces of reddish-brown mud in the fabric. Apparently her mom couldn't talk her into wearing another much cleaner pair. She wore a gold tank top with a short-sleeved, blue jacket over it. Her hair hung straight and long over her shoulders but pulled back from her sleek neck that was adorned by Taqa's azurite pendant.

Her mom came in from the back porch after setting the table for twelve—the eleven seniors and Royce. "Sweetie, most of the food is ready, but we'll serve it when everybody arrives," she said.

Desiree got up from the counter and asked her, "Will Dad be here to party with us?"

Janelle stopped long enough to check her daughter's attire, rolling her eyes at the sight of her daughter's jeans. But she decided not to lecture any of her family members tonight. "Babe, your father wouldn't miss this party for the world," she said, brushing by her and heading for the cupboards. "He just had to stop at the store for beverages and camera batteries."

Just then someone knocked on the frame of the open doorway. They both looked over to see Wes standing there. Desiree started towards him, but he surprised her with a bouquet of roses.

"I got these for you," he said smiling.

Desiree stopped and stared at them. *Roses! I hate roses! They gave grandpa that blood disease that killed him. And now Wes wants me to have them!*

"Did I get the wrong color?" he asked, confused by her reaction.

Desiree reached for the azurite pendant and nervously rolled it between her fingers. She then remembered Taqa's words:

*My people believe that wearing azurite can heal the damaged soul.*

She let the pendant drop to her neck. It nestled right in the middle notch of her collarbone. She thought about her grandpa's love for gardening. She resolved that his death from a rose thorn wasn't going to make this beautiful and fragrant flower loathsome. *Grandpa must have loved roses to be taking such great care of them.* She decided that she would, too. She finally smiled and looked up at Wes.

"This is a wonderful surprise, Wes!" She smelled the blossoms. The sweet fragrance filled her nostrils and she smiled. "They're so beautiful, thank you." She wrapped her arms around his neck. At the same time her mom took the bouquet from Desiree and went to the kitchen to find a vase. Wes and Desiree embraced, rocking each other while still in the doorway.

"You're so good to me," Desiree said. "Even though I never thanked you for helping my brother down in the canyon. There was so much excitement going on that I didn't get a chance."

Wes stepped back while still holding her hands. "I understand, Dizzy. Hey, isn't blood supposed to be thicker than water anyway?"

"Not in Clear Creek that day," disputed Desiree. "Royce won't admit it, but I'm sure that he was pretty scared at the time. I think he found his courage with you at his side. Thanks for being there."

Wes smiled. Royce did admit that he was scared, but to avoid any further ribbing between the two siblings, Wes decided not to tell her.

"You're welcome." Wes replied. "But I didn't come for your gratitude. I came to tell you that I love you."

Desiree's face lit up with delight for a quick moment, but then she dropped her expression to a calm and reserved look. After all senior girls are sophisticated—not primitive.

"I'm glad you told me," she said. She was so overwhelmed, that she couldn't think of anything better to say. All she could do was look up into his light-green eyes. To her they shone like peridot jewels.

Then Wes smeared his heart onto his sleeve—something he thought he'd never do. "Desiree, I have a confession: I should have told you long before this field trip, but I was a little scared. We always laughed and joked, and that hid my inner feelings. But I can't hide them anymore."

Desiree was stunned, not knowing how to reply. She just ran her hands up his forearms past his elbows and gently squeezed his triceps. Her movements caused the azurite pendant to roll slightly back and forth on her skin.

His arms felt wonderfully strong right now. It's no wonder he and Royce were able rescue Taylor. He, indeed, had an amazing physique to accompany his humor and wit. But at the same time, she couldn't help feeling infatuated with his body. She tried to fight her infatuation with sophistication because, after all, she was not a freshman dog.

She finally replied. "Wes, *I* should have told *you* before the field trip," she replied stroking his arms. She ran her arms up his chest to his neck then around it to the back of his head. "But I was too busy fighting my own personal demons. I'm sorry that it took me this long to say that I love you, too," she said as she pulled his face down to hers. *OK, maybe I still have some dog-like passions, too,* she thought.

He bent forward and she lifted her chin. She closed her eyes and offered her lips to him. He embraced her with both arms wrapped around her lower back. He looked at her lightly polished lips and grinned.

He was happy about her feelings towards him, but he was also feeling passionate. He closed his lips over hers. She felt them but arched her back more—enticing him to press upon her lips harder. Her long hair hung back towards the floor almost touching it. Her jacket fell slightly off her shoulders, revealing the lacey gold straps that lined her gently rounded muscles.

He slid one hand up to the back of her head while he used the other to support her spine. Pressed so hard against her, he felt her heart beating like the ancient drums of a lost civilization as it resonated through his ribs. His heart matched the beat of hers.

Their bodies were so tightly wrapped and arched that Taylor, who came up the steps from behind, was able to duck under Desiree's arched back and slip into the house. Taylor straightened back up and turned to see them in an extremely contorted position.

"Hey, you guys," said Taylor politely interrupting.

They stopped kissing but stayed tightly connected. "Hey, Taylor," they both replied simultaneously, not embarrassed at all by their romantic display.

"I'm looking for a freshman dog superhero. Seen any?" Taylor asked.

Desiree laughed, and while still in Wes' arms, she pointed towards the family room. "Yes, you can find one superhero back there in a video boxing match against *Geek the dwerb*," she replied.

Taylor thanked her and started heading that way, but she stopped and turned back to them. "By the way," she began, tilting her head sideways to mirror Desiree's position. "If Salvatore Dali were to write a steamy, romance novel, you two would be perfect on the front cover," she said, winking then heading towards the family room. Desiree and Wes laughed, not understanding Taylor at all.

Dominique and Perro were outside, waiting their turn to come through the door. Dominique, supported by crutches, had heard Taylor's comment and cleared her voice trying to get the couple's attention.

"Ahem—hey, you two, I can explain the Salvatore Dali thing…"

Taylor entered the family room and hopped onto the couch next to Royce, bouncing him. Royce hadn't noticed her; he was busily throwing punches, trying to beat the boxer on the video screen.

"Hey, Royce," she said, trying to get his attention. He landed a hard uppercut to his opponent. The round ended and Royce paused the game. He then turned and was surprised to see Taylor sitting next to him.

"Oh, Taylor, it's you," he said still holding the controllers but lowering them onto his knees. "Sorry, I thought you were my sister. She always bounces me off this cushion while I'm punching out my opponent."

Taylor batted her eyelashes at him. "Well, I don't want to get between you and *Geek the dwerb*, so go ahead and finish your match," she said. "Besides, you need to warm up with him before you move up to me." Her flirtatious comment caught him off-guard. She didn't sound all that sophisticated.

The final round of the boxing match started, and Royce put up his fists guarding his face. The TV screen mirrored his defensive posture. His opponent was making small circles with his gloves, looking for an opening. He made a right cross to Royce's ribs, but that was enough to leave an opening for a left-hook to *Geek's* jaw.

*Geek*'s head was knocked to the right and Royce followed with a right jab to the chin.

Taylor was getting excited about Royce's match. "That was a great punch, Royce! Ooh, and another one." She then punctuated her commentary with a light jab to Royce's ribs.

Royce flinched, holding out his controllers to protect his ribs. "Hey, Taylor, watch it—I'm ticklish, remember." The temporary distraction was enough for *Geek,* who landed a punch squarely on Royce's nose. Royce's character on the screen stumbled backward.

"Sorry, Royce. I forgot." She then smiled and added, "You realize that if you weren't ticklish I'd still be thrashing with the ice chunks and wood in Clear Creek."

She scooted closer to Royce on the couch. He felt her hip nudge into his, but he continued to dodge and weave defensively and ready himself for his next series of punches.

"Take this, *Geek, Unh! Unh! Unh!*" Royce grunted as he delivered a left cross, right jab and left uppercut to his opponent. *Geek* fell back into the ropes and then dropped to the canvas.

While waiting for the ref's count, Royce turned to Taylor. "Yeah, and I would have still been thrashing out in the creek with you," he said. "If I were going to drown, it would have been cool doing it with you."

Taylor immediately gasped with glee and hugged Royce so forcefully, that she knocked him into the deep cushions. With the controllers still in his hands Royce wrapped his arms around Taylor.

This happened just as more classmates entered the family room. They were puzzled to see *Geek the dwerb* on the video screen—not boxing—but wrapped up in a bear hug with his opponent. The classmates then realized that Royce still had the controllers in his hands while lying on the couch, hugging Taylor.

Walter Sumner soon arrived home and got his son to help pull out the fish cooler from the van. It was stocked with cold beverages and was quite heavy. While both were carrying it up the porch steps, the handle pinched Royce's fingers. He suddenly lowered his end and cussed at the cooler while squeezing his fingers.

"Ow—my fingers! You stinking aholehole bucket!"

As Royce tried to flick away the pain, his dad laughed. "Aholehole? Now that's a fish that never graced the insides of my cooler," the elder Sumner remarked. "But you never know—I just may book a tour in the South Pacific just to get some."

"I wanted to call it something else, Dad, but I'm in the presence of ladies," Royce whispered through his teeth.

Walter chuckled and pulled Royce aside. "Remember what you said about my fish cooler up at the Grand Canyon—about how your ma felt that I talked to it more than her? Now you're doing the same thing," he said.

Royce thought about his dad's words for a moment then replied, "Dad, remember, we never had that conversation." Both he and his dad chuckled together.

"Conversation?" Janelle asked, stepping out onto the porch. "What conversation?" Royce and his dad both shrugged their shoulders. Janelle looked confused for a moment then received two kisses simultaneously on both her cheeks. She hooked her arms up with theirs. "Who needs conversation when there's two of the world's most charming guys right here with me?"

The dinner guests were soon seated at the table out on the porch, which was decorated with the same Chinese lanterns as before. Candice, of course, sat closest to the green one with Aaron at her side. Dominique sat next to Perro with her leg cast extended across his lap. All the students signed the cast—including Taylor's sketch of Dominique's hanging from a cliff with ravens circling her head. Jeremy and Jace paired up with Martina and Sayuri. They each wore a musical note stickpin that Sayuri claimed was only to be worn at the *mother* of momentous occasions.

A large, digital photo frame was mounted on the windowsill between the kitchen and porch. It showed most of the pictures that Dominique and Taylor took of the field trip.

A few other photos were mixed in—including one of Royce with whipped cream on his nose that was taken by his mom at the ski lodge. He sat with his back to the frame, so he never saw his picture. No one else was going to mention it to him either. They just laughed every time his photo appeared, but by the time Royce turned to look, the next photo was showing.

The dinnerware and tablecloth were all in several shades of blue. Candice asked Desiree about her color choice. Desiree was prepared for a long explanation but decided to keep it brief.

"Blue has always been my favorite color," Desiree explained as she walked up behind Wes who was already seated. She then lightly massaged his temples as if trying to hypnotize him. "But lately I've come to believe it has mysterious healing properties."

"Wait a minute," said Taylor. "I can banter with that." Then she quoted Charles Dickens:

*"I have been bent and broke, but—I hope—into a better shape..."*

Dominique continued with a quote from Agatha Christie:

*"Under the circumstances I think it's really quite natural to do."*

Candice added a line from her favorite author:

*"...But like so many unfortunate events in life, just because you don't understand it doesn't mean it isn't so."*

The other girls cheered, recognizing that she quoted Lemony Snicket!

Desiree, totally overjoyed by the meaningful banter, concluded by quoting Shakespeare:

*"Now good digestion wait on appetite, and health on both!"*

The four girls applauded, knowing that their classmates would want to know why. Soon after, Janelle and Walter proudly served a barbequed dinner fit for a king—not the kind of king at risk on a chessboard.